CW00518323

HA-HA-HA-HA

TRIPLE THREAT MYSTERIES BOOK 5

TYLER COLINS

Copyright (C) 2021 Tyler-Addison Colins

Layout design and Copyright (C) 2021 by Next Chapter

Published 2021 by Next Chapter

Cover art by CoverMint

Back cover texture by David M. Schrader, used under license
from Shutterstock.com

This book is a work of fiction. Names, characters, places, and incidents are the
product of the author's imagination or are used fictitiously. Any resemblance to
actual events, locales, or persons, living or dead, is purely coincidental.

All rights reserved. No part of this book may be reproduced or transmitted in
any form or by any means, electronic or mechanical, including photocopying,
recording, or by any information storage and retrieval system, without the
author's permission.

This novel is dedicated to fellow mystery lovers/authors and aspiring writers.

PROLOGUE

"What an f'g jackass." Thumbs in ears, melodramatic [former B-actress] Cousin Reynalda thrust forth her tongue and wiggled long, slender fingers. Sparkly raspberry nail polish glittered under the bright lemon-colored sun.

Standing alongside a looming, leafy shrub that served as target practice for strident feathery friends gliding past, Detective Sammie Sallo chose to turn just then.

In went the tongue and out came the thumbs. With a Hollywood [dazzling] smile, Rey waved both hands, then tucked them into the pockets of daisy-imprinted cut-off shorts.

"Next time, sister, that tongue better mean business." With a camel grunt, he pulled out a mouth-to-lung e-cigarette bundle. Sallo resembled Stacy Keach's Mike Hammer right down to the mustache and fedora, an odd hat to be wearing on Oahu. It had arrived with him when he'd moved here two months ago from NYC to replace Devoy Hunt, a detective the three of us had barely gotten to know. He'd opted to move to Hawaii's Garden Isle, "quieter, calmer" Kauai.

"Jackass," she muttered, spinning sideways. "Why'd he have to choose the same time as us to come and check out the murder scene?"

"Timing's everything," Linda said gaily, giving him the finger when he turned back to view the canal.

The three of us—private eyes from *The Triple Threat Investigation Agency* (Rey's choice re name)—hadn't been officially hired for any particular case. We had, however, received an odd email at 8:30 p.m. two nights ago that read: *The game's afoot, ladies. Check out the area on Laau around the Ala Wai Canal. I suggest you head there now. HA-HA-HA-HA. Your loving GrimReaperPeeper.*

A "congratulatory" message from GrimReaperPeeper had been received at the completion of our last case, the third in the agency's short history that involved bad-ass murderers. And that had been that—until the other night.

Tourists, joggers, and strollers with frolicsome dogs utilized the sidewalk on the *makai* (ocean) side of the canal. On the *mauka* (mountain) side was a golf course, park and community garden, and boating facilities, among other things. Sadly, people didn't— couldn't—swim in the Ala Wai anymore. To do so could prove hazardous, because the 1.5-mile-long canal was a breeding channel for bacteria, heavy metals, and pesticides, never mind garbage. Kayakers and canoe paddlers, however, seemed fearless, overlooking the fact that getting canal water on your skin or in your mouth could result in rashes and gastro-intestinal issues. Hazards aside, it was a lovely stretch, although the three of us might never quite few it the same way again.

Curious, we'd driven to Laau Street and checked cautiously around. Given the vague directions, there'd been considerable ground to cover and when we were about to give up, Linda had stumbled upon four bodies stretched before the canal by the Fisheries Management area—four bedraggled, bruised, blotched bodies with loose puckered skin as white as the underbelly of a perch and as translucent as a jellyfish.

Countless hours in the canal, which served as both drainage ditch and tidal estuary, would have contributed to multihued patterns on regions still resembling human body parts after aquatic inhabitants had feasted. *Would have but didn't.* These four souls had taken their initial swim elsewhere, before necrophagous insects had come to feast and spawn.

The two couples had been missing since March twenty-fourth and had been dead since March twenty-sixth, Prince Jonah Kuhio Kalanianaole Day. That had been the initial determination and it hadn't, yet, changed. So where had they been those two days?

Detective Sammie Sallo drew on an e-cig and exhaled at length. Fumes twirled upward like coolant smoke from a tailpipe. Strolling back to join us, he eyed Rey's face with obvious interest. "Looked kinda like beached whales, didn't they?"

An image of the humpback whales that migrated to Hawaii this time of year came to mind. The migration was comparable to an Oregon cattle drive of yesteryear, a Macy's Thanksgiving Day parade, or even a run of the grunion, marine fish related to the mullet that spawned from March to August on the first four nights after the highest tide of each full or new moon. They were so predictable, the California State Fisheries Laboratory published a timetable indicating when they'd appear.

Well, these four grunion had made it to shore all right, but they'd not completed their quest. There'd been no dissolved oxygen to fan their blood, no sand from which to begin the regeneration process, no purpose or hope to keep them alive. And this ending was far from predictable ... although there had been a full moon that night. Given that unusual things reputedly occurred during one, was that significant?

It had been two days since the discovery of the bodies. We'd returned this breezy afternoon to take daytime photos, poke around, and get a feel for what might have happened; Sallo, unfortunately, had had similar thoughts.

The fifty-year-old believed that the four had partied hardy, so he'd stated a few times that night. Given his next words, he was still of the same mind. "There was probably a group of them. They got caught up in too much booze, maybe drugs too, and started playing weird cult games. Maybe they were paying homage to the great god of Ecstasy and/or praying to Mr. Full Moon. I've seen shit like this before. Booze and drugs make people do bizarre things." He picked up a large stainless-steel travel mug perched alongside a small plumeria tree, noisily gulped back what was left, and belched.

When it came to class, Sallo had as much elegance as Archie Bunker, a character that retro television wouldn't let anyone forget. Rey, Linda and I had met him three times in the last few weeks and while Detective Ald Ives (or "Hives" as Rey mockingly called him) seemed to get along well enough with his colleague, we found Sallo as abrasive as steel wool.

Linda smirked, tossing raspberry-red, shoulder-length waves. "You really think a group of them got into 'cult games'?"

"It sure looks that way, Royale. Remember the marks on their chests? In their fucked-up states, they'd probably thought it was a fun, freaky thing to do. Matches the tatts on their arms and probably other body parts we've haven't seen." He eyed her with dark amusement, like a deranged despot might his lackey.

"So a group of friends just left them there after moon-and-drug worshipping, and what? Went home to sleep it off? What about their state, that they'd been submerged in water for some time?"

He ignored the last question. "Why not? They staggered home and, come the morning, realized how carried away they'd got. They're now either having issues coming to terms with it or they don't give a rat's ass."

They'd been found facing the canal with arms folded neatly over chests. Four black fabric roses, glossy and delicate, had been pinned to tops and shirts and all four had had floral designs incised into chests, possibly with a roulette—not the gambling game, but a small toothed disk of tempered steel attached to a hilt and used to make a series or rows of dots, slits, or perforations.

I kicked pebbles as I eyed the crime area ahead, thinking it was time to visit an upset-irate client whose wayward hubby we'd finally caught being wayward—with her sister. We'd promised to arrive around 4:15 to provide a report and invoice, but given Mrs. Starzeneiss' "high-strung" personality, we'd probably have to stick around to smooth ruffled feathers.

"Isn't it possible they were murdered by a sadistic killer? A psychopath? Given the roses and all?"

He scowled, hung the mug from a thumb, and popped two ICE BREAKERS mints.

I swallowed a rebuke. Pulling a warm bottle of water from a Hawaiian print backpack, I took a long swallow and eyed fluttering, ripped police tape wrapped around several trees and shrubs. A yellow ribbon tied around an old oak tree it wasn't. What it was, was jarring. A reminder that something terrible had occurred.

There were obvious if not improbable gaps in Sallo's hypotheses, but he wasn't the sort you could argue with, not without wanting to bang your head against a wall or tree.

I nodded to my Jeep parked by a lonely palm several yards down. Thankfully, the sunroof and windows were open (I didn't much care for A/C).

"Catch ya later, Detective S," Rey purred, flipping her pretty wheat-color with sunshine-yellow streaks, which was now several inches below her shoulders. Sparkly pyrite drop earrings caught the sun. Cousin Reynalda was a salesaholic who couldn't resist bags and shoes; in the last month, earrings had become an additional passion.

"Whatever."

She blew a raspberry and the three of us moseyed to the car.

"Can you spell jerk?" Linda asked, pulling an apple banana from a large crocheted tote.

"Yeah. S-a-l-l-o," I replied wryly, opening the passenger door.

"What's up, buttercup?" a baritone voice boomed from behind.

Rey spun, ready to pounce.

Linda and I exchanged amused glances.

"Do you always pop out from behind parked SUVs like that?" I chided.

Jimmy Carcanetta—Jimmy C—was a freelance writer and blogger Linda had gotten to know in the last couple months. He grinned like a toddler who'd just been given a huge slice of icing-laden cake and his pumpkin-shaped head bobbled like a fishing bobber. "Nothing like the element of surprise."

"What brings you here?"

"The same thing that brought you guys here: a need to piece things together and get a feel for what happened."

"Your article on the murders was good."

"For a food and wine reviewer and blogger," he chuckled, pulling a new Canon camera from a faux-leather bag. "I came to take a few more pics, for context."

"Any new findings or thoughts?" Linda leaned into the passenger door and bit into the apple banana.

"Not yet. Just mulling over facts. They'd been missing two days and died on the twenty-sixth, or thereabouts. They'd been meticulously mutilated—and please don't attribute it to cult games or weird rites. I heard that crap from the ass back there the other day." With a glower, he jerked a thumb rearward. "Any thoughts about the fact they'd been so neatly arranged, with roses yet? That seems very specific, as if the killer were leaving a calling card."

"Maybe it's the creep's way of saying goodbye, a ceremonial or funereal kind of thing," Rey offered.

"Who said the roses came from the killer?" Linda added. "They could have been a club or party signature thing. The four may have been wearing them before they were done in."

"Yeah, but the incisions resembled flowery embroidery. And those flowers hadn't been as, uh, saturated as the foursome." He scanned the end of the street. "I'm thinking there was a connection between the two, even if Sallo won't admit it. Why though?"

"Why won't he admit it? Or what's the connection?" I smiled drily. "I have a feeling the detective's going to prove a thorn in many people's sides."

"Thorn?" Rey asked sarcastically. "How about curare-tipped *spike*?"

CHAPTER ONE

Who'd have thought a scrawny pimply-faced guy could have sent a Mack-truck-sized man into the pavement with such caliber and zeal? The impact had surely loosened a few teeth. Blood oozed from the prone truck's nose and lips like a Rocky mountain stream during spring thaw.

Pimple Guy shook his head, cursed three times, hawked loudly and graced Truck Man's soiled bargain-store running shoe with a large gob of phlegm before sauntering into an early evening that veiled the local world with a blackberry-plum shroud. Truck Man's friends appeared embarrassed and unsure as to whether they should assist their fallen comrade or maintain a semblance of dignity and walk away. Heat took its toll on some tempers, but then, so did a late afternoon of lagers and rum chasers under a baking sun.

"Clean up by the fountain!" Faith shouted to Wayne, an attractive beanstalk of a man hoisting a crate of wine bottles onto a rear counter.

"Hey, Shooter Lady! Three KDs, times three," Paco ordered hoarsely as he hastened past the bar with a sizable tray supporting frosty mugs of beer and fancy (pricey) appetizers.

Faith Suren, recently dubbed "Shooter Lady", was a former

9

diner waitress I'd met during the agency's first official case. Instead of slinging loco moco and burgers, these days Faith was serving different shooter cocktails—mini mixtures—each unique and each a specialty. One was the U.S. Kentucky Derby, or KD for short. While there was a shooter named after a special event in each state, KD seemed the most popular this balmy, breezy Saturday night.

Three months ago, my friend had ended up working at Flaming Daisies, a popular upscale lounge, when Rog's diner burned down, courtesy of an exploding oil vat. Faith and Pollo, the cook, had already left for the night after pulling double-duty, as had the customers. It was Rog's misfortune to have chosen that particular evening to [finally] perform minor maintenance on said vat. The greasy spoon had been leveled, much like Rog.

Having served greasy but tasty diner fare for too many years to count, it was a blessing in disguise when she had to find a new job. A friend of a friend of a customer of a cousin had recommended her to Ritch Lea and Izzie O'Rourke, owners of the popular venue. Customers had taken a quick liking to the amiable, even-tempered woman and Faith was given better shifts as well as bartending training from Josho, who thought she'd make a great replacement when he finally took early retirement.

It was 6:45 according to a huge prawn-shaped wall clock suspended on a rear wall above a long table where twelve young people sat, celebrating two friends' birthdays.

"Sorry I couldn't get out at 6:30, like planned." Faith topped off my wine glass. "Tamara's on her way, so we'll still make it to the theater in plenty of time, yeah."

"No worries."

With a wink, she went to see to a beckoning man's eager bidding.

A friend had offered Rey, Linda and me tickets to a classic comedy playing at Hawaii Theatre. Unfortunately Linda had eaten something that had disagreed with her, so she was bed-bound for the evening while Rey—who'd already seen the play twice—was on a mission to test domestic decorating skills by painting the laundry room and pantry in our recently acquired house in Kalama Valley, which was part of Hawaii Kai. We'd gotten the five-bedroom house—with *ohana*—for a song, as the saying went, but only because it was a fixer-upper ... in every sense of the word. When Faith had called the day previous to see about getting together, I invited her. The third ticket wouldn't go to waste; Sach Morin, our neighbor and new pal, would meet up with us in the lobby before the start.

"Hey, Shooter Lady, two times three KDs." Pierre winked and waited for Faith to fill the order. Young and cute, in an extraterrestrial sort of way (remember E.T.?), he loosened a lavender bowtie, part of the venue's white-shirt-black-pants ensemble and muttered something about wishing the gentle winds wafting through six open doors would pick up because the rapidly rotating fans above were doing dick.

A valid comment. The muggy evening felt like a layer of nylon clinging to sweaty skin: confining, cohesive, suffocating. The heat and mugginess magnified the usual scents and odors: smells of fried and grilled foods wrangled with hops and barley and malts while a sundry of scents wafting from foodstuffs and bodies fought for supremacy with a host of perfumes and colognes (some which may well have been applied with a soup ladle).

Faith motioned Felicity, a plump and pretty blonde bartender, to see to two arrivals on my left. They reminded me of young versions of Ricky Ricardo and Fred Mertz from *I Love Lucy*; the one seated was dark and handsome but solemn-faced, and the other standing alongside with an elbow on the bar, was dumpy but cute, in a Cabbage Patch doll sort of way.

I took a sip of Chardonnay. Custom-made glasses at Flaming Daisies were tinted gray-blue with a black-mesh pattern in keeping with the color scheme of the establishment. Glossy black molding complemented gray-blue walls. Fragile-looking bar stools with argent-gray patterned seats were supported by thin black chrome legs. Beams and rafters over the bar were black, as were pillars and posts that supported esoteric, customer-created paintings housed in black frames. It wasn't very Hawaiian, but it was rather cool.

Pierre wrinkled a flat, scrunched nose and set his tray on the corner of the bar, nearly upsetting a bowl filled with maraschino cherries. Resting one hand on a lean hip, he silently challenged Fred M with a sinister dare-to-say-one-word-about-me-standing-in-your-space smile.

"Hey, Felicity, grab me a couple of Wild Turkeys—and not those two leather-vested boys sitting by the pretzel bowl," Faith called over bottles of multi-colored ambrosias (or banes, depending on your viewpoint). With a weary chuckle, she motioned a glossy black door that led to the owners' offices, a change room, locker and storage areas, and rear exit.

I followed and waited outside a small change room for her to step out of her bartending uniform. Crash N. Bern, real name unknown, stepped from Izzie's office and offered a curt nod as he hastened past. A new addition to the bartending team, the twenty-two-year-old was damn skilled, not simply at the bar, but on the bongos, bass, and banjo. An aspiring musician, he looked the part with long mahogany hair, pierced ears (a skull hung from the left lobe, a saber from the right), muscles that would have made Mr. Universe jealous, and a colorful serpent tattoo that curled around the base of a long, heavily veined neck and slithered down to sights unseen. If he weren't so attractive, with a gleaming Crest smile and intensive grass-green eyes, never mind the obliging disposition, he could prove intimidating.

Faith opened the door, looking attractive in a rose-pink peasant blouse and gray straight-leg pants. During Rog's diner days, she'd looked weary, thin, pale. The new job agreed with her, so much so she'd decided to do things never dreamed of: have teeth fixed and whitened, face toned, new make-up regime acquired, and unruly curly walnut-colored hair highlighted and fashioned into a stylish bob.

"Remember the guy you called Howdy-Doody a few nights back when you were sitting at the bar with Rey and Linda?"

"Who could forget those crazy freckles? That beaver smile and mango-orange hair?"

"I was checking for a text re next week's schedule and accidently hit a news app. Look at this." She held up her cell phone. There was a small full-face shot of the fellow Rey had dubbed Howdy-Doody. His name according to the article was Van T.L. Quist. Very "was". Yesterday morning, his body had been found in an alley not far from the bar, under a pile of cardboard. Apparently, it had been a few days since he'd died. Speculation regarding cause of death: drug overdose. There'd been traces of a suspicious powder on his person, a short-needle syringe in a back pocket, and a crop of dot- or pin-like marks on his chest. Injecting into the chest was less conspicuous than an arm, I supposed.

With the island heat, you had to wonder why no one had discovered the poor guy; surely the stench from the ripening body must have been overwhelming. I mentioned this to Faith.

"They're often strewing garbage in that alley," she said, draping a polished-leather tote from one shoulder and closing the change-room door. "The smell of death wouldn't penetrate the smell of rotting foods, and whatever additional ugliness may lay there, yeah."

"But they must collect garbage on a regular basis," I pointed out as we stepped from the rear exit into a small, well-lit parking area.

"Way at the rear?" She appeared dubious and shrugged. "It does go to prove, though, that appearances aren't everything. Would you have thought that fresh-faced guy was a drug user?"

I recalled the young man who might have been labeled wholesome, like a choir boy or Boy-Scout leader. "No, but he was pretty good at tossing back the booze."

"He reminded me of a university kid, out for alcohol-infused fun. And an unwelcome morning hangover." She slipped into the passenger seat of my Jeep when I opened the door. "Do you suppose he bought the drugs at the bar? Or sold them?"

"Anything's possible." I got into the driver's seat. "I wonder when the cops will come calling at Flaming Daisies."

"They only just found the body, so they have to figure out the wheres and whens and whos. Apparently, the fellow who wrote the story was in the vicinity when it all came down and, so, the 'scoop'."

"My Vancouver friend would call him a keener."

Faith chuckled and adjusted the seat belt.

* * *

The following morning found the three of us at Flaming Daisies, where we'd agreed to meet Faith and an HPD detective who'd requested a meeting to discuss Van T.L. Quist. She, in turn, had requested we attend; given our profession, she felt we might have something of note to add.

Ritch and Izzie had personally opened the bar to observe the police investigation. Organizing bottles and jars, they not so surreptitiously watched as Faith sat with a new HPD detective, Detective Petroni Carter Hammill. Felicity and Paco were also there, waiting to be interviewed re the Howdy-Doody Murder, as Rey had labeled it, even if it hadn't officially been confirmed as one.

Save for the closely cropped chocolate-brown hair, the attractive man bore a striking resemblance to singer-songwriter-model Shawn Mendes. I tried not to gape, unlike Rey and Linda and Felicity, whose jaws were hanging between their navels and knees as they leaned into the bar counter. Faith simply sipped coffee and waited for the man to talk, her gaze as expressionless as her face.

"I understand you were serving Van T.L. Quist last Friday

night." His voice, somewhere between gravelly and raspy, wasn't asking a question but making a statement. The hint of an accent was hard to place.

"Mr. Quist was sitting at my counter for an hour, an hour and a half, give or take," Faith advised, gesturing the bar. "He was chatting with one of the regulars a lot of the time."

"What's the regular's name?"

"Morris. I don't know his last name, but I do know he works at the university in an administrative capacity." She glanced over at Felicity. "Do you know Morris' last name?"

She shook her head and started slicing limes.

The man's shapely sensual lips drew into a tight line as he keyed something into his cellphone.

I gave him a casual once-over. Defined facial features. Long thin neck. Adam's apple bearing a tiny scar. Broad shoulders that saw weights regularly. He was too attractive by half.

As he pulled a black lizard-skin card holder from the inside pocket of a trim-fit navy-blue blazer, eyes as black as eight balls and as deep as abysses glanced over and eyed Rey for several seconds. He then smiled tightly. "Can you three spare a few minutes?"

Grabbing chairs, we sat next to Faith and eyed Hammill expectantly. The man seemed in no hurry to ask questions.

My gaze traveled to the unbuttoned portion of a white linen shirt. His chest was smooth and brawny, and a partial tattoo—a red and black wing—was visible on the left breastbone. It probably belonged to a hawk or an eagle (couldn't imagine it being a sparrow or swallow). Noticing where my gaze rested, he smiled in a way I was tempted to call arrogantly smart. My eyes rolled skyward.

Rey crossed slender arms and regarded him intently. "You're here because Howdy-Doody was murdered. Are you thinking someone here committed the dastardly deed?"

He offered a fleeting smile and arched a strong shoulder.

"We're simply tracing the deceased man's last few days... *Howdy-Doody?*"

"The first nationally televised kid's show featuring Buffalo Bob Smith and Howdy Doody, a puppet, which ran from, oh, 1947 to 1960, thereabouts."

Linda slapped her BFF's back. "Your TV trivia knows no bounds."

Hammill gazed from Linda to Rey and back again. "She gives names to people?"

"We all do, when inclined."

He smirked. "Who do I remind you of?"

Rey smiled saltily. "Rocky Balboa. After losing a pathetic nine rounds."

He smirked again. "Cute."

"You asked."

"Yeah. Serves me right." Hammill turned back to Faith. "Okay, so you were his bartender that night. From?"

She drew a long breath and rubbed her thin face thoughtfully. "From 8:00 to 9:15 or maybe 9:30. Thereabouts. As I said, he sat beside Morris most of the time."

"Quist was drinking"

"Most people in a bar do that, yeah."

His eyes narrowed slightly and he scratched a sun-burnished cheek at length, as if he were contemplating something—like a castigating remark. "What was he drinking?"

"Red-Blue-Whites primarily. As opposed to White-on-Red-Blues."

Hammill held up a tanned and scarred hand that had surely kissed a knife blade or two. "What the hell are those?"

"Patriotic shooters. One type for those who don't want to handle something too intense and one type for those who do."

"Patriotic shooters?" He laughed. It was a pleasant, throaty sound, like a Porsche slipping into fifth. "Did the guy look like he was flying?"

"On the wings of some euphoria-inducing drug? Or on one of her shooters?" Rey asked bluntly.

He eyed her at length. "Are you always so cocky, Ms. Fonne-Werde?"

Placing a palm to her chest, she feigned child-like innocence.

With the shake of the head, he returned to Faith. "Was he on drugs? As far as you could tell?"

"He didn't look or act drugged, nor did he mention drugs. In fact, he talked mostly about his third-year med studies … and some commercial or ad thing."

Hammill stared at something beyond her shoulder. "Did he at all look or act suspicious, strange, like maybe he was doing something illicit? Was he talking to anyone who appeared out of the ordinary?"

"He chatted with Morris and the odd person that leaned into the counter beside him. No, he didn't look like someone doing something illicit or trying to buy drugs, but then I'd not have that emblazoned on my forehead if that were my intention. As for someone out of the ordinary, no, I didn't see or notice anyone I'd never seen before. I tend to remember new faces."

He rubbed his chin, looking pensive. "And he didn't appear depressed, down, suicidal?"

"The kid was into having simple, bar-time fun."

Tapping the table absently, the detective's gaze fell on a lithograph of an absurdly fat pink-faced man reclining in a tub with flabby arms outstretched. Hammill frowned. Either he didn't like the artwork or he didn't care for Faith's flat response.

"Do you recall anything of *note*, Ms. Suren?"

"Not particularly."

"Not particularly suggests a little something. Maybe you have a little Miss Marple in you, like your private-eye friends here?" He jerked a thumb toward us and, smirking, regarded us with a critical eye. "Did you 'not particularly' notice anything that night?"

"After Morris left, he talked to a woman and not long after her, a jock."

A perfectly shaped eyebrow arched. Did he pluck them? Probably. Vanity, thy name was not always woman. "A little something is better than a big nothing. Tell me about them. Maybe *they'll* be able to provide some useful information."

CHAPTER TWO

Linda turned to Faith. "Remember the Woman in Black and Jocko, the linebacker-looking guy?"

Faith nodded. "He actually is one."

"Both spoke to Howdy—I mean, Quist. For a few minutes. Both seemed to make him happy," I offered casually.

"Happier than he already was?" Hammill.

"Happier than he was tipsy, yes."

The detective looked from me to Faith. "Tell me about the Woman in Black first, maybe starting with her name."

"I've heard her called 'sugah', 'honey', 'love', and 'sweetness'. Pick one or all four." She smiled amiably and waved to Felicity, motioning her empty cup.

Felicity strolled forward with a steaming pot and refilled it, her gaze riveted on Hammill.

"The Woman in Black will occasionally smoke black cigarette on the patio. Keeps them in a gold-and-rhinestone case. They're English, so she probably has them specially ordered. She creates a very dramatic effect, dressed in upmarket vintage clothes— almost always black—and very high-heeled shoes. Long flashy black fingernails with sparkles add to the look." Meeting his keen scrutiny, she again smiled prettily. Faith wasn't easily rattled. There'd been too many dramas in her life to allow one arrogant detective to fluster her. "The few times I've seen her on my watch she'd set her sights on attractive, model-type men. Lets them buy her a couple of drinks, but rarely leaves with one."

"What made her chat with the likes of Quist?"

"I heard that she'd told him he reminded her of someone, and that got them to talking. It wasn't until that night that I learned she worked as a scout or agent for some production house... Or maybe it was an advertising firm? Anyway, she's not one to chat with staff. Only attractive men."

Hammill appeared bemused. "She wanted Quist for a commercial or something?" His eyebrows shot up so fast I thought they might leave that finely lined forehead altogether.

"Apparently. She gave him a business card and he got so excited, he had to share. He flashed it before me as I passed a drink." She smiled sadly. "He couldn't believe someone found him ad material."

"Neither can I," Hammill acknowledged with a frown. "But maybe she—they—wanted a certain look for a cookie-and-milk ad, or a front man for a new cartoon or comedy act. How long were Quist and this woman together?"

"Maybe ten minutes. She let him buy her a Bloody Mary, extra spicy. Then, off she went. That was around nine."

"You saw the card, Faith. Did you see a name?" I prodded.

Faith closed her eyes to replay the moment Howdy-Doody-Quist had displayed the card. "It was a unique black business card ... real fancy ... with raised red lettering. I see it, sort of. Zelde. Zee. Priz—uh." She sighed softly and reopened her eyes. "Nope, can't recall it. But there definitely was a 'z'."

"You're very observant," Hammill stated with a curt nod. "Now, what about this Jocko person?"

"When he overheard Howdy-Doody was studying medicine, he engaged him in conversation."

Hammill wiggled long fingers in a give-me-more gesture.

"Jocko seemed very interested in forensics. They were debating which of the *CSI* shows had been best."

"Anything else?"

"Other than the fact I'd thought it strange that Jocko was interested in the world of

medicine, no. His buddies had often joked about his mind being as vacant as his 'mug'."

"Is he?"

"Vacant?"

"Uh-huh."

Faith shook her head. "No. Although I rarely talk to him or his friends about anything but sports or the cute redhead or lovely blonde at the end of the bar, he seems articulate."

When she ceased speaking, he turned to us. "Is there anything you'd like to add?"

The three of us eyed one another and shook our heads.

"So, you're private eyes, huh?" The brow arched again, this time in amusement. "You save runaway Rottweilers and spy on disobedient husbands?"

Yes. But we'd never admit it. "We *are* private investigators and we're pretty good at it," I said bluntly.

Hammill rose and took a couple of steps towards us, then gazed around the lounge with a furrowed brow. I could smell cologne that had been subtly applied—Egoïste if I wasn't mistaken. A former weather-station colleague, Edgar, had worn it since its inception, up until the day he'd been felled by a giant shamrock during a Saint Paddy's Day parade.

"We have an agency," I stated evenly. "And we're bloody damn proud of it. And ourselves."

"I'll bloody damn bet you are."

"Don't patronize," Linda said brusquely, standing.

"Look, maybe you three *are* good at locating little old ladies' missing pension checks and runaway Pomeranians. Murder's another thing. It's not like *Murder She Wrote* or *Poirot* or *Nero Wolfe*. It's dangerous. It's ugly. And it's fucking real."

"We've had a few 'real' encounters and solved a few 'real' murders," Rey declared briskly. "*Successfully*. Maybe you should ask around the precinct. Start with Detective Hives."

"Ives," I corrected automatically.

Hammill stared at Rey, then turned to Linda and me. "If you remember anything, your bartending friend has my contact info." With a brisk nod to Faith, he sauntered over to Felicity.

Belgian. That was it. Out of the blue, it came to me—that whisper of an accent. It hailed from Belgium.

* * *

"Where to now?" Rey asked as the four of us stepped up to the Jeep.

Linda held up a hand to shield her eyes against the bright sun as she scanned the long one-way street. "How about lunch, maybe somewhere Kailua way?"

"That'd make for a nice drive," I agreed, hopping into the driver's seat.

"I'm in," Rey said, swinging into the rear.

Faith leaped in alongside her and Linda slipped into the front passenger's seat. "Man, was he a piece of work, or what?"

"Kinda like Sallo," Rey frowned, adjusting the seatbelt. "At least this dude's easy on the eyes."

Faith laughed and slapped Rey's thigh. "Is that why yours were twinkling?"

My cousin's response was to stick out her tongue and offer a raspberry, which prompted the rest of us to laugh.

"So, what do you think about Quist's murder?" I asked as I pulled onto H1-61.

"You mean, not-yet-officially-confirmed murder," Linda stated drily.

"The poor kid was in the wrong place at the wrong time," Faith said quietly.

"You don't think he had anything to do with drugs, do you?" Linda.

"No, I definitely don't. He enjoyed bending his elbow, but drugs?" She shook her head. "I don't buy it."

Recalling that face, I had to agree. There was something off and it wasn't with Howdy-Doody Quist. As Faith had said, he'd been in the wrong place at the wrong time.

"Well, it's not our case, so we'll have to leave it to Hammill et al to solve," Linda advised, watching the passing scenery.

"What about your case?" Faith asked.

"It's not our case," Linda responded. "GRP merely used us as some bizarre starting point."

"GRP?"

"GrimReaperPeeper."

Faith offered a flat chuckle. "You don't believe *GRP* will contact you again?"

Linda turned to eye the former waitress. "He hasn't contacted us since we called the police about the bodies we found by the Canal. If it was a game, like he'd stated in the email, you'd think he'd continue taunting and teasing."

Faith tilted her head one way and then the other as she considered it. "Maybe you're right."

"We should still try to find out who he—or she—is," Rey declared, opening a bottle of tepid water and taking a long swig.

"We don't have any leads and our IT expert-slash-pal had no luck tracing the URL," I pointed out.

"Some expert," Rey muttered.

"He's pretty good at what he does," Linda said in Rocky's defense. "And Ald and his team didn't do much better."

"Maybe one of Gail's IT buddies could check out things when she's back from Japan."

Gail Murdock was an HPD Administrative Specialist and good friend. Right now, she was on a three-week tour of Japan after breaking up with a fellow officer she'd been dating.

"We could text her now—"

"Let the woman enjoy her much-deserved vacation. She'll be back soon enough," Linda interrupted her BFF. "The poor thing hasn't had a decent break in three years. She needs the down time."

"No thanks to that jerk." Rey snorted softly and gazed out the window.

* * *

Lunch at a small café in the heart of Kailua had been delicious, pleasant, and just what was needed: respite from reality.

On a lark during the drive back, we stopped at a bustling souvenir shop and bought some un-needed things: salt-water taffy, mac nuts, and cute touristy T-shirts. After promises to get together again soon, we dropped Faith at her small Makiki apartment and drove back to the house that was in dire need of repair—from painting to refurnishing and some remodeling thrown in between. With time. After purchasing it for nearly 1.5 million, it would take time to earn the wherewithal to finance major house projects.

It was 4:15 when we stepped into the foyer and changed from sandals to slippers. Our agency's part-time cleaner/gofer/assistant, Eddy Galazie—"Red-Head" as we sometimes fondly called him, due to an amazing head of radish-red curls—hastened from the rear with Button and Piggaletto scampering behind.

The former was a young rescue mutt of Havanese, Schnoodle and Chacy Ranoir origins, the latter Linda's pot-bellied pig. Not far behind bounded Bonzo, Rey's Checkered Giant rabbit, rescued when its young owner had been murdered during the *Can You Hula Like Hilo Hattie* caper. Oddly enough, my cousin had requested—demanded, implored, and pressured as only Reynalda Fonne-Werde could—that the rabbit be placed in her "custody" when she'd heard he'd be removed to an animal shelter. She'd never been much of an

24

animal/pet person previously and what had changed her mind, and heart, I'd never know. But God bless her. Home to Oahu the rabbit came.

We greeted the kids with hugs while acknowledging Eddy. Linda gave him a playful slap to the back while Rey brushed her lips across his low, flat forehead. We'd grown quite fond of the young animal lover.

"Did the kids behave?" I asked, leading the way into the spacious, cupboard-heavy kitchen.

"For the most part."

"Oh-oh."

"Only one broken vase," he grinned, sitting at the blue-veined granite counter and watching me remove four cartons of coconut water from a large wheezing fridge (appliances were on the to-buy list, too). "You had a call."

"Anyone important?" Rey smiled, dumping the contents of the souvenir shop before her and ripping open one of three mammoth packages of Diamondhead Taffy. She tossed one to each of us.

"Strawberry-guava," Eddy said excitedly. He unwrapped it and popped it into his mouth before you could say taffy twice. The amiable fellow had suffered a head injury when he was eight, which left him challenged; his uncle, a former mob-type menace with a good heart had employed him until his unexpected demise during the *Coco's Nuts* case.

"Who was the call from?" Linda asked, squeezing his hand and pulling one of four adjustable-height swivel chairs alongside his.

"Some guy with a weird voice." Ash-gray eyes glanced earnestly from one face to the next. "It was like he had marbles or pebbles in his mouth. Said to tell you he was wondering what was happening with the game."

We stared, stunned. Linda found her voice first. "Did he say who he was? What the game was or what should be happening?"

"He didn't give a name and didn't say what the game was," he answered, eyeing the bag of taffy by Rey's slender hand.

She passed it over. "What else did he say?"

Eddy removed six candies. "Something about ... yeah ... it was time for the players to stop snoozing." He grinned and crammed two coconut-flavored ones between small, thin lips. "Was he talking about you?"

Rey and I exchanged concerned glances, then she casually said, "He sounds like the guy we met at the Center a couple of weeks back, when we were looking at board games."

Eddy chewed blissfully as he watched Button race past, Piggaletto at her heels.

"Maybe he'll call back," Linda said dismissively. "Would you like to stay for dinner? JJ's barbecuing."

"I am?" I asked flatly.

"Yeah, you love it," she grinned. "Why else would Rey have bought that six-burner backyard grill?"

"Because she was hoping to learn to cook the *easy* way?" I asked wryly.

"I can stay and help. Just tell me what to do," Eddy said cheerfully. "By the way, the guy said he'd try and contact you again sometime soon."

Rey, Linda and I exchanged anxious side-glances. Evidently, GRP was back.

CHAPTER THREE

Two burned pork chops out of eight wasn't bad. With the creamy-mustard sauce, you could hardly notice the "charcoal" flavor. That I'd managed to singe Eddy's shaggy eyebrows wasn't that bad, either; he liked the trimmed look. That Rey's were now non-existent, well, that was another thing altogether. But they'd grow back.

At seven, Eddy returned to his Waipahu apartment, three-dozen salt-water taffy candies happily in hand. At half past seven, the three of us—kids at our feet—were seated on the lanai, drinking iced tea with fresh lemon slices and watching a beautiful starry sky.

"There's no place like home," Rey said happily. Stretching long legs onto a birch-colored cushion of a long metallic-framed rectangular ottoman, she draped an arm along the top of the sofa, next to Linda's shoulders.

"Yeah, one we'll be paying off for the next four decades," Linda said drily, giving her leg a light kick.

Rey kicked back. "Pishaw."

"Pishaw?" I asked wryly.

"My new word for the year."

We all chuckled and settled back. Button rested her chin on

my bare foot while Bonzo hopped onto his mom's lap. Piggaletto snorted and started to slumber on the uncut grass.

"We need to mow the yard," Linda said.

"We need a lawnmower," I reminded her.

"Maybe we could go for the concrete look," Rey said. "I'm not keen on grass."

"You're just not keen on cutting it."

Linda concurred. "You're the one who wanted a house—with garden, lawn, pool and all. Now you have to pay the price, which extends beyond the financial."

Rey offered one of her water-buffalo snorts, then laughed. "You're right. I'll head out and buy one tomorrow. But when we pull in more cases, we're getting a landscaper."

"Fair enough," I said, sipping the last of my tepid tea. "We've been here almost ten weeks now. It's time we rolled up our sleeves and stopped living out of boxes and unpainted bedrooms."

"When we're on lawnmower patrol tomorrow, let's make an effort to get paint colors selected. Maybe Eddy would be willing to help here and there," Rey suggested. "He's pretty good at whatever task he takes on."

"Unlike you and your laundry room and pantry painting 'venture'," I jested, whacking her knee playfully, then motioning the fair-sized kidney-shaped pool. "We should get the pool fixed and filled. The tiles are looking pretty sad."

"So's the hot tub," Linda added.

"The pay from my in-between commercials and theater gigs will help a little with the smaller tasks, but we need to get some serious work happening," Rey said, stroking her bunny's large, long ears.

"Linda and I could take part-time jobs—"

"No, you couldn't, Cousin Jilly," she interrupted. "As private investigators, we can't be seen doing something other than P.I.ing. What'll potential clients think?"

"What about you and your acting?" Linda scoffed.

"It's not the same as you scanning products at the check-out counter or taking a burger order—"

"Of course it—"

"Let's not go there again, ladies," I advised. Before I could continue, my cell announced a text. I grabbed it from the base of the chair and eyed the display.

"One of those potential clients? Your 'sometimes boyfriend' from Florida?" Rey smirked.

"Adwin."

"*Adwin*? As in pastry chef and former 'beau', Adwin Beauregard Timmins?"

"Byron," I corrected mechanically, re-reading the message.

"What's *he* want?"

"Just reminding me we're meeting for dinner day after tomorrow."

"What!?" Rey sat flagpole straight.

Linda's latte-colored, almond-shaped eyes rounded in surprise. "When did you two start chatting again?"

"He emailed me about six weeks ago to see how we were doing." I shrugged and put away the cell phone.

"And you've been communicating regularly ever since?"

"Kind of, yeah."

"And he's *here*?" Rey demanded. "When did he arrive? Where's he staying? Does he want you two to get back together? I thought he'd met someone?"

"He emailed the other day to say he was on Oahu, staying with a foodie-friend in Mililani. He had met and married someone—Lizbeth was her name, I think. It didn't work out. They were divorced after five months."

My cousin and her BFF goggled.

"He just wants to have dinner and catch up. Nothing more, nothing less," I said with a dry smile. Adwin had been part of *The Connecticut Corpse Caper* entourage, but we'd parted on good terms after solving the murders at Aunt Mat's haunted mansion. "What's wrong with meeting an old friend?"

"*Everything*. Old-lover dates are never a good thing," Rey advised and looked at Linda.

Who nodded. "Never good, JJ. Never good."

I rolled my eyes.

* * *

At nine, Linda wanted to peruse food and wine blogs, and Rey intended to Zoom a couple actor friends. For me, it was time to call it a night. Just as we were about to part ways, we received a call from Detective Hammill: he was in the area and would be dropping by.

Five minutes later, frenetic knocking echoed throughout the sparsely decorated house. The three of us answered it to find the detective looking annoyingly cheerful and robust, and rather attractive in a crisp white shirt and Diesel jeans held up by a thick leather belt with an elaborate eagle buckle. The finely chiseled face was freshly shaven and radiating arrogance. A recently nicked hand supported a cardboard tray with four large coffees and a small brown paper bag.

With theatrical flair becoming my cousin, I motioned the tall man with the too-white teeth inward.

"Piggaletto! Come to Mommy!"

Hammill's eyebrows flew up as Linda swooped past like a bat out of hell.

Fleet-footed, but not always surefooted, she stumbled and sailed into the tall grass before a cluster of Frangipani. The pot-bellied pig, looking as innocent as always, ceased scampering, perched himself alongside her head and eyed her with soulful hound-dog eyes. I swallowed laughter as Linda lay there, not in the most flattering of positions. Rey simply tsked and moved toward the kitchen.

With a sigh, Linda got up, scooped her pet, and shuffled past a surprised and—gauging from the twinkle in those billiard-ball-black orbs—very entertained detective.

Placing Piggaletto on a small Persian-like rug before the entrance to the kitchen, she wagged an admonishing finger. "Do that again and no treats."

With a yeah-right-lady look, he scurried to the water dish. Bonzo and Button appeared from nowhere, soaring past Hammill with the speed of the SC-44.

"You're giving the Honolulu Zoo a run for their money," he smirked.

Rey looked like she might offer a barbed response, but my warning look stopped it. Sighing, she grabbed the stainless-steel cordless kettle. "Tea?"

Hammill placed the tray on a recently purchased rectangular rubber-wood table. "I brought coffees. Ives said you're into those sweet fancy ones, so help yourself to any cup with an X on it." He sat in one of the vertical slat-back chairs, looking overly cheerful. "A beautiful day, wasn't it?"

"I'm sure it was, Mr. Rogers," Rey purred. "And just how were our neighborhood friends today?"

"Mind if I sit?"

"You already are," Linda pointed out, plopping on a chair across from him. "So, Detective Hammy—"

"Hammill. Petroni Carter Hammill—PC for short. That should be fairly simple for those shootered brains to remember." Prying off the lid, he took a sip and remained silent.

"Just for the record, Detective, we don't do shooters," I stated.

"Not often, anyways," Rey winked, then looked at me. "Doesn't this guy remind you of someone?"

I sighed and focused on the latte.

"Come on, you gotta admit he's got a lot of your 'sometimes boyfriend' in him."

One of Hammill's contoured eyebrows arched questioningly.

Rey was referring to Cash Layton Jones, an undercover agent who played drug dealer "Richie J" or "Ricky J". Currently residing in Florida, the arrogant, audacious, and way too good-looking man and I had a tempestuous on-off relationship. At the moment, it was [once again] non-existent.

I remained mum and sipped ... and bristled upon seeing Button flop before the detective.

With a grin, he provided a thorough belly rub. "She's a cutie."

"Any progress on the Howdy-Doody case?" Rey asked, leaning into a wall.

"Since this morning?"

"Someone might have confessed, or something been discovered—"

"Right, and kangaroos can fly. Murders aren't often solved in a couple of hours."

"So, it *was* a murder? Not an overdose?"

Hammill's gaze met Linda's, but he said nothing and continued sipping.

As Rey was about to say something, there was a light rap-rap-rap on the rear kitchen door before it slowly swung open.

Chestnut-brown, owl-round eyes gazed from one face to the next. "I saw the light as I was walking back from Casper's and thought I'd pop by to invite you to a fitness function—uh, I'm not interrupting anything, am I?"

"Hey, you," I said with a limp wave. "Come in. Join the party."

Linda introduced Sach to the detective.

"Sach?"

With an impish grin, he took a seat at the counter. "Yeah. Sach Martin Morin."

"Isn't Sach the name of a Bowery Boy?" Hammill drained his coffee and rose. "Huntz Hall's character. Let's see. Horace ... Dubussy "Sach" ... Jones."

Our neighbor was visibly impressed. "Few people know or remember that."

My cousin cleared her throat.

Sach chuckled. "Except for Rey. She knows tons of film and TV trivia."

Hammill's smile was flat and fleeting. "When I was growing up, Grandmother Manon's idea of babysitting was seating me in front of the television so I could watch old movies featuring The Bowery Boys, East Side Kids, the Stooges ..."

"Yeah, I watched those, thanks to Uncle Shawn and Great-Uncle Conerie working in film. Hey, we've got something in common." The muscular man of 5'8" eyed Hammill closely. "So, you're a detective like the gals here?"

He didn't respond, simply scanned Sach's attire: a tight saffron tank top tucked into loose-fitting lavender-and-lilac jogging pants.

"What kind of business brings you here, Detective? You can tell me. The four of us are good pals."

Hammill cocked his head, his eyes expressing amusement. "You're a private investigator, too?"

"I'm a fitness instructor and personal trainer. But I've offered to help. I'm great at puzzles and I'd make for excellent security." He flexed his biceps.

"I'm sure," he said drolly and stood.

"That's it? You came to deliver coffees ... *PC*?" Rey asked sardonically.

He started to say something, then shrugged. "It can wait, *Reynalda*."

"Rey. And Sach won't share. Come on, Hammy, spill it."

Meeting Rey's saccharine-sweet smile with one of his own, he then turned to Sach and regarded him circumspectly. Again, he shrugged. "I wanted to get an account of how you got involved in the Canal murders... It appears the small mess of teeny marks on Quist's chest were made with a similar implement to the one used on the four bodies."

* * *

Hammill left fifteen minutes later with Sach on his heels. Nothing else of note had been revealed or shared, but the two gents now knew as much as we did about GRP and the murders. Yes, our new friend had indeed offered to assist, but we'd not yet taken him up on the offer. There'd been no need to.

"You think GRP will call soon?" Linda asked wearily as we climbed the winding stairwell leading to the bedrooms. Hers was in the northeast corner, mine the southwest, and Rey's on the east side, between two mid-size unadorned and unfurnished guestrooms.

"Bet on it," Rey murmured, rubbing her eyes. "What's that dude's 'game', you think?"

"Perverse fun," I muttered, opening the door to my room.

"Perverse something," Linda grumbled. "Night, ladies —crap."

She'd stopped so suddenly, Rey smacked into her.

"Take a look." Raising a toned arm, she pointed.

Attached to the exterior of the tall arched hallway window was a satiny black rose fastened with thick, clear industrial tape. A one-word question had been scrawled with a substance that looked suspiciously like dried blood: *howzit*?

Beneath the word, in the same substance: a happy face.

CHAPTER FOUR

"So much for an early night," Linda grumbled, waving farewell to Ald and Sallo.

The two detectives had arrived fifteen minutes after we'd called Ald to tell him about the rose and message. Both men had been wearing 50s-style polyester black-and-red bowling shirts. Funny, who'd have guessed either HPD homicide detective was a bowler? As Rey would say, ya truly do learn something new every day.

Pets on our heels, it was fifteen minutes after midnight when we finally locked up and trooped upstairs.

Leaning into the far wall, Linda frowned and appeared pensive. "GRP's becoming close and personal. I wonder whose blood he used."

I parked my butt on the edge of Rey's queen-size upholstered storage bed and wearily said, "I suspect we'll learn soon enough."

"Do you think they'll find anything incriminating?"

"That dude won't have left any evidence or DNA," Rey responded, removing a folded oversized T-shirt from one of two marquetry-motif nightstands. She started undressing. "Guess we can open an official case file, starting with the photos we took earlier."

"And the details Ald said he'd provide tomorrow," Linda added.

"*Limited* details," I emphasized. "He's not going to share all."

"There should be enough for us to begin some serious private-eyeing."

"Think we should get a security system, like Hives suggested?" my cousin asked, tossing a crimson lace bra across the room. It landed at the base of an "awesome mega-sale piece", a variegated solid-marble and brushed-brass floor mirror.

"Given our line of work, yes." I flopped back and stared at a ceiling in dire need of paint. Bonzo landed beside me, his face—whiskers twitching wildly—inches from mine. "Let's do it first thing."

Linda glanced at her ice-pink Coach watch. "I'm bed-bound. Nighty-night ladies."

"Who can sleep?" Rey asked drily, slipping the T-shirt advertising a local rib joint over her head.

"Count sheep."

"More like corpses," she said with a cynical smile.

Standing, I waved goodnight and tread to my room where I found Button already on the bed. With a pat to her head, I slipped into a V-back chemise and pulled aside the covers. An abrupt twinge—gut instinct—impelled me to check the agency website. The laptop, conveniently perched on a recently purchased diamond-patterned nightstand (Rey's "sales bug" had proven contagious), found its way onto my lap.

Sure enough, a message from GRP had arrived in the Inbox.

Need help with house renos? Climbing ladders is no big deal and I'm pretty good with tools as you've with seen my etching work. Let me know and I'll pop by. Your new playmate. GrimReaperPeeper. Or, as you've so fondly dubbed me, GRP.

I drew a deep breath and gazed around the dim bedroom. Obviously, GRP was watching. It appeared he was *listening*, too.

* * *

"Thanks for the update. We'll have the email checked out and have someone drop by to sweep the place in the morning," Ald promised and disconnected.

He sounded as tired as I felt. And yet I wasn't certain I'd be able to sleep. Wondering if Rey and Linda were feeling the same, I slipped into the hallway. Sure enough, diffused light emanated from the partially open door leading to Linda's room.

I found both wrapped in short fuzzy robes, seated on the velvet-seat bench while Piggaletto and Bonzo lay snug as two bugs on the porker's small designer sofa. Sweet-smelling hot cocoa wafted across the room.

"No invite?" I pouted playfully. "What's wrong with me?"

Linda smiled. "I heard you on the phone and figured you were talking to one of the two men in your life."

I dropped onto the edge of the double bed. "You mean Adwin or Cash, aka Richie-slash-Ricky J?"

"We didn't want to bother you," Rey said cheerily. "We were just shooting the shit. Didn't think there'd be much point in having you waste time with us."

"It'd be better than tossing and turning, and," I leaned forward and whispered, "wondering if GRP's listening."

Both pairs of eyes opened wide.

Quietly, I told them about the email.

Instinctively, they gazed around the room.

"Crap." Rey.

"Dang." Linda.

I hopped to my feet. "A security system's on the shopping list for tomorrow morning. No ifs or buts."

"And the firing range tomorrow afternoon," Rey added.

"Since when do you want to shoot a gun?" I asked with a dry smile.

"Since I suspect this case is going to be insaner than the last three."

* * *

Mulberry wisps spiraled through a grapefruit-pink sky while a pleasant breeze countered what might have proven an oppressive heat. Sunset wasn't far off.

The three of us were seated on a picnic bench in Le'ahi Beach Park, about to indulge in a Korean barbecue feast we'd just picked up. The small park had recently become one of our favorites. Even if it had no easy ocean access (fine for Rey and me, who didn't like the water that much) and a very small sandy beach area, it was quiet and had a lovely view.

Linda sighed appreciatively as she scanned the expanse. "Too bad Faith had to work today."

I concurred and opened a can of black-cherry soda.

"We did good today," Rey commented with a contented smile and started sipping a volcano-sized mango bubble tea.

"Security system bought. Installation of rear and front cameras tomorrow." Linda stretched toned legs along the bench. "Shooting practice completed. You did pretty decent, Rey."

"Yeah, I managed to shoot the target every time." She laughed. "You, Cousin Jilly, need glasses or tons more practice."

"Hey, I got the target—"

"In the balls when you were aiming for the side and in the neck when you were aiming for the heart, and—"

"We don't need a replay," I declared drily.

"Too bad Ald's folks didn't find a bug," Linda said with a wry smile, digging into a big bowl of Bibimbap.

"I'm guessing GRP removed it when he stopped by with the rose."

Rey regarded me intently. "That's so creepy that the guy actually got into the house. How, though? They didn't find anything out of the norm. No picked locks or anything."

I selected a long sliver of soy-glazed fried tofu. "He could have snuck in while we were on the lanai or in the kitchen. I often leave my bedroom window open when we're at home or at the agency; so do you two."

"Not anymore," Linda declared. "Not without us being there *and* vigilant."

"He might have made us the next three victims." With a glower, Rey sucked furiously at the bubble tea.

"He wouldn't do that, not yet anyway," I affirmed.

Linda agreed. "He needs us for some weird reason. Maybe to amuse himself."

"We certainly do something for the dude," Rey frowned. "So where are we gonna start, ladies? The facts Hives provided earlier today were borderline okay. They give us an idea about what a sicko GRP is, but they don't do much more."

"We can start with Woman in Black and Jocko, both who spoke with Howdy-Doody. They may have something to share about their chats."

"It's a start," I nodded. "Maybe Howdy-Doody had plans to meet up with someone later, after the bar, or had a project on the go, something he may have shared with one or both."

"According to our HPD dick, Jocko's camping on Big Island and is off the grid for the moment. And Woman in Black hasn't been reachable. Hopefully, Faith will call us when and *if* she returns to Flaming Daisies." Rey snapped her fingers. "And what about Morris?"

"Right." Linda gave a thumb's up. "He's a definite must-talk-to."

I smiled. "Requests for him were put in while we were in the food pick-up line-up."

Another thumb's up from Linda. Popping an edamame into her mouth, she stared across the ocean. "Why leave black roses? Is it something as basic as representing death?"

"Maybe, maybe not," I replied. "Black roses also have a positive meaning, like the demise of old habits, rebirth, or the end of a period or stage that leads to the beginning of a new one."

"They can also stand for tragic love or be symbolic of hatred and/or revenge," Rey added. When she noted our stunned gazes, she chuckled. "In one of my horror B-movies, we had black roses as the central theme. So I did research to get into the character and 'mood'." She chuckled again and opened a container of spicy barbecue chicken. "One fact: the Irish used black roses to symbolize courage and resistance during their battle against the British. Another fact: black roses also once served as a symbol of anarchist movements. A black rose can also relate to obsession. And it can be associated with—believe it or not—eternal love."

"Which 'meaning' do you suppose GRP is embracing?" I asked.

Linda shrugged. "Considering he's a crazy killer, the death theme makes the most sense."

"Crazy doesn't equal predictable," Rey stated. "Maybe he's going with the obsession angle—as in he's obsessed with mayhem and murder."

We shrugged in unison and chowed down.

Five minutes into the meal, a woman of medium stature, wearing a gingham-like side-buttoned dress with a big patch pocket, stopped before the table. The 1940s look was carried into two-toned shoes and a Cartwheel hat. The late afternoon light enhanced her looks; she was quite pretty in a Theda Bara sort of way, with overly dramatic make-up that drew attention to deep-set eyes the color of sea urchins and sultry lips stained damson-plum purple. I noticed lean muscular legs the color of Godiva white-chocolate liqueur, made paler by a burgeoning rose—a deep purple bordering on black—with a thick twisted stem, braided with what looked like dead nettles, that started at the ankle and snaked up the left leg. Intricately detailed, the tattoo was of quality artistry.

"I stepped into Flaming Daisies to collect my assistant, who was meeting with a client, and the bartender—Faye?—saw me and hurried over. She wanted me to contact you, but I thought I might perhaps meet you in person—she did call you?" Her voice was tempered, crisp, and held a slightly hard edge, like Lauren Bacall with a slight English accent (that didn't quite sound genuine).

Sheepishly we looked at one another.

"We'd decided to avoid calls and texts for a while," Linda explained with a rueful smile.

The woman offered a quick, patient smile.

We stared. We'd almost not recognized Woman in Black. Besides the fact she was wearing something light-colored, we'd never viewed her in daylight.

"The police have been looking to talk to you," Linda finally said, moving her legs and motioning for her to sit.

"I shall call them when I'm ready. For now, however, I'd like to speak with *you*."

Smiling graciously, I gestured the food. "We have more than enough. Join us."

She peered down her nose at it—in more ways than one. With a shake of the head, she looked from one face to the next, removed the hat, then sat. Even her raven-black hair, coiffured with little Betty-Boop flips, hinted of a bygone era when women played up femininity in a very different way from today.

"What can you tell us about your chat with Howdy—uh— Mr. Quist?" Rey asked.

"Mr. Quist?"

"The red-haired, freckle-faced guy at Flaming Daisies you were chatting with several nights ago."

"Oh, him… He was a nice young man who had the perfect face for an ad I'm spearheading," she replied casually. "I gave him my card, but I've not yet heard back."

"He's dead," Linda said flatly, eyeing her quizzically.

"I hadn't heard. I avoid sensationalized 'riff-raff' news," she said with a transient smile.

Rey, Linda and I exchanged amused glances.

Woman in Black glanced at the small tray of crispy spring rolls, took one, and eyed it skeptically.

"They're really good," Rey said flatly, regarding her guardedly.

"I'm certain they are," she said with a flip of her head.

"I don't believe we caught your name," Linda said.

"Caprize."

"I'm Linda. That's Rey. And this is JJ."

She looked from one face to the next, then shrugged. "Someone is following me."

Rey leaned forward. "Someone you're familiar with? An ex-boyfriend? A coworker?"

Caprize studied her, as if committing every pore and mark to memory. "I don't know him. He stands outside the office sometimes. Watching. Waiting. The odd time he's on the street when I'm shopping or jogging, but then when I draw close, he quickly departs. It's very … off-putting."

"Where's the office?" I asked nonchalantly.

"Bishop and King."

"Advertising?"

"Advertising and integrated marketing."

"Why not go to the police?" I inquired.

An odd smile—one of amusement, maybe tolerance—tugged at full lips. "You're private investigators, aren't you?"

"Yes, but stalking is something the police—"

"A friend of mine was stalked last year and she went to the police… Now she's dead."

"That's most unfortunate," Linda stated. "But—"

"I'd prefer *you* find out who he is and what he wants," she declared and rubbed a long, slender neck.

I noticed long fingernails black as night, save for a tiny red sequin on each. They brought to mind an image of a black-widow spider crawling languidly, determinedly, along a deadly course. Forcing my gaze back to her face, I asked what he looked like.

"I haven't seen him up close, but he's of medium height and build. He has black hair from what I've noticed sticking out from a Rainbow Warriors cap he's always seems to wear. And a dark hoodie. There's nothing remarkable or memorable."

"That should narrow it down to a few hundred guys," Rey said blandly. "You didn't notice any scars? That he walks with a limp? *Anything* that might make him easy to spot?"

She offered a dainty shrug.

"How long has he been following you?"

"I first noticed him five or six weeks ago."

Linda eyed her closely. "And you never called the police, not even for the record?"

"I'm a good-looking woman. Men regularly chat me up in bars and in stores. The police would merely claim I have an overly active imagination."

"And you'd like us to confirm you're *not* imagining him?" my colleague smiled.

"Exactly."

"And find out what he wants?"

"And insist he stops. I'll pay you for your time, gas, and whatever expenses you may incur." She reached into a Saint Laurent mini satchel and pulled out a card. "This is my work number and address." On the back, she jotted a number with a handsome brass-and-copper ballpoint pen. "This is my personal cell number."

"What time of day do you usually see him?"

"Outside the office after work, around six. When I'm jogging or shopping, it's more like seven."

"We'll start tomorrow."

With thanks and a smile that almost appeared grateful, she glided along parched grass to a shiny black BMW M4 parked close to the park entrance.

"She has a Morticia Addams thing going. Not just in terms of the frequent color of choice, but that weird walk," Rey commented.

"She also has a very dark, almost black rose on her leg." I told them about the tatt.

My cousin and best friend stared across the park in disbelief.

"What do you suppose she's not telling us?" Linda asked, her brow furrowed like a farmer's field.

I glanced at the elegant linen business card. Black with red raised lettering it wasn't. Had Faith been wrong? Or did this enigmatic woman have more than one calling card? "Caprize Marquessa … *de Sade*? Surely she jests?"

CHAPTER FIVE

Like a Jack-in-the-box, Rey's head popped between Linda's and mine, seated in the front of the Jeep. Our curious eyes were focused on Caprize's sizeable two-story Kahala house, situated several yards back on a sizable lot.

"We sure lucked in getting an address so fast," she said, an uneaten black Twizzler protruding from one side of her mouth.

"It helped that Gail's HPD pal has the hots for you," Linda kidded.

I chuckled, envisioning the IT-savvy fellow's sharp-nosed Pomeranian-face. Talk about lovesick puppies.

"Too bad we didn't luck in with Morris the same way."

"Yeah, that was a real dud. Talk about no-value add," Rey murmured.

"It wasn't a total loss. Morris reinforced the fact that Howdy-Doody is—was—a nice young man who liked to cut loose drink-wise now and again but was *not* a drug addict."

"That's true. He even stressed that Howdy-Doody was *very* anti drugs, because of a cousin that nearly died from an over-dose," Linda said.

"Which means that short-needle syringe they found was planted to make it appear he was a druggie," Rey said with a soft snort and looked back to the house. "Our client has some serious money."

"Or some serious debt."

"Good point, Lindy-Loo." Rey dropped back into the rear seat and started chewing the Twizzler.

It was just after seven. We'd been parked four doors down for forty minutes. It didn't appear the woman was home as no lights were on.

Linda drew up both feet onto the passenger seat. "You think the stalker will show?"

"She said she sights him outside the office after work and while she's jogging and shopping, but given she doesn't appear to be at home, who knows?" I scanned the well-lit, nicely land-scaped street for the umpteenth time.

"It's a fairly affluent area. Unless he's strolling nonchalantly or walking a dog, he'd look pretty suspicious hanging or standing around," Linda remarked.

Five minutes and seven Twizzlers later, a male of medium height dressed in jeans, a black hoodie, dark leather shoes, and cap ambled along the opposite sidewalk.

Linda sat upright. "Could that be him?"

"Could be him. Could be anybody," Rey replied dully.

"He does have a cap on," I pointed out. "But I can't tell if it's Rainbow Warriors."

"Even if it is, what are we gonna do?" my cousin demanded sarcastically. "Make a citizen's arrest?"

"Let's observe. For now."

"Take a pic, Lindy-Loo, for the file," Rey instructed. Taking photos was not a favorite pastime of my cousin; she habitually got thumbs and fingers in the way or ended up with blurry faces and bodies, regardless whether she used a digital camera or cell phone.

"It won't prove of much value, but what the hell."

I decided to check my cell and found an email from our neighbor. "Sach wants us to drop by tomorrow evening at seven for drinks and nibblies. He's throwing a farewell party for a fellow trainer who's moving to Singapore and wants his P.I. pals to make some new ones, because,"—I had to laugh—"we're socially inept."

Linda chuckled. "Tell him he's on." She gestured the man with the cap. "Given this guy's been admiring the Bird of Paradise and Naupaka for the last two minutes, can we agree he might be Stalker Boy?"

"He might be a flower lover," Rey offered with a snort.

"Or an amateur horticulturalist." Me. "They do have some impressive landscaping around here."

"Then why is he staring across the street at Caprize's place? Admiring the handsome diamond trellis panels?" Linda mocked.

"They do have a certain appeal," I joked.

"Ha-ha-ha-ha."

"Oo-ooh. Shades of our 'loving' GrimReaperPeeper and that message about the Canal bodies." Rey playfully smacked her BFF with a Twizzler. "Do you suppose *he's* watching us?"

A shiver skipped up my spine as we instinctively gazed around. "If he is, he's good at concealing himself," I murmured.

"It's dark out," Rey stated flatly. "That makes for primo concealment places."

"Mr. Flower-Lover's leaving," I advised.

"Should we follow?"

Linda shook her head. "It would be a guaranteed waste of time."

Rey sighed. "A non-event evening."

"Not necessarily. We got to see where Caprize, a.k.a. Woman in Black, lives."

"What about where she works?"

"Let's meet her there tomorrow before she leaves for the day," I suggested.

* * *

47

"There he is, on the bench right beside the fountain."

Standing behind a tall narrow tinted lobby window, we watched a dark-dressed man several yards across the street, seated on one of three benches. The streetlamps didn't provide enough lighting to illuminate his face, but then he was wearing a cap and peering in the opposite direction. It was impossible to tell if he was the same man we'd sighted last night, though he had a similar build. So did countless men.

"Has Stalker Boy been here long?" Linda asked Caprize, who was leaning into a wall, slender arms crossed, appearing blasé.

Once again, she was wearing black—a sable-black two-piece scallop-edge topper and dress set. Pretty. Expensive. So were the leather portfolio and Acne Studios bag resting on a nearby oval waiting-area table. "I was by the window when you called to say you were on your way up. I happened to glance down. There he was."

"Linda's Camry is in the car-park five buildings over. How do you feel about having him follow you two, *if* that's Stalker Boy?" Rey asked, regarding her closely.

Her smile bordered on scornful. "If it is 'Stalker Boy', then what? Make a citizen's arrest?"

"We'd thought of doing the same not long ago," Rey said blandly. "Let's see if he follows you and Linda … and if he does, JJ and me'll follow him."

"And then what?" she repeated.

"One thing at a time. For now, we're on his ass, uh, case."

"Sure. Let's go for it." She grabbed her belongings.

Linda motioned the portfolio. "Artwork?"

Caprize's smile was fleeting. "Illustrative work. Drawings, hand lettering, and photos. It's an advertising realm I recently entered. I'd always had artistic talent, but never did much with it. A former coworker was a fan of my art and suggested I apply myself. So I have. I've even set up a studio at the house." With a knitted brow, she peered outside again. "Speaking of house, I'm not sure I'd like to return to mine right now."

"Our neighbor's having a party this evening. I'm sure he won't mind if you join us," I said amiably.

She scanned my face, glanced at Linda and then at Rey, and finally nodded.

"Why don't you and JJ hide behind that banyan?" Linda gestured a magnificent tree fifty feet behind the bench. "As soon as you're in place, Caprize and I will stroll to the car-park."

Rey clasped my arm. "We're on it."

Leaving via a side exit, we melted into a crowd of workers heading home. Quickly, easily, we slipped behind a cluster of thick woody trunks.

"Maybe this guy's got the serious hots for her and nothing more," Rey murmured.

"Then why not make his intentions known? Lurking around, wishing for something that will never be, isn't going to win brownie points," I stated.

"He could be super shy."

"He could be super stupid."

"Say, weren't you supposed to go out with Adwin tonight?" she smirked.

"Not the smoothest segue, Cousin Reynalda," I smirked in return. "We've rescheduled. He had to attend some important food function."

Rey's elbow shot into my ribs.

"Hey, that hur—"

"Ssh! Linda and Caprize are leaving, and Stalker Boy's getting up."

Tucking his hands into hoodie pockets, he slowly, casually, started strolling behind the two women. Silently, we followed, careful to remain several yards back.

"Can you make out anything?" I asked softly.

"The cap's too low and the hoodie neckline too high. But he looks to be of medium height—5'10"—and medium build. Nothing distinguishing."

We continued pursuit, pausing behind a streetlamp when

Stalker Boy stopped by the car-park entrance and leaned into a Rainbow Shower tree. Unfortunately, the lighting was less than ample.

"He's pulling out a pack of smokes."

"And Linda and Caprize should be pulling out of the car-park any second," I said.

"Doesn't look like he's much interested in anything but sucking in nicotine." Rey nudged my arm. "There they are. And there he is ... inhaling feverishly ... like a firing squad's about to shoot."

"You're right," I frowned. "He really doesn't seem much interested in anything but smoking."

Rey scowled. "What gives?"

"If it weren't for the fact that he followed them here, I'd say we're mistaken in assuming he's Caprize's stalker."

"Let's ask!"

Before I could react, my melodramatic in-your-face cousin had all but jumped in front of the fellow. I heard her greet him as I slipped alongside.

It was impossible to see his eyes because of the cap and the fact he was holding his shadow-filled face low, but prominent acne scars zigzagged a rounded chin. The jawline was angular, the lips tight, and the nose exceptionally long and pointed, prompting an image of a fox to come to mind. Given the stance, the man didn't seem surprised or shocked. Simply sucked on the cigarette as if it were a lifeline.

"We were wondering why you're following our friends."

He merely stood, silent.

"You *are* following them, right?" Rey smiled prettily. "Any particular reason?"

"Don't know what you're f'g talking about." The accent sounded fake "Noo Yawk" while the voice and tone were heavy and flat, like a grease-laden burger. Tossing the stub near Rey's feet, he sauntered off.

Her questioning look asked if we should pursue. I shook my head and nodded to the remains of the glowing cigarette.

* * *

A text message from Linda had arrived while Rey and I were in a cab six blocks away: *Sach & Al low on rum & pineapple juice. Grabbed us to go get some. We're being social and getting drunk. Where the hell are you?*

"There soon" was our response. Pulling before our house, my cousin and I raced inside and changed into Ts and flats, and pulled out a bottle of never-opened vodka from a living-room corner that would one day host a bar.

"Let's make sure we drop that butt off first thing when Hives is in."

I nodded. "Here's hoping we learn something from the DNA."

"We already learned one thing: Stalker Boy likes French cigarettes."

"Which he probably buys on-line or has sent from abroad."

"Which means there's no chance of locating him through local sales. But let's call around tomorrow anyway."

We headed to Sach's house six doors down. The four-bedroom, single-level home was crisp and clean—paint fresh, garage uncluttered, lawn and garden immaculate. The rear of the house contained the master bedroom and a decent-sized fitness room, which had originally been two guestrooms. There was an impressive rectangular pool surrounded by lava-gray Italian-slate stamped concrete and Mexican river rock. Sighs of envy escaped both our mouths.

Hearing Latin jazz playing at a moderate level from the pool and patio area, we swung around. A cheery-faced party of fifteen milled around a large glass-topped table supporting a huge array of noshables. Six folks were laughing and splashing in the pool and another six, glassy-eyed and grinning, stood by a well-lit Tiki bar.

Viewable through the patio doors were Linda and Caprize. Frothy peach-colored cocktails in hand, they were chatting with Sach and a tall rugged fellow—Al, no doubt.

"Looks like they're enjoying themselves," I said.

"Let's do the same," my cousin said, taking my arm.

I pulled back when the theme from *CHiPS* announced a call (I changed ringtone songs repeatedly and these days I was into retro TV show melodies).

Rey snorted and waited, ear cocked.

Sticking out my tongue, I turned.

One minute later, I turned back, my face surely as pale as my egg-white T-shirt.

"Oh-oh. What's up, sweetums?"

"We've now officially *heard* from GRP."

CHAPTER SIX

Rey's jaw dropped. "What the hell did he want?"

"To ask if we're up for the challenge."

"The challenge of playing his game or solving the murders?"

"He didn't specify," I said flatly, glancing back at the four-some beyond the patio. "He chuckled, too, like Vincent Price in *Thriller*."

"Figures. What about his voice?"

"It sounded as if he were talking through fabric, but it seemed deep and throaty. I didn't detect an accent."

Rey's mouth pulled into a taut line. "Let's not share with Linda until later."

Before I could reply, a sequoia of a man drew before us. "Lovely ladies, you can't come to a party and not mingle." A warm smile greeted us. "I'm Jethro. Let me get you drinks." Not waiting for a response, he gently grabbed our arms and guided us to the bar where he asked a pretty redhead to pour two Mai-Tais. Introductions were quickly made.

And the Mai-Tais quickly downed.

Twenty minutes and countless cheese-and-pork-topped nachos later, Rey and I followed Jethro and Jake, another goliath, into the house. Both were fitness instructors at a newly-opened upscale fitness studio. While the latter hailed from California, the former originated from Iowa. Amiable if not charming, they'd insisted on showing us Sach's fitness room.

"Nice, huh?" Jake asked with toothy smile as he flourished a beefy arm like an enthusiastic church usher.

The pine- and sage-colored room was filled with state-of-the-art fitness equipment and weights. Three tall arched windows were bordered by faux-silk taupe drapes while rubber matting covered the floor. Impressive was the word that came immediately to mind.

"Sach's doing real well," Rey commented, stepping onto a rear-drive elliptical.

"He did have help," Jake said, stepping alongside and fingering the control panel. "May I?"

She nodded and he complied.

"What kind of help?" she asked, beginning to take long strides.

"The Dowager paid for the reno and equipment."

We looked at Jethro, who had removed two Bowflex dumbbells and was starting to perform bicep curls, casually and effortlessly. I couldn't help but stare at his upper arms. Damn, they were huge. Well-developed. And very, well, sexy.

"The Dowager?" I asked.

"Great-Aunt Leticia May Morton. She's a rich lady who never had any kids and never had family ties. She moved to England when she was like twenty," he explained. "When she returned ten years ago, the family didn't want to have anything to do with her. But Sach responded to a tea invite one day, about five years ago. They've been close ever since."

"And he calls her The Dowager?" Rey's brow furrowed like a crumpled linen skirt.

"*She* calls herself that," Jake laughed. "Not sure why. You'd have to ask Sach."

Jethro put the weights back. "You two interested in fitness?"

"Sorta," Rey smiled.

"Kinda," I grinned.

"We have great rates for folks we like," he winked.

"I bet you do," Rey purred, turning off the elliptical.

"You both look good," Jake said.

"But we could look *better*," she finished for him, stepping down.

"Stronger," he replied cheerfully. "You're private eyes. You should develop some serious muscle tone ... learn defense moves ... so you can *really* scare off bad guys."

My cousin and I burst into laughter, then eyed each other and sobered. Tasers and guns were one thing, but who always had a weapon handy? Yes, we had taken some martial arts lessons, but not enough to flip a "bad guy" on his back or knock him out cold. And while I was a decent "beaner", the element of surprise was part of the equation (you couldn't bean someone if they knew it was coming). Jake's simple advice was worth serious thought and I told him as much.

With a thumb's up, he gestured the door. "How about we get this party started and have another drink?"

When *CHiPS* resounded. I inhaled sharply and glanced at Rey, and pulled the cell phone from my jean pocket. The number on the display wasn't familiar. GRP again? If so, for the moment, I wasn't going to play "the game".

* * *

"You sure you put the butt in this drawer?" Rey asked, perplexed.

"You saw me do it," I replied, unease suddenly stirring like recently ingested food ... of the tainted variety.

It was 8:00 a.m. and we'd just finished coffees. Normally, we picked them up on the way to the Chinatown office, but we'd stayed at Sach's longer—and imbibed more cocktails—than intended.

The plan was to drop by HPD with the cigarette stub and

huddle with Ald, who I'd texted an hour ago. He'd agreed to see us at nine.

"You don't suppose Stalker Boy followed us last night?" Linda asked, hopping off a kitchen-counter stool and slipping beside her BFF.

"How could he have?" I asked, stymied. "This doesn't make any sense."

The three of us stared into the drawer, hoping if we gazed hard and long enough, the butt might reappear.

"Maybe GRP came here because he got pissed off when you didn't pick up last night," Rey suggested. "And he came here—"

"But that wasn't GRP," I uttered. "It was Adwin. He texted me this morning to say he'd called last night from that function. He'd had to use the host's phone, which is why I didn't recognize the number."

"How would GRP know about the butt, anyway?" Linda asked, grabbing her Michael Kors leather tote and car keys from the kitchen table.

"He would if he'd been watching. He may have seen us pick up the butt ... maybe that was even his intention, to see if we would."

"Possibly," Linda said with a frown. "But in terms of it missing from our house, that means he'd have to have been close to see you place it in the drawer. And, if this were the case, why take it? To ensure we couldn't test it for DNA." Her frown deepened. "Come to that, if this *were* the case, how'd he get past the alarm?"

"We didn't turn it or the sensor lights on," I replied sheepishly. "We were in a hurry to get to Sach's and given we were only going to be a few doors down ..."

Linda tsked.

"Man, this f'g sucks." Rey slammed shut the drawer, causing the contents to rattle as if a small earthquake had transpired.

"This is too weird." I looked from Rey to Linda, bemused. "Unless he *was* watching and wanted to rile us."

"Part of the game? Or the challenge?" Rey asked.

"We'll have to be more watchful." I sighed and grabbed three bottles of water from the base of an island cart. "First things first. Let's meet Ald and learn all we can about the four Canal victims. Next, let's take Sach up on his offer to help. He can follow Stalker Boy while we focus on this new case—"

"The *non-paying* one," Rey said with a wry smile.

"Nothing wrong with *pro bono* work now and again," Linda stated, slapping her heartily on the back.

* * *

"Thanks for the coffee and calories." Ald Ives offered a quick smile as we made ourselves comfortable on a large worn leather sofa in the corner of his tiny butternut-squash colored office, one I'd always thought was size-perfect for accommodating two Abyssinian guinea pigs.

The detective spoke with a mid-west accent that better suited his former appearance, that of a wrangler or ranch hand. Last year he'd lost his twin brother, Gerald One and, subsequently, left behind frumpy off-the-rack suits and thick messy hair. To honor Ger's deathbed request, he'd adopted a new look that incorporated upscale fashion and a $200 coif, wine instead of beer, and a fine car in place of a jalopy. Ald was Gerald Two, if wasn't evident. Mother had been a pathologist assistant and Father a chemist; both leaned toward eccentric and had given the identical twins nearly identical names. As the boys had grown older and developed distinct personalities, they evolved into "Ger" and "Ald".

The ruggedly handsome man (think Viggo Mortensen in *Eastern Promises*) removed one of two haupia malasadas from the bag and took a bite. "So, you managed to lose evidence?"

"We didn't lose it," Rey sniffed. "It was stolen and, before you ask, yes, we're sure."

Narrowed Maya-blue eyes looked from her to me. He requested details.

Which I provided. When I was done, so was the malasada and its mate.

"And you really think, uh, GRP took it?"

We glanced at one another, shrugged, and nodded in unison.

He sighed loudly, gulped coffee, and drummed the small L-shaped desk with recently manicured fingers. "I'd send someone to the house, but I'd bet serious dollars there won't be anything to find. This guy's good."

"And then some," Rey muttered.

"Moving on to the four victims, did any witnesses come forward?" I asked

"Who saw the killer do the deadly deed or arrange the bodies by the canal?" Ald asked dully.

"Were there *any* witnesses who saw *anything* at *any* given time related to the four?" I responded gruffly. "Maybe someone saw a man dragging four long boxes or bags that seemed strange? Or viewed a delivery van out of the norm by the canal?"

Ald pursed his lips, appearing to debate what he might wish to share. Finally, he shrugged. "Talk to Sallo."

I sighed. "Will you tell us what you have on the four victims?"

He regarded me suspiciously. "This isn't your case."

"GRP *made* it our case," my cousin avowed.

Ald drew a deep breath and leaned back in the high-back swivel chair. "I'll share some details, but if you go snooping around—"

"Hey!" Rey glowered.

"Pardon me. If you go *detecting*, and find out any little thing, I want to know about it." He glared at her, then Linda, then me. "And you also share it with Hammill and Sallo."

"If we must," Rey said with exaggerated annoyance.

"You *must*, Fonne-Werde."

Her response: placing a thumb to her lips and wiggling fingers.

I sighed, wishing the two would grow up and/or make peace.

"We have four young adults, friends, who were in the wrong place at the wrong time: John Meurto, Raine Sonne-Spitz, Les Rutgar, and Rona Plantene. Their parents weren't even aware that anything had gone wrong. Jane and Isaac Sonne-Spitz hadn't been heard from their daughter since the twenty-fifth, but they're television producers and have been in Spain for the last five weeks working on a documentary. The Rutgars believed 'ever responsible' Les had traveled to Florida with friends. He was always taking off, thanks to an extensive allowance and not enough parental direction, so one of the maids told Hammill.

"Rona Plantene hadn't called from Cape Cod, where she was to have headed with two friends the afternoon of the twenty-fifth: Jeannette Lindsmore and Pedro Reede. We talked to them, but they had nothing to share other than they'd changed plans at the last moment, had left messages and texts for Rona, and gone their merry way elsewhere."

"Do you have the autopsy reports?"

"With photos or without?" he asked cynically. "Nothing like looking at waxy, spongy, blistered bodies laid out on a gurney, sporting multiple incisions, among other things."

"We've seen worse," I stated flatly.

He scanned my face and pointed at his laptop.

Rey and I all but sailed across the room. We scanned report details that described the internal examination, body cavities, and weights of organs. Ald chatted with Linda about the amount of pressure it took to collapse an artery versus a vein.

Rey looked up and asked blandly, "Are you trying to impress us with your forensic knowledge?"

He offered a Cousin Reynalda response: a strident raspberry.

"Why don't you two just kiss and make up?" Linda asked tartly as she ambled over.

I turned back to the report with Linda peering over my shoulder. The summary of injuries was comprehensive, but it wasn't the number of scrapes, scratches and lacerations that attracted attention, it was a common phrase: *abraded and contused furrows present on both left and right wrists and ankles.* What suffering the four must have endured during those last living hours.

Autopsy-related words and terms swirled in and around alternating images: subdural hematoma, petechiae, brown vomitus, dry drowning, adipocere, anoxia.

"What can you tell us in a proverbial nutshell, in layman's terms?"

"A down and dirty?" the detective asked drily. "Meurto died of multiple injuries with drowning. There were hemorrhages in the bony middle ears and there was a fine, white froth present in the airway, indicating he was alive at the time of submersion but barely, gauging from the type, number, and severity of the wounds."

Linda took another look at the report. "The others?"

"Sonne-Spitz, like Rutgar and Plantene, had an absence of liquid in the stomach, suggesting death prior to submersion. You want details of the injuries, like the fracture contusions involving the right posterior ... ?"

"Whatever ya got, Hives."

The thick notched scar running along his right temple pulsed, as it tended to do when angered or stressed, but this time he ignored her. "Bruised muscles and injuries to the hands and fingertips showed that Plantene, who was very fitness-minded, had struggled violently before death. Unfortunately, she'd not managed to scratch her killer because no traces of skin were found under her fingernails, which were always chewed to the quick according to sources."

"Just our luck," Linda sighed.

He sighed softly. "Preliminary examinations revealed traces of alcohol and drugs in all four, but toxicology tests and the like are still underway and conclusive determinations are forthcoming. According to Doc Halston, the water they'd been submerged in held evidence of nitrates and nitrites—"

"Such as that found in processed food?" asked Linda.

"Yes, and like those found in fertilizer and manure, as well as the decomposition of plants and animal organisms." He smiled fleetingly. "I received a corresponding briefing on groundwater and surface water, point sources versus non-point sources, organic contaminants versus inorganic contaminants, non-pesticide compounds, heavy metals, and volatile organic chemicals or VOCs, information I'm sure will someday prove useful ... to *someone*."

"As if they'd been placed in a pond or a pool?"

"Considering acid rain, storm-water and pesticide runoffs, the traces of decaying leaves, Doc Halston suggested it was likely they were placed in a tank or a well." Ald rose and stretched his arms. "Surface water is cleansed by sunlight, aeration, and micro-organisms. This water source had been secured."

Linda sat on the corner of the desk and crossed her arms, looking thoughtful. "As in covered with a lid? Like a manhole cover leading to a sewer or a drain? Or a tarp on a pool?"

A weary smile pulled at his full lips as he dropped the empty coffee cup into a metal receptacle. "I'll provide more conclusive results when I receive them."

"Will tests be run to see what type of fertilizer and—"

"Already in process," he assured her.

She frowned. "Care to bet a lunch of Machete sandwiches the compounds and composites are relative to the vicinity where our victims of misfortune were murdered?"

"The killer could have transported the bodies over a considerable distance."

"Could have," Linda said, "but I'd be inclined to think he wanted to be rid of them as quickly as possible."

"That would imply the guy is slipshod and anxious. This is only my humble opinion, ladies, but this guy—GRP as you call him—seems systematic and, in common vernacular, cool as a cucumber." He held up a strong, scarred hand. "Only in *my* humble opinion." He glanced at his cell phone when it buzzed.

Three-quarters of the quartet had died from drowning, yet all four had been submerged in water, then stored somewhere, out of the heat. Not a freezer, but a cool place/space. A cellar? An air-conditioned room or refrigerated locker? … A cave? Certainly they'd not crawled along the Ala Wai Canal like B-flick zombies and through telepathic communication simultaneously agreed to pose in the same horizontal positions?

"There's a twisted mind at work here, which is probably as redundant a comment as 'looks like rain'," Linda affirmed, handing the tablet to Ald. "We've been discussing the black roses and their significance."

"And?" he asked.

"We didn't come up with anything notable, but we'll keep at it," she promised with a trim smile.

"What about the immersion? Was it a cleansing? Or something done on a whim?" I mused aloud.

"Your guess is as good as anyone's right now," Ald said wryly and stood.

The group huddle was officially over.

CHAPTER SEVEN

The day at the agency was spent making calls to various shops to see if any French cigarettes had been sold recently, as well as to the victims' family members. Providing heartfelt condolences didn't seem enough; their pain was so raw. Nothing new was gleaned from the fret-filled conversations, but we did acquire a handful of names of close friends. Contacting them seemed the next logical step. As for the cigarette queries, they proved a waste of time, much like we'd expected.

Meanwhile, the media was still featuring stories of the four murders, hypotheses that ranged from crazy party shenanigans gone freakishly wrong to vengeance killings to potential serial killer running amok.

After a briefing—and advisory call to Caprize—Sach was all in re surveilling Stalker Boy. He'd be meeting with our client at her home this evening.

Interestingly enough, Sallo promptly returned our call and agreed to meet us for dinner at six at a diner off Auahi, near Cooke. We'd be footing the bill, of course. We were fine with that; eating with Sammie Sallo, not so much.

The three of us entered the quiet diner at 5:45, intending to have a beer and relax a bit before the tiresome detective arrived.

No such luck. He was already seated at a large corner booth, eyeing his Smartphone and sipping coffee, his signature Mike-Hammer fedora suspended from a hook sticking from the side of the booth. Who knew he had hair? Thin and wispy, it was pickled-herring gray.

Small dung-beetle-brown eyes peered up when we stopped before the table. Uneven lips pulled into a saccharine smile, but the triangular jawline tensed. "Evening, ladies," came the gruff greeting.

"Detective," Linda nodded, swinging alongside.

Rey and I acknowledged him and sat.

"Food here safe, uh, good?" My cousin gazed dubiously around the sizeable eatery that smelled of grease and onions, stale coffee and flat beer. Though clean, the paint was an ugly industrial-green popular in the 70s, probably the same decade the owner had last bought new furniture.

"Chili's tasty. Lots of ground beef. Burgers are decent." Tucking the Smartphone into an ugly lightweight plaid jacket, he called to the solitary waitperson chatting cheerfully with a couple at a small window table.

The flabby, pimply twenty-year-old offered a [buck] toothy smile and passed four dog-eared menus. "Hey. Nice to have ya here, yeah. What can I do for ya?"

"Usual for me, Clem. And bring a light beer. I'm off duty."

"What's the usual?" I felt compelled to ask.

"Chili with cheesy garlic bread."

The three of us looked at one another, shrugged, and ordered the same. The orders arrived quickly, so small talk was—thankfully, painlessly—short. As he arranged the meals and drinks, Clem updated us on his part-time IT studies and a newly adopted mutt named Ponch.

When he toddled off to see to four new patrons, we got down to business.

"We asked Hives earlier, but maybe something happened since. Any witnesses or sightings re the murders or murderer?"

Rey asked, studying a large thick slab of cheese-heavy garlic bread as if it might grow teeth and bite back.

Which prompted a smirk from Sallo. Snorting, he said, "It ain't gonna chomp back."

Appearing doubtful, she took a tiny bite, chewed, and nodded. "Damn. It's good. Real garlicky."

"Told you so," he simpered, digging into the chili.

Linda and I followed suit. Sallo would share information when he was ready and not a blink before.

Half-a-bowl later, he motioned Clem for another beer and sat back. "Jo Belcastro saw a black van around 7:30 the night you found the bodies. He was jogging along Date, near Laau, heading nowhere in particular. He noticed it because it was standing alone, real close to that house that burned down last month. As a landscaper, he tends to notice things that don't fit well, but he didn't think about it again until he settled in with the news last night after his jog."

"He called the police simply because he remembered a van parked near a burned-out house?" Linda asked, skeptical.

"He heard of the murders—who hasn't?—but he wasn't really following the news. Too many landscaping projects." With a smirk, he started on the garlic bread and we returned to our chili.

A couple minutes later, he was ready to pick up where he'd left off. "When he caught up on them last night—and saw the request for people to come forward if they'd seen anything out of the ordinary—he remembered the van and decided to call."

"What could he tell you about it?" I asked.

He frowned. "Not a helluva lot. Black. No lettering. Basic windows. Didn't catch the license plate. Only noticed it because it was the only vehicle there—in the shadows, slightly off the street, near that house some ass had set a torch to."

"That sucks," Rey said.

"Yeah. But there's something positive. Belcastro tripped and another guy and his dog, who weren't that far away, went to his rescue. Belcastro was okay. Just a skinned knee and bruised ego. They chatted briefly. Belcastro patted the dog and asked his name and all that, and then they parted ways."

The three of us leaned in close—grateful we all shared the same garlic breath—anticipating something more useful was about to be imparted. "When Belcastro called to tell us about it, he mentioned Barty the Springer Spaniel. Seems Barty's a favorite in the area, so it wasn't hard to track down his owner."

Linda gave a thumb's up.

"Barty's owner, Murphy Geist, saw the same van that night. Considering he wasn't far behind Belcasto, how could he not? Anyway, just after the two parted ways, owner and pooch continued their nightly stroll. After circling around, maybe ten or twelve minutes later, Barty began acting a touch weird—straining at the leash, making whiney doggy sounds."

"And Geist didn't think to see what might be bothering Barty?" I asked, astonished.

"He'd been mugged a couple of times and figured it might be some thug lurking in the shrubbery with bad deeds on his mind. He decided it was a good time to head home and head home fast."

"And?" I prompted.

His expression bordered on smug. "He sighted a guy in the van."

Rey all but squealed. "No shit?"

Sallo simpered. "The guy'd obviously just slipped into the van—and it was long enough for Geist to notice a shape, a profile if you like, before he slammed shut the door."

"Was he tall, fat, ugly—"

"The guy was dressed in dark clothes. Geist couldn't make out height or size or anything, but noticed he was wearing a baseball cap, pulled low on his head."

An image of Stalker Boy came to mind, but a lot of men wore baseball caps. "Was he doing anything out of the ordinary?" I prodded.

"Nope." He eyed me closely. "But Geist heard music as he was leaving with his furry buddy in tow. Creepy classical stuff. Funeral like."

Rey speared a couple of fat beans with a chunky fork, eyed them fixedly and popped them into her mouth. "The creepy-sounding van didn't drive past him?"

"Nope. And he wasn't tempted to look back. Guess the music was the clincher in making him scurry home like a hen-pecked hubby."

"I wonder where it went," Rey murmured to no one in particular.

"We're hoping surveillance and traffic cameras caught it."

Linda shook her head. "I'm betting they didn't."

"You're probably right," he agreed with a grunt. "But we're checking it out anyway."

"Can we get a detailed description of the van?" Rey asked, looking hopeful.

"What I just told you is all what we have."

"But was it new? Boxy? Sleek? Maybe a weird shape?" she persisted.

"I repeat: what I just told you is all what we have. But if we see anything on camera, I'll share it." He looked at his empty glass and swore under his breath. "But if we see anything on camera, I'll share it." He eyed his empty glass and swore under his breath.

"It's a start, Sallo." She offered a dark smile. "As Enright, an actor friend always says: it's better'n a poke in the eye with a sharp stick."

He snorted. "You got that right, sister."

* * *

"Thanks for meeting me tonight, Jill—uh, JJ." Adwin sipped Chardonnay as he scanned my face. "That'll take getting used to. Who decided on JJ?"

"... A former legal associate." Otherwise known as Cash Layton Jones, agent/drug dealer, and colossal pain in the ass.

It was a little after ten and we'd been seated at a small corner table in McLord's for fifteen minutes, making how's-it-going, what-have-you-been-doing, you-look-great small talk while watching cheerful patrons greet and meet. As always, the Irish pub was bustling.

After Sallo, Linda had decided on a lengthy walk and Rey had determined a Macy's sale was in her best interest. My ex-beau had phoned three minutes after my cousin had excitedly flown out the front door like a parasailer taking flight. Considering I wasn't even remotely sleepy (and not inspired to do anything remotely challenging), it seemed as good a time as any to get together with my ex-beau.

I tried not to stare. The pastry chef had changed. Short straight hair the color of pitch had been shorn and a classic balbo graced a face I'd, in earlier times, thought a cross between Marilyn Manson and Matt Damon. The previously Ichabod-Crane skinny body was toned; formerly nonexistent shoulders were strong while previously willowy arms sported noticeable biceps. Cremini mushroom-brown eyes no longer hid behind square-shaped glasses and the sun had kissed normally pasty-pale skin. If I peered beneath the table, I was sure I'd find sturdy thighs instead of reedy ones. He was obviously into fitness and it looked good on him. *Real* good... Damn.

Apparently, he was thinking something similar. "You look amazing. I love your hair. It's kind of like a starting-to-grow-out mullet, but cool." He looped a strand around a long, slender finger. "I liked you Gothy, but this is ... really nice."

When Rey, Linda and I had moved to Oahu, I'd given up the Goth look sported for years and opted for chocolate-brown hair with honey highlights. Unruly waves usually hung well past my shoulders, loose and free, and fun—until an episode with a crazy gun-wielding woman resulted in seven stitches and one side of my head being shaved. To not stand out (too much) the other side had been shaved. I now sported a style I'd thought sort of resembled a 70s shag cut but maybe, more accurately, was what Adwin had called it, "a starting-to-grow-out mullet". It'd grow out ... eventually.

Sensing someone watching, I glanced around. My gaze fell upon a nondescript man at the bar wearing a Rainbow Warriors cap. He peered over, smiled, and raised his beer mug, then began chatting with an equally nondescript man beside him. Casually, I scanned the bar. Two other men wore caps. Three more, playing an enthusiastic if not strident game of darts, also wore them and one, again, advertised the Rainbow Warriors. Although I was certain I'd left my imagination at home, it was getting the better of me.

I chided myself and focused on Adwin. "I'm sorry things didn't work out with Lizbeth."

He shrugged. "It wasn't meant to be, but I don't regret it. We clicked as a couple for those few months." He eyed me intently. "What about you? Anyone?"

Cash came immediately to mind—like an icepick headache. Was he a boyfriend? No. A lover? Occasionally. In my life currently? No. Did I care? Yes. Frig it. "None of us is seeing anyone. We haven't had much luck in the relationship department to be honest, and that's okay. We're focused on making the agency a success. But Linda's made a new friend in our office building. Mink Ranch." I chuckled as I envisioned the eternally energetic woman and her four Lowchens: Snicker, Doodle, Peanut, and Butter.

"That's a name?"

"It is indeed. She's the proud owner of Minky-Dinky Doggy Dos—designer duds for discerning dogs."

Adwin laughed and nodded when the ever-grinning waitperson sauntered past and motioned our glasses.

"How long are you staying?"

" ... Indefinitely."

"Oh?"

"Blaze, an old culinary-school buddy, and I ... we're opening a restaurant on the waterfront in Kailua next month. Steaming Mimi's."

After picking my jaw off the floor, I managed to find my voice and ask when he'd made the decision.

"Last fall." He smiled ruefully. "I didn't want to tell you about it before, in case things fell through."

"Why here?"

"I kept hearing what a great place it was—from a number of people, including your mom when we'd bump into each other at the market. And Blaze always dreamed about living in a warm climate." He thanked the waitperson with a smile and a nod when the Chardonnays arrived. "I was hoping maybe we could, you know, be friends again. I mean, you know, do stuff together now and again. We had a lot of fun times."

"We did," I agreed. "But it'll cost you a few tortes."

"Heavy on the buttercream?" he joked, then exhaled slowly. "I have to admit, I was nervous coming here. I thought you might tell me to get lost or spit out something Rey-like." Adwin didn't care for swearing and cursing. He used to claim he worked with people who did enough of it to curl his naturally straight hair like that of a Bichon Frise.

"Why? We parted amiably." I toasted him. "Here's to friendship, tried and true."

He squeezed my hand and smiled gratefully. "So, tell me about this new life as a private eye."

CHAPTER EIGHT

"Very cool," Sach said, twirling slowly on the large Persian-green flatweave rug in the center of the main agency office. "Not what I'd expect a private-eye place to look like."

"You were expecting something à la Sam Spade?" Rey asked with a wry smile and dropped into one of four blended-leather chairs.

"Kinda." He grinned and sat on a rattan sofa.

"Coffee?" Linda held up a freshly made pot as she stood in our "sort-of" kitchen, a small niche with a counter and room (barely) for a small fridge, coffee machine and kettle, and toaster oven.

"Sure, with a little milk." He pulled down the sleeves of a raspberry-red quarter-zipper argyle sweater. "Who'd have thought it could get so cool so fast? My eleven o'clock client will probably nix the beachfront run."

I grabbed one of ten mugs sporting the agency's name and held it out for Linda to fill. "Are you finally going to tell us about your evening at Caprize's?"

"Your 'wait'll-you-hear-this' text got us *real* curious," Rey stated with an acerbic smile.

Sach grinned like a game-prize winner and accepted the mug

Linda passed. She sat alongside him and the three of us regarded him intently (and not necessarily patiently).

"Your Woman in Black is into flowers."

"She's into what?" My question had to sound as stupefied as my expression.

"Flowers. Roses. Lilies. But mostly orchids." He tested the coffee. A tilt of the head one way and then the other suggested he was okay with it.

I grabbed a haupia muffin from a box on the desk and perched on a corner. "So, she's an amateur horticulturist?"

"A damn good one. A few plants are in the studio, but most are in the basement—yeah, she actually has one. And what's kind of neat—okay, kind of weird—is that they're only in shades of dark red, deep purple, and near black. She's won a couple awards and even belongs to some society. It's called The Fellowship of Orchid ... Orchidaceae Voters."

Linda chuckled. "*Votaries.*"

"Yeah, that's it! Anyway, her studio's at the rear, in a two-story *ohana*. The top is a makeshift office and den, where she does advertising-marketing work. The first floor is a living and entertaining area, with lots of photos—primarily hers. The main house has a larger version of the same living and entertaining area, but no photos. Which is kinda odd. Anyway, the cellar, or basement, is where you'll find lots of plants and special lights to help them grow. To the rear is a pantry, or fruit cellar, or cold-room maybe. She closed the door as soon as we got down the stairs. Before she did, though, I saw dozens of bottles and jars on shelves. The cellar, I have to confess, creeped me out, because there were a whack of small surrealistic oil paintings—hers and a close friend's, she said—and the walls are in intense shades of purple and blue."

"Paintings of what?" I asked, curious.

"Bizarre creatures of the night. Fantasy stuff."

Rey, Linda and I looked at one other as if to say, "nothing surprising there".

Linda got up to top off mugs. "Any photos?" she asked.

"About a dozen, oddly in black and white."

"You think it's maybe strange that she's into dark flowers, especially roses?" Rey asked.

"Also lilies, but primarily orchids," Sach repeated. "You really find that strange?"

I shrugged. "Maybe we should check her out? See if there's anything weird out there?"

"I'll do some digging this aft, time permitting, and send an email to Sally. Maybe she can unearth something," Linda said. Sally was Linda's NYC friend, an ace freelance fact-finder and documentary research assistant.

"If there's anything to unearth," Sach said drily. He turned to me. "How'd I do?"

"Your details are amazing—you've got a P.I. eye," I replied.

He smiled proudly.

"What about Stalker Boy? Any sightings?" Rey asked.

"When we were back in the main house, in the living room, I looked out the window after hearing a crash, like a large bin overturning. There was a shadow of a guy standing four doors down on the opposite side of the street. He must have saw me at the window, because he hurried away."

"Was he wearing a cap?"

"Yeah. It was pulled low so I couldn't see the face, not that I'd have seen much anyway, given he wasn't under a street-light. I wanted to follow him, but Caprize—who was standing beside me with a glass of wine—got startled and spilled it on me."

"Bad timing," Linda murmured. "Did you notice anything else, anything of note?"

He shook his head. "Only that he wore dark pants and a dark baggy sweatshirt."

"We should talk to neighbors," Rey suggested, stretching long lean legs.

"They might confirm that they've seen him, but I'll bet they won't be able to provide any additional insight," I said with a soft sigh.

"Not necessarily," Sach said smugly.

"Spit it out, Morin," Rey ordered.

"When I left about ten minutes later, an old guy was letting his dog, Puckers, take a leak on the lawn. I went over to ask him if he'd noticed anything out of the ordinary, like a guy hanging around the street. He invited me in for tea. Jenners Altenmann is his name and he likes the History channel and chocolate-chip cookies." He smiled gaily. "He's become a self-professed busybody since his wife passed away three years ago, so he's always sitting on the lanai or peering out windows. He hadn't noticed anything or anyone out of the ordinary—except for a car the other night with three women in it."

The three of us glanced at each other, then giggled.

"Altenmann promised he'd keep his eyes open for lurking loonies. I gave him an agency card."

Linda gave a thumb's up. "Maybe you could drop by a few homes on Caprize's street if you have time later today."

"Be happy to."

An unasked question had been plaguing me for the last few minutes, sitting there like a bubble of air that refused to pass. "If she's a photographer, why'd she never take a photo of Stalker Boy?"

"Maybe she never thought about it. Or she felt there was no need to take one," Sach responded. "Considering he's always lurking in shadows, it'd be pretty hard anyway."

"Makes sense." Rey nodded and looked at me. "And why bother? She wasn't going to go to the police, remember?"

"I remember." Many things. None of them useful. Yet.

* * *

"Nice flowers," Rey commented, peering over my shoulder at the gold-flecked carton that had just arrived at the agency.

It was a few minutes before noon and Linda had joined Mink for a casual lunch in the doggy-wear designer's office. I'd declined as I'd already picked up shrimp wonton mein at a noodle house not far down the street and Rey had passed with a monotone "not hungry". Whether that was because she wasn't a fan of Mink or the fact her BFF and Mink were becoming good pals remained to be seen.

She dropped onto the rattan sofa beside me with a thud.

"Hey, we can't afford to replace broken furniture," I chided.

"You going to open that?" She poked the carton with a long apple-red fingernail.

"My, my, my. Aren't we curious?"

"We are. Now, open it!"

Chuckling, I untied the satin ribbon. Inside, wrapped in light-weight tissue were twelve long-stem crimson roses.

"Nice." Her tone was flat, her gaze narrowed. "What about the card?"

I passed it. "You do the honors."

She unsealed the small gilt-edged envelope like a pro. "Lovely flowers for lovely ladies." She turned it over and shrugged. "Looks like you have—hold on, it says 'ladies'. But the delivery was to you."

"Looks like *we* have a secret admirer."

She frowned. "They're roses."

"But they're not black," I said with a tight smile.

Her frown deepened. "You think they might be from GRP?"

"It's possible, but I'd expect him to enclose a taunting or sinister message. And the flowers would be black, or close to." I shrugged. "These could be from a former client or a mischievous friend."

"Our friends don't have money to blow on high-end roses," she stated, eyeing them circumspectly. "*Maybe* a client."

I stood. "May as well put them in a vase."

"We don't have one."

"Then I'll run down to the little trading shop next door and buy one. They're too pretty to let wither."

"Take 'em home." She smiled faintly. "The place could use some color."

"They still need water until we leave."

She shrugged and started to remove them from the box—and shrieked. "Shit! I forgot about thorns."

But it wasn't a thorn that was sticking from a bleeding finger when she held it up—but a mini razor blade for a snap-blade knife.

She looked at me crossly. "You were sayin' something about *friends*?"

CHAPTER NINE

"Too bad the kid's description isn't going to help much," Ald stated as he, Rey and I sat at a beachside café, watching people amble past.

The weather had changed dramatically since noon; it was pleasantly warm with no breeze or clouds. Sunset was but a few minutes away and several tourists were taking photos from various vantage points—beach, boardwalk, balconies.

Rey picked up a fat fry, jammed it into a SUV-sized mound of ketchup, and scrutinized it like a mycologist studying culture in a screw-top tube. "He earns a quick twenty bucks to run in and order flowers, pay with cash and provide a note regarding address and drop-off details. And all he remembers is that the guy who 'hired' him was of average height and build with dark hair peeking from beneath a beanie and dark clothes. Shit."

Ald smirked. "Young Keene had a date with a new girlfriend on the brain."

"That twenty no doubt made his day *and* date," I said with a wry smile. "I wonder if it was GRP who 'hired' Keene or if GRP had someone else engage him."

The detective finished his pint of light beer. "Hopefully, our team will find something on the carton or flowers."

"Besides my blood?" Rey held up her stitched middle finger before popping the fry between glossy pomegranate lips.

Ald glowered, then snickered and looked at me. "By the way, you *are* keeping GRP under wraps, right? No mention of your relationship with the killer to anyone, particularly the frothing-at-the-mouth media, right?"

"We haven't shared with anyone except the folks in blue and Sach," I replied. "We have no intention of adding fuel to the fire. The island's nervous enough."

Ald frowned. "Is Sach reliable? We don't need—or want—certain details finding their way into the media."

"… He's reliable."

"I hear hesitation, Fonne."

"Yes, he's reliable," I affirmed. "A tad excitable, and very eager, but he'll remain mum if asked. Count on it."

Rey met my gaze and we exchanged quick nods: a talk with Sach was on the agenda.

"Any news on Howdy, uh, Quist's murder?"

He eyed Rey critically.

"What about his personal stuff? Or Caprize's business card? Anything of interest found?"

"There was forty dollars, a receipt for a recently purchased sound system, and a Macy's card in the wallet. No business card."

"What about new leads regarding the Canal murders?" my cousin asked, leaning back and eyeing two twenty-something surfers saunter past.

"A bit young, Fonne-Werde."

"A bit not-your-business, Hives," she sniffed.

Ald chuckled. "Driscoll said the roses was comprised of material that was primarily fibroin."

"Silk?" I asked, motioning the waitperson for another round of beers.

"Silk," he affirmed, crossing broad arms across his chest. "The silk filament is composed of a thread-like protein called fibroin. Silk is a proteinaceous filament produced in the posterior silk glands of the larva of the silkmoth, or *Bombyx mari*." He smiled when he noticed my eyebrows kiss the top of my forehead. "Grade 10 chemistry, courtesy of Demers Driscoll."

"Were they store-bought roses? Hand-made? Are they common? Ones we could find in a multitude of places?"

"Ah, the detective mind at work. It's a beautiful thing." Ald eyed the pile of fries and took two. "They're hand-made, for sure. The flowers are small, tight, very delicate and intricate, and before you ask, no, they're not traceable, and, yes, we have been checking ... endlessly and tirelessly. The fabric comes from China in bulk and could have been purchased in numerous places. No clues re DNA. Whoever made these little 'accessories'," he grimaced, "knows not to spit, sneeze, or shed hair while craft-making."

"The same no doubt holds true when killing," Rey grimaced. "The dude probably wears a mask or some sorta protective face gear."

"Maybe HAZMAT gear," he scowled, "or a scuba-diving suit. In any case, he's careful and clever."

"Clever *and* lucky," I added.

"Maybe too clever by half," Rey murmured, then smiled. "Luck does wear down eventually."

"But when is 'eventually'? At body count number twenty-two?" I stared across the ocean. "Do we know of similar killings?"

Ald didn't respond.

"Spit it out, Hives," Rey ordered.

"Don't tempt me to spit it out ... in your face."

Her response was to stick out her tongue.

I rolled my eyes. "Come on, Ald, share. Please."

He gazed from her to me and shrugged. "Early last year, there was a nasty car accident on the North Shore that took the lives of three young people."

"I remember."

79

"So do I," Rey stated. "Two guys and a girl. They were coming home from a birthday party or something."

"A high-school reunion." Ald.

"They were full of cheer and booze." Me.

"Which lent itself to recklessness. They had the radio on loud as they rocked and rolled down the road."

"Yeah." Rey snapped her fingers. "Daddy had loaned his new Lexus to his son, and it ended up with deep dents, smashed windows, a missing door, and a demolished trunk. The thing looked like it had kissed the tail end of a twister."

Ald drew a deep breath and nodded.

"But it wasn't an accident, was it?"

"It was until very recently. The black roses on the Canal victims rang a bell for a cop who'd worked the accident."

"They weren't laid out and posed like the four we found. They were in the car," Rey stated, regarding him intently. "But there *were* roses, weren't there?"

"They were found in the stream still seat-belted, slashed and gashed, which wasn't surprising given the plunge taken down the embankment. It wasn't a pretty sight when the first responders got there."

Our waitperson swung around and placed fresh beers on the small round table.

"What about the roses?" I prompted Ald.

"Frank and Nico had ones pinned to their denim jackets, and Carolyn had one on her sweater."

Stunned, my cousin and I could only gape.

"Yeah," he nodded. "No one had thought anything of it at the time. Why would they?"

"But this cop remembered and brought it to someone's attention," Rey urged.

"He did and it prompted us to see if anyone else had died in the last while wearing a black rose."

"And?"

"Remember the two young homeless men—Ongelukkig and

Nestastny—found two summers ago near Point Panic, by the water's edge?"

"The ones who'd gotten into bad heroine and freaked out with a jackknife and penknife that were found nearby?" I asked with an involuntary shudder. "There was mention of whiskey bottles, too."

His gaze hardened. "It looked like a doped-up, drink-heavy free-for-all."

"... They were wearing black roses?"

He shook his head. "I called someone working that case. Photos showed that two roses were lying beside a broken bottle. Again, no one thought anything of it at the time. No reason to. I also had the autopsy reports sent over. It seemed the incisions and punctures were quite precise."

"Too precise for a 'doped-up, drink-heavy free-for-all'?" I asked darkly. "Didn't anyone think to question that?"

"They did, but nothing ever came out of it." After sipping beer, and a moment of reflection, Ald continued. "There was also a college-aged couple—the Daltons—who'd just flown in from Boston, found three summers ago by the Waihï Stream, not far from Manoa Falls. They'd been beaten and slashed. At the time it was labeled a mugging gone terribly wrong. But they, too, had been sporting black roses. Again, they'd been at a party, so the roses, at that time, were simply considered—"

"Party favors?" Rey asked sarcastically.

He gazed at the mug as if he were peering into a crystal ball. "We definitely have a long-term serial killer on our hands ... using the black rose as a calling card." He looked up and across the ocean with a glower. "The similarities, besides the cuts were found alongside rivers or waterways."

"So, we're looking at killings transpiring over a good three years, maybe more, yet GRP only recently made himself known," I murmured.

"He obviously never felt a need to announce himself before."

"I'm curious as to how the three in the car ended up going

81

down the embankment. Yes, we know booze and drugs were in their systems, but given the black roses, we also now know that the cause couldn't have been a result of an accident due to booze and drugs," I said. "There were no signs of another car having propelled them off the road?"

"Or could GRP have been with them?" Rey put forth.

"And taken the plunge with them *and* walked away?" Ald shook his head. "Not likely. Too bad there were no witnesses to advise about another car. But the reconstruction process, structural damage, and physical evidence suggested there'd been no other vehicle."

"What about the undercarriage of the car? Anything found there?"

"Dirt and debris. Fertilizer. Grass. The usual. Nothing that wouldn't have collected or come about after several hours on the road, and nothing out of the norm to suggest they'd been at a specific location or area."

"Sounds like they traveled along a rural road or two," I remarked casually.

"Hey, wasn't there talk about fertilizer in terms of the Canal victims?" Rey asked.

Ald nodded and shrugged. "Coincidence probably, but a comparison is on the agenda."

Her brow puckered like tightly stitched cloth. "What about that couple, the Daltons?"

"No trace evidence re a killer, not even a fiber. No visible,"— he held up a finger as he cited each type—"patent, latent, molded or plastic prints."

"Maybe you need to go back and review *all* the items found at the scenes," Rey suggested.

He eyed her critically, but evidently saw nothing in the relaxed expression to suggest she was mocking or patronizing him. "Yeah, maybe."

"Meaning you're already on it," I winked.

With a salty smile, he drained the mug, and strolled away.

* * *

Rey and I sat on the lanai with veggie burgers barbecued by yours truly (no singed-eyebrow incidents this time) and tomato-cuke salads prepared by her (only two nicks this time). It was just after seven and it was leaning toward cool again, the afternoon span of warmth now a memory. Sporting hoodies and jeans and fluffy slippers—dogs with floppy ears for me, bunnies with whiskers for her—we lounged under a star-speckled sky. Although Rey had offered the odd off-color joke, I could sense she was miffed that Linda had accompanied Mink Ranch to the "Canines to the Nines" fashion show.

I elbowed her gently in the ribs when I saw her spear the same tomato slice for the fourth time. "You've become a pretty decent salad-maker."

"I've come a long way," she smiled wryly. "Maybe I'll be able to move up to decent pasta-prep next."

I elbowed her again and placed the plate on the ottoman. "Too bad Linda's friend Sally didn't find out much about Caprize."

"Only that she seemed to have an everyday kind of life and was married in Cali a few years back. But then she did say she had little time to do much research. Should we ask Linda to have Sally dig some more?"

I shrugged. "It doesn't sound like there's much there, but we can do some digging too."

The theme from *Peter Gunn* announced a call (I'd recently added ringtones to the agency mobile phone, too). I hastened into the kitchen.

"Good evening, Ms. JJ."

"Good evening." I looked at Rey, who had followed and was watching. I arched a shoulder. I didn't recognize the baritone voice that seemed a little distant, as if he were standing away from the phone.

"Did you like the roses?"

I turned on the speaker and said tartly, "The razor blade wasn't very nice."

"I wanted to get your attention, but maybe that hadn't been the best way to do so. I'm sorry. I hope your cousin didn't experience too much pain."

"I didn't, thanks, but the intern did when I kicked him," she declared flatly.

"You've had our attention for some time, by the by," I added.

"But you're not playing the game." He sounded like a petulant child who hadn't received enough ice-cream.

"What *is* the game? You haven't exactly described the activity or sport, or set any rules. All you've done is asked if we're up for the challenge."

"True again." He inhaled and then exhaled dramatically. "To be honest, I was rather hoping *you'd* establish them as we went along."

"Why us?"

"Why you?"

"Why did you pick us of all the private investigators to be found on Oahu?"

"Besides the fact you're all easy on the eyes, you've been quite successful at solving cases in the short time you've been in business." He chuckled. "Granted, you've had to put in a lot of time and energy into each case, but ultimately, you caught your culprit."

I strolled to the door and peered out casually. Was he watching? Probably. "Do you want us to catch *you*?"

"I want you to try."

"That's the game, then?" I asked bluntly. "To nab a nutcase?"

"Ha-ha, ha-ha. I'm far from a 'nutcase', Ms. JJ."

"You kill people on a whim, Mr. GRP."

"Never on a whim, oh fair dearheart. *Never* on a whim," he said theatrically and disconnected.

CHAPTER TEN

Rey leaned into the kitchen counter. "He's getting overconfident."

"*Getting*? He already was," I responded drily. "What he *is* getting is outright cocky. I hope he's not planning to do this daily."

"Let him. The cockier he gets, the easier it'll be to catch him." She stepped onto the lanai to collect plates and cutlery.

"How's that?" I asked when she returned.

"The more self-absorbed he gets, the more likely he'll slip up."

"Good point," I conceded. "Let's review what we learned to date and see if there are any similarities between the victims."

"You mean discover something the police haven't?" She pulled out two bottles of water from the fridge. "Speaking of, maybe you better call Hives."

I accepted a bottle and left a voicemail when Ald didn't pick up. I was just about to place the cell phone on the table when *The Love Boat* pulled into port. Exchanging an anxious glace with Rey, I answered.

It was Adwin, asking if I'd like to meet him for lunch on the weekend. I did.

She eyed me suspiciously. "You two getting back together?"

"We're just friends," I assured her. Fortunately, before she could pursue it, Sach knocked on the kitchen door and slipped inside before we could invite him in.

"I met with more of Caprize's neighbors," he announced gaily, swinging around the counter and plopping onto a kitchen table chair with a thud.

"And you learned a shitload of stuff about Stalker Boy," Rey said with a droll smile.

"Not a shitload. But two people confirmed they saw a guy dressed in dark clothes hanging around, admiring flowers and shrubs."

"But they didn't get a real good look, right?"

"Mrs. Kotter did. She and Angheim walked past the guy—Angheim is her Dalmatian—and being a happy-go-lucky gal and greeter, she said 'good evening'. He reciprocated."

Excited, Rey and I took seats across from him.

"Could she describe how he looked and sounded?" Rey asked eagerly.

"Medium height, youngish, with dark eyes and hair. She recalls the voice as being really deep, with an exaggerated British accent. He didn't stick around to chat, though. As soon as he said 'good evening' in kind, he turned and walked down the street."

"Was he wearing a cap?"

"She didn't mention it." Sach gazed from Rey to me, appearing slightly perturbed. "Did I do okay?"

"You did good." Rey patted his beefy hand and looked at me. "He kinda sounds like the guy at the parking garage the other night."

"Kind of," I nodded. "No mention of acne or long nose, though."

"She may not have noticed. Or maybe she did and didn't think to mention it at the time we talked," he said. "Let me ask her. I said I'd drop by the Tinkers—her neighbors—tomorrow afternoon. They're returning from Maui tonight."

"Do you want to stay on top of Stalker Boy?" I asked, smiling. "You'll get some practice playing P.I. and the three of us will have more time to focus on GRP."

"You bet! Thanks for the vote of confidence and opportunity." The elated smile flipped into a troubled frown. "You're seriously going after that crackpot?"

Rey and I looked at each other and smiled darkly.

"He wouldn't want it any other way," I declared.

The following morning found the three of us going our separate ways. The gray, cool Saturday had Linda taking a "health day" on the North Shore, which included eating well, meditating on a quiet beach, walking 10K, and playing with Piggaletto (she thought the little porker might enjoy an outing). Rey was spending the day with an actor she'd met at the theater late last year: Brie Kaese. I'd decided to take Button to the Canal, enjoy a long walk, and then meet Adwin on the beach; he'd called early that morning asking if I'd like to indulge in shave ice and a stroll. It might not have promised to be an exciting day, but it would certainly prove a tranquil one.

Just before I was about to chug an industrial-size coffee, Caprize had phoned to provide positive feedback re Sach and request the four of us come over for Sunday brunch. She seemed amiable if not animated, as opposed to lofty, and we chatted about plans for the day, the weather, favorite foods, and upcoming/hoped-for vacations, everything and anything but Stalker Boy. In terms of finding something out-of-the-ordinary re Caprize on the local front, we hadn't lucked in; we did find mention of her flower photos (she'd had an exhibition had a popular café last year), a promotion at the agency, and had shared credentials in an award-winning commercial about caffeine-infused pralines, but nothing remotely suspicious.

Walking along the Ala Wai Canal, from Kapahulu Avenue to McCully Street and back again, I couldn't help but recall the murders, try as I did to dispel the grim images. Finally, the two of us settled on a bench near the Honolulu Zoo, not far from the car. My fuzzy friend was delighted to meet and greet fellow canines; I was simply happy to veg.

Ald had called late last night and I'd given him a rundown on the conversation with GRP. The plan was to pinpoint the killer's location next time he called, but gut instinct advised GRP was too smart to continue calling; he'd find other ways of communicating.

I had to laugh as Button and a playful Collie, aptly named Colleen, struck up a friendship. His owner, a middle-aged gent with face and hair not unlike his charge, sat down and shared his life story as an inventor and manufacturer. I learned more about portable forehead un-furrowers and mini coconut mallets in those twenty minutes than I'd ever need to know. Nothing like expanding one's knowledge. When Mr. Hund and Colleen finally decided to return home, Button and I strolled toward the beach, where Adwin would be waiting.

The pastry chef was sitting cross-legged on the sand, not far from the Kuhio police station. Dressed in jeans, a white-and-navy striped shirt, and a denim jacket, he was engrossed in a young couple playing Frisbee. Whether it was the string-bean guy's colorful 80s Mohawk or the girl's short shorts and 38C chest that had his full attention was anyone's guess.

I gave his backside a light kick.

A frown twisted into a smile when he saw me. "Hey."

"Hey."

"How goes detecting?"

"It doesn't." I sat beside him. "For the moment, anyway."

"Things'll pick up." He hooked a strong arm around my neck

and kissed my temple, letting his lips remain a second longer than a casual peck normally necessitated.

I eyed him, surprised. Public displays of affection had never been in his make-up. Interesting. People truly did change.

Button demanded attention and he offered it with a chuckle. "Oh, almost forgot." He pulled a small card—the sort found in a carton of flowers—from a shirt breast pocket. "A little friend left this for you about ten minutes ago."

I drew a sharp breath and glanced at the card with "JJ" in Jokerman font. "Which little friend?"

He pointed at four young boys scampering along the Waikiki Wall. "The one with the crazy curls and plum-red T-shirt. He stopped by maybe five minutes ago."

How detailed a description would the "little friend" provide if asked for one re the person who'd enlisted his assistance? "Would you mind bringing him over here? Tell him he'll earn some money if he spares a couple minutes."

"Sure." He hopped to his feet.

I peered around and saw no one of note. But then GRP wouldn't be standing in the open, sporting a sandwich board advertising "nutcase at your service". Drawing a deep breath, I removed the card. A detailed metallic-gold lily lay across a thin embossed black line that ran along the edge of the classy—pricey—camel-colored card. The message: *Ms. JJ, given your fellow detectives and friends are out and about, perhaps you and your boyfriend (?) could do the honors: please proceed to Flavo's Fish Flakers past Mikole, toward Sand Island SRA Park. You won't be disappointed, just as I know you won't disappoint me.*

Without thinking, I took several quick photos of it. As Rey might say: ya never know what can happen.

"Hi auntie."

I looked up to find a television-cute, pre-teen face. Round bear-brown eyes watched me eagerly.

"Hey." I offered a sunny smile. "What's your name?"

"Niko."

"Nice name." I patted the sand beside me, and he fell to his knees. Button took an instant liking to him. "How would you like to earn $20?"

He hugged Button and started scratching her ears and nose. "Sure!"

Adwin chuckled and pulled out his wallet.

"Tell me about the person who asked you to drop off this card?" I held it up.

He looked worried. "Did I do something wrong? The dude seemed okay. Even gave me $10 to do it."

"You did fine," I assured him, devising a quick lie. "I have a secret admirer. He sends flowers and cards regularly but won't tell me who he is. I thought maybe you could give me a description. I'm dying to know who he is."

Niko brushed heavy chocolate-brown curls from his eyes and returned his attention to Button, now lying on her back. "Like I said, he seemed okay. Nice."

"What did he look like? Tall? Short? Fat? Thin? Gray eyes or brown? What was he wearing?"

"Black jeans and a black sweater. He had dark eyes, I think. He wasn't tall, but he wasn't short."

I tried not to appear discouraged. "Would girls think he's cute?"

Niko stopped rubbing Button's belly and studied my face. "Maybe. He wasn't ugly or anything."

"Maybe he had a scar or marks on his face?" Adwin asked with an easy smile. "Did he have an accent? A soft or high-pitched voice?"

I looked at him, impressed. Who'd have thought the pastry chef had a detective mind?

"He rubbed his face a few times, like I do when I get an allergy attack because I ate fruit I wasn't supposed to." Niko shrugged, then smiled. "And he sounded like someone on TV or radio—you know, a nice, kinda smooth, deep voice. Like a singer maybe."

"Would you recognize him if you saw him again?" my former beau asked.

"Maybe." Another shrug. "Yeah. Probably."

I motioned Adwin and he handed Niko the promised twenty dollars. "Do you hang around here a lot?"

"As much as I can," he grinned, hopping to long, slender bare feet.

"I come here as much as I can, too. Maybe I'll see you again."

"You never know." He grinned, thanked Adwin for the money and raced back to his friends.

"Cute kid."

I agreed and stood. "Care to take a drive?"

"Yeah."

"Even if there may be something grisly when we arrive at the intended destination?"

He eyed me curiously, then gestured the card I still held. "Bad news?"

"Probably."

"Should you call the cops?"

"Probably."

"But you won't."

"Not until I'm sure there's a valid reason to call them."

He tweaked my chin. "I did see some 'grisly' things back in Connecticut. If I could stomach that, I can stomach this." Taking Button's leash, he wrapped an arm around my shoulders, and we proceeded towards the Jeep.

* * *

Adwin gazed around and leaned into the vehicle. "Pretty quiet around here."

Button, front paws on the open passenger window, barked once in agreement.

"I don't imagine many places around here are open on a Saturday," I said, glancing at *Flavo's Fish Flakers*, a small ware-house-type building situated between a large storage facility and a recycling plant.

There were a few cars sporadically parked along the street, suggesting some people were working. Pruned bougainvillea hedges and chain-link fencing ran the length of both sides. Everything about the area screamed "industrial", save for a small park in the nearby distance.

"What do you suppose Flavo and his fish flakers do?" Adwin asked with a wry smile.

I smiled in return and Googled. "It appears that fish flakes, or rather freeze-dried fish scales, are a new and popular flavoring."

He grimaced. "For what?"

I quoted Flavo's landing page, "To flavorfully season a sundry of savory dishes."

He shrugged and, with a pat to Button's head, strolled toward the front entrance. A long, narrow window ran alongside a thick frosted-glass door advertising the company name and logo: a frolicking fat fish shedding scales. He peered in. "There's a small linoleum-floor foyer with a two-seater bench and umbrella rack, and a closed door farther on. I see nothing grisly within immediate view."

"I suppose we should swing around the back."

"You sound as eager as you look," he said drily.

I extended both hands in a what-can-I-say gesture and nodded to an interlocking-concrete walkway that led to the rear.

Adwin swung around and we made our way past a row of sad-looking date palms, plastic bins in various sizes and conditions, a pile of crushed boxes advertising Flavo's and, oddly enough, a rusted red wagon listing like a reef-stuck ship. A few yards farther were six stacked metallic chests.

"Not much to see," he commented quietly.

I agreed and sighed, perplexed. Had GRP evolved into a joker? While I didn't appreciate taking an unnecessary trip out here, better he play prankster than murderer.

"Let's look at it positively. I got to visit a part of Oahu few tourists or visitors do," he said blithely, squeezing my shoulder.

"And Button enjoyed the ride," I said, squeezing the hand that lingered.

"So did I."

The tone was casual, the expression serene. There was nothing to read in either … thankfully. I gazed over his shoulder and noticed even darker clouds rolling in. "Let's grab a shave ice before I drop you off," I suggested as we started walking back to the Jeep.

"Sounds like a—"

The theme from *Cannon* announced a call.

"Yeah?" I growled, knowing who it would be.

"That's just shy of rude."

I could hear the smirk in the tone. "I'm not a fan of practical jokes."

"*What* practical joke, sweetheart?"

"I'm hanging up, GRP."

"Come on, JJ. Don't be a sore loser. Besides, if you look a little harder, you'll hit a 'Community Chest'."

As in Monopoly?

"'*Life insurance matures—collect $100*' for you." He disconnected.

I swore softly.

"Problem?"

"Looks like." I began retracing our steps and stopped before the six chests. All had locks on the sides. save for one, because it had been recently removed. Metal shavings lay at the base.

We stared at it for several seconds, then at each other.

"I guess it's time to find something 'grisly'," Adwin said dully.

With a quick breath, I grabbed the heavy lid from the left; Adwin took hold on the right. With simultaneous nods, we lifted the lid.

A loud "crap," leaped from his mouth like a mullet fish jumping out of water.

Inside lay a young man with a black rose pinned to a white shirt stained with red. Slender hands with long fingers, like those belonging to a pianist, were crossed over the ribcage. The handsome face appeared peaceful, despite an obviously violent death.

Interesting. Previous "Black Rose" victims had never been found alone. Why a solo murder now?

My cell advised a text had arrived. GRP had obviously anticipated the question. It read: *A spur-of-the-moment thought and gift. HA-HA-HA-HA.*

I phoned Ald. Fortunately, this time, he picked up.

CHAPTER ELEVEN

Rey dropped a faux Prada shoulder bag the same second she dropped her mouth. Grass-green eyes gazed in surprise from one face to the next. "A pizza and beer party? Thanks for the *non*-invite."

I toasted her with a bottle of Longboard. "It was very impromptu."

"I see some of my favorite people ... not." With a cynical smile she nodded at Ald, waved limply to Sallo and Hammill, greeted Adwin with a quick kiss to the nose, and high-fived Sach.

"Four extra-larges just arrived. There are also two tubs of poke: spicy salmon and musubi tuna. Grab some food and a drink."

"Looks like it's still raining cats and dogs," Adwin said when she returned with a plate and glass of red wine.

"More like giraffes and elephants. We'll need to build an ark if it keeps up." She glanced down at her wet jeans and sighed. Taking two veggie slices, she slipped alongside Sach on the dusty-pink two-seater rattan sofa that had accompanied me from the condo (it still had a few years of good sitting left). "What'd I miss? Another murder?"

I nodded grimly and, leaning back, crossed my legs. I was seated against the far wall, away from the testosterone-infused bunch.

"I was just joking." She looked at Hammill for verification. When he nodded, she cursed softly.

"GRP 'invited' Adwin and me to Sand Island. We found Jon Doe just after noon."

"Someone's gotta be missing him." She sighed. "No recent missing persons' reports that might possibly identify the poor dude?"

"He *was* missed and Jon Doe's his *real* name," Hammill stated gruffly.

"No shit?"

"Jon Flannigan Doe," Ald affirmed. "His girlfriend, Olivia, was supposed to meet him at a Kapolei bar Thursday night, but he never showed. Never called. When there was no word by mid-morning the next day—they'd planned to drop by the hospital to visit a sick coworker—she called 911."

"Then he was on your radar."

Ald murmured accord.

"Fill me in, guys."

We did, concluding with the sad fact we were no further ahead in figuring out who GRP was.

"So you're all here sittin' around and shootin' the shit, basically?" she asked drolly.

"Pretty much," Hammill replied with a grim smile and sauntered into the kitchen to get another beer.

Rey sipped thoughtfully. "He's never gone with a solo murder before."

"I'd thought the same earlier," I said drily. "His text said Doe was a 'gift'."

"Some gift," Sallo grumbled, pushing back the signature hat and grabbing another slice before returning to the rattan armchair across from Ald.

Lightening lit the street and sky like a powerful monolight

strobe, and thunder lashed the heavens like dynamite razing a concrete structure. We jumped. Then laughed.

"The Black-Rose Killer's getting to us," Adwin grinned.

"We're calling GRP the Black-Rose Killer now?" Rey asked with a furrowed brow.

"JJ called him that on the drive back. I guess it stuck in my mind, but it's an appropriate epithet, given he uses black roses as a calling card."

"The media would certainly like that," my cousin declared. "I'm surprised they haven't given him a name yet."

"They're still not stating that the four murders are courtesy of a serial killer, just tossing the idea around," Sallo grumbled.

"Give it another day or two," Ald muttered.

"Say, any news on that card we got at the beach?" Adwin asked him.

On the promise he'd return it the following day, I'd given it to him earlier so he could check it for prints and origin. "Checking ... checking," he replied.

Rey's Clara Bow lips drew into a tight line as she scanned his face. With a shrug, she looked from face to face as she spoke. "You know what we haven't considered much?"

We waited for her to elaborate.

"Howdy-Doody and the marks on *his* chest." She turned to Hammill. "Wasn't it you who told us the 'mess' of marks were similar to the ones found on the Canal victims' chests?"

"Similar yes, but there was no black rose and nothing to suggest he was another victim of the guy who did in those four."

Rey looked at me. "What about that card Faith said Caprize gave him? There was none found on him. Doncha think that's weird?"

I stared at her for several seconds, then turned to Ald. "Considering he was found in the alley wearing the same clothes he'd had on at Flaming Daisies that night, and nothing else appeared to be missing—"

"That we're aware of," the detective said pointedly.

"The card may have fallen out of his pocket or wallet when he left the place," Sach offered.

Hammill added, "There was a ten and a five in his wallet and a Macy's credit card. Nothing else. No one at the bar—or from the family members we connected with—could corroborate what the guy actually had on his person, save for the wallet they saw him pull out to pay, so who knows if something was actually taken?"

"Maybe we need to revisit him," I suggested.

"We haven't left him," Sallo said derisively.

"But you haven't considered him in terms of GRP," Rey pointed out sharply.

Sallo exchanged a glance with Hammill, who exchanged one with Ald, but no one responded.

Sach rose and stretched. "Here's hoping he's nabbed before he kills again."

"Do you have a profile going?" Rey asked Hammill.

"We do," Ald acknowledged.

"You planning to share?" Rey's tone was as flat as a flapjack.

So was Ald's when he replied, "Don't I always?"

"No."

His silent response: a flip of the bird.

* * *

Given Linda had decided to stay on the North Shore until Monday morning and the rain hadn't ceased teeming, Caprize changed Sunday brunch to Wednesday dinner. Rey and I were fine with that, as was Sach, who'd dropped by to chat over mid-morning espressos and home-baked cookies courtesy of Uncle Chin Ho, a local bakery that created everything "from scratch and heart".

The Dowager, his great-aunt, had called as we were putting away dishes and had invited him over for afternoon tea. When he'd cheerily explained he was hanging with new friends, she'd graciously insisted he bring us along.

The immense living room - dining room combination better belonged to a Canterbury countryside manor than a luxury condo. Main colors were muted shades of apple green, lingonberry and pineapple yellow, with a multitude of lovely small watercolors—floral arrangements and countryscapes—adorning high walls. Furniture was classic, of course, with an elaborately carved credenza, hutch, table and chairs. Everything about the place [loudly] whispered "Old [Moneyed] English".

Adding to the hominess were a multitude of well-tended plants that lined four acacia-wood ladder bookcases on the far wall … and Piddles. The white Standard Poodle, resting on an attractive Archie & Oscar Corvus dog sofa, had a blow-out going that had to cost more than my highlights and cut combined. Sach thought the furry fellow had attitude, but he seemed amiable enough as he daintily gnawed a sweet-potato chew while keeping curious eyes on us.

While waiting for Great-Aunt Leticia May Morton to finish in the kitchen, Sach mentioned how much she enjoyed afternoon tea—with a hint of VSOP. Evidently, when it came to get-togethers, festivities and fêtes, the old gal could drink most people under the table, *if* so inclined.

"Reynalda, would you mind bringing in the teapot and cups?" The Dowager asked as she carried in a highly polished, hand-carved Koa tray. The accent she'd acquired while in the UK was a bit strange—a collection of oddly pronounced words and phrases she'd gathered from numerous places she'd lived. "You possess a most curious sense of fashion, my dear."

Perplexed, Sach peered down at the papaya-orange stretch top he'd tucked into wide-legged black denim pants with red stitching, secured by a blinding white vinyl belt.

"He does possess an intriguing wardrobe." I patted his shoulder and swallowed a smile as I organized exquisite gold-edged plates and silver cutlery on a fine linen tablecloth.

Rey entered and she and The Dowager arranged pretty porcelain Minton Ware cups and saucers.

Great-Aunt Leticia proved a blend of dry, droll and quirky, and after sipping and nibbling and chatting and laughing, Sach revealed another fact about his beloved relative: she was "seriously into flora and flowers and all things blossomy".

"The Dowager knows a ton of stuff about them—you know, meanings and messages," he announced, arcing a bushy eyebrow that would have made Groucho Marx proud.

Rey and I gazed at her, awed.

Her laughter was as delicate as the teaware. "My nephew exaggerates."

"Hardly," he said with feigned affront, then winked. "Your cop pals chatted about roses last night, so why don't you ask The Dowager about them?"

He was referring to the ones GRP fashioned and fastened to victims. "Sallo said they were 'teas' and Hammill said they were miniatures," I advised. "But, first, I have to ask: why 'The Dowager'?"

She twittered. "I always wanted to be a woman of a high social station. So … I decided to become one."

Rey laughed. "Fair enough. Now, back to the roses …"

"Many people merely see a rose as a rose as a rose," she said with a sad smile.

"And that black only relates to death," my cousin added.

"But that makes sense, given the guy pins them to his victims," Sach said.

A pencil-thin eyebrow lined with a light-brown pencil arched slightly and a transient frown pulled at the septuagenarian's slender lips. "Did they finally agree as to whether it was a tea or a miniature?"

"When Hives finally returned from that long call he'd made in the mudroom, he confirmed that it was a tea, based on some expert's input," Rey replied, taking a petit four, her fifth, but who was counting?

"By the way, this business about the roses is highly confidential." I offered a significant look.

The Dowager waved a slim heavily-veined hand as a queen might when dismissing her audience. "You can trust me —implicitly."

Rey leaned forward eagerly. "What can you tell us about them?"

"Hybrid teas are very fragrant, very dainty. Pointed buds and beautifully formed single blossoms. Miniatures are not as fragrant, but very hardy. They're perfect when you wish to have a profusion of blooms, but only have a small space. Most grow on their own rootstocks." The Dowager gazed across the vast room in contemplation. "There is a similarity. The miniature simply isn't as full as a tea."

"Is there a black miniature?" I asked.

"The Black Jade," she answered with a soft smile. "It's an intense, rich, velvet-like red with atramentous features. There is no actual black rose, my dears."

"It sounds exotic." Sach.

"It's a breathtaking rose, although some have referred to it as a charming novelty. The Black Jade produces blooms singly and in small clusters, and it does well in pots or in the garden."

I asked the next obvious question. "And the significance of color? Black meaning death?"

Sach's great-aunt tsked. "Oh my, we have much to discuss. Black roses can signify death, yes. They can also stand for hatred, or farewell, or refer to the color of the crone, the sage woman of death. Some view it as an evil or bad omen."

"Then it's not necessarily a portend of death?"

"That's correct. Flowers are messengers, JJ, messengers of our deepest feelings. Over the centuries, countless metaphors were assigned to the rose. Actually, the language of flowers has a long history going so far back as to fifteenth-century Persia, but it was during Queen Victoria's reign that the language of flowers reached its zenith. Flowers became a form of communication between lovers and friends."

"Who knew?" Rey asked, awed, leaning forward on both elbows, icing gracing her lower lip. "Tell us more."

"How the flower was presented, worn, the color, and the type of flower or mix of flowers, all played a part in the meaning of the message. And speaking of meanings, they have been passed on through myths, legends and folklore—"

"We'd love to hear the history, but maybe could we stick to the black bloom?" Sach rubbed his temples, obviously wanting to get to the nitty-gritty.

A triple tsk. "I'll provide an ultra-condensed version, although I'm certain you'd find the imagery of the rose throughout the ages fascinating. Given you're anti-history, however, I won't relate the fascinating Talmudic legend of how the rose became red. Nor will I share the first historical reference of the rose, rose myths of Greece, and the Egyptians—"

Sach cleared his throat.

Deep-set nickel-gray eyes narrowed for a twinkling. "Skipping empires and the like for my impatient nephew, the rose ended up a predominant symbol of Christianity and the Virgin herself became known as *La Rosa Mystica* or the Mystic Rose."

"You're a wealth of information," Rey complimented, gently squeezing the woman's hand.

She beamed and wiped the icing from her lip with a linen napkin. "Hybrid tea roses can mean, 'I'll remember you always' or 'always lovely'. A single rose can stand for simplicity. If it's a rosebud, it can relate to beauty and youth. A rosebud with leaves, but no thorns, may mean there is nothing to hope or fear."

I recalled the night we'd found the foursome, the roses, and the description reiterated by Ald last night. GRP's hand-fashioned roses had neither thorns nor leaves. There was a six-inch stem and the rose itself. I provided details to The Dowager.

"No leaves, as well as no thorns, can signify 'I hope' or 'I fear no longer'. A thornless rose, if I'm not mistaken, can also refer to early attachment or ingratitude."

"Fascinating," Rey and I murmured simultaneously.

"A faded rose means beauty is fleeting. Google, my dears. You'll be amazed at what you'll learn."

"You're a much better source that the Internet," I said with a cheery smile.

"Say, that flower guy you dated with the big gold chain necklace, Horace What's-His-Name, have you heard anything from him lately?" Sach asked.

"I received another lengthy email about three weeks ago, with the usual begging and threatening."

"Is this dude dangerous or weird, or something?" Rey asked with a creased brow.

"Horace leans toward eccentric." She chuckled softly. "Now, how were the roses positioned?"

"Pinned to a garment on the upper portion of the torso, much where brooches would be," I answered.

"Pinned on the left or right? Over the heart? Bent one way or the other?"

"Bent? Not sure." I glanced at Rey, bemused.

"We'll get back to you," my cousin promised.

CHAPTER TWELVE

Early evening found Rey and I sipping Mai-Tais at Lily Pad, a quaint lounge a few walkable blocks from the house. Sach had wanted to catch up with friends visiting from Denver, so he'd left us after high tea with The Dowager. Despite pelting rain and a gray drab day, my cousin and I were feeling fine—and no, it wasn't the rum that was contributing to it (though it didn't hurt).

"What do you think about the fact they were bent to the right?" Rey asked, playing with the pretty plumeria that adorned the thick glittery tumblers. "And who's 'I'? GRP?"

When Ald had confirmed that the roses pinned on the victims were bent to the right, we'd called back Sach's great-aunt. She'd advised that bent to the right meant "I", while to the left meant "you".

"Maybe. But who does the 'I' signify? *I* am the killer? *I* am the one in control?" I shrugged. "Maybe he simply shapes them all in the same fashion, with no deliberate significance at all."

My cousin drew a long breath. "What's the plan of action?"

"Getting drunk," I joked.

She offered an impish sneer. "We *need* a plan."

"For what? Catching GRP?"

"If *we* don't, who will?"

"Duh—the police, maybe?"

She chuckled and motioned the bartender for another round.

"Where should we start, dear Cousin?"

She stuck out her tongue. "Darlin', how about the card missing from Howdy-Doody? It's very curious."

"It's missing. How's finding it—which would be like looking for a penny in a pit—going to help?"

"He may have left it in the bar washroom or lost it somewhere between the bar and that alley."

"They never did find it at Flaming Daisies—I called Faith while you were in the ladies."

"I'd suggest checking the laneway where he was found, but even if the card is there, *somewhere*, it's of no informative value. So it would be a colossal waste of time."

"But if we search for the card, maybe we might find something else of note."

"After so many days?" I smiled saltily. "After the police combed the area?"

"What's there to lose?"

I stared through a large square window, onto a waterlogged street void of people. Rey was right; there was nothing to lose and maybe even something to gain. "Let's do it tomorrow morning. Later, we can pour over the reports of all the victims. Make some calls for clarification, if necessary."

"I'd like to focus on GRP." She nodded to the waitperson when he placed the drinks and a bowl of mac nuts on our small round table.

"Thought you might like something salty with the sweet," the attractive thirty-something winked. "I'm referring to the drinks, of course, and not myself."

"Come on, sugah, I'll bet ya'll sweetah than molasses and honey combined," Rey replied with an exaggerated Southern accent, offering a flirty smile.

Laughing, he offered a casual salute and returned to the bar —with more swagger than earlier.

"Back to GRP. Do you think we could trick him into showing his hand?" Rey asked, popping a nut in her mouth.

"How do you mean?"

She frowned, pressing the plumeria to her nose as she considered it. "I'm just thinking out loud. If we could get him angry enough, maybe he'd want to meet up face-to-face or—"

"Or pin roses on us after he kills us, because he lost his temper when we royally pissed him off?" I interjected drolly.

"Okay, so maybe we *flatter* the dude. He likes and wants to play games. Let's tell him how good he is at it and that we don't think we're up to the challenge—"

"He'd see through flattery in a blink."

She eyed the plumeria as she twirled it. "You're probably right... What's up with Linda and Mink, ya think?"

"A budding friendship," I replied with a placating smile. "She's entitled to have friends outside our teeny circle."

Rey frowned and focused on the Mai-Tai.

So did I, listening appreciatively to the soft jazz playing in the background while I watched heavy rain, resembling translucent silver-tinged cords, twine beneath a street lamp.

Several minutes later, Rey's cell phone trumpeted a call, as in swing-time boogie-woogie bugles.

I turned my attention to her when she asked, "Would we see you if we looked?"

"Uh-huh... Sure. Thanks for the compliment... Uh-huh. You're not fond of GRP, huh? ... Kamahkay? Really?" Placing the cell on the table, she met my curious gaze. "He was watching. Said we looked very pretty in our 'casual off-the-rack wear' and hoped we were enjoying a pleasant, relaxing evening."

"Great. We've become a fixation."

"He said he didn't want us to feel ignored," she declared with a flat smile. "And not to make me or Linda feel left out, he's decided he'll call any one of our three cells when he's 'so inclined'." She exhaled slowly. "I'm not liking the fact he's watching."

I agreed. "Kamahkay?"

"That's what he prefers we call him going forward. Nice Hawaiian name."

I rolled the name around on my tongue, then smiled bleakly. "*Ka make* means death."

"*Not* nice Hawaiian name." She turned to the window and toasted our unseen fan—with a raised middle finger.

* * *

"You two look like you bent the elbows a bit. Maybe you should have slept in." With a chuckle, Sach placed coffees and croissants on the agency's "sort-of" kitchen counter. He'd called twenty minutes ago to say he was training a client in the area at ten and would stop by beforehand with caffeine boosts.

Rey's response was to blow hair from her eyes and lean back on one of the blended-leather chairs lining the meeting table. Mine was to grimace and sink farther down on the rattan sofa. Thanks to a car crash not far from the house—courtesy of four impatient businesspersons in a major hurry to get to the office— we'd been awakened at six.

Laughing, he brought over the medium-size coffees and sat on the edge of a desk. "You should get a motto."

Rey eyed him as if he'd grown an extra arm.

"*Really*. Branding and all that. A motto would define you." He cocked his head and contemplated. "How's this? No catastrophes too big or complaints too small to handle."

"We're not FEMA," my cousin said dully.

"We'll work on it," he said brightly, biting into a croissant the size of a coconut. "Where's your fellow private eye?"

"Linda's returning around noon." I took a hesitant sip of the cinnamon-flavored coffee. "Hey, not bad."

"New place off Ward."

Rey tried hers and gave a limp thumb's up.

"Question about a guest last night?"

We gave the go-ahead.

"Adwin. Is he, like, unattached?"

"Physically no, emotionally yes." She crooked a thumb in my direction. "He's still got a thing for that one."

"Still?" With a drawn brow, he scanned my face.

"They had a long-time relationship back on the Mainland."

"Too bad for me." He sipped and sighed appreciatively. "So, besides Caprize's for dinner at eight on Wednesday, what's up? Anything I can help with?"

An eager, childlike expression prompted Rey and I to laugh.

"Unless you know where to find GRP—or *Ka Make*, as he requested—there's little to be done. We're going to review reports after we head over to that alleyway where they'd found Howdy-Doody." I looked at Rey. "Maybe we should have done that before coming here."

"It was raining, remember?"

"So it was." I peered out the window. Heavy gray clouds were dispersing and it appeared as if the sun might make an appearance.

"I wish I could come with." Sach sighed. "I don't suppose you want to wait until this aft, when I'm free?"

"We're meeting a possible new client later," Rey replied. "Next time."

The eager, childlike expression returned. "Who's the client? What's the case?"

"Possible wayward hubby. She's rich, he's not, but he's cute and sexy, and very hot."

"Which is why she married him," he snickered. "And now he's developed a roving eye, right?"

"He's developed a roving something," she said with an acerbic smile. Taking several loud gulps—like a caffeine addict in need of a serious boost—she plonked the cup on the table and hopped to sneakered feet. "So, Cous, ready to go laneway trolling?"

* * *

It was nearly 10:00 a.m. when the cab pulled up before the alley, three blocks from Flaming Daisies. The sun had finally made an appearance and the few remaining clouds were no longer dark and ominous. A sign of good things to come?

Rey adjusted tortoise Ray-Ban sunglasses and peered along the street. Various bins were neatly stacked where the alley met the sidewalk, while crates and cartons lined one side for several yards.

"It looks rather neat," I said cheerfully as we strolled forward.

"Yeah? Take a gander past the rolled-up fencing that's beyond the boxes."

Farther in, neat gave way to disordered. Cracked concrete was littered with paper, bottles and cans, and dried foliage propelled from parts unknown. A half-dozen fire exits appeared ineffective with metal doors, dented and rusted, permanently sealed. Iron steps, some corroded, seemed as if they couldn't support much weight.

"Charming," she murmured, motioning the left.

A grizzle-faced man of indeterminate years, with toilet paper adhered to a worn runner, was scrounging through a large battered suitcase.

"This may be his home," I whispered.

She frowned, nodded, and straightened her shoulders. "Hey, Charlie?"

Rheumy winter-gray eyes studied her for several seconds. "Name's Chuck." His voice was as thin as his frame.

She smiled warmly. "Know anything about the dead guy they found here a few days back?"

He scratched thick scabs on his lower left arm and looked from her to me.

"We'll compensate you for your time," I stated.

"I don't need the money, but if you don't need it either, I'll take it." He offered a jovial smile that revealed uneven teeth stained by time and nicotine.

I laughed and pulled out twenty dollars from my colorful knapsack. "Do you know where he was found?"

A slim, scored thumb pointed to the rear. "Past that wrecked newspaper box, beyond that stack of broken tiki lights, to the side by that recess."

"Were you here?"

He stuffed the twenty in his timeworn shirt pocket. "I was putting stuff away when a pal of mine, Emme, found him. His shriek—like a Western scrub jay—sent the hairs on my neck and arms shooting straight up. He ran out of here like a feral pig biting his butt, and before you could say my name five times, folks were coming and running from every which way."

"Did you see the body?"

"I did and I'll never forget it. Young guy lying there with eyes wide open. A combination of fear and woe permanently frozen on that freckly bruised face. Blood on the open shirt. Blood all around. Hand clutched tightly, like he was trying to clasp life."

"You have an awesome memory." Rey.

"I'm homeless, not stricken with Alzheimer's," he said gruffly, then smiled.

"Was most of this stuff here that morning?"

"Yeah, except for the stuff they took away as evidence."

"Did you notice anything odd? Like somebody weird lurking nearby? A weapon maybe? A card? Anything at all?"

He gazed to the rear, as if collecting thoughts. "I remember a couple of guys. One was taking pictures; a super snoopy media sort. Another one was leaning into the wall not far from the newspaper box, hands jammed into the pockets of a really nice cotton jacket, watching what was happening around the body—like we all were before the legal sorts made us leave. He was, well, intense."

"Intense?" Rey prodded.

"He wore super large, dark, squarish glasses. And a black

trucker hat, pulled low on the forehead. It was jet-black like his jacket, T-shirt, and pants. He seemed real intense, yeah. Didn't jabber like everyone else. Didn't seem as curious as everyone else."

"Trucker hat?"

"Yeah, they look like baseball caps, but fuller … rounder top, flat brim."

Rey nodded, her gaze in the distance as she envisioned it. "Was there a logo or design on it?"

He, too, looked into the distance. "Nope. It looked new, though. Crisp. Like it just came out of a box."

"Was he young or old, handsome or ugly, short or tall?"

Chuck's laughter was hollow, staccato, like a toy machine gun. "He wasn't young or old, handsome or ugly, short or tall."

Deflated, Rey and I gazed at each other.

More laughter. "Medium height with an oval face. Thirtyish if I had to guess by the smooth, lower face. Thin lips. Hollywood nose. Sunglasses cost more than I scrounge together in a month. The jacket more than two months."

Rey's eyes widened in admiration. "You *are* good."

He shrugged. "I was a photographer once upon a time. I notice things."

Rey pulled three tens from her jacket and tucked them into the pocket that held the twenty. She smiled and turned to me. "Care to nose around?"

"You cops? You looking for something your friends might not have found?" Chuck asked, curious.

"We're private eyes," she said proudly and winked. "Sometimes cops can't see for looking."

He grinned and returned to the suitcase.

Passing latex gloves to my cousin, we began poking and prodding and shifting, trying not to be repelled by unpleasant, malodorous items. Nothing of note was to be found in the recess, nor in the hindmost part of the alley.

"This is a dead end, Rey. Literally." Frustrated, I slapped a graffiti-covered wall and grimaced, and pulled a tissue from my knapsack to wipe the gunk from my hand.

"We gave it our best." She peered around. "Did we miss anything?"

"I don't think so." I scrutinized the area we'd covered. "Save for that thin layer of garbage over there and those two crumpled shoe cartons and the old broken-down newspaper box on the opposite side."

We regarded each other, then hastened forward and struggled to open the battered door.

"Crap. And I mean *crap*." Crouching, my cousin took photos with her cellphone, swore softly, and got close.

"Since when do you get down and dirty?" I joked.

"Since this." She held up a gloved hand. "As good ol' rube Gomer Pyle would have said, 'Shazam'!"

Between a thumb and forefinger was a dirty, crumpled hand-crafted black rose.

CHAPTER THIRTEEN

It was noon and steel-gray clouds had rolled in. The sun made feeble attempts to show itself now and again, but rain was imminent. You could sense it, smell it, feel it. The air was thick, as if a giant aerosol can had sprayed its dense contents across the region.

We'd called Ald Ives about the rose found in the newspaper box and he'd ordered us to stay put until Sallo and Hammill arrived—and arrive they did, in not so record time. Both were dressed in jeans and blindingly loud Aloha shirts. Undercover?

"Ladies, you did good," Hammill said with a trim smile as he carefully placed the crushed rose in a printed paper evidence bag.

Tilting back the signature hat, Sallo muttered under his breath and scanned the alley for the umpteenth time.

"We're not just pretty faces," Rey stated coolly.

Hammill tucked the bag into a worn leather messenger bag. "Where's this Chuck guy you told Ives about?"

"He left after Rey woo-hoo'd," I replied with a droll smile. "I think her 'earsplitting' roar of excitement was too much for him."

Rey snorted.

Sallo slipped alongside her. "Looks like we have another official Black-Rose victim."

Rey snorted even louder.

"If you need an official statement or anything," I advised, "We'll be at the agency until five."

"That's JJ's way of saying, we're outta here," Rey stated with a brittle smile.

Hammill offered a swift salute, and my cousin and I ambled back to the main street.

"Sallo made a pretty obvious statement," she said blandly.

I chuckled. "An 'official' for-the-record comment, you mean —that GRP *is* responsible for the death of Howdy-Doody?"

She too chuckled and motioned. "Care to walk back to the office?"

"Why not? Let's grab bubble teas along the way."

"Why do you suppose GRP jammed the rose in there?" She hooked an arm through mine. "It's not like him to be so slapdash."

"Maybe he got spooked."

"Yeah, someone could have surprised him … come into the alley unexpectedly," she submitted as we crossed Kuhio with a dozen excited, chattering tourists and surfers.

"But does he strike you as someone who'd become startled or agitated so much so he'd get flustered and do something sloppy?"

"No."

"Maybe he was going to pin it on Howdy-Doody and dropped it, then accidentally stepped on it. Being the 'precise' whacko he is, maybe he got p'o'd because it got bent or mangled, and so he flung it in the box."

Rey's expression said she wasn't buying it. "I'd expect someone that's as 'precise' as GRP to carry extra roses, just in case. The guy'd want everything to be perfect." She shrugged and stopped. "What if someone pulled it off Howdy-Doody and threw it in there?"

"Why? And why?"

"Just throwing around ideas," she said with a sigh.

I nodded. "What do you think about what Chuck shared about GRP?"

"We're of the same mind, Cousin Jilly, that it *was* GRP?"

"We are—and it *was*—Cousin Reynalda."

We began walking again. "Okay, so what's up?"

"Chuck gave a pretty decent description."

"He did. Hey, you're a good sketcher. Why don't you draw something from the details?"

"I will, but did anything stick out about what he'd shared?"

Rey glanced over. "Besides the fondness for dark clothes and accessories?"

"Uh-huh."

She chewed her bottom lip as we ambled along the heavily populated sidewalk. "Shit! Sure! The guy's got money."

"You got it, sistah." I gave a hip check. "Not that it will necessarily narrow down the search, but it may help."

* * *

"Look what the cat dragged in," Rey said sarcastically when Linda strolled into the office with Mink at 2:30 that aft. "Twins, no less."

Both wore lilac sundresses with a hibiscus theme and similar sandals. Faces were highly polished with sun-kissed cheeks and noses. While Linda was toned and athletically built, Mink was buxom and hippy. And happy. Shiny watermelon-pink lips perpetually smiled.

"Someone's in a snarky mood," her BFF commented drily, placing a bakery box on the counter. "We brought malasadas."

"And frosty-cold drinks," Mink added gaily, holding up a large paper bag.

"Bully for you."

I shot my cousin a withering look, to which she arched a

shoulder and returned to the last of the reports she'd been scanning.

"We haven't had much sleep," I apologized on behalf of my cousin.

"We can see that by those humungous bags under your eyes, honey." Mink's sing-song voice held a hint of a Texas twang. Opening the bag, she pulled out bottles and a package of long, thick plastic straws.

Rey shot her a look; if it had been a fist, Mink would have been out for the count.

"Well, honey, it's the plain ol' truth. Concealer would do wonders."

Another look.

"Good weekend?" I asked, accepting two bottles and straws, which I plonked in front of Rey.

The two women glanced at each other and something unreadable—but emotive—passed. Rey hadn't noticed, because she was opening a bottle. She leaned back and sipped. "I believe my cousin asked if you had a good weekend. Actually, a *long* weekend, wasn't it?"

"It was good." Mink removed a malasada. "Haupia. Yummy. I'll see ya'll at the luau in two weeks."

"Luau?"

"Linda'll tell ya'll about it." With a wave of the malasada, she left.

Rey was about to speak, but the agency phone—thankfully—announced a call. Hastily jamming a straw between my lips, I motioned my cousin to take it.

As she went to speak with the caller in a corner, I gave Linda a thumb's up and strolled over to the box. "Lookin' good."

"The sun and rest did wonders," she said nonchalantly, then motioned. "Is she mad?"

"Miffed, more like."

Linda sighed. "She's being silly."

"She's being Rey."

She sighed again and eyed her best friend, whose back was turned. "We'll always be best friends. Sometimes, though, we need to do things … differently … with different people. Know what I mean?"

"I know. And she *will* get over it." With a squeeze to her arm, I leaned into the counter and began nibbling. When the call ended, I glibly asked, "Anyone important, Cousin Reynalda?"

"Just Hammill. He and Hives are dropping by the house around seven. You can show them that sketch you've been working on."

"Are we throwing another pizza party?"

She smiled darkly. "Why not? We don't have dinner plans. Obviously, they don't, either."

The phone announced another call.

She sunnily asked, "Aren't we the popular ones today?"

A minute later, she announced drily, "It's Lover Boy #2, who also goes by the name of Adwin. I told him to drop by. Maybe we should recreate the other evening and have Sallo and Sach come as well."

"Why do I feel like I've missed out on a few things?" Linda asked with a casual smile.

"Because you have," Rey replied blandly. "We have a wayward spouse case, we think, but we won't know for sure until tomorrow. We had to reschedule the meeting."

"We're good at waywards. Who's cheating on whom?"

Rey shrugged. "Wifey's rich and he's hot."

"And young, no doubt," Linda smirked. "So, he's the cheater."

"JJ'll catch you up," Rey replied blandly and turned to me. "It'd sure be nice to have Gail back. We could use her help and insight … and friendship."

Linda snuck a quick look at me.

It was going to be a long afternoon, but at the end of it, Rey would once again be her old self. Of this I had no doubt. … Well, maybe a little.

* * *

We'd opted for a homemade menu instead of pizza, with Hammill and Adwin preparing hamburgers and steaks on the lanai barbecue. Thankfully, there was a canopy to keep the persistent drizzle from dampening food and enthusiasm. The three of us had prepared a trio of salads: fruit (with enough Vitamin C to stave off colds for a month), mixed greens (nothing like a healthy dose of folate and potassium), and Caesar (with enough garlic to ward off vampires in the Pacific Rim). Buffalo-chicken dip, guacamole and fish tacos—courtesy of Sach—were also on hand. Beer, in abundance, had been supplied by HPD's finest while we'd seen to the wine. Simple but filling fare.

"Nice spread," Sallo said, chomping on a dip-slathered chip. The requisite Mike Hammer fedora was perched awkwardly to one side, as if he'd yanked it on his head before dashing to an important meeting. Bonzo had perched himself on the man's bare feet (he'd stepped in a huge [unseen] puddle coming up the driveway). Both bunny and bozo, uh, detective, appeared content.

Rey looked from the two to me with a what-the-bleep expression.

Ald strolled into the living room with a fresh beer and fat burger oozing mustard and grilled onions. "Next time I throw a get-together at my place, *you* two are cooking."

"It'll cost you a couple of weekends on that sleek Catalina you just bought," Hammill joked, slipping onto a circular rattan armchair with a heaping plate.

"I didn't know you were into boating," I said.

"It seemed worth pursuing, given I'm living on an island," he said drolly, taking a seat alongside Linda on the dusty-pink two-seater rattan sofa. "A guy needs a pastime or two."

"Can deep-sea fishing and golfing be far off?" Linda grinned.

"I hope so," he winked.

Smalltalk and jokes eventually gave way to discussion of the case and killer. I pulled out the two sketches I'd done earlier: one a close-up, the other a full body. Rembrandt I wasn't, but I drew well enough to make GRP seem real.

"Not bad, but not sure it's enough to go on," Sallo commented as he passed the sketch to Adwin.

"It's more than we've had," Ald said, offering me a quick smile.

"If we all show it around," Rey proposed, "maybe others will recognize the dude and add some particulars, and we'll end up with a more detailed sketch."

"It's a start." Hammill got up to fetch beers.

"You were saying you think the guy has money." Ald.

"His clothes suggest it," Rey responded.

"I wonder how he earns money to buy them," Sallo said. "Executive type? Broker? Rich kid?"

"Maybe he has a rich daddy … or steals money from the victims," Adwin suggested.

Ald regarded him intently. "Wallets and/or purses were usually there. Nothing was readily missed. That is, those in the know, like family members, couldn't see anything suspect. All seemed to be in order—licenses, some money, and/or credit cards."

"But family and friends wouldn't know *every little thing* that might be in a wallet or purse," Rey pointed out. "Maybe something less 'noticeable' was missing … like a library card."

Ald smirked. "People still have those?"

She gave him the evil eye.

"Rey may on the right track," I said. "If our killer collects trophies, maybe they're items not that 'missable'. A grocery card, a points card—"

"A gym or health card," Adwin threw in.

"Or a key," Rey nodded. "He may even have simply taken a sawbuck—who'd miss that, right? Just a little something to confirm his kill."

He looked from Adwin to me, and then to Rey, and frowned. "Okay, I'll buy that as a possibility."

"That'll keep you busy ... revisiting." Rey presented a pretty [and exaggerated] smile.

Ald glowered.

Which resulted in my cousin's smile widening. "So, you know that the *victims* all came from money?"

Ald eyed her as if she'd morphed into Batgirl.

She turned up her nose and then looked at me. "You wanna tell him what we found?"

"You may have seen this, but we scoured the records and backgrounds of the various victims. They were either financially well-off or came from fairly well-to-do families."

"*All* of them?" Sach asked, bemused (we'd not had a chance to update our budding gumshoe).

"*All* of them," Linda affirmed.

Sallo looked skeptical and turned to Ald. "I know the four at the canal had rich folks, but what about the kids in the car and the two homeless guys, and that freckly-face kid, uh, guy?"

Ald gestured Linda.

"Re the kids in the car: Frank Hitenmis' mom was a judge and dad a lawyer, Carolyn Kleid's mom was a fashion model turned successful photographer, and Nico Ungluck's parents were high-end real-estate agents. No lack of allowances there. Howdy-Doody's dad was a dentist and mom a denturist. So, again, they weren't suffering financially," Linda explained. "As for the two 'homeless' guys—Ongelukkig's father was the CEO of a bank and Nestastny's parents owned a winery in Europe."

He snorted. "Those two must have made *really* bad choices and taken very wrong turns."

"Big time," Hammill agreed.

With a furrowed brow, Sach asked, "And wasn't there a couple a few summers ago?"

Linda nodded. "The Daltons. Her parents owned a small chain of restaurants along the east coast; his had died when he was six, but his grandparents, who raised him, owned a flight school." She looked at Ald. "What about Jon Doe?"

"He had a successful security business." He sighed and rubbed his temple. "Saying this is true—that, in addition to the victims having come from money, that the killer has money— why shouldn't we assume it's simply coincidental?"

"It may well be," I acknowledged. "But it could also lend itself to a profile of the killer."

"I'll run it by Singh tomorrow," Ald said.

"Don't crazies like GRP usually take—what do they call it —trophies?"

We all turned to Adwin.

Who smiled and toasted us with a glass of red wine.

Ald looked at his empty beer bottle and rose. "I'll give the crazy this: he's *really* good at what he does."

CHAPTER FOURTEEN

Mid-morning Tuesday, Rey and Sach went to meet with our potential wayward-spouse client, Hardena Antigua, at her substantial Kahala home. Linda and I had decided to stay at the office to do more research re similar Mainland murders, specifically any found near water. We discovered there'd been many—too many—and a number involving mutilations too, but given roses weren't part of the equation, we didn't pursue them.

"Most likely, GRP started killing here on the Islands." Linda sucked back the last of a kiwi bubble tea and, plopping onto one of the rattan sofas, sighed. "It's kind of sad, isn't it? All the murders that take place, *all* the time?"

I extended my legs sans ballerina flats onto the desk. "I'm inclined to agree that he probably started here. Maybe with animals to start. Got used to killing—"

"And perfected it," she finished sourly.

I smiled drily. "Rey back to full BFF mode?"

"She's still 'miffed'."

"It does seem like you and Mink are becoming rather good friends."

"I really like Mink. She's a wealth of information, has a fun sense of humor, and offers awesome support." With a pensive brow, she scanned the office for several seconds. "We should get Eddy in tomorrow to clean."

"He can help with supplies, too."

"Maybe we should revisit those cards," Linda said with a shrug, her expression deflated.

"Yeah, we didn't spend too much time checking them—"

"Because we're expecting Ald and his people to luck in," she interjected wryly.

When her cell phone shrilled a call, I winced and got up to peer out the window. At 2:30, the street was busy and the sky cloudy and gray. No rain yet. Across the street, by a small florist shop, stood a man dressed entirely in raven black: trilby, long-sleeve crew-neck shirt, boot-cut jeans, and leather low-top sneakers. He was vaping, chatting on the phone, and staring this way —to the second floor office. Or so it appeared, given the angle of the head and dark aviator sunglasses, Gucci if I wasn't mistaken. I tensed but didn't move.

"Linda, grab the camera, will you? Fast!"

"Yes, I understand, thank you kindly," she said as she hastened to a cabinet and handed it over several seconds later.

I grabbed the Sony and zoomed in—and succeeded in shooting a few seconds of video before he whirled and darted into an adjacent laneway.

Linda peeked outside. "What did I miss?"

"You missed a possible serial killer," I grinned. "But *I* didn't."

* * *

"If we view it on a large screen, we might have something," Linda stated, squeezing my shoulder.

"That wasn't GRP calling, was it?"

"No. Why?"

"The guy outside was on the phone at the same time."

We viewed the vid showing a male of medium stature with

lips I'd describe s flabby, and a long, odd, pointy chin, and that was about it.

"What do you think?" she asked, peering closely.

"I think he bears a slight resemblance to the guy outside Caprize's building the other night."

"Him and a few thousand on Oahu," she affirmed with a weary smile.

"Fair enough." I pointed. "The hat's hiding the forehead and brows, the glasses are concealing the eyes ... but those lips and that chin."

"I don't know. He doesn't have a long pointy nose like you described that night near Caprize's office. Or acne scars. Not that I can see." She studied the face. "Then there's that Chuck guy who said something about an oval face, right? This one leans toward oval. So ... are we talking about the same guy at the parking garage and in the alley? Caprize's stalker and GRP?" Camera in hand, she walked to the window and looked out. "The guy may have been looking up this way, but at something entirely innocent. Maybe a pigeon on the window ledge or someone on the roof had his attention."

I chuckled. "And maybe I'm paranoid, right?"

"Maybe." She returned to the camera and watched the brief vid again. "You know ... there's something about him. Not sure what ... but it's off."

"Let's show this to Ald later. Maybe he can use it."

"Let's do up some close-ups and see if we can't get a better picture." Linda sat on the corner of the desk. "Do you think GRP will contact us again soon?"

"If his intention is to kill again, he will."

Perry Mason announced a call.

"That's the best ringtone yet," Linda chuckled.

I winked and saw a number I didn't recognize. "Hello?"

"Hello, my dear JJ. Missing me?"

"Not in the least. How're tricks, GRP?" I asked curtly, putting on the speaker and jotting a note to Linda to contact an HPD colleague.

"It's Ka Make."

"We prefer GRP and will stick with that."

He chuckled. "Fine. Whatever."

"Why didn't you simply come up when you were outside just now?"

"Outside just now?"

It was my turn to chuckle. I was fine with playing games; that's how he wanted it. "Is it hatred of money that makes you kill? Given the clothes you wear, you're not poor. Maybe it's that you don't believe others are worthy of having any."

"Leave psychology to those that have appropriate training and credentials," he said briskly.

"Does Daddy-Dear know what you do?"

"*Daddy-Dear* has better things to do," he replied snippily.

"Hit a nerve, did I?"

"Bitch."

"Ooh, someone's not happy."

He disconnected.

"We may regret that," Linda said somberly.

"We may." I bit my bottom lip. "I hope I didn't just push him into doing something deadly."

"Chances are he'll kill regardless of mood."

"… If he hasn't already."

* * *

"You think it's him?" Ald asked with a furrowed brow, watching the video for the fifth time as he sipped coffee.

Linda and I had met him at a favorite bakery near the office. The place, as always, was hopping, particularly given it was lunch hour. We'd grabbed large cups of caffeine and several mini *pao doces*, also known as sweet breads—as opposed to sweet-

125

breads or thymus glands, yuck—and taken them to a bench under a lush monkeypod (or rain) tree.

"I do," I replied, watching Nimbus clouds scud past. Rain couldn't be far off. Thankfully, Linda and I had brought umbrellas.

"Gut feeling?"

"Gut feeling," I confirmed.

He exhaled slowly. "I'll get a composite and run it through various databases."

"Did you find anything of use from the alley?" Linda inquired. "What about the crumpled rose?"

"Nothing of note from the alley, but we're still checking," he replied wearily. "We're also still running tests on the rose. The only thing I can confirm at this time is that it's identical to the ones found on the victims ... a small, tight and delicate—hand-fashioned—silk rose."

"And how's the investigation re similar murders on the Mainland and abroad. Anything stand out?" I asked casually, wondering if he'd had better luck than us.

"There were five murders in England last year, where bodies were found with silk lilies, but they caught the perp, even if he's claiming innocence."

"We didn't have any luck in our search for identical murders either," Linda advised, taking a bite of freshly baked sweet bread. "Dollars to donuts he started killing here."

"Quite possibly." He stared across the busy boulevard. "So you pissed him off today?"

It was my turn to shrug. "It proved he's sensitive re talk about 'Daddy-Dear'."

Perry Mason announced a call and we glanced at one another before I answered.

"It's me," GRP announced casually.

"I suspected it would be," I said with equal ease.

"Am I getting predictable?"

"Kind of."

He chuckled. "So if I tell you to go to the bridge by the Kahe Stream, you know what you'll find?"

"Pretty much," I said evenly. "Just not how many."

"That's good. Then I'm not *that* predictable." Another chuckle.

"Should we go there now?"

"Why not? You're almost finished your coffee and nibbles. Take your detective friend with you."

"If I ask you *why*, would you tell me?"

"Why I do it?"

"Uh-huh."

"That's part of the game. I can't hand you everything on a silver platter, can I?"

"You won't elaborate on the roses, either, will you?"

"You're the detectives," he stated matter-of-factly.

"Does it all have to do with Daddy-Dear?"

"… Nope."

There was something there in the hesitation that suggested it did. "Are we ever going to meet?"

"Count on it." With what sounded like a kiss, he disconnected.

"Trouble?"

"Yeah, and it's spelled G-R-P." I hopped to my feet. "Let's go check out our next body."

Linda grabbed Ald's elbow. "This may be a needle-in-a-haystack mission, but what if we looked at rich kids being arrested for animal abuse and violent crimes—"

"In and around the time the first murders here began?" he asked cynically.

"Maybe two-three years before, to start. Maybe Daddy-Dear didn't come to Junior's rescue when he was arrested and that stuck—and flourished—in the kid's craw."

* * *

Two hours later, Linda and I were standing in the background waiting for Ald to finish conferring with the ME and Sallo. Only one body had been found and from the immediate looks of it, it had been lying at the base of the bridge since last night. Fortunately, it hadn't started raining, so evidence—if there was any— wouldn't be lost or obscured.

The unfortunate victim was a male in his mid-twenties. We'd only viewed him for a couple of minutes before Ald delegated us to the tree line, but gauging from the leather shoes and clothes, he wasn't struggling financially. A rose was there, as expected, pinned to a snazzy satin bomber jacket that had undoubtedly sported an eye-bulging price. Floral designs etched into the chest could be viewed where the jacket and shirt were unbuttoned. The young handsome face was marred by dirt and flora, but the expression was almost serene, as if he knew death was coming and accepted it.

"GRP probably intended to tell us about this guy the first time he called, but when you brought up Daddy-Dear, he got flustered and hung up," Linda murmured, watching legal sorts engaged in the collection process.

"Probably … but why was he standing outside the office?"

"*If* it was him, maybe he was waiting for us to leave, then follow."

"For what purpose? Surely he has better things to do?" I could feel my forehead crease. "I don't get it—"

"You're not supposed to. He's crazy," she stated flatly and, glancing at her watch, leaned into Ald's Audi A-5 coupe. "Maybe we should call Rey and let her know what's happening."

"According to that text, she and Sach are having a late lunch with Ms. Antigua at her—as Rey called it—hoity-toity club. Let's call her when we leave here."

She nodded. "We can catch up with them at the house later, after we 'casually' drop by Caprize's to say hello and see if there have been any Stalker Boy sightings."

I watched Ald, grim-faced and stiff, approach with small bags in hand.

"What's up?" Linda asked.

He rubbed his temple. "This guy's really pissing me off."

"That may well be the intention."

He eyed her for several seconds, then swore softly and held up the bags. "There's a small card in this third one with your names on it. It was tucked in the victim's back jean pocket, the part of the body not in the water."

"Did you find out about the other card yet?" Linda asked as she peered closely at the tiny cream-colored card sporting our names in bold 8-Arial font. "This one looks like a mini version."

"The card the kid gave JJ is high-end … a favorite of a stationary supplier … has been available in the New York region for a few years now. It can be purchased on-line now, as well as via card and gift sellers."

Linda smirked. "But no luck re who might have purchased them."

He smirked in return. "No luck. They could have been bought years back—or recently—in person or on-line."

"But you'll stick with it?"

"Of course. As will you," he chirped.

"Did you open and read it?" I asked, curious to know the message.

He smiled sourly. "Simon says pull up your socks."

CHAPTER FIFTEEN

"Your flowers are just stunning. The colors are so intense," I said.

Caprize beamed and motioned a teak-and-metal two seater on her small but lengthy lanai. She handed Linda and me small frosty bottles of Perrier and parked herself on the matching lounge chair opposite.

A few days ago, Linda, Rey and I had discussed the flowers Sach had mentioned viewing upon his visit here and wondered if there might be a connection to GRP. Then we decided there was probably nothing there; her love of dark red, deep purple, and near-black flowers was likely coincidental and lots of people had rose-nettle tatts on their legs. Still, the flowers had us curious, so we'd determined to view them, if no other reason but to appease curiosity. We hadn't gotten around to it until, on the drive over, Linda and I elected to ask if Caprize might allow us to see them. She'd been "absolutely delighted to".

"Why have them downstairs, though, where no one can see or enjoy them?" Linda asked.

"When I'd grown them on the ground floor—in an appropriate enclosure—I had people peering in. Somehow, word got around. I even the odd theft, if you can believe it. I didn't so much mind curious admirers, but why steal flowers, for heaven's sake?" She smiled sadly. "So, I moved them into the living room and *ohana*, but several friends and clients reacted negatively to them, thanks to allergies. Downstairs they went." She smiled sadly again and motioned. "Except for a couple I just brought back up."

"That's a shame, but they are stunning," I repeated and pointed. "What is that black orchid in that openwork hanging basket called?"

"Dracula vampira is the lesser known name. It's endemic to Ecuador, specifically mountain rain forests."

"You know a great deal about flowers," Linda stated nonchalantly. "How about their meanings?"

"I can tell you how to maintain flowers, where they originate from, and some history, but *meanings*?" She looked blank. "I can't say that's ever interested me."

Linda smiled amiably. "Any sightings of Stalker Boy?"

She chuckled gaily. "No sightings of 'Stalker Boy' since last Wednesday, or maybe it was last Thursday. In any event, he appears to have given up. Wouldn't that be wonderful, if that were the case?"

I scanned the attractive woman dressed in a pretty black-and-white polka-dot flare dress. Very 40s and very chic. Despite the friendly demeanor, there was an undercurrent of cold. It wasn't evident in the words or expression. It was—buried deep within the sea-urchin-colored eyes, like speleothems in a deep dark underground cavern.

"What can we bring for dinner tomorrow?" I sipped cold bubbly water and regarded her closely. An intriguing woman, this one.

"Just yourselves." She held up a slim hand before we could speak. "But given you asked, and people hate to come empty-handed, please feel free to bring wine or champagne. Everything else will be provided—in abundance."

Her cell phone chimed, but she didn't answer, simply smiled.

"That may be important," said Linda.

"If it is, they'll call again," came the simple response. "How is that case of yours going?"

"It's not really our case," I replied casually. "Just something we were ... pulled into."

"I heard another body was found this afternoon."

Linda looked at me and grimaced. "It doesn't take long for news to travel, does it?"

I smirked. "Not if he was found by four high-school students —social media enthusiasts—taking a roundabout way home—"

"You mean *playing hooky*," she threw in with a grin.

Caprize's laughter was throaty and deep, like a rumbling train. "No wonder it made the news so quickly." She shook her head. "What a shock it must have been to stumble across a body at the water's edge. Such a tranquil setting with a bridge and trees ... and *that*." She shook her head.

"They probably texted their friends the second reality set in," Linda said. "And taken photos to boot."

Caprize tsked softly. "That poor man has to be all over social media right now."

Perry Mason announced a call. I glanced at call display and saw an unknown number. With a deep breath, I answered.

"Are you up for a late dinner tonight?"

It wasn't GRP, as anticipated, but Adwin. With a sigh of relief, I advised him I was and agreed to meet him by the Tapa Bar in the Hilton at nine.

"You two are getting serious," Linda joked.

"It's just dinner with a friend," I advised.

"A *boy*-friend?" Caprize asked with a sly smile.

"*Ex*-boyfriend. Buddy-pal now."

"Bring him along tomorrow evening."

"I don't think—"

"Nonsense. The more, the merrier."

* * *

Linda and I stopped in our tracks when we entered the house a few minutes after seven … and found Rey and Sach half seated, half hanging off the living room three-seater soft velvet sofa (Rey and her sales had recently moved on-line), tall icy-filled drinks in their hands. Given the glassy eyes, this wasn't the first round.

They reminded me of grade-school kids. Sach's thick, sandy waves were tousled, like a little boy who'd been in a playground free-for-all while Rey's messy ponytail looked as if it had been yanked, repeatedly, by the little smart-alecky boy in the desk behind. He had a split lip and she a bruised chin.

Linda and I looked at each other, ambled into the kitchen to pour two large glasses of wine, and returned to sit on the rattan two-seater.

Linda looked from Rey to Sach and back again. "Dare we ask?"

"Shoe sale at the mall." She exhaled loudly, gulped back half the glass, and sucked in a small globular ice cube.

Linda and I exchanged that-explains-it glances and toasted each other.

"It was crazy-nuts, but we got great deals," Sach announced with a triumphant smile. "I got three pairs of runners, two pairs of loafers, and one rain boot."

One of Linda's thin eyebrows arched questioningly.

He smiled ruefully. "I lost one in the fracas."

Linda turned to Rey with a please-explain gesture.

"The prices were too good. The mall-mob sales-seekers went ballistic."

"Including you?"

"Of course," Rey snorted. "How'd you think I got this?" She gestured her chin.

"And that." Sach clasped her arm and showed a discolored wrist. "One woman was bound and determined to get the stunning Valentino shoes Rey had in her hand." He shook his head. "Who'd have guessed that petite middle-aged lady had it in her?"

133

"Meaning she got the shoes," Linda affirmed with a droll smile.

Rey nodded grimly. "What's that broad gonna do with ultra-high heels? Use 'em as canes?" The last of the drink flowed past glossy lips.

I struggled to contain the guffaw.

"What about you two?" Sach asked. "You texted Rey something about stopping by Caprize's?"

"We wanted to see the flowers you told us about and find out if Stalker Boy's been around," Linda replied easily.

"And?"

"They're quite lovely and he hasn't."

He nodded and gestured Rey's empty glass. She passed it over and he got up.

"You're back to rye and ginger?"

"It seemed appropriate, given our harrowing evening and experience."

Linda bah-hah-hahed, prompting me to crack up and Sach to stare, stunned. (It was a most, hmm, unique sound.) When her cell shrilled, she didn't answer, and we all eyed her curiously. "Nothing important."

Rey scanned her friend's suddenly strained face, shrugged, and swung one long leg over the other. "Tell us about this latest victim."

Linda glanced at me and I offered an it's-all-yours gesture.

* * *

"Super breezy tonight. Good thing you called and told me to bring a jacket," Adwin smiled over the glass he was holding.

We'd met at the bar five minutes earlier than planned and decided to eat at The Tropics, a Hilton restaurant located on the beach boardwalk. We'd both opted for burgers and frivolous cocktails; his a Blue Hawaiian, mine a guava daiquiri.

"Here's to a lovely evening and woman."

I toasted him in return, my smile amused as I scanned his attractive face. "You've changed. And I don't just mean physically."

"Is that a bad thing?" he grinned and took a sip from a tall, fat straw.

"Not at all." Feeling eyes on me, I glanced around.

"What's the matter?"

"Just … nothing." I shrugged and acknowledged the server, who placed a sizeable Caesar salad on the table with two plates.

Adwin's cremini mushroom-brown eyes gazed to the left and then the right. "Do you think you're—we're—being watched?"

"If we are being watched, there's little we can do about it." I glanced around. "But I don't see anyone even remotely suspicious."

His thin lips pulled into a full smile. "Not even that guy with the two-sizes too-small John Wayne T-shirt, draining the pitcher of beer—with a straw?"

Three tables over sat a chubby twenty-something with two pals. They weren't being nuisances, but it was obvious from the tomato-red faces and hands they'd had too much sun and frolic. Pal #1 was sucking on a wing with great gusto while Pal #2 was chomping nachos with abundant delight.

I chuckled. "Not even him. Or them."

He began to divvy the salad. "Do you ever miss what we had?"

I drew a slow breath. "I try not to look back—at anything. The past can provide wonderful memories, but it's just that: the past. I don't see any good in stepping back … know what I mean?"

He nodded and pushed over a plate. "I totally agree, but does the past have to deter someone from moving onward, along a similar path?"

I squeezed his slim hand and smiled kindly. "This is more than the 'let's do stuff together as friends' from last week, isn't it?"

He offered a trim smile and shrugged. "I really don't know, to be honest. I just, well, I suppose I'd like to think that maybe I could see you as more than friend ... eventually." He chuckled. "Damn, I thought I'd left awkward moments back in my teens."

"Let's just see where life takes us, one day, week, month at a time. Fair enough?"

"Fair enough," he smiled. "I just wanted to put it out there, you know?"

I smiled in return. "I know."

Just as I knew there was someone *definitely* watching, despite what I'd claimed earlier.

CHAPTER SIXTEEN

"Not like you to be late," Rey commented over a huge cup of take-out coffee. She sat in one of the blended-leather chairs at the black pedestal table in the main office, a pumpkin-sized muffin perched on a paper plate before her.

"Not late," I muttered, dropping my new Jones New York hooded raincoat on one of the rattan sofas and stepping into the "sort-of" kitchen to prepare a pot of coffee. "It's not even nine."

"Usually, you're in before us."

I glanced around.

"She dropped by Mink's," Rey said sourly, then shrugged. "How'd your date go last night?"

"It wasn't a date, silly," I chided, removing a small carton of milk from the fridge and checking the date. Today. Hmmmm. I sniffed. Hmmmm.

"He doesn't want to get back together?"

I watched coffee drip-drip-drip into the glass pot. "What makes you think that?"

"Just a hunch," she simpered. "Maybe it's a P.I. gut thingy."

"It's a we'll-take-it-day-by-day-and-see-what-transpires kind of thingy," I said casually.

She picked off a piece of muffin. "Are you interested in getting back together?"

"I'm interested in getting GRP and helping Hardena Antigua. And what's up with that?"

Rey popped the muffin into her mouth and chewed for a few seconds. "Lance's the guy's name. Saw a pic. He's serious drool material. I can see why the woman would worry."

According to my cousin, Hardena was fifteen years Lance's senior—a mature, wise fifty-five to an immature, oblivious forty. The two had met on a Mediterranean yachting adventure fourteen months ago when he'd served as deckhand. It was love at first sight ... or rather upon winch cleaning. Engrossed in a fashion magazine, she'd not seen him and literally walked into him. The rest was, as the silly saying went, history.

They'd been married ten months and after eight, she was certain he was two-timing her. Hardena had turned a blind eye for a while, but finally decided it was time for action; she wanted photos of Lance "in the act".

"I don't think we'll be peeking in any bedroom windows," Rey chuckled, "but we'll definitely give the woman what she's paying for."

I smiled, poured a mug of coffee, and took a seat at the table across from her. "It felt as if someone were watching us in the restaurant last night."

She snorted. "Probably because someone was."

I concurred. "I just don't get GRP's obsession with us."

"The guy's a fruitloop. Do we need any other reason?"

I sighed and sipped.

"Oh, I got a part in an ad for a local business. Nancy-Anne, my agent, texted my last night. Said the guy had seen a few of my commercials and thought I was prime for his."

"Congrats. What's the business?"

"A hardware and garden center. She's arranging a time for us to meet tomorrow or Friday." She smiled and sighed. "I guess we'd better buy a couple of bottles of bubbles for tonight. I gotta admit, I'm not really keen on going. The woman's a bit of a snot and bore."

"Caprize's a client." I frowned, wondering if Stalker Boy had ceased being an annoyance. "Was a client?"

Rey arched a shoulder and straightened when *The Mod Squad* announced a call.

* * *

"Thanks for letting me us know," I said to Ald and disconnected.

Rey gestured me to reveal all.

"No leads on the cards and the latest victim is twenty-seven-year-old Burt Fayne, a real-estate broker. He went missing after an early dinner meeting. His partner, Ned Marvin, called the police this morning when he didn't find Fayne at the condo after he'd arrived home from a two-day business trip in Seattle."

"Did he actually make the meeting?"

I nodded and got up to stretch my legs. "The client, Ed Melville, saw Fayne walk to his BMW in the parking lot. After that, he wasn't seen again. Ald's got everyone on it."

"I should hope so," she sniffed. "Linda's tailing Lance this afternoon; he's playing tennis at four and then has some boating event to attend at seven. She'll leave the event after checking it out for a while and take a cab to Caprize's. What about us? Any ideas how to pursue this case?"

"It's not ours," I reminded her.

"Maybe not technically, but Mr. Fruitloop made it ours."

"I suppose he did." I peered onto the street below. Another gray, cloudy day. And, hopefully, an uneventful one.

* * *

And uneventful it was. Linda took a few photos of Lance snuggling up to a blonde and a redhead at the boating event, Rey secured a time to meet the businessman interested in her acting talents early Friday afternoon, and I updated our site and blog ... and connected with Gail, our HPD pal who returned from Japan. She'd meet the three of us for drinks at RumFire at nine Friday evening.

Adwin accompanied Rey and me to Caprize's, where we enjoyed a delicious (abundant, as promised) dinner complemented by very fine wine. Caprize was quite the hostess: thoughtful, joyful, and rather amusing, sharing surprisingly funny anecdotes. At eleven, everyone departed with full bellies and smiles and that was, very happily, that.

* * *

Thursday was equally uneventful, except for tailing Lance and taking a few more photos of him—flirting with a barista, chatting to a pretty brunette, and sitting at a busy bar sipping Chardonnay. Nothing incriminating. We'd keep at it.

Upon arrival at home at six, the three of us took the pets for a long walk, ate Edam-and-avocado sandwiches and green salads, and did personal errands. At ten, we reconvened in the kitchen in our nightwear to enjoy caramel-white hot cocoa before officially calling it a night.

Linda, dressed in cotton pajamas with a sashaying squirrel theme, stirred the sweet and fragrant beverage while Rey, sporting a silky chemise nightgown, searched the well-stocked (for once) fridge for canned whipped cream, one of our new "indulgences".

"Can't wait to see Gail," she said, pulling out the can and shaking it close to her ear to determine if there was enough whipped cream left.

Linda murmured agreement and removed the steaming pot from the stove. "None for you," she told Button, who had parked herself at her feet. My fuzzy honey shook her head and scrabbled over to nudge Bonzo, nibbling grapes in a corner.

As I placed a bag of super-size marshmallows on the table

and she filled three mugs, my cell advised there was a text. We groaned simultaneously.

"Doesn't that guy ever rest?" Rey griped.

"May not be him," Linda murmured, topping the cocoa with whipped cream and passing it to her.

They both turned to me expectantly.

"Well?" my cousin asked when I placed the phone on the counter.

"No one important."

"Share, Cousin Jilly."

"... It was Cash with a how-goes-it-with-the-new-case and stay-safe message."

Rey's brow furrowed. "Your sometimes boyfriend hasn't kept in touch quite like he used to. What's up with that?"

"You'd have to ask him," I said sharply. "I won't."

She scanned my set expression and shrugged. "Lindy-Loo, where's that third mug?"

"Uh."

"What's up, buttercup?"

"Uh."

My cousin and I glanced toward the window, which had her attention. Attached to it, from the outside, was another satiny black rose fastened with thick, clear industrial tape. This time, a small picture of a chessboard accompanied it. Scrawled on it, with a substance that, yes, once again resembled dried blood, was one word: checkmate.

Rey said blandly, "Thank goodness we'd gotten the security system or that rose and message might have been inside. That'd have really ticked me off."

"Ditto," Linda and I responded in unison.

* * *

Three large pots of hot cocoa kept Sallo and Hammill—and a couple of forensic folks—going as they checked out GRP's latest rose offering, the house and lanai. The three of us had opted for herbal tea—to relax and keep warm on the increasingly cool night. It was close to two a.m. by the time we climbed the stairs to go to bed.

"Like you said, good thing for the security system. It makes for a definite deterrent," Linda muttered through a yawn.

Rey swore softly. "Mr. Fruitloop must have been right behind us when we got home, managed to sidestep the outdoor motion sensor, peered in the kitchen window and when he saw we weren't there, fastened the flower to the glass."

"The stupid f'g shit," Linda grumbled.

We stopped in the middle of the dimly lit hallway and Rey and I looked at her in surprise. Linda rarely used bad/foul language.

"He's pissing me off."

Rey snorted. "He's not doing much for me, either."

I agreed and rubbed my face. "I'm hoping we'll have something to work with after we meet Ald tomorrow."

She snorted again. "Yeah, like he really wants our help."

"Well, he's got it, whether he likes it or not," was my flat response.

Linda smiled drily. "Sallo said Ald had been digging into detained and/or arrested male teens and young men who came from money—"

"Whose rich daddies didn't bail them out," Rey interjected with a sneer. "I got the impression the dick found someone."

With a light slap to her arm, I chided, "You really should stop insulting the guy."

"I meant 'dick' as in detective, that old time word. You know, like gumshoe. But if the shoe fits, or something like that." She watched Bonzo bounce past, followed by Piggaletto and Button.

"Bedtime beckons," she announced with a light whack to our backs. Off she ambled.

CHAPTER SEVENTEEN

"Couldn't sleep, either?" Linda asked, removing two slices of overly crisp toast from a retro-style two-slice toaster—as in charred-shingles crisp.

"I've been awake since five," I confessed, glancing at the new coffee-cup kitchen wall clock; it read seven on the nose. Turning to the window, I noticed sunlight, which was welcome, and it was also very breezy ... and cool, according to the thermometer hooked outside. I was glad I'd opted for a ribbed seamed sweater and ponte pants.

"The winds kept me up, strangely. I guess GrimReaperPeeper got into my head." Nodding to the coffee pot, she plopped a huge tablespoon of grape jelly on the flat charcoal that was once bread. No butter or margarine. Ugh.

"You're looking very professional. That a new outfit?"

She glanced down at her cocoa-colored roll-cuff blazer and sleek skinny pants, complemented by an animal-print blouse. "Bought it three weeks ago. Thought it might be nice for business meetings."

"Do we have any?" I asked with a yawn.

"Not yet." Her smile fleetingly.

"There was an email and voicemail from Hardena on the

agency laptop and voicemail on the agency phone last night. Lance is going to the yacht club mid-morning. Apparently, a friend of a friend wants him to look at the engine before he calls in service personnel. I guess even millionaires like to save a buck." She smiled drolly and sat at the table. "I'm going to see that he's doing exactly what he said he'd be. Mink and I are going to meet downtown at half past eight; she wants my opinion on a new line she's considering carrying."

I poured a big mug of coffee and sniffed. "Vanilla?"

"Tahitian."

"I didn't know we were into flavored java."

"Sach dropped it off the other day. A gym buddy just opened a café. Thought I'd give it a try. It's not bad by half." Linda bit off a corner of toast.

"Rey still asleep?" I took a seat across from her.

"She muttered something about a shower when I peeked in, but then rolled over with a grunt."

I chuckled. "You and Mink are building quite a friendship."

"I like her. A lot." She held up a hand. "But I love Rey. She's my best friend and always will be."

"I think she's feeling *un*-loved." I took a sip and tilted my head one way and then the other. Not bad. "As in *jealous* un-loved."

"She's being silly."

"She's being Rey." I winked.

Linda scanned my face for several seconds. "Could I share something with you? Just you?"

"Of course."

"Mink's funny and easy to be with. We get along well and … and I'm kind of, well, attracted to her."

I arched an eyebrow. "Really?"

"Really. I know, I've never really been attracted to women like that before … and it's something I need to … think about."

I squeezed her hand and returned to the coffee.

"That's not the only reason I've been hanging around with her."

"As Frasier Crane used to say," I smiled, "I'm listening."

"She's been supporting me through ... a medical issue I have ... I mean had."

Linda went on to explain how a few weeks back she'd discovered something unexpected and unwelcome on her torso —or rather Mink had noticed it when Linda was changing tops, courtesy of a tea spill. Given three close relatives had died of different cancers, Mink had all but dragged Linda to the doctor. Thankfully, tests proved it benign and she had it removed, but the wait for the final results had taken longer than expected or hoped for; hence, the weekend away. Linda hadn't wanted Rey and I to see how anxious—petrified—she'd been.

Stepping beside her, I hooked an arm around her shoulders. "You really didn't feel you could share with us?"

"I figured if I did, you'd both worry too much, and watch my every move. That would have been way too intense. And I didn't want you two to mollycoddle or follow me like the kids do." She gestured the threesome, who were lying nearby, looking overly eager to indulge in treats and walks, and changed the subject. "Do you think Lance is cheating on Hardena? Or is he just a major bad-ass flirt?"

"We haven't seen any sign of cheating so far, but never say never." I shrugged and topped off my mug. "What does he do for a living, anyway, if anything?"

"He's CMO."

"CMO?"

She smiled drily. "Chief Money Overseer."

I chuckled and glanced at the clock. "I hope Rey gets her butt in gear. We're meeting Ald at nine."

"When does she meet that business guy re that ad again?"

"Today at two, I believe. And we have Gail at nine tonight."

"It'll be nice to see her again."

I concurred.

Linda looked at her Olivia Burton watch, also a recent purchase. "I guess I better mosey."

"Good luck with the line and Lance."

She smiled. "Good luck with getting closer to GRP—so we can nail the SOB."

* * *

Rey's cherry-red lips pulled into a trim line as she watched Ald re-enter his office. He'd stepped into the hallway to confer with Sergeant Culum Beau about a hit-and-run that had just transpired outside HPD headquarters as we were about to sit down to talk.

My cousin was still upset that Linda had opted to join Mink to review a line of dogwear. "What the hell does she know about doggy fashion?" she'd demanded as we'd parked ourselves on Ald's all-too-familiar worn leather couch.

"She'll provide a 'fresh' take," I'd said, patting her hand. "Don't fret. Linda's not in the market for a new best friend."

Ald shook his head as he took a seat behind his desk.

"Is the victim okay?" I asked.

"The victim, a six-foot-tall meerkat, got himself flattened like a flapjack by a manure truck."

Rey appeared puzzled. "A meerkat got manured to death?"

"The guy was late for his first day at a new job; hence, the costume. He's—was—greeter at the zoo."

"What a spot of damn bad luck," Rey stated with an exaggerated British accent.

"Majorly," he said with an acerbic smile, leaning back.

"You're looking rather dapper today," I smiled.

"You trying to butter me up?" he smiled in return.

"Yes ... but you do look rather nice. The suit's nice."

Absently, he glanced down at the Bonobos two-piece blue cotton ensemble. "I've got a meeting with a hotshot at the DEA this aft. Thought I'd look," he simpered, "*dapper*."

"Sallo told us you might have something."

"Did he now?"

"He said you'd been digging into arrested young dudes who came from money," Rey said flatly, crossing her arms and one long leg over the other.

"Did he now?"

"You hard of hearing, Hives?"

Ald smirked. "I came across four that fit the bill."

Rey and I glanced at each other.

"You going to provide details?" she asked with a scowl.

"You going to play nice?"

A raspberry rang forth. "JJ'll buy you a fancy-schmancy dinner. How's that for 'nice'?"

"Any place you like, Ald." I interrupted as he started to speak. "Now, come on. Share. Please."

He smirked again and grabbed a 9" x 12" brown envelope with clasp from the corner of his neat desk and held it up. "Four names with background re arrests. I'm providing them because I'm a super nice guy … and I can do without the whining and pleading," he gazed balefully at Rey, "and *insulting* that'll surely come my way if I don't."

It was Rey's turn to smirk. She rose and ambled over to accept the envelope. "Thanks, Hives."

He rolled his eyes. "Just make sure you three follow up in a professional manner."

"We're always professional," we said simultaneously.

Another roll of the eyes.

Rey perched herself on the edge of his desk, much to his visible annoyance, and looked at me. "Anything else?"

I shook my head. "Not until the next body."

"Or bodies."

"This is one bizarre game," Ald said sourly, hooking his hands behind his neck. "No rhyme, no reason."

"That we can perceive," I stated.

"Random murders. Prosperous victims." He scanned the ceiling with a furrowed brow.

"A moneyed and clever killer," I added.

"Moneyed and clever *fruitloop*," grumbled Rey.

He looked at her, then me, but remained silent.

"We're meeting Gail tonight." I stood.

"So she told me."

"Want to join us?"

Rey shot me a look.

Which he caught.

"You bet I do," he grinned.

* * *

Rey zipped up her royal-blue hoodie advertising L.A. and scanned Ald's list one more time before returning it to the envelope. We'd decided to grab coffees and sit on a bench on the *ewa* side of Ala Moana Beach Park, not far from the water.

"Think it'll ever get warm again?"

I scanned the cloudy sky. "Let's keep the faith."

"Whatever," she sighed. "I wonder if one of these guys on the list is GRP."

"When you head over to your meeting this aft, I'll research the names and family. Hopefully, one of them will prove to be our guy."

"Pretty impressive names, huh? Henry Wickenhauffer IV. Joseph Reichmann. Franklin Czerwony Sledz III. Luc E Mei, no period after the E."

I chuckled. "They do tend to scream 'money'."

She smiled and tucked the envelope into my Nordstrum leather tote. "Guess I'd better get ready for the meeting. What'd you think—professional or casual?"

"His biz is hardware and gardening, so something casual. Maybe those new white pants of yours with a floral top and lightweight sweater. Not too much make-up. Think wholesome."

"If you drop me on Ward, I'll grab a cab. You head back to the office and start researching." She stood and stretched. "We'll catch up at RumFire."

* * *

"You sure you want me to leave?" Eddy Galazie asked, grabbing an icy soda from the small office fridge. "I don't mind staying. I can vacuum."

"You did that the other day," I reminded our young part-time assistant and motioned the room. "It looks great, Red Head."

The twenty-four-year old beamed.

The agency phone rang, which he answered with a cheery, "Hey, TTIA. How can we help?"

I swallowed my smile. He was too sweet to admonish.

"Uh-huh. Sure … okay. Uh-huh."

When he hung up, I looked at him expectantly.

"That was Linda. Her car died and a tow truck's coming. She won't be home as planned. She's not sure how long she'll be, but said," he frowned as he recollected, then smiled, "she'll definitely meet you at Fireplace."

"You mean RumFire?"

"That's it," he grinned.

I grinned in return. "How about you run by the house and take the pets for a walk, feed them, and maybe keep them company for an hour or so?"

"Sure!" He scanned me closely. "You going to sit at the laptop and keep Googling?"

"For a while," I nodded. "You okay with the new security system?"

He looked thoughtful, then gave a thumb's up.

Come four o'clock, I'd learned a few things about the four young privileged gents and their families. Maybe not enough— yet—to determine if one was indeed GRP, but with more digging, it was possible we'd unearth a vital link.

Henry Wickenhauffer IV was arrested five years ago for setting fire to a friend's BMW after they'd had a drunken argument. This was the third time he'd played arsonist and Papa, a fourth-generation lawyer, was *not* amused. It was Mama-Darling who'd bailed him out, but not until he'd sat in a cell for three days; Papa had wanted Henry to learn a lesson.

Given a vintage Vette was torched a few months later, it was evident HW IV hadn't learned a blessed thing.

Now twenty-three, the poor guy had absolutely nothing going for him in the looks department. In the few photos I'd seen, he had thin walnut-colored hair, a long gaunt face, a bulbous nose and flabby lips. Something in the demeanor suggested he had low self-esteem, not something I'd associate with a cocky serial killer. And given that he was currently working as a security manager at a resort in Bermuda, it was a pretty sure thing he wasn't GRP.

Joseph Reichmann had been born into a family that had been in aerospace for decades. Omar, the father, had worked in the industry for a dozen years, but decided to try his hand at real estate—with winning results. When his health had declined, but his wealth had (progressively) grown, he moved the family to Oahu. Seven years ago, Joseph had been arrested for running down a middle-aged couple while under the influence and driving without a license. The husband had survived but was wheelchair-bound; the wife hadn't known what hit her. At the time, Daddy Omar was in Spain re a business deal and didn't fly home. In fact, not even the family lawyer came to bail out Joseph —not for a few days, anyway.

Joseph, now twenty-five, was medium height and medium weight. Dark eyes and thin lips. Not attractive, not ugly. He did sport a haughty screw-you expression, at least in the social media photos of him standing in front of a gleaming white Porsche. He'd not entered the aerospace or real estate realms but had chosen to become a writer ... of books that would make even Cousin Reynalda blush.

Franklin Czerwony Sledz III was heir to a successful software throne, er, company. His father, who preferred to be called "Big Fish", hadn't been overly pleased to hear that his son had been arrested for drug trafficking. Franklin claimed innocence. Stated (emphatically) he was just hanging with friends. How did he know they were doing a deal in the back room of the restaurant? Powerful lawyers got him off on probation, using the reason of "affluenza" (used to define psychological problems that can afflict privileged offspring). No time served.

Twenty-three-year-old, Franklin was of medium height and medium weight, with onyx-black eyes and fairly thin lips that were, in the six photos I'd viewed, pulled into a perpetual sneer. His hair was lustrous, black and wavy. Again, not attractive, but not ugly.

He was studying Applied Mathematics at the local university.

Luc E Mei had been arrested for mischief one Halloween at the age of seventeen with three friends—one of them Henry's brother, interestingly enough—for smashing pumpkins and creating mischief. At nineteen, he was arrested for screaming obscenities while drunk. The yacht club might have let it go, as it so often had with young Mr. Mei, had he not thrown bottles at yachts and, subsequently, beaned one well-to-do captain. Given the gent was a hot-shot CEO, Richard Rijk [Highly-Successful-Cosmetic-Surgeon] Mei decided to let his son cool his heels for three days; pretty, young Step-Mom didn't care one way or another. Unfortunately for Luc, he'd encountered Angry Anson while in the pokey, who didn't have much love for spoiled rich kids. One broken nose and arm later, Luc was released, lesson most unequivocally learned.

Also medium in stature, Luc was extremely good-looking, as in GQ-cover good looking. Brilliant blue eyes the color of the Pacific and soft, full lips. Nice cheekbones and smooth skin. Easy come-hither smile. Had the pater's talented surgeon hands worked on his son's face? I pulled up a pic of the successful man.

Father and son had exceptionally similar features, maybe too much so; I suspected both had been enhanced and not by familial genes or the forces of nature.

He wasn't following in Daddy's footsteps, not even close. He'd acquired a Creative Media degree and had started a video-game design and development firm with two graduates, Henny Spieler and Beck Bild.

I tucked printed photos and docs into a folder to take home; the three of us could review them tomorrow at the breakfast table. Tonight, we'd sit down with Gail, kick up our heels, and bring her up to date with our current cases.

CHAPTER EIGHTEEN

"I hear you got the job," Gail said, raising a glass of Pineapple Mana Wheat beer as Rey, beaming, slipped into the seat across from her.

"And I hear you had an awesome time in Japan," my cousin said, requesting a glass of Australian Chardonnay from a passing server. She was still wearing the outfit I'd suggested for the meeting but had added a pretty silk shawl to the ensemble.

"Your news is more exciting," our reedy fifty-some-year-old HPD pal chuckled. Her cranberry-glossy lips pulled into a smile as she peered over the rim of round black-rimmed glasses perched on a Roman nose. Her orb colors changed with the outfit and this time her eyes were fern-green.

"Hardly, but we're filming the ad on Tuesday."

"Nice guy?" Linda asked over her Longboard.

Rey nodded. "We met in a coffee shop across from his huge place, Mapunapuna way. Bought me a large latte and awesome home-baked banana bread, and herbal tea for him. The poor dude had a cold, thanks to a hiking adventure on Big Island. He had a scarf around his neck and chin, and a wool hat. We sat outside, a few feet apart, so I wouldn't catch any germs. He thought he might still be contagious. I told him we could postpone, but he said the studio was booked and too many people had been scheduled.

"Anyway, we didn't talk long, maybe ten minutes. Said he'd heard good things about my acting and loved the few ads he'd seen, so he was good to go. He just wanted to meet me first. He's going to have the contract drawn up and at Nancy-Anne's Monday."

We toasted my cousin and then demanded Gail tell us about Japan, after which we promised to fill her in with details about Lance and GRP. Before she could begin, Ald swung by and said he could only stay for one drink, much to Rey's observable relief.

The night ended with Gail agreeing to come to the house the following day and staying through Sunday. We'd pursue Lance for a few hours in the afternoon when he'd be attending a charity event without Hardena, then hunker down and find all we could about the four young men. If nothing of note was unearthed, we'd expand our horizons; it was entirely possible, after all, that Ald et al had missed someone in the Flush-Boys-Behind-Bars search.

* * *

Saturday morning proved routine, which suited the three of us fine, though we did grumble—just a bit—about wanting to acquire a new case or two. It was too nice a day to grouse much, though; a dazzling sunflower-yellow sun and bright azure sky were accompanied with a soft breeze and much-appreciated warmth. It was decided that Linda and Rey would follow Lance in the afternoon while Gail—who'd arrive at three (after making a stop by HPD)—and I would prepare dinner. Gail's barbe-cue/grill skills were better than mine, so she was in charge of shrimp and sea bass and veggies, while I'd pull together a potato salad and cold cucumber soup.

Kojak announced a call as I started peeling cukes. Oddly, I didn't flinch or grimace, simply answered with a typical Rey greeting, "Yo."

"Yo?"

"Oh."

"Oh?" Cash laughed. "Try not to sound too excited, hon."

"What do you want?" I briskly asked my "sometimes boyfriend". As much as Rey and Linda might joke, I didn't find the relationship anything to josh about. I considered myself a fairly strong individual, so where the bleep was that strength when it came to Mr. Agent-slash-Drug-Dealer? I was as attracted to the arrogant ass as I was aggravated. Sure, the guy was f'g hot, as Rey would say, and sexy, but he was also, hmm, irresistibly irritating. Or was that irritatingly irresistible?

"I called to see how you were doing."

"You should know I'm doing fine. You have eyes everywhere, don't you?" I put the phone on speaker and placed it on the counter.

He laughed again. "I'm flying over next Saturday."

"Bully for you. Have a nice, safe flight," I said impassively and returned to peeling—and cursing, when I sliced my finger. I eyed it critically. No stitches required, but a few bandages for sure. With a sigh, I stepped over Piggaletto, contentedly perched at my feet, and ambled over to the far cupboard to get the first-aid kit.

"Speaking of eyes, I understand an old boyfriend is back in town."

"Your spies tell you that?" I asked brusquely, pulling out an antiseptic wipe.

"Don't be silly. But I do like to know what's happening on the other side of the world," he replied flatly.

"… How's Florida and the drug biz?"

"Going way too well."

I added the second bandage, not sure what else to say. Okay, there were some questions, but they were ones I'd never pose: do you miss me, do you care, who else is in your life, why do you call so sporadically?

What are you thinking, JJ? I slapped my head and winced.

"How's the new house?"

"Needs work."

"Think maybe I could drop by when I arrive? Maybe stay a night or two?"

I drew a deep breath. I *really* needed to walk away from this bad boy. Once and for all. "No." With that, I disconnected and finished bandaging my finger.

"Males," I spat, glancing at the porker, eyeing me. "You're an exception."

Piggaletto snorted and smiled and scampered to the water bowl.

Ten seconds later, *Kojak* was back.

"I said 'no'," I huffed.

"I didn't ask you anything," GRP laughed heartily.

"Oh, it's you. How are things?" I asked casually, wondering if he'd announce another body was to be found.

"Going, going," he replied cheerily, sounding like a friend or colleague. "You?"

"Everything's peachy-keen."

He laughed again.

"A friend found out that chessboard pic you left with the rose on the window was of the Short-Timman game in '91. Any particular reason you chose that one?"

"It was an outstanding game, with Short's quick control—his King supporting the Queen to win the day. He marched his king for g1 to g5—how I could go on. In any event, it was a king walk extraordinaire."

"You're a chess fan?"

"I'm a fan of many things," he replied.

"Particularly games, though?"

"I like challenges."

"Which others do you enjoy?" I asked casually. "I'm rather fond of Monopoly and Scrabble."

"They can prove fun."

I suspected he wasn't going to reveal more, so I switched gears. "Did you call to advise of another victim?"

"Not today. I'm taking a little time off. I need a rest. A diversion if you like."

"Diversion?"

"Why don't we call it a mini vacation?"

"So you're merely calling to say hello?"

"Pretty much," he replied simply. "I didn't want you to forget me."

"I—we—could *never* do that."

"That's so nice to hear," he said gaily. "I'll call you early next week, JJ, when I'm back to work. I just wanted to wish you and your police pals a pleasant weekend. Take care."

I eyed the phone, puzzled. This was getting way too weird.

* * *

"We go out for a few hours and look what happens: we miss Cousin Jilly's calls from Lover Boy and GRP." Rey stuffed spicy falafel into her mouth.

We were seated in the kitchen, starting on the soup course, which was accompanied with cold deep-fried chickpea balls. The three of us had changed into jeans and T-shirts, before sitting down with Gail. The kids were in a corner, cuddling toys, happily stuffed with too many treats.

Before gearing up for dinner, Gail and I had spent an hour on her laptop, checking out our four young men and not finding anything of major relevance. Rey and Linda hadn't lucked in re Lance. He'd attended the social event—a charity fundraiser for deserving kids and their families—and while he'd chatted and flirted, as seemed to be his common way, nothing of note transpired. The twosome arrived home, deflated, wondering how much longer the "hunk" should be followed.

Gail dipped a spicy deep-fried ball into a bowl of tahini. "Too bad we can't zero in on GRP's calls. He's clever, like you said. He knows about burner phones, security and VoIP technology, DNA and forensics, among other things. But Rocky's good. I'll have him drop by tomorrow, late afternoon. Do you have any Scotch? He likes to sip when he's focusing."

"We'll get some," Linda promised.

I rose to clear soup bowls. "I can't help but feel we're missing something."

"That's because we're missin' a shit-load," Rey snorted. "Facts. Evidence. All things solid."

"We'll get them," Gail said cheerfully. "Keep the faith, ladies, keep the faith."

* * *

"I haven't done this in too many years to count or admit," Gail laughed, repositioning the laptop on her lap as she pulled a thin blanket with a grinning kitty-cat theme across her slim legs.

While cleaning up after dinner, we'd decided to put on pajamas and have an easy-going girls' night with wine, nibbles, and K-pop playing in the background. Gail wore a plaid pajama set, Linda a cotton lace-trimmed calf-length nightgown, Rey a soft ribbed-knit sleepshirt, and me a striped top and shorts sleep set. Seated on the hand-twisted wool rug in the living room, we'd assembled blankets, sheets, and cushions—and a white marble wine cooler (a gift from Gail) keeping a couple Chilean Chardonnays nicely chilled.

"You know what we haven't searched?" Linda asked over her wineglass.

We eyed her questioningly.

"Games."

We continued to eye her questioningly.

She chuckled, looking at me. "You told us GRP is fond of chess—"

"And challenges."

"We haven't checked on the four guys' history regarding games, specifically chess."

"Yeah," Rey said, straightening. "We've got some background re their college and university studies. We should check to see if one of them was on a chess team or something. And go back to high school if possible."

Gail gave a thumb's up and started keying. I got up to refill glasses and find more nibbles; we'd pretty much sucked back the bowl of Kasugai roasted nuts and plate of Pop Pan, nummy scallion-flavored crackers. In the kitchen I found two more items to keep the Asian-treat theme. Arare, Japanese-style rice crackers, and shrimp chips found their ways onto plates, and a new bottle of wine graced the wine cooler.

Gail focused on the screen and Linda peered over her shoulder. Rey munched shrimp chips and petted Bonzo, who'd hopped over to warm her legs and I checked email. Nothing of note had arrived, thankfully. Just as I was about to put the cell on the ceramic-top coffee table, *Adam-12* announced a call.

Gail chuckled. "You change ringtones like I change contacts." (Sapphire-blue today, in case you were wondering.)

"And the rest of the world underwear," Rey said jokily. "Is it some sort of ODC thingy?"

"OCD."

"Whatever."

Linda looked over with a furrowed brow and I gave a fingers-crossed sign. "Hello?"

"It's Sach."

"What's wrong?"

"Why should anything be wrong?"

"It's Saturday night and you're calling," I replied.

He chuckled. "My date canceled. You want some company?"

"It's girls-only night. Sorry."

"I can put on my Liza Minelli or Chita Rivera Halloween wig and make-up. And I have a lovely peach-mango sheath with sequins along the bosom—"

"Sounds intriguing, but even if you sang a stellar rendition of 'All that Jazz', sported a 38-C chest and waxed your legs, it would still be no."

He chuckled again. "Guess who dropped by yesterday."

"Peter Pan? The Tooth Fairy?" I asked drily.

"That'd be cool, but no. Caprize did. She decided she wanted to start training, get toned and gain strength, and after we chatted a bit, she signed up for three-month personal training package."

"That's great, I guess."

"You guess?"

"To be honest, I can't imagine her training. She's not the sort that ... sweats."

Sach burst into laughter, which was funny in itself, given he sounded like Donald Duck. "She probably doesn't."

We chatted a little about nothing in particular and then disconnected. When I looked over, Gail and Linda and Rey were looking at me triumphantly.

"You scored?"

Linda squeezed Gail's shoulder. "Our friend did. Luc Mei played a few scholastic tournaments back when—he's mentioned on a few sites—and belonged to a couple of clubs. There's no mention of him in relation to chess after the age of eighteen, though."

"Given he's into video games, maybe that's when they caught his attention and he gave up chess."

"Quite possibly," Gail said. "But he wasn't the only one. Henry Wickenlaufer played in one scholastic tournament, but didn't seem to pursue it after that. Franklin Czerwony Sledz III —is that an amazing name or what?—is *still* a member of the ChinHo Chess Club."

Linda looked from me to Rey to Gail. "Maybe we should check out these guys firsthand."

"Let's tail Luc and Franklin for a day or two, just to see what they're up to and into," Rey suggested.

"That's a great idea," I said.

Linda appeared pensive. "But if one of them is GRP—"

"He'd welcome the change of rules," I grinned.

"And resulting challenge," Rey added with a tart smile.

CHAPTER NINETEEN

Noon the following day, the four of us were seated on a bench in the beautiful, bustling Ala Moana Center, sipping smoothies— avocado for me, banana for Gail and Rey, and berry-blend for Linda. Franklin, who we'd followed from his parents' opulent estate to the shopping mall, appeared to be on a casual shopping spree. He'd purchased two shirts at Neiman Marcus, a pair of shoes at Cole Haan, and mochi in the food court.

"That bag in the window was so-o sweet," Rey groused. "Thanks for making me leave my credit cards at home."

"You and malls, and those cards, are a dangerous mix," Linda declared. "You know it, I know it—"

"And so do all the stores in here," Gail interjected with a giggle. "They must love you."

I all but chortled. "Do they!"

Rey shot me a withering look.

"Our boy's leaving Prada's," Linda announced.

"With a purchase," Rey noted, eyeing the tiny bag closely.

"Good things come in small packages," I said with a wry smile, standing.

"How long should we keep following?" Linda asked as we

began to tail him again. "He doesn't appear to have any nefarious plans."

Gail chuckled. "You never know. He might be on his way to slice and dice his next victim, dressed to the nines."

"GRP said he was taking a mini vacation," Rey reminded her. "I don't know, ladies. You think this shopaholic might really be GRP?"

We glanced at one another and shrugged simultaneously.

"You know what might help?"

We turned to Linda.

"Hearing him speak. GRP's voice is pretty deep."

"But the guy outside Caprize's office had a flat, heavy voice … with what sounded like a fake accent."

"Maybe GRP uses voice enhancers. And if he *was* that guy, he could have changed his voice a bit. I can change mine, just as you can," she said, speaking from low in her throat.

I had to concur.

"Hearing his voice, though, is a great idea. Ya never know." Rey slapped her friend on the back and pushed her smoothie into her hand. "Let me at 'im".

"Oh no," Linda murmured, watching her best friend sprint forward.

"Oh yes," I sighed.

"If he is your guy, and he recognizes Rey—which he will, of course—for sure he'll change his voice," Gail advised, motioning us to stop as Rey all but leapt before the young man.

"Still, maybe she'll hear something familiar in it," I shrugged. "As she said, 'ya never know'."

We slipped alongside a koi pond and watched as she presented an engaging smile and chatted him up. They talked, smiled, chuckled, and then Rey casually ambled to the front of the pond, where she took a seat and pulled out her cell. Franklin looked back and they waved at each other, then he continued on.

The three of us waited until he was gone from view and hastened to Rey's side.

"Well?" we asked in unison.

"He's not our guy."

"Are you sure?" Linda asked, eyeing the crowd pensively.

"He has a slight stutter and a really low, low voice. Could be a tenor with that bass-y voice."

"Like one of your beloved Il Volo?" I jested.

"I'd rather not put him in the same league as my cuties," Rey sniffed.

Linda and I laughed. She'd developed a real "thing" for the attractive men who comprised the Italian operatic pop trio.

"Might he have faked it?" Gail questioned.

"Of course he might have," she retorted, then grinned and elbowed her lightly. "He's into shopping and designers, much like me, but I can't usually afford the *real* deal. But something tells me he wasn't faking."

"Did this guy say anything of note?"

She shook her head. "He's taking a couple of evening courses and has an exam to study for. He's going to do it with a class-mate this afternoon." She chirped. "Otherwise, he'd have asked me for coffee."

"Do we want to try for Luc today?" I asked.

"It can't hurt to swing by his place and hang around a bit. If we sight him in a reasonable amount of time, we follow. If not, we call it a day," Gail proposed.

We agreed and hastened to the overfull parking lot.

* * *

Just before two, we were in my Jeep, watching Luc. We'd lucked in. Five minutes after parking near his upscale Hawaii Kai condo, he left the garage in a gleaming white Porsche Boxster. We followed him to scenic Wawamalu Beach Park, a rocky place with little sand and few trees. The beach, fairly empty, had a lovely grassy area for sitting, relaxing, picnicking.

He'd met two young men there, and the threesome sat on

rocks near the water. They were dressed similarly, with patterned board shorts, pressed T-shirts, smart Ray-bans, and flip-flops with serious names like Versace and Gucci. All that was missing from the [swank] beach look was a baseball or Frisbee—with 24K-gold stitching or lettering.

"Henny Spieler and Beck Bild confirmed," our HPD Administrative Specialist announced, looking from the trio to the laptop and back again. "Obviously, they work and play together."

"So do we," Rey said with a quick smile.

Gail gave a thumb's up.

"He's hunky."

"Which one?" Linda asked, opening a bottle of water and sipping.

"Actually, they all are, but Luc's *über* hunky."

Linda bah-hah-hahed, prompting Gail to snort with laughter and me to choke on mine.

"Sssh, we don't want to attract attention."

"You don't think we already have?" Rey asked smartly, chomping a strawberry Twizzler for a rare change. "Four gorgeous women sitting at the side of a parking lot, watching young guys at the shoreline?"

Another bah-hah-hah from Linda and snort from Gail. I rolled my eyes and slid down in the seat.

A quarter of an hour later, the threesome went their own ways. Spieler and Bild started ambling in the direction of nearby Sandy Beach, known for awesome bodyboarding and bodysurfing, while Luc sat in his open-top car, chatting on the phone.

"Man, those teeth are blinding," Rey murmured, grabbing Linda's water and chugging.

"They weren't cheap," I said.

"Nothing of his is."

"How long should we follow?" Gail asked.

"You got somewhere to go?" my cousin asked, turning to her with a raised brow.

"We have Rocky dropping by your house around three."

"Crap, I forgot." Rey leaned forward and looked at me. "Whadya think?"

I shrugged. "It depends on this guy's schedule, not ours. Isn't the plan to get an idea of what he's into?"

"I think he's into himself, if you ask me," she sniffed.

I was inclined to agree. For the fourth time, he eyed himself in the rearview mirror, checking his smile, his hair, and how the glasses embellished that perfectly sculpted face.

"Do you think he's your guy?" Gail asked, pulling her wide-brim floppy straw hat lower onto her forehead.

"Hearing the voice would help—"

"Let's give his office a call tomorrow," Rey suggested.

"Good idea. It can't hurt," I said, "but my instinct says he's not our killer."

"I'm inclined to agree." Linda.

"Yeah, ditto." Rey.

"He's too I'm-too-Good-Looking-to-be-True," Gail said glibly. "How would he find the time to break away from the mirror to do any killing?"

I chuckled and said, "The chess angle has me curious, though."

"Lots of folks, including Franklin, play chess," Rey pointed out. "Probably a coincidence."

"Let's see if we can find out everyone who played with the two."

"I'll get on it," Gail advised and we pulled away.

*   *   *

At six, a glassy-eyed, grim-mouthed Rocky called it quits. He'd not lucked in re GRP from what we had to offer but had organized it so that we could record all incoming calls on our cells with ease. He also took the vid of the guy outside the agency and said he'd check with a colleague who could tap into "private" databases to ascertain if the facial features showed up elsewhere.

"He won't give up," Gail assured us as we watched the boxy man amble to the waiting cab at the curb.

We returned his wave and tread back into the kitchen.

"Hey, it wasn't a total bust," Rey said, gesturing Gail's laptop on the counter. "You got some names of fellow chess players."

"More leads to follow," Linda added with a smile.

Gail pulled up the list of eight. "I'm not sure where these will lead, but I'll check them out, starting with Slim Mei, Luc's brother."

"Funny we didn't come across him before," Rey said.

"We didn't look that hard because we were focused on jailed sons and non-bailing fathers." Linda scanned the list. "These others have to be former classmates, given the years."

Gail hopped to her feet. "I'll catch up with you tomorrow night. How about a bite at the Zippy's near the station … around 6:30?"

Rey nodded. "I could go for oxtail soup."

"What are you three up to now?"

"A long bubbly bath and an early night of sleep," I replied.

"Think I'll curl up with Piggaletto in bed," Linda said. "I'm reading *To Kill a Mockingbird* for the third time."

Rey grinned. "I'm gonna research garden and hardware centers to prep for the commercial."

Gail gave two thumbs up and we walked her to the door.

CHAPTER TWENTY

Monday morning proved uneventful, with the three of us organizing reports and paying bills and indulging in an hour-long
meet-and-greet with a few local businesspersons. At noon, Rey
left to drop by her agent's office to pick up the contract and
Linda got ready to tail Lance again; he was helping a friend at a
wine expo in the afternoon. If nothing of note transpired today,
we'd advise Hardena that it might be best to drop the case: why
take money if nothing was happening beyond Lance's silly but
seemingly harmless flirtations?

Eddy dropped by to ask if it was okay to visit a relative on
Big Island for three days, which I assured him was more than
fine (the guy rarely took vacation). As we sipped frosty sodas, I
listened to him chat gaily about Cousin Petro and his papaya
grove and found myself wanting to spend time on a plantation
or farm. It would be pleasant, relaxing, to be somewhere remote
and quiet for a few days, not thinking about anything but respite
and nature, food and drink. Sure. In my dreams. I chuckled and
waved Eddy off—with $50 to treat himself and Petro to lunch.

I found myself checking the names that Gail had located re
Luc's and Franklin's former chess associates. I dug into every
one of them and learned they'd moved on to jobs and/or fami-

lies. Nothing out of the norm or even remotely curious ... save for Luc's brother, Slim Mei.

When Dr. Richard Rijk Mei divorced Alaina-Lei, she'd moved to Cali with thirteen-year-old Slim (Luc would have been fifteen). Interesting, splitting the sons like that. Alaina-Lei had been an artist while on Oahu but had later become a nurse. Old photos showed her to be a beautiful redhead, tall and lanky; later ones showed her to be more zaftig, and still quite attractive. A full toothy smile graced the screen as she stood with Slim at two local theater productions. In the first, he was dressed as Geppetto, the woodcarver from Pinocchio, with a woolly beard and hat. In the second, he was sporting a woolly cape and tinny crown, perhaps playing a prince or king. She seemed quite proud. There was no tension visible in the eyes or expression, as there had been in the other shots with her former hubby, except one I came across post-dating these two.

Standing before a crowd, she shielded her son from the media, one palm outstretched to the camera, her expression resolute and defiant. Slim had been found in the yard with a dismembered cat, Tosco, a beloved neighborhood tabby. Given several pets had gone missing over the last few months, it was believed he was the culprit. I hated animal-abuse stories, but felt compelled to read on. As it turned out, two days later, Meyers "Juniper" Beenie, a quiet man who lived alone down the street in an upstairs flat, was found dead with several stuffed animals (as in taxidermy stuffed and not plush retail stuffed). A nearly empty bottle of gin was clutched in a hand when they found him at the base of the stairs; in his drunken state, he'd tumbled and smashed into a large three-piece hear-no-evil, see-no-evil, speak-no-evil gnome set. He'd been known for bending the elbow and then some, but had never been verbally offensive or physically cruel, at least that anyone had observed.

"Ya just never know by looking at someone, do you?" a wizened, pockmarked neighbor, identified only as Flange, had asked, grabbing the mike and peering into the camera with exaggerated disbelief. "The guy was real quiet, stuck mostly to himself, but would always wave or say 'hiya' if ya passed him on the sidewalk or street." Flange shook a bald, eggshell-shaped head. "Yeah, ya'd never have guessed he'd be the sort to massacre animals."

Aliana-Lei had demanded a public apology for the stress and humiliation Slim and she had endured. Who could blame her? It must have been awful to be accused of such a heinous crime. Curious, I pursued Alaina-Lei a little more and discovered she had once—before Slim was born—claimed domestic abuse. Sadly, the case had never made court and was, like many similar ones in those years, swept under the rug. She was currently living in Santa Monica and was a critical-care nurse at UCLA Medical Center. Good for her.

Slim was hard to track after the incident. Prior to leaving Oahu, he'd played in a few chess tournaments and proven very skilled for someone so young; the title grandmaster had been given to him in one article. It was unknown if he'd pursued chess once on the Mainland, but I assumed he'd have let it go, given the new life/lifestyle. Maybe he'd pursued theater, but if he had, he'd done so under another name. Perhaps he'd changed it given the unwanted and unwarranted publicity. Who could blame him?

Did Alaina-Lei and Luc keep in touch? I couldn't imagine a mother not doing so, but something about the overly attractive surgeon—perhaps the grimness in those sapphire-blue eyes—suggested she'd probably been cut off from any ties. My gut said this gifted specialist was not a nice man, and definitely a force to be reckoned with.

A knock at the door preceded Mink's entry. The pretty, buxom woman smiled and waved a manila envelope as she entered. "Found this inside the outside door. How goes, hon?"

"It goes. You?"

"No complaints. I thought I'd check to see if ya'll were still attending the luau next week? 'Cause if you are, I'm going to ask if I could drive over with ya'll."

"No worries," I replied, standing and stretching. "What happened to Cousin Arnold, your ride?"

"His mom, Joelle, is feeling poorly, so he felt obliged to fly back to Texas and keep an eye on her."

"What a nice son."

"He's a good boy," Mink grinned and placed the textured earth-colored envelope on the corner of the desk. "Our Linda still on wayward-spouse patrol?"

I nodded and decided to make a fresh pot of coffee. "She's keeping an eye on him at a wine expo."

"Oh-oh. She does enjoy a good glass or two. Hopefully, you won't have to pick her up … as in off the floor."

We chuckled and I motioned one of the rattan sofas.

"Naw, I gotta run, but we should have a drink together one night this week. You three come over to my place. We'll chat, get silly, check out my new Ouija board, and make plans for the luau."

"Text me and we'll set a date—"

"Hey!"

We turned as Linda bound into the office.

"You lose Lance?" I jested.

"Yes!"

* * *

Linda dropped into one of the blended-leather chairs and slumped across the pedestal table with a loud sigh. "I was chatting with a vendor about coconut wine—"

"Pee-yoo!"

"It's not that bad, surprisingly," Linda told Mink. "A little over an hour ago, Lance was chatting up some important-looking patrons, and then a dynamite brunette. I had my eye on him as I sampled Sammy's fare, but then he wanted me to view a short promotional vid. I couldn't have looked away more than fifteen seconds, tops, and when I did, Lance wasn't there anymore." She sighed again. "I promised Sammy I'd buy a case and hurried off, but couldn't sight Lance anywhere. Nor could I see the brunette."

"So they may have scurried off together?" I asked with a dry smile.

"Maybe. Probably." She smacked the table. "Do you think he knew he was being followed?"

"It certainly seems like it, given the fast exit. Did you ask around to see if anyone had seen them?"

She gazed over angrily. "Of course I did. The only one who had was Charles Vin, a longtime seller of wine cabinets. He said he saw them walking in the direction of a nearby exit—he noticed her more than him because she was 'dishy'."

"Dishy?" Mink asked dully.

"Dishy."

We all laughed.

"I guess we'd better try to find out who she is," I said. "We'll need to locate her, keep tabs and take photos, and all that."

"I hadn't seen her face, but she had a nice figure and the salmon-colored outfit wasn't cheap—couture, for sure. Charles Vin said she had dark sultry eyes, lovely lips, and perfect make-up."

"That limits it to a few hundred women," Mink declared wryly.

Linda sat up straight. "Maybe Gail can get us security footage. There were certainly enough cameras around."

"That's a big ask, given we're simply pursuing a wayward hubby," I said.

"You're right." Linda appeared dejected. "We'll have to wait until his next outing … and be better prepared."

"Don't fret, hon. Ya'll catch the jackass in the act next time," Mink smiled. "He just gave you the slip. It happens in your biz, doesn't it?"

She nodded glumly.

* * *

"Looks like Hardena's settling into enjoying a glass of red on the balcony," Linda said as the three of us watched the well-maintained two-story abode from the other side of the street. We were seated at the base of a banyan tree on an expansive, deserted for-sale property. It was just after four and, given nothing was happening at the agency, we'd decided to drive over to Hardena's to see if Lance came home any time soon. Of course, he might have already arrived, but given she was alone up there, it wasn't likely.

"How long do we want to stay?" Rey asked, blowing a bubble. The not-so-subtle scent of watermelon wafted past. "We've got Gail at Zippy's at six-thirty."

"I don't see this guy returning anytime soon. The expo's on until nine, so he's free to take full advantage of that time," Linda stated.

I had to agree.

"You gotta wonder what she saw in the guy," Rey said.

"Besides him being exceptionally good-looking, virile, and young-er?"

She popped a noisy bubble.

"From what I could see and hear, he wasn't that smart," Linda offered, "and he was very much into himself. Not to the same extent Luc E Mei is, but there's definitely a hint of vanity there ... and gruffness. I got the impression he could be quite insulting if he wants to be or doesn't get his way."

"You think the guy low-brows Hardena?" Rey asked.

"You mean browbeats?" I asked.

"Whatever."

"From the interactions I'd seen him have with others, I could easily see him badger her," Linda said.

"So, he can prove to be an *un*-nice man," I stated.

"He can appear nice enough—even charming—but if he doesn't get things his way, I could see him getting his knickers in a knot," Linda explained with a salty smile.

"You watching PBS again?" Rey asked drily and hopped to her feet. "As they used to say, let's shake this pop stand."

* * *

Dinner at Zippy's was a quiet, relaxing event, even with rambunctious four-year-old triplets a couple of tables over. Per Gail, Rocky had been called into a special assignment and hadn't had time to check out anything related to GRP, but we were okay with that (we doubted he'd have much luck).

At nine, we sat in the living room in long T-shirts, and slippers, drinking hot cocoa, which was becoming a regular favorite. The kids were curled up nearby, fed, and walked.

"Ready for the shoot tomorrow?" Linda asked sleepily.

"More than," Rey answered. "We can put the money toward the house."

"What? No new purses or shoes or earrings?"

"Ha, ha, ha, ha."

"Oooh, shades of GRP," I said with a dark smile.

"He really must be on vacation. He's certainly lying low."

"He'll be back ... unfortunately," Linda said, draining her mug.

"Do you think Lance has returned home now?" I asked.

"Probably. And no doubt kissing up to Hardena." Rey sighed softly. "The poor woman."

"She knows what she's up against. I hear 'divorce' blowing in the breeze."

"You know who's been pretty quiet of late?" Linda asked.

We looked at her expectantly.

"Ald."

Rey snorted. "That's coz Hives is too busy pretending to do cop stuff."

"Don't be so mean. He's a decent guy."

She shrugged. "Come to that, we haven't heard from Hammill or Sallo either."

"They do have other cases and are probably as stumped and unlucky at finding information and evidence as we are," Linda said in their defense.

"This guy's gotta slip up at some time."

"He will," I assured them.

"But at the cost of how many more lives?" Linda asked quietly.

"Too many," was my cousin's soft response.

CHAPTER TWENTY-ONE

"She must have headed out with the production team after the shoot," Linda said, glancing at the pretty Coach watch that graced her slender wrist. "They were starting at one and it's eight now."

She, Gail and I were seated on the heavily packed patio of a small cozy Mexican restaurant off Kuhio, sipping fruit-dense sangria and munching jalapeno- and cheese-laden nachos under a ginormous tomato-red sombrero that served as an awning. A light drizzle that had started falling earlier had now stopped, and the night was sultry warm.

"They may still be shooting." Gail motioned a passing server for more salsa. "Or had technical issues. Six hours doesn't seem that long to film a commercial and get it right."

I nodded. "She did this hulaing ham ad that took twenty hours because the preening pineapple, the director's partner, kept flubbing the lines—all two of them."

"Well, she'll certainly be sorry she's missing out on these." Grinning, Gail raised her blue textured retro goblet.

"I just texted her again and said we'd be here until ten." Linda glanced around the hopping eatery abounding with luscious scents of roasted vegetables and grilled meats and filled with happy-looking patrons outside and in. "Oooh, that *tinga des res* looks delicious."

"Let's wait another half hour, then order."

I agreed with Gail's suggestion.

"So, no case nibbles today?"

Linda shook her head. "We worked from home today. No calls, emails or texts. Even our current case seems to be on hold because our client didn't call back. Too bad Betty, her house-keeper, took that three-day vacation." She sighed. "Timing's everything."

"You're talking about that woman whose hunky hubby has a roving eye?" Gail pulled a pineapple spear from her drink, eyed it critically, and took a bite.

"It's more than a roving eye," Linda responded flatly.

* * *

Half past ten, we called it a night. We parted company with Gail on the tourist-heavy street, who promised to check in with Rocky the following day and let us know if he'd unearthed anything.

Upon arriving home, Linda and I took Button and Piggaletto for a quick walk under a starry sky, and then prepared a pot of passionflower tea. We weren't overly sleepy and thought the soothing brew might help.

"It's odd she hasn't texted or anything." Linda placed the teapot on the kitchen table, her brow lined like an okra pod.

"She might not have her cell handy while they're filming. And you know what a social butterfly she can be. She may have joined the crew at a bar or something."

"She can be irresponsible sometimes."

"She can be many things sometimes," I winked.

"I guess she'll come home when she's ready." Linda chuckled

and poured tea into two large mugs sporting a surfboard theme. "Should we swing by Hardena's tomorrow?"

"If she doesn't call back in the morning, let's drop by at noon."

"Maybe she confronted Lance and they had a row."

"Maybe."

"Should we be worried?"

I scanned Linda's impassive face. "Should we?"

"I don't know. She's always responded in a timely manner and given Lover-Lance left with that woman, maybe she caught wind and a scene erupted. Or maybe he didn't return home at all yesterday and she decided not to stick around."

I glanced at the clock. It was rather late to call, but better to be safe than sorry. I dialed Hardena and received no answer. "You up for a drive?"

* * *

We took Linda's black Camry, which would blend nicely into the night, and parked it in front of Hardena's dark and still house.

"You think they're asleep?" Linda asked.

"No."

"You think we should check it out?"

"Yes." I pulled two small flashlights from our handy-dandy P.I. carryall, as well as latex gloves, a new B&E kit (Rey had insisted—whined and wailed—re have a second one, just in case), and two black ribbed beanies.

As she pulled one on, she said wryly, "This wouldn't be considered trespassing, would it?"

"We have a legitimate concern about a client."

"Right. We're concerned citizens … about to commit B&E."

* * *

Linda took the Diamond-Head side and rear, I the *ewa* and front. Fortunately, it appeared everyone on the dim, quiet street was asleep, so we'd not attract attention. Hopefully. As Linda scurried to the back, I peered into the living room windows, but saw nothing thanks to heavy, gauzy drapes. Nor did I sense movement inside. Not that I'd actually expected any.

Where had Hardena gone? Had she and Lance fought? Or, at the last moment, had they decided to take a mini vacation or go visiting or something? Either way, why not return calls?

I moved to the dining room and then the salon windows, and had no luck. This was a fruitless venture. Still, I told myself, it couldn't hurt: better to be safe than sorry, right? The pool and cabana were dark; no lanai or patio lights. The last window was beside a narrow door, which was near the pantry leading to the kitchen. I'd not used the flashlight as yet, but turned it on as this window had no drapes or blinds. At the same second I shone it inward, a flashlight beam shone outward. My eyes grew owl-round as I gazed into someone else's. Our mouths rounded into tremulous ovals, but no sounds were uttered (a shriek was trapped in my throat).

Suddenly, recognition set in and Hardena and I simultaneously twittered. She hastened to the door and flung it open.

"Good Lord, I thought there were prowlers on the premises! I was ready to use this." The fifty-five-year-old laughed, holding up a mezzaluna. I eyed the curved blade that glimmered in the light. That baby could do some serious damage if used quickly and constructively.

"Why no lights?" I asked as she turned them on.

The handsome woman was dressed in white cropped cotton pants with a one-button cutaway jacket, which surely cost more than the monthly agency rent. "I'd arrived home about thirty minutes ago and was so exhausted, I fell asleep on the salon settee," she said ruefully. "I'd not wanted to awaken Betty."

"But she's on vacation, isn't she?"

She smiled ruefully. "She is, but I'd forgotten; the dear rarely goes away."

Linda strode in and looked relieved. "You're all right!"

"I certainly hope so," Hardena said with a droll smile. "Drink? I could use one."

We followed her into the salon, where a vibrant-colored, well-stocked bar lined a far wall. "Name your poison, ladies."

"I'm fine," I said.

"Me, too." Linda sat on a sleek dark bar stool. "Why'd you not call back?"

She poured brandy into a tulip-shaped cognac glass. "Lance didn't come home last night."

Linda and I glanced at each other.

"When he'd not returned by ten, I called Barry, our friend who'd organized the wine expo. He said he hadn't seen Lance since late afternoon and seemed reluctant to provide details, so I became rather insistent. It appears my husband was last seen chatting with a 'luscious' brunette. I sat on the balcony a long while, thinking, drinking, then decided I'd visit my insomniac cousin Florina."

"He didn't return home at any time, you're sure?" Linda pressed.

She shrugged. "Maybe he did and left again. It's conceivable that when he saw I wasn't here, he figured I'd put two and two together, and decided to stay clear for a while." She chuckled darkly, toasted me, and sipped. "I should have called, but I wasn't up to it."

Linda nodded with understanding. "What will you do now? Wait for him to return?"

She took a small sip and stared across the vast room, her brow knitted. "I should probably call Nadio, my lawyer, and set things in motion."

"You'll set divorce proceedings in motion?" Linda studied the slender woman's unlined face.

"I believe I will." She took a seat beside her. "Lance is an excellent excuse-maker and very smooth talker. He knows how to charm. Maybe she truly caught his eye and then some, and the two ran off together." She frowned, then shrugged. "But he'll have to return sometime, if only to collect his things."

"He will," Linda affirmed with a tart smile. "When he finds the courage.

CHAPTER TWENTY-TWO

At six a.m., Linda and I were in the kitchen, she absently stirring oolong tea in a chipped Wonder Woman mug, me sucking back Kona coffee from caffeine-stained Batman and on the phone with Ald. "But I tell you, it's *not* like her."

The detective groaned. "She's a grown woman, even if she does act like a spoiled brat. She probably met a guy and—"

"That's not like her," I shrilled. Taking a deep breath, I gulped back the last of the coffee and forced myself to calm. "My P.I. gut senses something is *very* off."

"It hasn't been twenty-four hours—"

"*Please.*"

He groaned again. "Give me the name of the hardware-garden guy, and details where she was filming, and I'll have Hammill check it out."

"I don't know the exact details," I confessed, meeting Linda's concentrated gaze. "But I'm sure they're in the contract."

"I'll wait while you find it—you do have it, right?" he asked tetchily.

"It's probably in Rey's room."

"While you're looking, tell me about your latest case."

Mechanically, I described the "Lost Lover-Lance Case" as I

hastily checked Rey's room. Fortunately, the document wasn't hard to locate; it lay in a nightstand drawer. "Got it."

"Well?"

I scanned the two-page, word-dense contract. "Uh ... oh, here it is. The guy's name is Slank Roos. Sunset Gardening & Hardware Center is the place and it's off Waialae."

"Did they film there?"

"It doesn't say, but I'd have to believe so, given he's promoting the business."

Ald tsked. "The place won't be open yet, but I'll have Hammill drive by anyway."

"Hell, *we* could do that," I said crossly.

"Hammill has a badge. You don't," he said crisply.

"But—"

"I will personally call this dude Roos, okay? Why don't you two head to the agency? Call anyone and everyone you think may have heard from your cousin. You're professional P.I.s. Start private-eyeing."

"But—"

"I'll drop by the agency around ten. Go!"

* * *

Fresh coffees in hand, Linda and I sauntered into the agency a little after eight, concern lining our faces.

"What if—"

"Nothing's happened," I said firmly. "She's just ..."

"Being Rey?" came the crisp question.

"Nothing's happened," I repeated sternly.

Linda pulled out her laptop from a new Swiss Gear laptop case and sat at the pedestal table. Before logging on, she took a look at her cell. Her forehead crinkled like a cruller and, exhaling noisily, she scrutinized the room as if hoping it might offer an account of what had transpired. "Hey, there's an envelope by the umbrella stand. Someone must have slipped it under the door."

Placing the cup on the counter, I retrieved the textured earth-colored envelope. It seemed familiar—right. Mink had brought up one like it recently. I glanced at the desk and noticed the identical envelope laying there. I grabbed the unopened envelope; it, like the one in my hand, had the agency's name and address typed in gold French Script font. Fancy.

I started to open the one Mink had brought when Linda took a call on the agency phone. Curious, my ears perked and I perched on the corner of the desk. The conversation was quick and, from the tense expression on my colleague's face, not positive.

"That was Hammill. He'd checked the center." Her forehead crinkled again.

"And?" I urged.

"Although the place wasn't open yet, he did sight a middle-aged man unloading mulch and fertilizer, so he chatted with him. Turned out Max McCabe has been an employee for twelve years."

Anxious, I leaned close.

She met my worried gaze. "While the place is indeed called Sunset Gardening & Hardware Center, the owner's name is Pete Smith. There'd been no plans to advertise."

I swore under my breath.

"Ditto." A tense smile pulled at those unusual button lips. "Hammill said he would check with businesses in the immediate area to see if they'd sighted anyone filming in the vicinity or noticed any suspicious people hanging around … or if someone observed Rey in the area."

"He called Ald, I assume?"

"He did." She scanned my face. "Should we head over to the station?"

"No, let him do his job. He's due here at ten and I'm sure he'd call immediately if he heard something."

She pursed her lips, then slapped the table. *"We need to do something!"*

"Let's continue to contact everyone and anyone who knows Rey. Maybe someone heard from her."

Linda stood up, then noticed the partially open envelope in my hand. "Anything important?"

I shrugged and pulled out a folded page. Also textured, it was without a doubt expensive. I swore again, this time not so softly, and passed it to Linda. The message: *I thought it might add a new and fun dimension to the game if Rey and I spent a little time together. Now, don't worry. Per the "contract", she'll receive $850 for her services. I honor my promises. If you want to play the game, which I'm sure you do, then follow the rules. Be by the Waikiki Shell in Kapiolani Park at 8 p.m. tonight. On the nose if you please.*

"Dang," Linda murmured. It was a word she didn't use often anymore, but I suspected I'd hear it often today. "We screwed up."

"I did. Big time. I didn't open the envelope in time."

She got the other envelope, met my apprehensive gaze, opened it, and began reading aloud. "I was astounded when you didn't show up at the Shell, then concluded that you'd not opened the envelope I left earlier. That's rather unprofessional, but you might have thought it a bill, or a request for money, so I'll forgive you this time. I must say, Rey's quite delightful—a bit of a firebrand—but I did enjoy our time together, even if her language is a little colorful for my delicate ears. LOL. You know, she's rather like Lady Macbeth: strong and dominant, able to accomplish what needs doing, and not at a cost of madness. I like her mettle. Your Rey has definite pluck. I digress. Given you've ruined the game, I'll let her find her own way home. Do remember this, lovely ladies: I could have easily killed her. I could still. Next time I say 'play', play!" Linda muttered something indistinguishable under her breath. "He signed off with HA-HA-HA-HA and hugs and kisses."

"How sweet," I said flatly and grabbed my bag and paused. "Did he really call her a firebrand? Who uses that word anymore?"

"He does, apparently," she responded drily.

"Forget waiting for Ald. Let's head over to his office," I suggested, pulling out my cell to inform him of our plans. "We need him to ramp up the search."

"Hopefully, he'll get some prints or DNA off the envelopes and notes."

"Hopefully, but—"

"Not likely?"

I smirked, tweaked her chin, and affirmed resolutely, "Let's never say never. This guy *will* screw up."

* * *

"He didn't say, just raced out like a flamethrower was blasting his butt," Gail said with a quick smile as she leaned into the corner of her boss' desk.

"Do you think he found Rey?" I asked hopefully, leaning forward. I was seated on the sofa alongside Linda.

The Administrative Specialist arched a slender shoulder.

"Has Hammill returned?" Linda asked.

"I haven't seen him." She arched a shoulder again. "Sallo's MIA. Seems half the force is."

I stood and looked down at Linda. "Want to stick around?"

She shook her head. "Let's sit in the park and text everyone to keep an eye and ear open for Rey."

"She'll be all right," Gail said optimistically, hopping to her feet. "As crazy as he is, I'm inclined to believe the whack-job's a man of his word."

Linda and I gazed at each other, and she nodded. Gail was right: GRP was many things, but not a liar.

I placed the envelopes on the desk. "Tell him to call us as soon as possible."

Gail saluted smartly and led us down an unusually empty corridor.

* * *

"Where the hell are you?" Linda bellowed, jumping from the metal perforated bench.

Hastily I disconnected from Adwin, promising I'd see him tomorrow, if doable. "What—"

She held up a hand and nodded as she listened. "Uh-huh ... really? You're kidding?"

More nodding and uh-huhing. "We'll drive—what do you mean 'no'?" She looked over, her expression one of utter disbelief. "What?" The nodding and uh-huhing were replaced by soft curses and swearwords. From Rey, they sounded forceful and scary; from Linda, silly and unpersuasive.

"Well?" I demanded when she finally jammed the cell in her bag.

"Ald said Hammill located Rey near the Hawaii Kai Marina. They're taking her statement over coffee at a nearby station. Ald was on his way there when a call came through regarding a body having been found by the Kuliouou Stream in Hawaii Kai."

I drew a deep breath. GRP at work again? So much for a mini vacation. "Why doesn't he want us to drive there?"

"He doesn't want us getting underfoot. Said 'enough people are running amok—er—around'. His words, not mine." She smiled sourly.

I rolled my eyes and called Gail. "Where's the body?" I demanded before she could say a word.

* * *

Numerous legal and media sorts milled near the stream, at the base of a parking lot not far from the Kalaniana'ole Highway. Two TV vans were pulling up behind another two already in full, enthusiastic news-reporting swing, as Linda and I parked by an ironwood tree, several yards from the action.

"Do you see anyone we know?" she asked, after we'd checked in with the crime scene security officer.

"Just Jimmy Carcanetta," I motioned as we began to meander over. Our budding young blogger/writer was standing by an army Jeep, taking photos as he spoke with a female police officer. "I wonder where Ald—ah, there he is with Officer Macmillan."

"Looking efficient and p'o'd," she chuckled when he glanced over and scowled.

"Something we said?" I asked sarcastically as we stepped alongside him, pushing hair from my face. The breeze was picking up.

"Didn't I tell you to stay put?" he questioned Linda gruffly.

Her response was an expression of Hello Kitty innocence.

His response was to gaze heavenward.

"Who's the victim?" I asked, motioning to a group examining remains.

"We don't know yet," Macmillan replied matter-of-factly, cola-brown eyes scanning the crime scene perimeter. "There's no I.D." With a nod, she walked over to a colleague when he beckoned her.

"It's someone who fits the usual victim description, isn't it?"

With a frown, Ald ran a tense hand through his James Dean coif and nodded. "Designer clothes, expensive haircut, nice manicure ... floral carvings, perforations, on the chest. Black rose pinned to the shirt."

Linda peered over Ald's broad shoulder. "Our friend's been busy again. Man? Woman?"

"Man. Late 30s, early 40s."

I asked when he'd been found.

"Two hours ago by a recycler. He'd parked his truck to suck back a donut, a Cocomac, to be exact." He sighed wearily. "I could use a couple of those. Maybe I'll drop by the bakery on the way back to the office."

I swallowed a smile and made a mental note to pick up a dozen for him later. "No cards or anything?"

"Nothing … well, not yet, anyway."

"Could we take a look?" Linda inquired with a doe-sweet expression.

He scanned her face, then mine, and shrugged. "A quick one."

We hastened over to find a once virile, exceptionally good-looking man was no longer "serious drool material". He lay on his back. His legs, encased in designer jeans, and feet sporting expensive leather shoes, were immersed in the calm stream. Muscular hands were folded neatly across his upper chest while a handsome Burberry shirt, with the signature black rose attached, was unbuttoned to display six-pack abs … and the infamous carvings.

"Crap," we said in unison, surveying Hardena's wayward hubby, Lance, who was staring up unseeingly at a topaz-yellow sun.

His final expression suggested abject fear.

CHAPTER TWENTY-THREE

"See something interesting?" Ald asked cheerlessly as he stepped around Linda. "Or are you consigning the poor guy's face to memory?"

"We know him," I replied quietly and provided background.

He rubbed a scarred hand along his full lips as he studied the corpse.

"Why Lance?" Linda mused aloud. "This is getting weird-der."

A strident ringing, like old civil-defense sirens, erupted. Everyone on the scene gazed wildly around. A couple of forensics folks determined it was coming from a patch of dense shrubs and a grim-faced gent hastened forward. He located an Android cell phone amid several 'ulei plants. Holding it gingerly, he brought it over to Ald.

"Yeah hello?" the detective demanded gruffly, scanning strained faces and inquisitive eyes as the team peered over from various investigative positions. "Listen here—shit. Yeah, okay." He held out the cell phone to me.

"Hello?" I asked tentatively, scanning the detective's dour expression.

"You found my present. I'm so pleased."

"You really shouldn't have," I said sarcastically. "It's a bit much."

"He had it coming," GRP said casually. "Cheating on his wife. Exuding over-confidence and attitude. Taking someone else's money for granted. One should always acknowledge one's background and demonstrate gratitude for all that's been received."

"Lance Antigua was many unfavorable things, I'll give you that, but it's not for you to dispense punishment simply because he was a self-centered ass," I stated matter-of-factly.

Ald and Linda stepped so close, they practically trod my toes, their ears but an inch from my mouth.

GRP chuckled drily. "Rey must be chatting up a storm at the station."

"We haven't had a chance to connect with her, but no doubt."

"Not to worry. As I wrote, she's fine. Even the drug I administered—something from the benzodiazepine family, in case you were curious—will have little residual damage, considering the amount. Oh, I mentioned I'd reimburse her for her time, didn't I? It'll be on your lanai, under the cushion of that metal lounge chair. It's only fair, given I'd 'hired' her. You know, you really need to get that place fixed up, outside *and* in." He disconnected.

I stared at the disposable phone in disbelief.

"This just keeps getting *weird-der*," Linda repeated with a shake of the head.

* * *

"Was that the killer?" Jimmy Carcanetta asked, striding alongside us as we headed back to the car.

"You know it was," I told the freelance writer and blogger with a tight smile.

He blew a strand of fine mocha-colored hair from his face. A second later, it returned, thanks to an increasingly strong breeze. "Wanna share?"

"Not much to share."

"Come on, JJ," he wheedled.

We stopped before the ironwood tree we'd parked under and I shook my head. "Detective Ives prefers we keep details quiet for now."

"Figured as much." He shrugged soft shoulders. "So, any clues as to who this guy is?"

"Not one," Linda answered, absently checking the square neckline of her tank top and wincing upon seeing pepper-red skin.

"Forget the sunscreen?" he joked.

She sighed. "What about you? See anything of note at the scene?"

"I took photos of footprints I found a few yards from the body. Given the tread and size, it looks like a size eleven running shoe. I checked the footprints and shoes against those of the investigators and none are wearing runners, so I'm thinking they might belong to the killer."

"Maybe you can send us a pic or two? We'll see if we can find out what type it is; maybe the runners are unique and there'll be a sale trail," Linda said.

He nodded and pointed down the stream. "I'm going to head that way and see if I can find more of the same ... and hopefully something of weight."

Dubiously, I scanned the stream. "I can't see GRP lugging Lance's body a great distance."

"Lance?"

Crap.

"Come on, JJ. Lance who? Please? I'll share anything I find— or hear—with you. Promise." Jimmy C crossed his broad, unfit chest.

I looked at Linda. She shrugged.

"The victim's Lance Antigua—"

"*Hardena Antigua*'s husband?" Fuzzy eyebrows all but leapt from the high gleaming forehead.

I nodded grimly. "I don't believe she's yet been informed—"

"Don't worry. I'll check with Ives before I post anything."

I squeezed his flaccid arm gratefully.

Jimmy C gazed into the distance, his brow furrowed like a freshly plowed field. "There has to be a way of catching this creep."

"Yeah, one of us volunteers to be the next victim and then proclaims a citizen's arrest," I joked blandly, nudging him with an elbow.

"We wouldn't live to take him in, much less reveal his identity," he responded with equal blandness. He ran the tip of his tongue thoughtfully over uneven lips several times. "What if we called him out?"

"How do you mean?" Linda asked.

"What if we challenge him to explain the motive behind these senseless doings, openly criticize him maybe?" He snapped soft fingers. "Or maybe we tell him we can make him famous—post about his exploits, possibly even write a book."

"Are you volunteering?" I asked dully.

"I've got quite a following, so yeah, why not? If I promise a feature that explains his side of—"

"You may be asking for *serious* trouble," I interjected.

"Definitely," Linda affirmed. "This guy's no fool—"

"No, he's a narcissist, among other things," he broke in.

I had to agree. "Maybe you better discuss it with Ald Ives and get his perspective before you do anything."

"Maybe." He offered a strained smile. "So, what are you two up to now?"

Linda exchanged a glance with me and answered wryly, "Collecting a colleague."

* * *

Quarter after two found us back at the house, with Rey tucked in bed. No, she wasn't shaken up or anything after the ordeal—just drunk. She'd opted for that former favorite drink again: rye and ginger. Three ounces in one shot. On an empty stomach. Given she hadn't really eaten since yesterday, she was pretty much out for the count. Linda and I half-carried her upstairs and slipped her under the covers, Bonzo on her head, Button at her side, and Piggaletto on her stomach.

"It's nice to see the kids care," Linda chuckled as we stepped into the corridor and made our way to the lanai with a pitcher of iced tea and Pop Pan, buttery crackers with a hint of scallion flavor.

"The money's actually here," she announced after pulling out a textured envelope like the two we'd received at the agency and peering inside. "Think it's worthwhile having Ald check for fingerprints?"

"Nope."

"Didn't think so." She sat on the two-seater sofa and sipped tea. "To think Rey was actually in GRP's presence."

I leaned back in the lounge chair and recalled Rey's recounting of her abduction adventure ...

* * *

... As agreed, Rey sat on a metal-meshed bench outside the coffee shop where she'd recently met Slank Roos and kept an eye open for a white Benz. It pulled up shortly and Roos waved her over from the open window.

"The crew's beachside. The director wanted to include an additional venue," he explained with a voice still strained from the cold as he opened the passenger door from the inside. He sported the same wool hat and scarf he'd worn the first time they'd met, but was dressed in a blended textured cardigan and AG Everett straight-leg jeans.

"For a commercial?" she asked, slipping into the leather passenger seat. "Going all out, are you?"

"CDS has the creative eye and insisted on it," Roos chuckled. "I'm just the business guy."

"You up for it?" She scanned his face. "You're looking more pasty than the last time—like you have on pancake make-up four shades too light."

"The worst of the cold is over," he assured her. "Seatbelt, if you please."

As Rey adjusted it, she felt a prick in her upper arm, and that was the last she remembered until awakening in a small, dim dwelling with a planked hip roof that reminded her of Aunt Sue Lou's Maine cottage. A mirror ran the length and height of one wall. There were three tiny windows draped with speckled-gray linen fabric and two doors—one three feet from the first window, likely the entrance/exit, given there was a fancy brass coat rack beside it, and one by an overarching metal-shade floor lamp in the corner to her right. Where did it lead? To another portion of the house?

Beside her stood a fake-oak, gate-leg table. She was seated in a cushioned, ash-gray armchair that looked like something out of a 50s sitcom. Her ankles and wrists were bound with braided nylon rope, and twisted manila rope was wrapped around her waist, securing her to the chair.

"Friggin' great," she murmured, gazing around to see if there were any viable means of escape.

"So nice to see you awake," Roos' voice now non-scratchy voice rumbled from beyond the mirror.

"You wanna show yourself, jackass?" she hissed, struggling to loosen the bindings.

"Not at the moment."

"Scared?"

"Actually, you *are* a bit intimidating, Reynalda dearheart."

"… So, I get to officially meet GRP?"

"Pretty *and* astute. I like that."

Rey scanned the room but didn't see anything of note. The hardwood floor was scraped and scarred while the walls, a light charcoal-gray, were freshly painted, gauging from the slight chemical smell. "Am I your next victim?"

"You're part of the *game*."

"Lucky me."

"Why don't you relax for a while? I'll be back later."

"Don't rush on my account, jackass."

"This promises to be most interesting."

When Rey awakened later—she was sure something had been pumped into the room to make her sleep—she was still in the chair, but a bowl of chicken-noodle soup was on the table, a bottle of water, and a cheese scone. Her hands had been freed, but she was still attached to the chair.

"I thought you might like some sustenance."

Rey scanned the humble meal. "Thanks, but no thanks."

"Go for it. You're my guest. The least I could do is feed you. You'll want your strength."

"For what?"

"Whatever comes your—*our*—way." He chuckled. "I'm afraid your colleagues haven't partaken of the game as yet. I suspect they may not, given the time. I'm rather surprised … and not at all amused."

Rey offered a loud raspberry and eyed the soup. It was steaming, so it had only recently been placed there. Truth be told, she was hungry; she'd not eaten since breakfast and then it had only been a cup of coffee and a mini biscotti. With a frown and a sigh, she leaned close and sniffed. It smelled good, herbally and comforting. Maneuvering as best she could, she managed a few spoonfuls and found the soup quite delicious: homemade, rich, and satisfying.

A crash—like something small falling and shattering on the floor—prompted her to look at the mirror. She thought she'd heard a curse, but the voice was different from Roos'. A woman maybe? A *partner*?

"Drop something, jackass?"

"Really Rey. Could we *please* stop with the 'jackass'?"

"Sure. How about we try something different, like these?" She offered a few choice obscenities and heard him draw a deep if not shocked breath. "Checkmate ... *dearheart.*"

Silence ensued. So did darkness a few minutes later. Damn, she realized—and should have known better—that the soup had been drugged.

When she awakened, it was early morning. she was on a small wood bench by a beach near a quiet marina, her bag beside her. Surprisingly, a compact mirror confirmed she looked none the worse for wear.

CHAPTER TWENTY-FOUR

Hammill called at 3:30 with an update. They'd not found the cottage or house that Rey had been kept in. Not that they'd thought they would, given it truly could have been located *anywhere*. Nevertheless, they'd scoured the marina and vicinity where she'd been found.

There'd been nothing new regarding Lance Antigua either, although Hardena had been informed. She'd taken the news with a stiff upper lip and a shrug; evidently, she'd already consigned him to memory.

While we were in no-luck mode, Gail called to tell us that Rocky had found "squat". The face in the vid taken from the agency window wasn't in any database.

Jimmy C called two seconds after Gail bid goodbye.

"I posted an invitation to GRP on my blog just before noon ... and got a bite," he advised excitedly. "Three, actually."

"You're kidding?" I sat upright. Linda mirrored my move. "Did Ald agree to this?"

"Well, he wasn't around to ask if it was okay, but I had left a message."

I put on the speaker. "Share, Jimmy C, share!"

"Someone named Whacker Wally is up for being featured

about his 'electrifying murderous exploits'. So is Slicer Sam. He'd love for people to know what makes him tick and turns his 'dark thoughts to the cheering pleasure of cutting and carving'."

"Lovely," Linda murmured. "I bet you'll get more of those."

"No doubt," he concurred. "The third one, though, may be our guy."

Doubtful, I asked, "What moniker did *he* use?"

"He didn't. He called," Jimmy responded somberly. "I don't know how he got my cell number, but anyway, he's up for being featured."

"Did he say he'd meet with you?" Linda.

"He said he'll call back. Maybe we'll meet at a bar he likes."

"When?"

"He didn't say."

"What makes you think he's our guy?" I asked.

"I asked him to provide proof he's our killer," Jimmy replied, his tone overly serious. "He told me to ask the pretty private eyes from Triple Threat Investigation Agency if I like games and flowers … and make a knock-out chicken-noodle soup."

"It's him," I confirmed.

* * *

Adwin, Jimmy, Hammill and Ald joined Linda and I for take-out Thai at eight that evening. Rey had made a brief appearance, uncharacteristically silent, grabbed a large rye and ginger, three spring rolls, and hustled upstairs with a determined Ald at her annoyed side; he wanted to review a couple of facts.

He returned to the living room ten minutes later, sporting a good-grief-Charlie-Brown expression. With a sigh, he seated himself on the three-seater sofa across from Adwin and me, lounging on the matching loveseat. With an abundance of local beers in two ice-filled buckets, we dug into the delicious fare, and chatted about all that had transpired. Nothing new or earth-shattering was revealed, but it felt like we were making a concentrated effort to put the pieces of the perplexing puzzle into place.

Adwin slapped my thigh playfully. "You'll nab this guy. I have absolute faith."

I smiled drolly. "At least *someone* does."

"He'll screw up," Ald nodded, eyeing the fare on the coffee table.

"I can't help but feel we're missing something," Linda said softly, scanning the ceiling as if hoping it might reveal that "something".

"Of course we are," I stated. "I, for one, am going to review the guys on our list again."

"The ones with rich daddies who didn't post bail?" Adwin asked glibly, spooning chili chicken onto his plate. "You really think the guy'll call back?" he asked Jimmy C.

"I do."

"And when he does, we'll trace the call," Hammill affirmed.

"Any luck with that prepaid phone you found this morning?" Linda asked. "It had to come from *somewhere*."

"No luck at all." Ald chuckled darkly. "We did receive a photo at the station, by the way."

"I don't suppose it was one of our killer?" I quipped.

"It was of an upright cartoon *finger*," he smirked, holding up a spring roll. "Guess which one?"

* * *

Sach dropped by the agency at nine the following morning. The three of us were drinking Kona coffee and going through emails, texts, and voicemails. Nothing of major significance had arrived, save for a new case: following another wayward spouse. Hey, they helped pay bills. Linda and Rey would meet with Thomas M.G. Namm III on his yacht in the afternoon.

"Oooh, pass me my shades," Rey simpered, placing her bare feet on one of the blended-leather chairs.

Our neighbor was dressed in a radish-red stretch polo shirt and slim-fit plaid pants; rutabaga-red, low-top suede runners adorned his feet while a straw boater hat graced his head. He stuck out his tongue and moved to the counter and poured himself a cup of coffee. "I'm feeling shunned."

Linda chortled. "Shunned?"

A petulant pout pulled at his wide lips. "You guys are ignoring me."

"Hardly," I said. "We've just been caught up in … business."

"I thought I was part of it?" Another pout.

"You are. We just don't have anything for you to do right now."

He sighed and, leaning into the counter, sipped. "What about Caprize's stalker?"

"We haven't heard anything from her recently. He must have lost interest in her," Linda stated.

"Maybe I should confirm that?" He looked hopeful.

"Sure. Check it out," Rey replied merrily. "We can close the case if all is good."

"I'll ask her when I see her later today; she has a training session."

Rey gave an A-OK.

"What about you guys?"

"Linda and I are meeting a possible new client later. JJ's Googling some more, I think."

He gazed from my cousin to me. "Like what?"

"I'm going to revisit a few people we've already looked at and then branch out from there. I sense there's something there, but *where* has me stymied," I advised. "I can't help but think about the word 'firebrand'."

"What about it?" he asked, bemused.

"It seems an old-world word. Why not use hothead or troublemaker, or bitch?" I replied. "Given GRP's literary reference—"

"Or theatrical," Linda interjected.

"Or theatrical," I repeated. "I can't help but believe there's another dimension to him, one we have yet to explore."

"Okay, we know he likes old words, is into chess and games, likes to kill and decorate people, and—say, did you provide the police with a detailed description of the guy who kidnapped you?"

Rey nodded and looked from face to face. "The more I think about it, the more I'm sure this Roos guy had altered his face. The pale skin should have been a giveaway, but he was sick, so he said, and his rough voice certainly suggested it, so I didn't think on it too much—guess I didn't want to. But later, when I was on the bench waiting to be found, I couldn't get that face out of my mind."

"Did you notice anything outstanding?" Sach asked over his Waikiki skyline mug. "What about his neck? His hands? Feet?"

She gazed at the black sideboard and drew on her bottom lip. "He had a scarf both times and that wool hat, like I mentioned. There was really no skin to see, except for the face. No visible scars there. The eyes were dark brown and close-set. I didn't look at his feet, but the guy had a medium build."

I snapped my fingers. "Reminder, folks. We need to check that footprint Jimmy C sent."

"Leave it to me, but don't expect much, given we haven't lucked in so," Linda said with a rueful smile.

"Yeah," Sach sighed. "Like the medium build ... like Caprize's stalker and a thousand other men in a four-block radius."

"Like." Rey chuckled gravely, then snapped her fingers. "Say! Let's compare that sketch—the one they did at the station and yours, JJ. And let's look at some frames of that vid of the guy you took outside the agency, the one Rocky was useless with."

Checking my emails, I brought up the sketch Hammill had sent and printed it. I did the same with a video frame and grabbed the sketch I'd made several days back. Placing them on the counter, the four of us studied them.

"There's a similarity in the facial structure," Linda stated, running an index finger along the jawline. "And the eyes are close-set."

"But different colors," Rey said.

"That's easy to change, isn't it?" her BFF challenged.

Rey chuckled. Her own eyes had once been pigeon-gray.

"I don't know a lot about theater or film make-up," Sach offered, indicating the cheeks. "But these seem somewhat high … except on the video guy, where they're kinda pudgy. It's like cotton balls are lining his cheeks."

"You could be right." Rey turned to me. "You never did one of that guy you and Linda met that night by the parking garage?"

"Mr. Fox-Face?"

"He did have that exceptionally long nose," Linda nodded.

"And tight lips," I added. "And a pointed chin."

"And acne scars." Rey scanned the sketches again. "Those could have been added at that time or concealed later. Hell, anything could be rearranged or altered if you're a talented make-up artist."

"You know, somewhere I've seen someone similar," I murmured, racking my brains. *"Where?"*

Sach stretched and patted me on the back. "If anyone can figure it out, you can." He walked to the window and peered below. "Any more thoughts about those floral-type designs etched into the chests of the victims?"

"It could be something as simple as adornment," Linda responded.

"But why *adorn* dead people? And when were they carved? After or before death?"

"After," I replied, stepping alongside him and looking onto a busy street.

Sach frowned, then pulled out his cell and made a call. "Hey Auntie, it's your favorite nephew." After putting her on speaker, he quickly explained about the incisions and asked her opinion.

"They could be a farewell to the dead, or a beautification of death, something the killer acknowledges is final, and/or something he may view as loathsome and undesired." She drew an audible breath. "To repeat a few facts touched upon previously: flowers are symbolic of life, nature, and earth. And flowers that are in perpetual bloom are representative of the resurrection. One of the major images of water is that it gives and sustains life. Water can also relate to the flow of life and the force of nature."

"So maybe our killer is granting them life again, or thinks he is?" Sach asked, puzzled.

She clicked her tongue. "Perhaps he's feeling remorse after the killings, and the flowers and water typify new life so, in essence, he is giving back that which he has taken away—thereby erasing the act and the guilt, and washing his bloodied hands clean."

"Wow, that's deep, Auntie," Sach said admiringly.

"Hardly. I'm merely offering thoughts, disjointed ones."

"GRP, the killer, keeps referring to this as a game. I'm not so sure about remorse and cleansing, or the re-granting of life," I stated.

"As I said, disjointed thoughts." The Dowager chuckled. "I wish you much luck, my dears."

"We need it," Linda and Rey said in unison and high-fived each other.

CHAPTER TWENTY-FIVE

"What a great idea. Haven't had a dog in what seems like eons." Grinning, Rey licked French's mustard from her fingertips and leaned back on the three-seater.

The three of us were seated on the lanai under a wonderfully warming sun. We'd left the agency at two when a small fire in a vintage-clothing shop three doors down had created minor chaos in the vicinity. We'd seen enough blazes to last a lifetime, courtesy of our last case, when two art galleries, and bodies, had been torched. After stopping off at a couple of stores and making a few fervent purchases, home we hurried, gleefully slipping into cut-offs, tank tops, and flip-flops.

"These fries are pretty decent for frozen," Linda chirped, popping a curly one into her mouth.

"Button's liking them, too." I offered her one more and then told her to join her friends stretched out in the corner by the scalloped picket fence and clump of crotons.

"Looks like he can't get enough of you," Rey said under her breath as she nodded to Adwin, who was rounding the corner. "If he were smaller, he could be your lap dog."

He smiled and waved, and we responded.

"Help yourself," I gestured the barbecue and square birch-colored wood side table we'd picked up at Nemo's, a small high-brow odds-and-ends shop beside our favorite grocery store.

"What brings your obviously way too happy self our way?" Rey asked with a bland smile.

"I'd called Sach to invite him to a party I was planning to invite you three to and he mentioned he saw you arrive home. I had nothing on my to-do list, so I thought I'd drop by." He spooned mango chutney onto a bun and placed a hot dog on top; a thin precise line of red-wine sauce graced the top. "Blaze and I are having a party to celebrate the opening of Steaming Mimi's, which is coming up fast. It's at the restaurant on Saturday at eight." He wedged himself between Rey and me.

She gave a Reynalda Fonne-Werde look that would have made anyone else jump up and sit far, far away. Adwin merely winked, grinned broadly, and toasted her with the hot dog.

Not thirty seconds later, Ald popped into view, two bottles of red wine in hand. He looked quite smart in designer jeans and a floral-print short-sleeved Billabong shirt; a nice-looking leather messenger bag was suspended from one broad shoulder. He placed the wine on the table, pulled out a fancy electric corkscrew from the bag, and sat on the ottoman, situated beside Linda, reclining on a hot-pink lightweight chaise longue (also picked up at Nemo's).

"Looks like no one has to work this Thursday afternoon," Rey said with a flat smile.

"Looks like someone hasn't been waxing lately," he said with a quick smile as he glanced at her legs.

She lifted one and eyed it critically. "I'm rather getting to like the … organic look."

Ald smirked.

I jerked a thumb sideward. "Help yourself, Detective Ives."

He did—with a wink and a grin.

"What brings you our way?" Linda asked, reaching over to plop pickled asparagus spears on her plate. "You've got good news, like you've caught GRP?"

Ald took a bite while Adwin grasped the corkscrew and opened a bottle of Barolo.

"I wish I could answer with yes, but our elusive killer is now posting on social media."

We looked at him, all eyebrows raised.

He chuckled and popped a radish in his mouth. "GRP posted that his 'exploits' would soon be available on-line and in stores."

"That's good, isn't it?" Linda asked, looking thoughtful if not hopeful.

"No. Now he's got the media chomping at the bit … like he didn't already." He shook his head and sighed. "Well, now it's official serial-killer fodder."

"But at least you can track him—"

"It should be so easy." The flat remark was accompanied by a grimace. "He's likely using a burner account and laptop … maybe a library or university one, but that means there'd have to be an ID card or something. He'd be using Tor, a Linux live image—Tails it's called—and other components to ensure he's not being tracked. That guy won't leave an online footprint." He met Rey's penetrating stare. "One of our computer forensics guy, Nat, gave a quick refresher course on what activists, journalists, military and the like do."

"Well, if nothing else, Jimmy C's plan to entice GRP worked," she muttered with a limp shrug.

Ald frowned, bemused. "Care to share?"

She looked from him to me, shrugged again, and related what the blogger-writer had proposed by the crime-scene stream. "He did say he tried to get hold of you."

Ald offered a rigid nod and exhaled noisily. "My bad for not returning the call." He accepted the square-bottom plastic tumbler Adwin passed him, eyed it, and chuckled. "Never sipped a sixty-dollar-bottle of wine from one of these before."

"Big spender," Rey sniggered.

He toasted her, holding up the middle finger as he did so.

She reciprocated and accepted a similar tumbler from my former beau. "So that's it? That's all? No more news re GRP?"

"The post was short, to the point, with a pic of a pretty forbidding-looking Grim Reaper."

"I'd expect someone like that to post pics of his victims," Adwin said, reclaiming his seat.

"Do you think he takes any?" Linda asked with a furrowed brow.

"I'm inclined to say no, because if he did, he'd have ensured we and/or the public saw them," Ald answered, sniffing the wine and smiling. "What about you three? Learn anything new?"

"Not yet, but we will," she affirmed

"Hear, hear." Rey.

He gave a stiff nod and settled into enjoying the hot dog.

* * *

The following late morning found Linda and I at home, entertaining Adwin, who'd slept—passed out—on the lanai three-seater, and Sach, who'd sighted the Jeep and dropped by to ask why we weren't at work. The one-word explanation: hangover.

Ald had called at 8:30 to advise they believed they'd found the dwelling where Rey had been held captive and requested she accompany him to the place to confirm this was the case. Two coffees and Advils later, she'd grabbed a cab to the station.

"That's amazing news," Sach said, pouring a large mug of fresh coffee before taking a seat at the kitchen table.

"How they managed to locate the place GRP held Rey is short of a miracle," Adwin said and stifled a yawn. He forked a black-edged waffle from the platter Linda placed in the middle of the table and eyed the crisp store-bought item critically.

She caught his disapproving, bleary-eyed gaze. "It's the best I can do with this katzenjammer," she mumbled, slipping into the chair beside him. "Who suggested Lava Flows after the wine?"

Sach chuckled and poured milk into his coffee. "I'm *so* glad I wasn't here last night."

Adwin rubbed his bristled face. "At least I had the sense to stop after the first one."

Linda made a face and sucked back the steaming contents of her mug. And belched.

He smiled wearily. "I'd expect that of Rey, not you."

Her response: another belch.

"How'd they find it?" Sach took a waffle and poured enough coconut syrup over it to accommodate a foot bath.

"It was an incredible fluke," I answered. "At sunrise this morning, a hiker found a credit card on a narrow path. It was Lance's. He recalled the name from the news and called the police."

"What a stroke of luck."

"An extraordinary one," I concurred. "The trail was a half mile from the cottage-like residence, which is near Makaniolu Place and not that far from the stream. They quickly surveyed the area and checked out nearby homes. They were speaking to a man when Sergeant Sen Oope, who happened to be at the station the morning Rey was providing a statement, recalled the hip-roof description as he surveyed the immediate vicinity. He headed across the street and knocked. No answer. No surprise. He inspected the grounds while his colleague ran a check on the owners—"

"Who are off in Scotland, conveniently," Linda stated wryly.

"But they did rent out the place to a man by the name of S.G. Strong. Ald's team is following up, before you ask."

"Did they find something else of significance, from this Lance dude maybe?" Sash asked eagerly, leaning forward.

"Oope noticed wagon tracks leading from the rear of the dwelling to the path, which ends—or starts, depending on your perspective—about fifty yards *makai*," Linda replied, getting a bottle of water. "Oope followed the path, searching with a critical eye. Not far from the credit card, hidden by jimsonweed, was an unzipped calf-leather BVLGARI credit-card holder. Hardena confirmed that Lance always carried his one-and-only credit card in it."

"Fascinating." Sach's Groucho Marx eyebrows drew close. "Are they thinking the guy was offed there?"

"They didn't mention it, but we certainly believe that," she said, nodding at me. "In fact, we're thinking that maybe GRP killed all his victims there. We're heading up in the next hour."

He whistled. "This could prove a big break."

"*If* it pans out." Adwin reached over to squeeze my hand. "We're hoping it will."

"I wish they'd call to tell us what's what," I grumbled, feeling impatience creeping in.

Linda glanced at the coffee-cup wall clock. "Maybe those on the scene might share. It's 10:45 so why don't we head over?"

"Why don't I drive you?" Sash asked, a hint of eagerness in his tone and expression.

"Given those lovely red-rimmed eyes, ladies, you might want to take him up on it," Adwin suggested with a trim smile.

Linda glowered and I stuck out my tongue.

He chuckled. "I'll join you."

Sach gave a thumb's up. "Do you think GRP's aware?"

"That he may have slipped up?" I asked drily.

He nodded.

"That might peeve him off," Adwin suggested. "Big time."

"I wonder if he'll try to connect with Jimmy C again," Linda mused aloud.

I hopped to my feet. "We better warn him"

"Warn?" Sach asked, concern lining his square-shaped face.

"If he gets peeved off, GRP's going to want to lash out. And if he lashes out, it may be at Jimmy C," I explained, grabbing my cell phone from the counter and calling.

"Or us," Linda added flatly.

Sach swore under his breath and Adwin blanched.

And I went straight into the blogger-writer's voicemail.

* * *

The drive to the crime scene in Sach's 2017 Nissan Murano S was smooth. We got there in decent time and found the property cordoned off with the usual crime-scene tape and two officers alongside a cruiser, chatting with a woman typing on a laptop. Three media vans were parked down the road. We pulled a few yards away, to the side, under a Loulu palm, and stepped into a hot and humid day, feeling all the hotter upon leaving an icy-cold vehicle. Thankfully, the brisk breeze made it bearable—and wearing shorts and lightweight T-shirts didn't hurt either.

"Hey, there's Jimmy C," Linda gestured.

He was seated on a stump, sketching. A shiny silver Vespa Elettrica was parked ten feet behind. So engrossed was he in the task, he didn't hear us step up. The blogger-writer jumped when we greeted him. "Crap, you scared me."

"Evidently," I grinned. "What have you learned?"

He shrugged a soft shoulder, closed the small sketchpad and tucked it in his large tactical army backpack. "The boys and girls in blue haven't been forthcoming."

"How long you been here?" Sach asked, pulling on a Dodgers baseball cap as he glanced around the foliage-dense neighborhood with fairly spacious lots.

"A couple of hours, give or take."

"What happened with GRP?" I asked.

A mix of concern and excitement glimmered in his mocha-brown eyes. "When I opened my condo door around nine this morning, there was a small fancy envelope on the welcome mat. In it was an equally fancy card—"

"With a metallic-gold lily and thin black line? Camel-colored?"

"Exactly like that," he confirmed, regarding me intently. "It said, 'I'll be in touch late today re drinks and discussion. You want a great story and I want long-lasting fame. Don't blow this mutually satisfying opportunity by telling anyone'. Silly me, though. I left my cell phone and that card at home when I heard about this place and raced over."

"How'd you hear?" Adwin asked, nodding to the small dwelling that had seen fresh paint in the last year. "This just hit the news."

He offered a knowing smile. "I have my sources."

I scanned the property and noticed Detective Hammill rounding a corner, talking on his cell phone. Dressed in jeans and a sweat-flecked sky-blue T-shirt, he wiped his brow with an arm, said something, and tucked the phone in his back pocket.

"Think I'll mosey over and get us logged in," I said.

"Think I'll join you," Linda said softly with a nod.

She fell in step alongside me, Adwin and Sach behind us, and Jimmy C at the rear.

Hammill stopped in his tracks when he saw us draw close, annoyance darkening his attractive face. He met us at the tape. "Taking a scenic tour?"

"What have you got?" I asked with an amiable smile.

"A raging headache," he responded gruffly. He eyed the media vans where two men were talking to someone inside the first one, then turned to us and sighed. "It looks like this was most certainly the place your friend was held. There was an unwashed bowl and some noodles in a sink. We took the usual photos, bagged stuff."

"Any fingerprints? Footprints?"

"Some fingerprints, but they probably belong to your cousin. We'll know soon enough. This is priority number one," he affirmed, wiping away sweat beads trickling down his temple.

"Anything of note found?"

"The place, for the most part, was extremely well cleaned, with industrial-grade products." He pulled out a pocket-sized tin of mints bearing a pretty hula dancer and popped two into his mouth.

I took one when he held it forth. "Ald said he posted on social media."

Hammill arched a shoulder.

Jimmy C slipped around, small notebook and pen in hand. "Would you like to comment on the type of serial killer you think our guy is, Detective, uh, Hammer, is it?"

He simply stared.

"There are four main types, as we know. Is he a hedonistic, mission-oriented, visionary, or a power-and-control guy?"

Hammill's stony expression didn't change.

"Okay. No comment." Jimmy C offered a casual smile. "Do you think we could look around if we promise not to touch anything?"

"*Ple-ease*," Linda beseeched.

"And if that sweet appeal doesn't work," I clasped Linda's chin and pulled her close to Hammill. "How about a bribe? Dinner and drinks, our place or yours?"

Hammill's billiard-black eyes rolled heavenward, much like Ald Ives' often did. "I see you logged in with Officer Dowling, so you can have five minutes. Walk around outside, look, and do *not* touch or take. You can also peek inside the door, but do *not* enter! And don't share what you see with anyone. Keep an eye out for evidence markers. I'll be in the shade of that koa tree over there, watching closely." He looked at his chronograph stainless-steel watch. "Your time starts *now*."

CHAPTER TWENTY-SIX

Like inquisitive tots curious to see what the parental units were up to, the five of us peered warily past the front entrance into the dim dwelling. Silly, yes, considering the police were all around, but given the circumstances, understandable. Linda and I took a few quick photos for what it was worth, which was probably nothing. Drawing simultaneous deep breaths, my colleague and I took one side of the property while the men took the other; we'd meet at the rear.

"Not much to see," Linda murmured, keeping one eye on the ground and one on the wall.

I had to agree. I took a few more photos—wall and roof, grass and soil, trees and shrubbery.

At the rear was a small vinyl deck that might have once held lanai furniture. Four large natural-stone planters, urns with ribbon laurels, stood empty in each corner. Nothing much of value to be seen or found.

We saw Adwin, Sach and Jimmy scour the terrain where the trail began and, respecting the time limit, quickly continued our own search. To the side of the deck, a few yards from the rear door, I noticed an access hatch lid for a water-storage tank. I took a photo of the cistern and moved over to Linda, who was peering in a small square window.

"Nothing remarkable," I murmured, dejected.

"Nothing extraordinary," Linda concurred, turning to me with a downcast smile.

The trio sauntered over, and our blogger-writer's words were all too discouragingly familiar. "Not much to be found."

"It was worth a try." Sach offered a reassuring smile and we started back to the road.

"What's next?" Adwin asked as we strolled past an irritable-looking Hammill, grousing into his cell phone.

"Maybe we should interview neighbors," Jimmy C suggested, nodding to the detective. "If this was GRP's killing base, maybe someone saw him or something unusual."

"Like GRP wheeling around bodies?" I asked drily, slipping under the yellow tape.

"It's worth a shot," Sach asserted. "Nancy Drew would do no less."

Linda bah-hah-hahed, prompting me to laughter. Adwin grinned and Jimmy C snickered.

"The police have already asked around but, okay, why not? It couldn't hurt. You three take the homes on either side of this one. Linda and I will pursue the four within sight range," I motioned. "If anyone witnessed anything, they'd likely be living in one of those."

* * *

Twenty minutes later we reconvened by Jimmy's new Vespa. Linda and I hadn't lucked in, save for the delicious and cooling glass of homemade sage iced-tea Mrs. Brosnan had provided, but the guys had. Mr. Noel C. Parker, who lived two doors down and was also an insomniac, had noticed a black SUV on the driveway in the house in question on more than four occasions.

As he'd told the police earlier that day, it was always parked on the driveway after ten in the evening and gone come sunrise.

No, he'd never seen the owner himself, not close up, anyway. As he was taking a midnight stroll along the road three or four weeks ago, he'd seen two people dressed in black alight from the SUV. A man and a woman. Or maybe it was two men. No, not two women. Well, maybe.

Instead of entering the dark abode via the front door, the duo had sauntered to the back. Given it was a clear and starry night, it hadn't been hard to see. No, he'd not heard them talk, nor had he seen anything unusual like them carrying or pushing something. Just two people walking.

It wasn't much, but it was better than nothing. We'd asked him to call if he thought of anything he'd not yet mentioned.

We watched Jimmy C get on the Vespa.

"Do you want to come by later tonight—with your cell this time? We can wait for GRP's call together," I proposed.

He appeared to think about it, then shook his head. "The guy said 'late'. That could mean any time between nine in the evening and four in the morning." He smiled wryly. "It's all in the perception."

Linda frowned. "Don't meet him alone, though, if that's what he requests."

"I can't call the police," he advised, adjusting his backpack and turning on the ignition.

"Then call us," I said. "We'll join you. I'm sure he wouldn't mind if we were there."

"I'll check with him first. Remember, I want a story and he wants fame," Jimmy C stated matter-of-factly.

"At what price?"

He smiled darkly and repeated, "I'll check with him first."

We watched him head down the road.

"He's asking for trouble," Sach murmured.

"Big time," Adwin muttered.

* * *

The drive back was a leisurely one. We stopped before a colorful beachside food truck with equally colorful service and enjoyed icy-cold sodas and delicious fish tacos while sitting at a picnic table twenty feet from the rolling Pacific. The topaz-yellow sun sparkled on the vast sapphire expanse before us. Somber situation aside, who could ask for a more beautiful day?

Talk started with the events of the morning and then turned to the forthcoming party once the tacos had been gustily devoured. Adwin and Sach chatted excitedly about the menu, plans for the restaurant, and their favorite foods. Linda and I smiled and nodded a lot and focused on emails and texts.

"Rey'll be back around six," Linda announced, looking up from her cell phone. "She and Gail are just about to have a bite— Korean for those who need to know—and then she and 'Hives' are meeting again. He wants to review all the events that transpired before and after the abduction."

I had to chuckle. "She must be gritting her teeth to the point of lockjaw, being in her not-favorite detective's presence for so long."

Adwin grinned. "And he must be grinding his teeth to nubs."

Sach adjusted his Dodgers' cap and motioned my face. "You're getting a bit of a burn."

I touched my nose and cheeks. "So I am."

"Should we head back?"

Linda glanced at her cell phone and announced it was almost 2:30 p.m. "Seems too nice a Friday afternoon to head home. I'm rather liking it here." She smiled appreciatively as she gazed across the Pacific.

We agreed, turned to the ocean, and smiled contentedly.

"What's that?" Sach frowned. "The theme from *The A-Team*?"

"I'm surprised you know it," I said, pulling out my cell phone.

"I'm surprised you're using it as a ringtone."

I stuck out my tongue and answered.

"My bad. You're good."

"Hello GRP."

"My bad for being careless. You're good—for being smart, persistent, and pretty."

"I hear you've taken to social media," I said casually.

"I may post a pic of you enjoying those tacos. Were they as good as they looked, what with you sucking them back like that?"

I gazed around.

"You can't find and won't spot me, but I *do* see *you*."

"You just love showing off how crafty you are, don't you?" I asked with a dark smile.

"I prefer the word ingenious."

I felt compelled to nip that smugness in the bud. A couple of questions popped into mind; maybe they'd catch him off guard. "May I ask you something?"

"Go for it."

"Why four bodies?"

"… A matter of convenience, let's say."

"Seems like three too many for one killer," I commented nonchalantly.

"… Likewise a test, let's also say."

"Why the funereal music?"

A sharp breath suggested the question had caught him by surprise. Gotcha!

"It was heard coming from your van," I said nonchalantly.

No response.

I swallowed my smile and took another route. "Maybe we should finally meet face-to-face?"

"We will soon enough," he responded brusquely and disconnected.

"Our favorite serial killer?" Linda asked blandly as I checked "Recents" for a number.

"Who else?"

"Better call it into Ald or Hammill."

"Later," I replied and began to re-examine the photos we'd taken earlier. There had to be something of note in one of them, just as there had to be something in the information we'd collected so far. But *what*?

Sach grabbed the ring of keys from the table and gestured the Nissan. "Let's go, kids."

I plodded behind the foursome, my eyes on the photos and not on the ground. Two seconds later, I tripped over a large piece of driftwood and ended up on my butt.

The others laughed and Adwin extended a hand, which I ignored. I was too busy staring at a photo.

"Earth to JJ?" Sach joked.

"A cistern."

"Huh?"

I hopped to my feet with Adwin's help and turned the screen toward them.

"Yeah?" Sach asked, perplexed. "It looks like a large underground, water-storage thingy."

"A cistern." I turned to Linda. "Do you recall a conversation about those?"

She thought, then nodded. "We'd talked about acid rain, storm-water and pesticide runoffs. Dr. Halston had suggested it was likely the victims had been placed in a tank or a well … or a cistern."

I gave a thumb's up.

She returned it. "Do you think Hammill will let us back on the property?"

"We can only ask," I grinned in return.

Sach looked skeptical. "Don't you think he—they—might get p'o'd if we check it out?"

I squeezed his shoulder and winked. "No question."

"Don't worry. We'll tell them," Linda grinned. "Later."

* * *

"Smart thinking, having Sach park at the end of the trail and us two looking like joggers. We can enter here, from the back," Linda whispered as we stopped behind a Hala tree at the far rear of the property.

"Equally smart thinking, stopping at a store to pick up small plastic jars and rubber gloves so we can take samples from the cistern," I complimented my colleague.

She smiled and motioned. "We've got that officer talking to a nosy neighbor over there and two more casually clothed guys eating burgers on the driveway. Detectives, you think?"

"Probably. Hammill must have headed back to the precinct." I noticed a cruiser parked farther up the road. If we walked along the shrubs that bordered the property line, we could then sneak over to the cistern, take samples, and no one would be the wiser, as long as everyone stayed where they were.

"Ready?"

I nodded and we quickly but cautiously strode forward. Upon reaching the water-storage tank, we crouched by the vinyl deck. I kept watch and Linda quickly slipped on rubber gloves and accessed the tank to take samples.

"It's low, but reachable," she said softly, lowering a container. "How many samples? Two? Three?"

"Three to be safe," I responded, scanning the area.

"This thing smells a bit funky."

"Like death?" I asked wryly.

"Like something," she replied sardonically, pulling up the first filled jar. The water wasn't terribly clear.

I passed a plastic bag to hold them and scanned the property again. So far, so good.

"Are we going to take these to Ald?"

"One of them, as a peace offering. The others we'll have analyzed by two alternative sources to detect contaminants and elements."

"Just to be sure?" she smiled thinly. "Okay. Why not? But Ald's people must already have samples?"

"Most likely. But the 'offering' may save our hides."

She shrugged and continued with the task.

CHAPTER TWENTY-SEVEN

After calling Francis Xavier Shillingford, an insurance adjuster friend of ours who we'd worked with on our last case, and getting names for two analysts—one at the university and one with a government agency—we dropped off the jars.

Professor Jerome Vatten had left at noon to enjoy a long(er) weekend, but his assistant said he'd "nudge" the professor to test the water on Monday. Nasa Wasser said she had an urgent project to complete before leaving for the day and had plans for the weekend that couldn't be altered, but she would make testing of the cistern water a priority the following week.

It was almost seven by the time we pulled into Sach's driveway, so we decided to call it a day and part ways. We'd catch up at the restaurant bash tomorrow evening.

"You should have taken him up on the offer to drive you home," I told Adwin.

"The guy's been driving all day. Besides, I could use a walk. Just let me grab a bottle of water and I'm good to go." He slipped an arm lightly around my waist as we started up the footpath. "Gorgeous night."

Glancing at the star-studded sky, I agreed.

Linda pulled her lips into a tight line, obviously attempting to contain a grin or chuckle as she eyed the two of us.

Ignoring her, I looked ahead and noticed the blinds hadn't yet been drawn and the living room light was on. "Rey's back," I said casually, digging the key from my bag.

"I can't wait to hear about her day with Ald Ives," Linda snickered.

"I'd be kind of interested," Adwin admitted with a chuckle.

"I'll make tea," I offered.

"Herbal. I can do without caffeine."

Leaving our footwear and bags on the laidback floor tiles under a hyper-realistic portrait of the pets in the small foyer, Adwin's arm once again hooked my waist and we sauntered into the living room.

"Hey-ho." Rey smiled puckishly. Dressed in a black and tangerine polka-dot front-top and shorts pajama set, she was seated on the three-seater, holding a tall icy glass of what appeared to be cola, one leg draped over the armrest. She nodded to the side. "Look what the cat dragged in."

We turned and found Cash Layton Jones, aka Ricky J / Richie J, seated on the ottoman, a bottle of Longboard in one hand. Dressed in a subdued but expensive Aloha shirt (the agent / drug dealer normally opted for bright/colorful ones) he raised the bottle in toast. Peeking from the shirt was an intricate wolf pendant he'd been wearing since we first met at a dive when the three of us had been entrenched in our first case, determining the "secret" of William Pierponce Howell's pretty, young trophy wife ... before she ended up dead.

The subtle scent of *Bleu de Chanel* wafted across the room. Jade-green eyes glanced from me to Adwin and a smirk pulled at those sensual lips. "Hey, Sunshine."

* * *

"You may want to pick your jaw up from the living-room floor," Rey snickered.

I drew a deep breath, unable to look away from Cash. Damn, he looked good. Sounded good, with that deep-toned voice bearing a hint of a Southern accent. I drew another breath and shrugged, hoping my deer-caught-in-the-headlights look had dissipated. "You're one day early."

"Finished up early," he said casually, looking from me to Adwin and back again. "I've seen you before."

"I don't remember you." Adwin eyed him curiously.

Cash pursed his lips as he scrutinized him from head to foot. Then he snapped his fingers. "I remember, yeah. Photo of you and JJ in North Carolina. You've filled out some. You used to be scrawny, thin, no muscle. You're a former boyfriend. A short-order cook or something."

Adwin's arm left my waist. "Pastry chef. Now restauranteur."

"Anyone for tea?" I chirped, turning toward the kitchen.

"Make it a big pot. We have some catch-up to do," Rey replied and sipped cola.

"How'd things go with Ald?" Linda asked, dropping beside her best friend.

Rey's head tilted from left to right. "We got facts sorted and stuff." She then eyed Cash, her expression suggesting she wasn't sure if she should tell us anything, given our guest's presence.

He smiled disarmingly and the fine lines around those intense eyes crinkled attractively. "Feel free to share in front of me. You know I'll learn about it anyway … if I haven't already."

She offered one of her raspberries, extra loud and long.

"I'll pass on tea, but does anyone want to introduce us before I head out?" Adwin asked crisply.

Cash offered his "drug dealer" moniker and held out a hand but didn't get up. "I'm Ricky J. Or Richie J. Pick one."

Adwin strolled over and shook it. "Adwin. You're a client? Neighbor?"

Cash peered straight into his eyes. "JJ's lover."

Adwin looked at me, hovering in the kitchen doorway, to Cash, and back. "She never mentioned you."

"Really, honey-bun?" He smirked and turned to me. "You still angry because I won't marry you? I thought you got over that after we spent that awesome week at that clothing-optional resort?" He winked. "Remember how we brought new meaning to the word 'optional', sweetie-pie?"

"You're insufferable." I stomped to the kitchen counter.

Cash's rich temple-bell laughter rang forth as did Adwin's terse "see you tomorrow night" before the front door shut with a resounding jackhammer-loud bang.

* * *

Linda waved off my offer of a refill of lemon-lavender tea. "Two mugs are enough."

"I'm kinda liking it. I'll have another." Rey held out a chipped mug promoting California.

Popping a Royal Creem cracker into his mouth, Cash rose to fetch another beer. "Sounds like you've got one frigging sicko on your hands."

After Rey had updated us about her "non-eventful" day with Ald Ives, save for a ten-second ha-ha-ha-ha call—taunt—from GRP, we'd filled him in about the serial killer. He, on the other hand, didn't provide an update of his undercover work, but we'd not really expected it.

"Cunning, clever, and calculating," Linda added with a glower.

"And pretty damn lucky," Rey snorted, watching Cash re-seat himself across from her. "So Mr. Cuteness, wanna help?"

"Wanna," he smiled ruefully. "Canna."

She chuckled darkly. "Not your jurisdiction, or something like that, huh?"

"Something like that." His grin was fleeting. "But, over the weekend, I'd be happy to look at what you've got and see if anything stands out. Fresh eyes and all that."

Rey looked at me. I gazed at Linda; we shrugged simultaneously and nodded.

My cousin took a cracker and eyed it circumspectly. "You here just for the weekend?"

"I'm leaving Tuesday, late afternoon."

"I'd ask where you're staying," she simpered, "but I got a feeling it's here."

"We've got a couple of nice, new sleeping bags. We can put you in the guest room," I offered with a salty smile. "The kids can keep you company."

Before he could respond, *The A-Team* announced a call. Rey, Linda and I exchanged anxious glances before I hopped up to grab the cell phone from the counter.

I drew a quick breath. "Hello?"

"He called," Jimmy C announced breathlessly.

"When?"

"Five minutes ago. He said something came up so he had to rearrange plans, but he'd be interested in getting together sooner than later. He'll call in the morning to schedule something."

"I don't like it. If he meets with you, you'll know who he is—"

"And then he'll have to kill me?" the writer-blogger asked solemnly. "Then who writes his story and 'promotes' him?"

"The guy can 'promote' himself," I stressed. "He doesn't need you."

"I can give a sympathetic spin—"

"Bull! He's up to something and it's not good."

"I have to see this through, you know that, don't you?" Jimmy C asked solemnly.

"Did you give that card to the police?"

"Not yet. JJ, they won't find anything. The guy's good. He doesn't leave prints or DNA."

Unhappily, I had to agree. "Will you call after he does and let us know what's happening? Don't go off without telling anyone. *Please.*"

He promised and wished me a good night.

I met Cash's curious gaze and gave a quick rundown about Jimmy C's plan re GRP.

"He's asking for trouble if he goes it alone," he said grimly.

* * *

"You're really going to make me sleep in this unfurnished guest room?" Cash asked with a wry smile as we stood in the doorway of the darkened room. He extended an arm over his head, along the doorframe. "*Alone?*"

"It's clean and the sleeping bag is soft and warm."

"So are you."

"Ha, ha."

The free arm pulled me close and those sensual lips drew on mine. There was a faint taste of beer in the kiss and the subtle scent of that wonderful, heady cologne. I could feel resistance dissolve. Where was that no-more-Cash resolve?

"You won't be alone. Button's dying to keep you company," I smiled, nodding below. She was seated on his left foot, a look of affection in those soulful eyes as she peered up. "She hasn't forgotten her 'boyfriend'."

He winked. "Let's make it a threesome—in *your* room."

"I think—"

"Oh, for the love of God," Rey groused, peeking around a corner. "You two'll kiss and make up before long, you always do, so stop wasting time and keeping me and Bonzo up! Just head over to Cousin Jilly's room, will ya, Mr. Secret-Agent-Drug-Dealer?"

"You've got no argument from me," Cash grinned.

"And I don't want one from *you*, Cousin Jilly," Rey declared, pointing a finger. "Now, go!"

"You heard the lady." He hooked an elbow through mine and pulled me down the hallway.

"How do you know where my room is—never mind," I sighed. "You just ... always ... do."

* * *

When I entered with Button behind me, the nickel-based nightstand lamp was on, providing the room with a soft cantaloupe hue. I noticed a leather satchel before the three-drawer TV stand. "Nothing like making yourself at home."

"*Tu casa, mi casa,*" he said airily.

Glancing back to the nightstand, I noticed one of our pewter ice buckets with a bottle of champagne leaning to one side. Two handsome flutes Linda had recently purchased sat before the bucket. "How romantic," slipped from my lips with a hint of sarcasm. (Yes, as I'd often confessed, I was [majorly] attracted to Cash, but I didn't want him thinking I'd be awaiting his arrival like an eager, lovestruck schoolgirl. Note to self: consider psychotherapy.)

He moved to the nightstand and sat on the edge of the bed as I dropped into the soft linen-upholstered armchair I'd purchased on a whim (courtesy of Rey's perpetual sales-purchasing enthusiasm). "What's up with this ex-beau of yours?"

"He and a friend decided to open a restaurant. Oahu seemed as good as any place," I replied casually, leaning back. All I wanted to do was climb into bed—*alone*. "There's a party tomorrow to celebrate the soon-to-be-open Steaming Mimi's."

"I could do with a party." He pulled up the bottle. "Dom 2008."

"Big spender," I smirked.

"Big tastes."

"Big jackass."

He feigned hurt. "Aw, hon, is that any way to treat your boyfriend?"

"You're hardly that," I smirked again.

He scanned my face, undoubtedly discerning the weariness —and annoyance. "Keep the bubbles for another time?"

I stifled a yawn.

He smiled fleetingly and pulled up his feet.

I glanced at the socks. "Gucci?" I all but snorted. "*Really?*"

"I'm a drug dealer with expensive penchants for many things."

"Evidently," I said drily, regarding him closely. I used to think he looked a bit like Jeffrey Donovan of *Burn Notice* fame and a little like Timothy Olyphant of *Justified*. With the stubble beard, I was no longer quite sure. He'd acquired a few more fine lines (I supposed playing a hardened drug dealer took its toll). Cash's buffalo-brown hair had always been thick and wavy, hanging 2" below the ears. Now it was messy and textured and ear-length. That guy'd look good with a bad, cheap peruke.

I watched Button pad across the floor and leap onto the bed beside him. "How's the wife?"

"The *ex* is fine. The kids are great." Pride was etched in the expression. "Nathan's thinking he might like to work in the world of science while Madison's started piano lessons and plans on being the next Yuja Wang; she's a big fan."

"Impressive for one barely ten," I smiled wearily.

"She's got a good head on those small shoulders." He eyed me intently. "Bedtime?"

He held up a hand before I could reply. "It's okay. Sleep's fine with me. Just an FYI, though. This *may* be the only night I can spend here. There are people to meet with, things to tend to."

Even to these tired ears, he sounded evasive, but I was too drained to care. I narrowed one eye as I watched him remove the Aloha shirt and slide under the covers with his jeans on.

I took off my shorts and climbed into bed beside him.

He hooked an arm around me and tugged me close. Damn, he smelled good.

"Night-night, Sunshine."

I didn't respond but drifted into Slumberland.

* * *

"Snap to it! Jimmy C's in trouble!"

Startled, I fell out of bed and Cash hopped to his feet, gun poised. Where the <bleep> had he hidden that?

"What's up?" he demanded, his voice husky with sleep but his eyes alert.

Rey stood in the doorway, doing up jeans. Button barked once (that was about as excited as the dear girl ever got) and dropped before her feet. A plum-purple hoodie hung from her shoulders. I could hear Linda running down the hallway (a ballerina she wasn't). A curse erupted as she banged into Rey with the velocity of a bumper car and they crashed to the floor.

Linda pulled herself up with the help of her best friend and then quickly said, "GRP called on my cell. Said he'd tried you and Rey, but no answer at either."

"I left my cell in the washroom," my cousin stated with a limp shrug, slipping the hoodie over a black camisole. "Not awake enough."

I raced to the closet, grabbed a pair of leggings and a floral-print sweatshirt, and pulled both on; Cash did the same with his clothes.

"I take it there's a good reason we're getting dressed so quickly at quarter to one in the morning?" he asked with a tense frown.

"GRP said Jimmy C has a story to tell. How he was abducted by the—what did he call himself? Right. The *Rose-Pin Killer*. I guess that's what he and Jimmy agreed to call him for the story." Linda's expression grew grim. "GRP said Jimmy C would be able to provide a firsthand account. There'll be pics, too!"

CHAPTER TWENTY-EIGHT

Cash and I exchanged apprehensive glances before the four of us scurried downstairs.

"We better call Ald," Linda said, turning on the farmhouse-inspired pendant lights over the counter.

I blinked at the sudden brightness. "You do that while I try Jimmy C."

"He didn't answer when I tried him after the call from GRP but go for it! I'll try Ald again." She raced into the living room to make the call with the mobile phone.

Rey pulled out one of the many organic cotton lunch bags we had stuffed in a bottom drawer and quickly jammed four water bottles and two boxes of Pot Pan crackers into it. "Let's head over to his place."

"He's not likely to be to be there," I stated uneasily, visualizing a very unpleasant scene as I dialed Jimmy C's number again.

"Sounds like GRP got to him." Cash looked solemn. "No doubt he'll let you and/or the police know where to find the body."

Rey and I gazed at each other with lined brows as I went into our blogger-writer's VM.

"It'll be us he'll tell," she said with flapjack flatness. "It's part of the *game*."

Cash leaned into the counter, his expression dour. "Game? Seems you might have forgotten to mention that."

I nodded to Rey as I left an urgent message—for what little it was worth—and then filled the coffee pot with water. Linda wandered back in, looking discouraged. No answer on Ald' Ives side either. This promised to be a long night, er, morning.

Not one minute after Rey had provided Cash with a *Cliff-Notes* version of the "game", her cell phone burst forth with "Reveille". We looked at her with eyes wide open and she merely stuck out her tongue.

It was Ald returning Linda's call. I eyed my cousin curiously, wondering why he'd called her, but as it turned out, Linda had left her phone in the foyer. Good Lord, we were evolving into a forgetful threesome. And speaking of forgetful, where was *my* phone?

As if reading my thoughts, Cash held it up. An arched brow asked what my lips didn't. His silent response was to gesture the top of the coffee machine. Really? I'd left it *there*?

Rey looked from him to me and shook her head. "The detective's going to Jimmy C's place and is sending Hammill to check in with the officers posted at the house of death, just in case."

"House of death? *Really*?" I asked, grimacing.

"It's only a matter of time—like hours—before the media calls it that," Rey said tartly. "They're having a field day as it is, now that it's a known fact that Fayne and Antigua were murdered, and decorated, in a similar fashion to the four by the canal."

"He *is* starting an official search, isn't he?" Linda asked her best friend, her expression tense.

She nodded solemnly. "If people weren't panicked before, they will be now. This is going to blow up majorly, especially when GRP posts pics and whatnot."

"Jimmy C doesn't have friends in the 'real' world," Linda

told us as she got milk from the fridge. "I'd opt for social media to help find him."

"Surely the guy has *some* friends?" Cash asked.

Linda eyed him for several seconds. "We qualify. There's also a restaurant blogger, Rouge Framboise, but he's in Paris for the month. And there's that crime writer Jimmy C met last year in the park. Simone Tempe Lerre."

"Track her down. You never know," Rey opened the cupboard door to get sugar, sweetener, and mugs. "We should cover all bases."

"We warned him not to meet GRP alone." Linda shook her head and moaned softly.

"He wanted a story," I said dolefully.

My cousin blew a soft raspberry. "Yeah. The biggest—and last—of the dude's not-yet-started career."

"Say, didn't he say that GRP was going to call him in the morning?" Linda asked, visibly bemused.

"Obviously GRP changed his mind."

My cell announced a call and we jumped.

When I answered, maniacal laughter greeted me. I couldn't help but snicker. "Cheesy, *very* cheesy."

"It seemed appropriate," GRP said gaily.

"You killed our friend."

"I gave him the story he wanted … and I'm now getting the fame I wanted."

"You have it—and it's called notoriety, Smart Ass."

"It's called *fame* and you can never have enough of anything. And calling me 'Smart Ass' isn't very nice."

"Where's Jimmy C?" I demanded. "Which stream did you lay his body alongside?"

"He's close, sweetie. *Very* close. Seek and ye shall find."

"He didn't deserve that."

"You're quite right. He didn't deserve that. And he didn't receive what the others did because he's not like them … even though he is in some respects. Don't worry your pretty selves. Until we talk again—or meet—my dear, *dear* JJ."

* * *

Before sharing GRP's remarks, I put in a quick call to Ald, who picked up on the first ring.

"I'm—"

"GRP just called!" I provided a quick rundown.

"Sounds like he's somewhere in your neighborhood."

"That'd be my assumption," I concurred, ambling over to the now full coffeepot and pouring the dark fragrant brew into four mugs.

"I'll send Sallo to your place with some officers to conduct a search. I'm en route to Carcanetta's place. I'll up meet with the two men I sent over, then head over to your house."

I took a big gulp of burning-hot caffeine and grimaced.

Cash came over to claim a mug, followed by Linda. Anxiously I scanned the kitchen, wondering what horrid fate had befallen Jimmy C.

"Maybe we should check the front yard and lanai," Rey suggested, eyeing the mug that remained unclaimed on the counter.

"Let me do it. Do you have a flashlight?" Cash glanced at his feet.

"Your designer loafers are in the mudroom, bottom shelf, by the storage bench," my cousin said flatly, gesturing the rear. "You can find flashlights in the storage bench's middle compartment."

He saluted and hastened from the kitchen.

"Damn, he's hunky. Especially with that three-day stubble-beard look."

"It does give him a certain appeal, but he's JJ's," Linda pointed out with mock sternness.

"She can keep him," Rey said with a dismissive wave. "But a gal can look."

I took two more bracing gulps. "Maybe we should search the house? Despite the call, GRP may have left a message or something."

"Something as in Jimmy C' body?" she asked sarcastically.

I bit my bottom lip.

"Let's head upstairs. Linda, you take the *makai* side and I'll take the *mauka*."

"I'll check around downstairs," I said somberly. "Meet you back here in ten."

Leaving my colleagues at the stairs, I entered the living room. A scrutiny of the room revealed nothing, nor did a peek behind the solar roller blinds. Cabinet shelves, throw blankets and cushions hid nothing out of the norm. The same held true for the under the rug and around the rest of the furniture. All was as it had been earlier.

I popped into the mudroom after checking the laundry area and Cash entered, a Fenix flashlight burning brightly in his hand. "Anything?"

He turned it off and shook his head. "Get me the key to the *ohana*, will you?"

"If it's locked, then it's—"

"Unlikely anything—or anyone—is in there?" he asked loftily.

He had me. "A good private eye leaves no stones unturned, right," I murmured, suitably chastised.

He tapped the tip of my nose with an index finger and I hurried to get the key.

Linda and Rey caught up with us as we were about to leave the mudroom, and advised they'd not found anything out of place upstairs. Reaching into the middle compartment of the bench, Rey pulled out another flashlight and we headed to the *ohana*.

As it had been the last few days, the night was breezy and the sky star-filled and bright, the temperature pleasant at 70 degrees Fahrenheit. As Cash beamed the light on the lock, I inserted the key. The guesthouse was in major need of work, a project we'd agreed to take up at the end of summer, once we [hopefully] had more finances in place. Inside were assorted boxes, some with tools and equipment to help with the project, others with old knick-knacks, clothes, and equipment. Against the far wall were pieces of furniture from the Ala Moana condos, draped with old bedsheets.

Cash flashed the light around and discovered a light switch. He tried it and was visibly pleased when a dim apricot glow warmed the main room. "You look around here and I'll check the other rooms," he instructed.

The three of us had just started to remove sheets when he called us into the next room. Gauging from the tone, he'd found something and it wasn't good.

We ran to the rear, what would one day be a bedroom, and crashed into Cash when we simultaneously sighted Jimmy C lying on the scratched hardwood floor.

"Great. The *four* Stooges," he sighed, pushing us away gently.

"Is he dead?"

"He appears to be breathing," he replied to Linda's softly voiced question as he crouched alongside the unconscious man. "Call 911 and your police pals, will you? And maybe you'd better go to the house to wait for them." He checked the young man's eyes and gently moved his head from side to side. "He's been drugged, and he'll probably hurt some, but I believe he'll be okay."

"And he'll have a 'memento' for the rest of his life," I gestured.

The top three buttons to Jimmy C's Sun + Stone patchwork shirt were unfastened. On his hairless chest were blood-encrusted incisions that resembled flowery embroidery; there weren't as many as on previous victims, just three "strands" like the chains of a delicate necklace. On his jeans, near his hip, rested a cell phone with a faux koa case cover. On it was a sticky note with "blgrME2B", written by a clumsy hand, intentional no doubt.

Figuring it was a password, I entered the PIN into the cell phone, which I held with the edge of my sweater.

"There won't be prints or DNA to find on that, I'd bet big bucks on it," Cash said gravely.

"Me, too," I murmured. The screen advised of a text. It read, "Check the photo gallery."

I did as instructed, with Rey and Cash standing on either side. There were three photos. One was of Jimmy C prone on a dark floor, bound and gagged, before any incisions were made. His eyes were wide with fear, yet there also seemed to be a sense of curiosity and interest … and acceptance. The second one was of a chess board with the pieces very specifically laid out. A winning game? Whose? The third photo was of a small round table sporting a dozen black roses, identical to those found on previous victims. The message at the bottom: *Reserved solely for the deserving.*

"Shit," Rey said under her breath.

Cash and I dittoed the sentiment.

CHAPTER TWENTY-NINE

The police and ambulance arrived within seconds of each other. Officers Lee Murr and Armad Dyllo were greeted by Linda and Rey while I accompanied the paramedics to the *ohana*, where Cash was seated on a windowsill, checking emails and texts.

With a nod, he hopped to his feet. "Your friend opened his eyes for a fraction of a second, mumbled something about 'two-faced killer', and winced with obvious pain."

The female paramedic, who'd said her name was Helga, gave Cash an approving glance, obviously liking what she saw, then got down to business. As her partner, Rada, crouched alongside Jimmy C to perform a swift assessment, I heard Rey call from the yard.

Cash nodded for me to go and I slipped from the *ohana*. At the edge of the lanai stood my cousin and Detective Sallo. Even under the dim lighting, it wasn't hard to see his dung-beetle-brown eyes narrow and his expression change from grim to dour as he peered over. He'd been following the sharp beam of his Maglite along the edge of the house. Dressed in a gray-striped shirt under a thin black cotton jacket and black pants, the trademark fedora was tilted at an awkward angle to the right.

"Look who's arrived? Our favorite flatfoot," Rey said with feigned cheer and gestured. "Detective Flatfoot-er-Sallo saw some footprints, but I told them they belonged to our cutey-pie visitor, who I'd found peeking into the window earlier today before inviting him in."

I offered a huge fake smile as I stepped before the detective. "Coffee?"

"Black. Extra-large."

Brusque as ever. With a quick nod, Rey, Sallo and I entered the kitchen to find Linda passing mugs to the officers. The pot was empty, so I set about making another one as she explained what had transpired. Rey grabbed three bottles of chilled water, placed them on the table, and took a seat. She motioned the chair across from her. Sallo sat. With a grunt.

"Don't you want to check out the *ohana* yourself?" I asked.

"The what—oh, the guesthouse." He clucked like a chicken, placing his flashlight on the table. "I'll wait for Ives. He should be here any minute."

"Anything new in your investigation?" Rey asked casually, taking a swig of water.

He shrugged. "Nothing of note in the Makan-uh-whatever Place house. The guy—or guys—must have sanitized the place regularly. They must have gotten quite their jollies, watching their doped-up victims squirm and flinch beyond the two-way mirror."

Rey arched a thin, shaped brow. "You believe there are *two* killers?"

"According to one of our witnesses, he'd seen *two* people out there one night."

"You mean Mr. Noel C. Parker?"

Sallo glanced sharply at her, sneered, and grabbed a bottle of water.

"But there's nothing to substantiate that theory, is there?"

"Didn't you mention hearing another voice?"

She pursed her lips, glanced at me, then nodded.

He sighed, then frowned as he removed the cap. "We have to work all angles. But if you think about it, it'd make sense. There were four bodies by the canal. Two people could handle moving them much better than one, if only to serve as a look-out."

Rey tilted her head one way and then the other, as if weighing his contribution, then gazed at me. "Maybe Jimmy C will have something worthwhile to share when he comes out of it."

"He did mumble something about 'two-faced killer'." I put milk, sugar and sweetener on the table.

"That makes sense. GRP tricked him with the promise of a story and therefore proved to be 'two-faced'," my cousin offered.

Sallo looked from her to me and back again. "You wanna fill me in on this promise of a story?"

She took another sip and relayed what we knew about the two men's intended meeting, which had obviously proven no longer "intended".

"Hey," Ald muttered as he strolled in from the living room, dressed in jeans, a Bonobo slim-fit plaid button-down shirt, and crocodile leather penny loafers. He might have been coming from a dinner or concert rather than bed.

"Fancy-schmanzy," Rey said drolly, eyeing him up and down. "Those Mezlan?"

"If you got it, flaunt it," he said with equal drollness, leaning into the counter.

"Anything at Jimmy C's?" I asked.

"Nothing on his laptop or tablet, which were in his office. We're checking out the place. It doesn't look like there was a fight or anything. The place is pretty neat and clean for a guy living alone."

"You won't find anything related to GRP," Rey said flatly.

"Probably not. GRP's good."

"Or *they're* good."

He looked from her to me to Sallo but remained silent.

"The paramedics just took him away," Cash announced as he entered the kitchen. Sighting Ald Ives, he smiled haughtily and stood beside me.

"Look what's back in town," Ald scowled. "Just what we need, Sallo. Serial killings and a scumbag drug king."

"That's *alleged* scumbag drug king," Cash grinned, hanging an arm around my waist. "Hon, we should make it a priority to get the *ohana* fixed so we can have privacy when I visit." He brushed his lips across my cheek and beamed with sunshine brightness at the detective.

Ald's expression darkened. "I *will* get you."

Cash's smile broadened and he turned to me. "I'll wait for you upstairs." With another kiss, he left the room.

"When did that arrive?"

"Today," Rey answered for me.

"He sticking around?"

"For a couple of days it appears," she replied.

I gave her a look and poured Sallo the big mug of coffee he'd requested earlier. Shall we compare notes before you and your colleague join the others searching for evidence?"

"Evidence of the *non*-findable type," Ald stated with a sour smile.

* * *

Three a.m. saw Rey, Linda and I finally plod up to bed. I slipped off my leggings and sweater and slipped into bed alongside Cash, who was fast asleep, snoring softly—and wearing nothing. Great. He must have been bordering on exhaustion not to have awakened; it wasn't like the vigilant agent. Or perhaps he was merely feigning sleep, wanting me to have quiet time. Whatever the case, I was grateful but far from sleepy.

Slipping away from him, onto my side, I thought about what had transpired. Jimmy C's words about "two-faced", the non-findings in the *ohana* and around the property, save for one pair of footprints to the far rear. Had GRP slipped? Or was it a "pretend" clue, something he'd purposely placed there as part of the game? When had GRP overpowered Jimmy C? How, for that matter? A knock-out drug had undoubtedly put him under, but when had our clever villain administered it?

You're quite right—he didn't deserve that. So, he didn't receive what the others did ... because he's not like them ... even though he is. GRP's cryptic words started tumbling through my mind. He's not like the others. What did the others have in common? Right! The others were rich and/or came from money. Note to self: find out more about Jimmy C in the morning.

* * *

Linda, Rey and Cash were at the kitchen table, drinking coffee and POG (papaya, orange, and guava juice) and eating boiled eggs with toast when I entered at seven a.m. My cousin and her best friend were wearing scoop-neck sun dresses with bright floral motifs while Cash wore designer jeans and a mesh-stripe crewneck sweater.

"Where were you?" Rey demanded.

"And good morning to you, too," I said merrily.

"You have bags the size of parasails under your eyes," she said flippantly.

"Much like yours, but not half as colorful," I responded with saccharine sweetness, grabbing an Aloha mug from the cupboard and pouring vanilla-scented coffee.

Cash took a bite of butter-slathered toast and eyed me keenly. "Congrats for not waking me when you slipped out. That took some skill. Where'd you go?"

"I couldn't sleep." I poured milk into the steaming coffee. "I drove to the hospital and saw Jimmy C."

"How'd you get past reception at this time of the morning? And surely they have an officer watching, too?" Linda asked, pouring more POG into her tall ice-filled glass.

"Where there's a will, there's a way." I pitched my eyebrows a couple of times à la Thomas Magnum and leaned into the counter. "He's doing okay, by the way. Groggy from the meds, but he'll be fine. He said he may post photos of the chest scabs, soon-to-be scars, as proof he'd met with the serial killer terrorizing Oahu." I smiled trimly, envisioning his proud expression as he displayed the perforations.

"The visit couldn't wait?" Cash cracked an egg against the table.

"GRP said something last night. 'You're quite right—he didn't deserve that. So, he didn't receive what the others did, because he's not like them, even though he is'. So, I considered what the other victims had in common ... and that was that they had money, or came from rich families."

"Is *Jimmy C* rich?" Rey asked with a brow creased like parsley.

"His parents are. They're philanthropists. Provide lots of money to very worthy causes, including homeless shelters, animal shelters, and residences for abused women."

Linda's brow arched.

"But Jimmy C never allowed them to pay for anything. He paid for college. And he rented a one-room flat when he graduated, paid for through part-time jobs. He wanted to make his own way. Said he didn't want to end up like his self-centered brother, Sloan."

"I never knew that about him. You truly learn something new every day," Linda said with an amused smile. "So, his brother's spoiled and all that?"

"Besides owning his own helicopter tour company, which is quite successful with twenty choppers on the various islands, he has his hands in a few tourist-oriented businesses. He obtained an MBA from UCLA—"

"All financed by Daddy?" Rey asked sarcastically.

I nodded. "He's quite the playboy, too, apparently. Two years older than Jimmy C and not one bit like him. They don't get along particularly well. Never did. Sloan always thought he was privileged; Jimmy C thought wealth was earned and shared." I smiled. "Jimmy C's name at birth, by the by, was James Constantino Carcanetta III."

"How very highbrow," Linda giggled.

"All which makes him like the others, but not," Cash said, salting his egg.

I nodded. "So, by GRP's standards, he *didn't* deserve to die."

"Interesting," Linda murmured, eyeing her juice. "Good for him."

"GRP or Jimmy C?" Rey asked drily.

She shrugged. "Both."

"What now, ladies?"

We all eyed Cash, then looked at one another.

"If GRP hates the rich enough to kill them, then wouldn't that mean he came from a poor home?" Rey asked.

"Possibly," Linda replied. "But he could be someone who simply holds disdain for the wealthy."

I added, "Or someone who was once rich himself and lost it."

"But got it back." Rey snapped her fingers. "Remember the description we got from Chuck, that homeless guy? He mentioned the pricey sunglasses and jacket. It sounded like the man—if he *was* GRP—had money."

"Then why the disdain for moneyed folks, if he has it?" Linda asked, perplexed. She sighed softly. "What did Jimmy C mean by 'two-faced'?"

"He didn't recall saying it or giving his cell-phone password … or much of anything that transpired. He said he remembered going to the kitchen at home to make a pot of tea because he was going to blog-hop for a few hours, but when he entered, he noticed the light was no longer on. Then, his own lights went out. He doesn't remember being hit on the head—an injury by a blunt object was verified by the ER doctor. Nor does he recall having something pressed to his nose or a prick to his skin.

Everything is hazy, with lots of weird images, but nothing more." I sighed softly and sipped. "He fell asleep and I left."

"He'll probably remember with time." Rey mashed an egg onto her slice of toast. "What's on the agenda for today?"

Dragnet announced a call and a breath caught in my throat. "Hopefully, not looking at another body."

CHAPTER THIRTY

Big sigh. There *was* another body. By the Kalihi Stream, not far from the Waipuhia Falls. The three of us grabbed sweaters, a laptop and cell phones, bags for collecting our own evidence (if possible), and bottles of water. Cash accepted a men's denim jacket from Rey; a date had forgotten it and she'd decided to keep it when he advised her they wouldn't be seeing each other again as she wasn't his type.

We scrambled into the Jeep, my "sometimes boyfriend" at the wheel, and headed over. Ald Ives, Sammie Sallo, and PC Hammill, would already be there, along with the usual assortment of legal sorts and keen media personnel.

"I wonder who it is," Linda said with a frown. She was seated alongside Rey in the back, who was staring out the window.

"We'll find out soon enough," her best friend murmured. "Man, this dude's on a major spree, isn't he?"

Cash smiled drily. "You three never seem to have a dull moment as P.I.s, do you?"

"I'll take dull moments to psycho killers any day," Linda declared with a lower as he pulled onto the Likelike Highway.

"Strange, though, that he hasn't called to impart the news like he usually does."

"Maybe he's tired of the game," Rey suggested, leaning forward, her mouth close to my ear.

Cash motioned Linda's laptop. "We've got a good fifteen minutes before we arrive. Why don't you list particulars, names, anything that you think are worth checking and rechecking? We can hunker down later, after we find out what's what."

"We already have a log—notes—of what we've investigated and learned, but why not?" I glanced back at my colleagues. Both perked up, eager for the assistance. "Let's review what we have and add what we've missed."

Rey hooked her hands around my headrest and started listing names she could easily recall, which Linda cross-checked. Then she provided point-form details, and I added my two cents.

"We've already got all that," Linda stated. "But a revisit's always worthwhile."

"Maybe we should start by returning to the chess players and those guys with the rich daddies," I suggested. "I still can't help but feel there's something there."

"Gut instincts have their merit." Rey motioned with a rueful smile. "But now, the next body awaits."

We'd arrived. Cash pulled over to the side of the small parking lot and parked.

The area was abuzz with activity. We jumped from the Jeep and looked for familiar faces, like the three detectives who were supposed to be there. A couple of officers we knew from the station were talking to a handful of reporters who'd heard the news. Three media vans were in the distance, hastening to join their associates.

I whirled upon hearing my name. Ald, wearing the same ensemble as last night, er, morning, stood by an HPD Crime Scene SUV, waving off someone I recognized from the pathologist's office. He scowled upon seeing Cash and shook his head. I could hear the silent curses. He drew a deep breath and marched over and stopped but an inch from Cash's feet.

"I'm not going to waste my breath on you," he hissed, then turned to Rey. "What did our killer say this time?"

"He didn't, because he never called."

"That's not like him," Ald lowered.

Linda concurred. "Something's up."

Curious, I checked my cell phone. No missed calls. No texts or emails. Very strange indeed. Rey and Linda checked theirs. *Nada.*

"Who's the vic?" Rey gestured the stream.

"A young woman."

"Who found her?"

Ald regarded her cagily. "We got an anonymous tip."

"Ri-ight. GRP called it in, I'd bet. He's changed his M.O." She watched an Evidence Specialist marking physical evidence. "How long's she been dead?"

"Doc Terry figures she died around three or four."

"And the call?"

Ald bristled and turned to Cash. "When'd you become a P.I., Mr. Jackass Drug Dealer?"

"That's *alleged*," he smirked.

Ald darkened and before they could get into a verbal—or physical—sparring match, I asked, "When did the call come in?"

"A little after five," he replied flatly, forcing his irritated gaze from Cash and focusing on me. "Our guy was a busy boy."

"Do you know who it is?" Rey asked, looking beyond the yellow tape several yards away.

"Not yet. There was no wallet or anything." He rubbed his temples. He looked beat. "As I said, she's young ... and likely moneyed, because she's wearing diamond earrings and designer clothes. Too bad her face is obscured."

The three of us glanced apprehensively at one another.

"Obscured?" Linda asked with a furrowed brow as she

shielded her eyes from the sun, which was beginning to slip from beneath a cluster of gray clouds.

"The incisions that are usually on his victims' chests are on her face—in multitude. If she was pretty, she's not now," he said flatly. "There are a few scrapes and scratches on the arms and legs, like maybe she was dragged or fought, and marks on both wrists and ankles."

"If her face is obscured, how could tell she was young?" Rey pulled out her pretty Bottega Veneta sunglasses (the real deal for a change) and put them on.

Purposely, the detective peered at the square-framed glasses, then at the left hinge and then the right. He smirked. "Well-toned figure, nice hands with pricy manicured fingers, very few wrinkles on that long slender neck. She was probably in her late twenties or early thirties."

"Any distinguishing marks?" Cash asked, then clamped his mouth shut.

Ald scowled as he scanned Cash's face.

"Were there?" I prodded.

The detective inhaled slowly. "Tatt on the left leg."

An unpleasant, queasy feeling spread through my stomach, as if I'd eaten bad oysters. "It wouldn't happen to be an intricate deep-purple rose, braided with nettles, that snakes up to the knee?"

A well-shaped eyebrow arched. "You know the victim?"

"Caprize Marquessa de Sade," Linda answered.

"Shit." Rey appeared stunned. "*Why her?*"

"And why no call or message this time?" I mused aloud.

"You better give us the details." Ald beckoned Hammill, who'd been heading over to the medical examiner.

"Yeah?" The attractive detective looked from one face to the other, resting on Cash's before looking him up and down. "Who are you?"

"A friend of JJ's," he replied casually. "Some people call me Richie J, others Ricky J. Take your pick."

Remaining silent, Hammill turned to Ald.

"It looks like our private eyes here know the victim."

Still silent, Hamill turned back to us.

"Maybe one of us should take a look and confirm," I suggested. "While it's a unique tatt, it's possible it's another woman with a similar design."

"You want to do it?" Ald asked, watching me intently.

I nodded and Hammill clasped my arm lightly, leading the way.

The flurry of activity was orderly, efficient. Every person had specific tasks to complete and did so with focus and determination. We stepped alongside the gurney that would soon be transported to the morgue and I felt a stab of woe and worry.

Hammill asked the two men standing by the body to move back and motioned me to take a look.

I did and blanched, grateful I'd not had breakfast. Caprize's once classically pretty face was a mass of teeny perforations. Flowers, like those of a child's drawing, decorated her forehead and cheeks. Around them were fancy curlicues. The canvas of tiny scabbed incisions resembled one of Aunt Ruth June's cross-stitch or needlepoint patterns.

Had Caprize suffered? Or had GRP drugged her beforehand? I opted for the latter; that's what he normally did, wasn't it? He'd probably bound her after administering the drug, as a precaution, to ensure she didn't wake up and escape, or fight. But, as Rey had asked, why her?

Given GRP watched us a lot, he had to have known we were helping Caprize with her stalker ... could it be, he *had* been her stalker? It was an idea we'd tossed around, but maybe it was *fact*. But even if that had been the case, once more: why kill *her*?

"It's Caprize, all right," I confirmed, peering down at her wrist to find red, broken skin. I'd been right about her being bound. "It seems that she may not have suffered, or at least not as much as the others." I knew the answer but asked anyway. "She wasn't tortured, was she?"

"It doesn't appear so, but the autopsy will tell us more," he replied, looking at Caprize with a frown. "Strange. Given the guy's previous victims, you'd think he'd have wanted her to hurt." He scanned the unsophisticated flowers. "I wonder if she was awake when he did that?"

A chilling shiver soared up my spine like a 747. Hopefully not. "She seems to be—like Jimmy C—an atypical victim." I sighed noisily. "Will you let us know what the autopsy reveals?"

Billiard-ball black eyes scanned my face for several seconds. "Will you let us know when you hear from him?"

"*If* we do, sure."

"You *will*."

"You're that certain?" I asked gravely as we started walking in the direction of my colleagues. "He hasn't called yet."

"He *will*." A tense smile tugged at his mouth. "He's fixated on you three."

"Maybe he's become *un*-fixated?"

"I doubt it. He's changed the rules of the game." With that, he strolled over to an officer arguing with a ruddy-faced reporter who might have stepped out of a 40s B&W mystery. Another fedora? *Really*? Had they suddenly become a new fashion craze?

CHAPTER THIRTY-ONE

Cash was perched on one of several large rocks lining the side of the road while Linda chatted on her cell to the side and Rey waved to someone in the distance. I peered over and saw Jimmy C paying a cab driver.

Surprised, I stepped beside Rey. "What's he doing here?"

"You don't think he'd miss this, do you?"

Dressed in a flamingo-print short-sleeved shirt and black flat-front shorts, he slung his messenger bag over one shoulder and shuffled over. "I can't believe it! I got a call about another victim! Who is it? What did I miss?"

"Whoa!" Rey pressed a palm to his forehead. "Where's the fire?"

"Over there," Jimmy C pointed. "Getting ready to be taken to the morgue."

"How you feelin'?"

He looked at Rey solemnly. "Better than that body did before it became a dead one."

She nodded, her expression grave.

Cash stepped alongside me. "Why don't I take you all out for lunch?"

Jimmy C looked at me questioningly.

I smiled and introduced them.

With somber smiles, they shook hands and Jimmy C turned to Linda. "Do we know who the victim is?"

"Caprize Marquessa de Sade."

Cola-brown eyes rounded like golf balls. "You're kidding!" He turned to watch a vehicle marked "Medical Examiner" drive off.

"You know her?" I asked, stunned.

"Besides Linda having told me about her in terms of your stalker case, I'd once done a feature on her ad company and her —both up-and-coming."

"Small world," I murmured.

"And getting smaller—and weirder—every day," Rey said softly.

"How about we pick up stuff for a barbecue and lounge on the lanai? We can put our heads together for a few hours before we have to leave for the restaurant do." I poked Cash's arm. "You, Aloha Shirt Man, are in charge of grilling. Rey, you're not too bad with salads these days, so make one or two. Linda, you can do alcohol-less drinks. And you, Jimmy C, you sit and rest."

"And what about you, General JJ?" my cousin asked blandly.

"I'm on cutlery and napkin duty."

"Ni-ice." She slapped me lightly on the back. "Let's get this party started."

When we stepped up to the Jeep, Cash stopped and stared upward. Prompted to see what had captured his attention, I stopped as well, which prompted Rey, Linda, and Jimmy C to do the same. Four mouths dropped open, wide as manhole covers, while Cash merely watched the single-seat turboprop-powered monoplane—an agricultural aircraft—fly overhead with an egg-white banner reading "HA-HA-HA-HA" in blood red.

"Son-of-a-gun," Jimmy C said under his breath.

"I'd have opted for SOB," Linda murmured.

"What a ballsy prick," Rey declared.

"Hammill was right. He's changed the game." I glanced over to see if the detectives had noticed.

They had. Ald was pointing and Hammill was barking into his phone as an officer sprinted to her cruiser.

"I'm guessing Ald'll be checking out aerial advertising companies."

Linda gazed at Rey in surprise. "When'd you stop calling him 'Hives'?"

"I haven't," she sniffed, looking from the detective to the disappearing plane and back again. "Five'll get you ten he won't luck in."

Her best friend's eyebrow arched, but she simply opened the door and climbed into the rear of the Jeep. "As you said, let's get this party started—"

"And nail this f'g sucker," Rey affirmed flatly, hopping in.

* * *

A little after eleven, the four of us were seated on the lanai, drinking lemon-basil iced tea, googling, checking databases, and reviewing notes.

We'd called all the local aerial companies and lucked in. An hour of flying/advertising time cost approximately one-thousand dollars, validating yet again what we'd assumed—that GRP had money (or was stealing it). The "HA-HA-HA-HA" order had been received two weeks previous and paid in full, with the date TBD. Given Mr. G.R. Pea—"yeah, like the veggie" —had paid in full and promised to pay extra if the flight had to be made with minimal notification, they'd been happy to oblige. Business had been somewhat slow this month according to Jeb, the owner. Neither Jeb nor Ralphie, his partner and pilot, had met G.R. Pea. Everything had been done online and via courier.

Cash was seated on the chaise longue, barefooted with legs crossed and laptop perched on top. Linda was propped up alongside, peering over regularly, obviously fascinated to watch him wear his agent hat; he was tracking down the courier that had delivered the payment to Jeb. Jimmy C was editing an afternoon post about the latest victim, which Ald had okayed for early evening release, given the name would soon hit screens.

Leaning against the rear wall, Rey and I were cross-legged on the square slate stone tiles with the "kids" scampering on the ragged-looking grass nearby. We'd only been here for thirty minutes when Sach wandered into the yard.

"Man, are you colorblind or what?" Rey asked, pretending to be dazzled by his apparel.

Bemused, he looked down at his coral tropical-print shirt and lobster-print pants. "No like?"

"No!" she and I answered in unison.

He shrugged and, noticing Cash, smiled from ear to ear. "Ooh, *me* like."

"Down boy," Linda advised, patting Cash's shin. "He's taken."

"Yeah. Meet JJ's 'sometimes boyfriend'," Rey said.

"Only *sometimes*?" he winked.

Cash winked in return and returned to the laptop.

"I noticed the Jeep in the driveway, so I thought I'd stroll over to confirm a time for heading over to the restaurant tonight," Sach explained, pouring himself half a glass of iced tea.

I glanced at Rey, having forgotten about Steaming Mimi's.

"Six," my cousin stated. "Can we use your Nissan? It's got more room to accommodate the five of us. Jimmy C, sure you can't come?"

"Uh-huh." He didn't stop keying. "Going to visit with a blogger buddy at six."

Sach sat on the edge of the ottoman. "I heard there was another murder, but they haven't released the name yet."

"Yeah ... and you'll never guess who."

He eyed Rey expectantly for several seconds. "Are we waiting for a drum roll?"

She drummed on her thighs in response.

"Come on! *Who*?"

"Caprize," Linda replied before her BFF could.

Sach goggled. "No!"

"Yes!" she all but shrieked.

His silver-gray eyes bulged like bocce balls. "No!"

"Yes!" we all roared.

Shotgun Slade announced a call (I'd changed the ringtone on the drive back from Foodland).

"Guess who's back?" Rey singsonged.

Everyone leaned forward as they watched me reach for the cell phone.

Turning on the speaker, I dispensed with the usual greeting and took a chance by saying, "What kept you, *friend*?"

"You knew it'd be me, how nice," GRP chirped.

"You hadn't called earlier, and given you'd flown that banner —how very theatrical of you—we figured a call was due," I said nonchalantly, grinning as Rey all but sat on top of me to hear.

"I thought I'd change the game a little."

"Why? You're not having fun anymore?"

"I didn't want you to get bored or me predictable."

"Are you nearby? In some shrubs maybe? Up a tree? Or maybe under a rock?"

"Ha-ha."

I met Cash's concentrated gaze and offered a salty smile. "You never stalked the others like you did Caprize. What made her worthy of your fixated attention?"

No response. Had I stumbled on the truth—GRP *had been* Caprize's stalker? If so, then he was the fellow Linda and I had met that night by the parking garage. We'd have to revisit the sketch again.

I tried another question. "Did *she* deserve it?"

"She did," he replied icily, "but for an entirely different reason than the others."

"Care to elaborate?"

"How's Jimmy C?"

I chuckled darkly. "Wearing his soon-to-be-scars proudly."

"Tell him I like the photo he posted this morning from the hospital room, the one he took of himself in the mirror. The short post didn't highlight me, just offered a nonspecific overview. Great by-line though: 'The Mesmerizing Mind of a Meticulous Murderer'. It has a certain alliterative appeal."

"He had to keep mum; hence, the non-reference to you," I advised nonchalantly. "Why'd you call?"

"I missed your voice and pretty face—well, *all* your voices and pretty faces, for that matter. How long's that new guy hanging around?"

"Does it matter?"

"I suppose not. He looks quite intense, and kind of dangerous. He can play as well, if he wants. I'll be calling again soon."

"Don't make it *too* soon."

He chuckled merrily and severed the call.

* * *

At two, thirty minutes after finishing lunch, Cash and I were lying on the grass, him staring at the sky with one arm casually draped over my upper chest while my head rested on his stomach. I'd been reviewing what we knew, or suspected, about GRP but frequently found myself drifting to thoughts of Cash—how pleasant it felt to be mellowing with him like this, enjoying the moment, and the tranquility.

He'd located the man—Bez Orger—who'd delivered G.R. Pea's payment to Jeb and left an urgent message with him to call him as soon as possible. Fingers crossed Orger would call soon, and with something worthwhile to share.

My colleagues were on the three-seater, sipping lemonade and reading—Rey a highbrow fashion magazine, Linda a James Joyce novel, and Sach napping on the chaise longue, a bunny on his belly. Jimmy C, who still hadn't recalled much of the night previous, had just left. He'd catch up with us tomorrow.

"Do you miss being a weathergirl, uh, meteorologist?"

"Sometimes. I really liked being on the scene and doing community features."

"Let's test your memory. What's the name of those clouds?"

I scanned the sky, recalling how often I'd informed viewers about cloud formations. "Cirrocumulus stratiformis, a type of cirrocumulus cloud."

He chuckled. "Care to elaborate?"

"Would you like me to?"

"Not really." He chuckled again. "This is quite nice, lying here, being in the moment."

I brought a hand to the arm crooked around my chest. "I'd had a similar thought. And it is quite nice. You're not your usual demanding, abrasive self."

Rich temple-bell laughter rang forth.

I smiled, enjoying the sound. "You're an odd man, Cash Layton Jones. Why'd you come back to Oahu? To meet with people and tend to things, like you so casually advised?"

His smile was so fleeting, I'd have missed it if I'd blinked. "To an extent ... but also to see you."

"I don't buy that."

He grasped my chin and turned my face towards his. "I care about you more than I'll ever admit."

I scanned an unusually solemn face and, unable to resist, rolled over and pressed my lips to his. "It appears you just did."

His arms curled around my back.

"Hey! If you're going to get smoochy, do it inside!"

We gazed up to find Rey peering down, the magazine curled in one hand.

"Don't make me beat you." The magazine rose threateningly. "We've got a good three hours before we need to get ready to leave. Why don't you two use it to get reacquainted?" She pointed to the house with the magazine and smiled impishly.

Cash looked at me. "Why don't we?"

CHAPTER THIRTY-TWO

"This place is quite something," Sach murmured as we walked along the winding path illuminated by metallic LED tiki torches that simulated flickering flames. "I'm glad we opted for dress-up instead of jeans and Ts."

Linda concurred as we stepped up to Steaming Mimi's two-door glass entrance, etched with the restaurant's name and abstract swirls representing steam. Tall, floor-to-ceiling windows ran along the entire restaurant as did *alahe'e*, which had been pruned into hedges.

"Quite something," Sach repeated as he opened the door and we stepped onto a vast terrazzo-tiled floor.

Inside, ambient lighting was provided by suspension lamps with interlocking squares of vibrant amber. Soft jazz played in the background as four-dozen guests—well-dressed and well-heeled—milled about, laughing and chatting and sipping from flutes decorated with plumeria. A long buffet table at the far rear was being organized by three women in cobalt-blue tuxedos. To the side of an open window, stood a tall slim but well-toned man with long blond hair and a GQ face; he was welcoming people with kisses to cheeks and hearty handshakes. Blaze?

"They've got enough lights in here to illuminate Broadway

and then some, but considering the amount, you'd think the place would be brighter," Rey said as she scanned the long, curved bar to the right that opened onto a covered rooftop deck. On it was a small, curved bar with five curvy, molded plywood chairs and a dozen metallic high-top tables with tall twisted candles on them.

"It's very futuristic, in a subtle sort of way."

Linda agreed with Sach. "The way it's laid out, with the double-high ceiling and niches, it's almost like a spaceship pod." She motioned to the far left. "The lounge reminds me of Ten Forward."

Sach looked blank.

"The lounge in *Star Trek: The Next Generation*."

"Not my cup of tea, but I am all for that miniature Niagara Falls of flavorsome bubbles." Sach gestured a four-tier silver champagne fountain at the lounge entrance. "Shall we?"

"Let's!" Rey hooked an arm through his and another through Linda's and led the way.

Cash chuckled and we followed. The two of us never did get "reacquainted". When we'd slipped into my bedroom, he'd received an "urgent must-take" call. It lasted longer than me, because after three minutes, I'd climbed into bed and fallen into a deep sleep. When he finally did return, fifteen minutes later— so he regretfully admitted—he'd tucked the cover under my chin and returned to the three-seater on the lanai with the intention of pursuing leads for us ... then, too, had dozed off.

I scanned nearby faces as Cash and Sach filled fancy flutes but didn't recognize anyone. Adwin was likely overseeing the food preparations in the kitchen.

Cash passed me a full flute and nodded to the far wall decorated with dozens of sable-black wood panels placed at angles to create a fin-like design. Subdued lighting flowed from behind. Impressive, to say the least.

A man resembling bearing a resemblance to a young Karl Lagerfeld, with ponytail and high stand-up collar, engaged Sach in an animated conversation; the four of us were fine with simply standing at the side of the lounge and observing the crowd and new arrivals.

"Oh my. Can you spell awkward?" Linda asked quietly as my ex-beau sauntered in view.

"Yeah. A-d-w-i-n," Rey answered.

He stopped five yards away and gazed from me to Cash, and back again, his expression neutral. The handsome plaid Marc New York suit, a pale pink tea rose affixed to the jacket, suited him well. As he took a step toward us, a handsome couple glided before him and began to make conversation.

"I could use a refill." My cousin held up her flute and peered at me. "You?"

I swallowed the remaining champagne, an extra-dry one with hints of crisp citrus, apple and toasty flavors. Not cheap. "Fill 'er up."

"It's too bad Jimmy C decided not to come. He'd have enjoyed this," Linda said with a frail smile.

"I think the reality of what transpired has only started to sink in. He needs quiet time," I said casually.

"Didn't you say earlier you were going to share a theory?" Cash asked.

"Didn't *you* say you were going to reveal some findings?" I asked drolly, recalling the brief exchange. Sach's arrival to drive us here had put a halt to the conversation.

"You first," he grinned.

"I wouldn't call it a theory on my part. More like a notion. I—"

Adwin stepped before us. "I'm glad you could make it."

"Did you not expect us to?" Rey asked drily as she strode around him and handed me a filled-to-the-brim flute.

Before he could respond, the GQ-faced kisser-greeter ambled up. "Errol wants to see us in the kitchen."

"This is my partner, Blaze." Adwin made quick introductions.

"Interesting name," my cousin commented. "Your dad a fire-fighter or something?"

Blaze winked and, holding a hand to Adwin's back, led him to the kitchen.

"He reminds me of Fabio."

"Your ex?" Linda asked, watching them slip behind a slate-black swinging door.

"No. The *I-can't-Believe-it's-Not-Butter* guy … a coupla decades earlier."

* * *

"Huh?" I forced open heavy eyes and found myself in Cash's arms in my bedroom. "What happened?"

"You and your cousin partook of the champagne fountain a few too many times … when you weren't dancing," he replied with an amused smile as he propped me in the armchair. "You two made quite a hit. Who knew you had moves like that?"

"We had a good time?" I hoped we'd not done any lamp-shade-on-the-heads hopping or limboing.

"I'd say so."

"Other's were dancing, too, right?" I oh-so wished.

"They were," he grinned. "Thanks to you two pulling them onto a makeshift dance floor. I'm not sure your ex-boyfriend was too pleased, but his partner seemed to be enjoying himself with his two lovely dance partners."

I groaned. "I feel a hangover coming on."

"So soon?" He chuckled and removed the Nine West dot-print shirt and hung it in the closet. Kenneth Cole pants followed.

I turned away when he started slipping off boxer-briefs. "I think I need a wake-up, sober-up shower."

He donned a black knee-length silk robe that I always kept on hand for his visits (yeah, psychotherapy was a definite must). "I'll come along to make sure you don't slip down the drain."

"Ha-ha—ah." I clamped my lips as I heard GRP's familiar taunt slip from them.

He took out a fleecy robe and draped it over his shoulder, then grabbed me gently by the hands and pulled me to my bare feet. Not wanting to disturb Rey or Linda, or the kids for that matter, we strolled silently into the dark hallway and to the bathroom.

The metallic three-light vanity light above the circular glass vessel sink provided subdued, no smack-in-the-face lighting. After gulping back a glass of tepid water and splashing my face several times, I pulled out two fluffy bath towels from the free-standing bathroom floor cabinet.

Not as self-conscious as I might have been [had I been more clearheaded], I slipped off my clothes and stepped into the clear-glass panel shower enclosure, Cash on my heels. Hot water on, I poured soft soap on a natural bath sponge.

He took it from my hands and began to lather my neck and shoulders. Suddenly he frowned and sniffed. "Rose ...?"

"Rose-plumeria."

"Great."

I slapped suds on his cheek, and he reciprocated. Within seconds we were full of fragrant lather, acting silly and feeling [relatively] fine—so much so, we'd not noticed the arrival of my cousin.

We jumped when we sighted her, dressed in a short-sleeve V-neck nightie, her nose pressed against the glass.

I swung open the door. "For the love of—"

"As Lindy-Loo might say, don't get your knickers in a knot." She peered from me to Cash and then down the length of his frame. "Nice chassis."

"You looking for a threesome?" he asked sardonically.

"I'm done with those, thanks."

He and I exchanged glances and then looked back at her with questioning brows.

"On the drive back, you said you had some info on Caprize,

but before you could share, Sach burst into the Village People song that had started playing. Linda and then you two joined in and all was forgotten. By the way, don't quit your day job, Cousin Jilly."

"Speaking of, where's your sidekick?" Cash peered over her shoulder.

"Putting on a pot of tea and waiting for us in the kitchen."

"This couldn't wait until the morning?"

"Curiosity got the better of me. I couldn't sleep. Then it got Linda, too. And it's only a little bit after midnight."

He rolled his eyes and asked brusquely, "You want to give us five?"

"I'll give you fifteen, if you like," she said with a Pikachu smile. "Meet you downstairs, honey-buns."

He watched her step into the hallway. "That cousin of yours has the same effect as a cold shower."

"Which might prove perfect for a full wake-up." I cranked the tap to cold, prompting us to screech simultaneously.

CHAPTER THIRTY-THREE

"Welcome," Linda smiled, pouring mint-fragranced tea from a high-gloss three-quart tea kettle. She nodded to the kitchen chairs and motioned a tray of cookies and crackers on the counter. Rey grabbed it, placed it on the table, and took a seat.

I glanced out the window as I sat, noticing rain had started to stream. "At 12:30, this *really* couldn't wait?"

"Of course not." Rey bit into a no-name ginger cookie. She eyed it critically for several seconds, then jammed the remainder in her mouth and eyed Cash. "So? Spill."

He smiled smugly and spooned manuka honey into his mug of tea. "There's not that much to spill, but I did find out a few facts about your dead stalkee."

We leaned forward like eager gamblers watching a spinning roulette casino wheel.

Which prompted him to smile smugly again. "She was married three-and-a-half years ago in Cali, which is where she lived since the age of nine—"

"Surely not *alone*?" Linda interrupted.

Cash shook his head. "With her mother. They'd moved there from here after a piece-of-work father left them—"

"For another woman?" she interjected.

"Unknown." His gaze narrowed. "What *was* known: he got very nasty when drunk."

Rey tsked and chewed another cookie.

"Caprize studied marketing and theater and appeared to do all right after graduation. Got a job in a small, established advertising firm. The mother, Maranza, worked in a magazine kiosk until she died—she was hit by a bus one night after work. One witness said he'd thought he'd seen someone push her, but there was nothing to substantiate this and no one to back him up."

"That sucks," my cousin murmured, peering at the rain thrumming the window.

Bonzo hopped in and onto his mom's lap, his whiskers twitching furiously. We chuckled and offered the longed-for pats and coos.

"It's really odd that she never mentioned being married." Linda got up to make more tea.

"Maybe it didn't end well, and she preferred to forget it," Rey offered.

"There's nothing to be found about a divorce," Cash said.

"Maybe the hubby died," my cousin suggested, tugging Bonzo's ears playfully.

"Then why is there no mention or obit?"

"What was his name?" I asked.

"S. G. Maye."

We stared at Cash.

"Yeah, same last name as one of your chess players, but different spelling."

"Same initials," I put forth.

"That's no coincidence." With a furrowed brow, Linda spooned loose-leaf tea into a second teapot. "But let's verify. Was he someone of note? What did he do?"

"Unfortunately, I haven't heard back from my contact. She said she'd be checking to see if more info can be found."

"Anything about *Slim Mei*?"

"The last thing she had on Slim was that he was working in

community theater, doing make-up and set design, and playing small roles. That dates back about six years ago."

"It's got to be him," Rey stated firmly.

I had to agree. "He must have kept his hands clean, though. Nothing became of that animal-abuse charge when he was younger—"

"Because Meyers Beenie was the perp," Linda stated.

"It appears this guy was never arrested for anything." Cash patted Button when she flopped onto his feet. "But then he's not been on the radar for a few years, either."

"Maybe the guy became a recluse," Linda offered with a shrug.

"How does a 'recluse' end up marrying someone like Caprize?" Rey sniffed. "*If* your Maye and our Mei are one and the same."

"Given the two had theater in common, maybe they met at one," I put forth, eyeing my untouched tea. With a sigh, I gulped back half.

Rey slapped the table, making us jump and Bonzo leap from her lap. "Why don't we call his mother and see what we can find out?"

Linda slapped the table with equal fervor. "What a great idea."

"You three ladies aren't all good looks," Cash smirked.

"Ha-ha." Rey stuck out her tongue and looked at the clock. "Think she'd like to be awakened before sunrise?"

"Not likely." I stood and stretched. "Speaking of awakening, how about we do that in a few hours? I'm all for bed."

Cash rose, extended his arms, and offered an exaggerated wink. "So am I."

* * *

I was pretty certain we'd all slipped into a deep sleep as soon as our heads hit the pillows.

Eight the next morning saw Rey, Linda and myself awake and alert, once again in the kitchen, with coffee, whole-wheat toast and boysenberry jam, my cell phone and Linda's laptop. This morning found us in jeans and T-shirts; the day, though cloudy and breezy, promised to be hot. Cash was AWOL. Apparently, "duty" had called during the wee hours.

Rey nodded to my phone. "Ready?"

I nodded and had Linda read Alaina-Lei Mei's number out loud. Three rings later, a deep husky voice—like someone suffering from laryngitis—answered.

"Ms. Mei?"

"Yes?" Her wary tone suggested she suspected a telemarketer was calling.

The four of us had invented a story re the phone call. I wrote under the name of Jimmy C and was doing a series on critical-care nursing from different perspectives—the job and responsibilities, the required skills, the personal life apart from the professional. Her name had been acquired courtesy of a colleague at UCLA Medical Center. The problem? I didn't feel comfortable duping someone of Alaina-Lei Mei's background. She didn't deserve that.

"I was a friend of your son's wife—Caprize Marquessa de Sade. My name's JJ Fonne and I work with the local police here on Oahu."

My colleagues dropped their jaws.

She didn't respond. Not a sigh or inhalation, or word.

"I wouldn't have called, but no one can seem to locate him, and I wanted him to know that she … passed."

"I haven't heard from Slim in a few weeks," she said, scraping something—a chair probably. "But his wife's name is Pree. I have no idea who this Caprize Zadie is."

"Oh, I must be confused. Perhaps she was a *friend* of his?" I asked gently.

"Possibly but, as I said, I don't know that name."

"Hmm. Well, maybe she knew Pree, too. How is Slim's wife?"

"I haven't seen her or my son in some time, but she was quite in love with my Slim."

I could hear the smile in her voice. "Well, given we can't locate Slim, we're not sure if he's aware … about Caprize, I mean. That's why we thought we would reach out to you," I said quietly.

"A year ago, he received a good part in a popular play in New York, and he wanted to pursue that—his big break, if you like. They decided to part ways for the time being, amiably of course, until he was settled and all that. He calls me from there every week, always excited about the theater and the city," she chuckled. "I believe he's still there, because he's not mentioned anything about moving the last couple of times we spoke."

"Do you have a number?"

"For his virtual call-answering service, yes. He's so busy, you know? It's right here, hold on." She came back fifteen seconds later and provided the number.

I took a stab. "When was the wedding and how was it? Did Pree look as pretty as a postcard with that lovely, luxurious hair?" I'd have added the color, but if I was wrong, I might have made her suspicious.

"It was almost four years ago and was a city-hall affair," she said with a wistful sigh. "They both looked so handsome—him in that white tuxedo and she in that vintage beige two-piece, which set up her caramel-brown hair quite nicely."

"… Slim really enjoys acting, doesn't he?"

"As much as he enjoys doing make-up. He's so very good at both." Spoken like a proud mother.

"You must be very pleased with all he's achieved so far."

"He's not achieved half the things he's hoped to," she confided. "But he's been such a blessing to me. Calling and sending flowers and/or chocolates regularly." A pensive sigh. "Taking care of me when I was stricken with cancer."

269

"He moved back home for that period?" I asked casually.

"No, I couldn't have him give up his life like that. He paid for someone to stay with me while I was recovering. But he called daily and made sure I was taking my medication, eating properly, that the caregiver he'd hired was doing a good job."

Could someone doing theater and make-up in NYC make enough to afford a caregiver? Not likely, but as I always said, never say never. "He's been very good to you, but then he's been very lucky to have a loving, giving mother like yourself. It wasn't easy, was it, raising him alone after your husband divorced you?"

"We managed," she replied simply. "I have no regrets, or anger, and I certainly bear no malice towards my ex. He is … was … what he was."

"A self-centered and greedy man with an eye for younger women, among other things."

"You know him?"

"I've had the non-pleasure of knowing him," I said evasively. She twittered.

"Would you happen to have a recent photo of Slim? It would be nice to add him to a photo collage made for Caprize's services."

"Just one of him as Donalbain in *Macbeth* that's about four, maybe five years old. He was performing in a theater in Boston, I believe."

"That will do nicely." I gave her Linda and my email addresses. "Hopefully, I can connect with him and he can get here in time, if he plans to attend."

Alaina-Lei Mei wished me luck.

"Oh, one last question?"

"Yes?"

"Does he still play a mean game of chess?"

She laughed. "He was a remarkable player, my Slim was. Come to that, so was Pree. The last time I saw those two, at their Astoria apartment, they'd played for four hours straight."

She chuckled again, then exhaled slowly. "That's such sad news about his friend. Too young, I'm sure, to have passed. You know, I'd best call him myself and let him know. Why don't you give me your number, JJ, and I'll have him call you?"

"I believe he already has it, but sure."

After providing it and wishing her well, I decided to make one more call—to an associate we'd met at a private-eye conference.

"Shane, would you mind looking up a marriage license. The fellow's name is S.G. Maye and the girl's name is Pree. That's all I know about her. Please try S.G. Mei and Caprize Marquessa de Sade, too."

"You got it," the forty-seven-year-old said gaily. "Next time I'm in town, you owe me a night on it—dinner, drinks, *and* dancing."

"You got it. Dinner, drinks, and a hula lesson!"

* * *

Cash and I decided to walk along the Ala Wai Canal mid morning and then have Mai-Tais on the beach. At 10:30 we were parked by the Honolulu Zoo and strolling, hand-in-hand, toward the narrow waterway.

He picked a plumeria from the first tree of many lining the sidewalk and tucked it behind my left ear.

"Since when did you become a romantic?" I joked, touching the flower. "And I'm not married."

"But you're unavailable." He smiled fleetingly and scanned the golf club on the *mauka* side. "Ever play?"

"Never had an interest," I confessed.

"Me either." He gestured. "Weren't those four bodies—the two couples—found somewhere nearby?"

I motioned toward Laau Street and we resumed walking, remaining silent, nodding to passersby, enjoying the early day despite the clouds and lack of sun. Still, it was hot and humid, and I was glad I'd decided to wear shorts.

"Penny for your thoughts?" he asked after several minutes.

"I've been reconsidering everything that's transpired since that night we found those four." I stopped and eyed the Ala Wai Community Boathouse. "As well as Jimmy C's comment re 'two-faced'."

"And?" He slipped an arm lightly around my waist and we resumed our stroll, nearing the McCully Bridge.

"Given GRP—if he's indeed Slim—was married, might it not be possible that his wife was also his partner in crime? Jimmy C didn't mean two-faced like Janus, but literally, *two faces*."

"If, JJ, if. But you may have something there; maybe someone *was* with him—that partner in crime, wife or otherwise." He glanced sideward. "What about his mom saying he lived in New York and giving you a number to reach him?"

"You're testing me." I smiled. "She gave me the number to an answering service there. That doesn't mean he's still living there, if he lived there at all."

He smiled. "Go on."

"What if he was *here* all along ... with Caprize?"

"As in hubby and wifey?"

"Or boyfriend and girlfriend." I offered a limp shrug. "I can't wait to hear the name on that marriage license."

We reached McCully Street Bridge and I motioned *makai*—we could head to Kalakaua, maybe do a bit of window-shopping and then go over to the beach.

"Why kill her if she was his wife or girlfriend? But, if neither, why *her*?"

"Maybe, as said wife or girlfriend, she didn't want to continue," I replied. "Maybe she said or did something to piss him off. Maybe she was no longer of use to him." I sighed at length. "And, if neither, maybe he thought she was worth sacrificing. We knew her, so that may have played a major reason. And she could seem a little standoffish, so that might have galled him. He has something against moneyed people and, while she was far from having Richard Rijk Mei's level of wealth, she was doing decently on the financial front." I chuckled wryly. "I'm picking at straws."

A soft drizzle began to fall, but we continued walking.

"Picking at straws can sometimes provide answers. But something certainly ticked him off," Cash said. "Unfortunately, we might never know the extent of her involvement or what she did to end up becoming a victim. Because, even if she was involved, it will be solely his word."

I concurred and sighed.

"Where to?"

I motioned the main boulevard. "Let's walk to the Cheesecake Factory and then turn back to the beach."

"So, what's with Adwin?"

I smiled and hooked an arm through his. "Jealous?"

"Should I be?"

I shrugged. "I like his new look and personality. But I'm not feeling attracted, if that's what you're asking. But, then, we haven't spent a lot of time alone since he arrived."

"You think he might spark something ... with time?"

I stopped before a shave-ice kiosk across from the International Market Place and regarded him intently. "What if that happened?"

His lips pulled into a tight line. "I'd be ... sad."

"Sad?" I snorted, then laughed. "I retract the comment about 'romantic'."

He smiled, but not with cheer, and motioned the kiosk. "Shave ice?"

"With boba and mochi?"

"Of course."

CHAPTER THIRTY-FOUR

Cash gestured the dark clouds hovering above Magic Island, a small man-made peninsula bordering Ala Moana Beach Park and the Ala Wai Yacht Club. "Think we're in for more rain?"

"Yes, but we have the handy-dandy covering above." I gestured the market umbrella and toasted him with one of the just-arrived Mai-Tais.

We were seated in the Barefoot Bar at a round table before the boardwalk. So were two dozen others, most of them happy [glassy-eyed] tourists. *The Saint* announced a call.

Cash arched an eyebrow while his expression asked, *"Really?"*

I winked and greeted Rey, whose number was on display.

"You'll never guess!"

"Of course I won't, unless you give me a clue."

My cousin offered a moderate raspberry. "Our detective pal called—"

"Hives?" I asked drolly.

"Hives-Ives, whatever. They found something in Caprize's mouth. You'll never guess what."

"You know what? I'm going to take a stab and go with a rose."

"Nope. It was a—"

"Chess piece!"

"Pretty good. You should become a psychic," she laughed.

"Yeah, it was a sterling-silver pawn to be exact."

"Interesting choice."

"Maybe it has something to do with the message our friend texted Linda an hour ago: *A sacrificed pawn.*"

"That's even more interesting."

"You want something even more, *more* interesting?" Rey asked, suddenly sounding solemn.

"Do I?" I asked tentatively.

"I found a sterling-silver chess piece just before I called you, by Bonzo's basket. Apparently, he or one of the other kids, found it and thought it was a new toy. Wanna guess which piece?"

"I'm going to go with … a king. Am I right?"

"Did you have a vision or something? Because you got it," she confirmed.

"Any notes?"

"If there was one, it was probably chewed or eaten, and/or tucked where we won't find it for days to come, if ever." She exhaled loudly. "Do you think Ms. Mei got a hold of her son?"

"She left him a message, to be sure."

"Should we be sharing our thoughts with our friends in blue re the wunderkind being GRP?"

"We should, but let's hold off another day," I replied, scanning the ocean, wondering what the next steps ought to be. "Although a lot suggests he's GRP, we really have no proof, just a lot of coincidences and suppositions … and our P.I. gut instincts. Let's not inflict our lovely selves and beliefs on Ald just yet. He's got enough on his hands."

"Fair enough. Linda's calling me from the lanai. Catch ya later, alligator!"

I grinned and placed my cell on the table, envisioning my cousin's long, toned legs carrying her through the house with that Reynalda Fonne-Werde melodramatic flair.

"What's up, buttercup?" Cash asked airily.

My grin widened. "You been spending time with my cous?"

He chuckled and I relayed what she had told me.

The Saint blared forth again and Cash picked up the phone and checked the display. "It's your cousin again." He answered the call. After three uh-huhs, two grunts, and a farewell, he passed the cell. "Linda received a photo of Slim, as did you. She wants you to check your email."

Excited, I opened the pic. Slim was smiling for the camera, dressed in a dull-toned seventeenth-century costume, arms crossed. Theatrical make-up was thick, exaggerated, as were the shadows created by stage lighting. "You know, given Slim does make-up, I bet you he's good at disguising himself."

"It's too bad we don't have a clue where to find him."

"He's close by." I took a long sip of the delicious, icy cocktail. "I can feel it in that private-eye gut of mine."

He smiled wryly. "Do you really want to hold off telling Ives and his team? This ass could take another life, or more."

I gazed across the beach where a group of teens were tossing a Frisbee. "He won't, not yet. It's our move."

"And what *is* that move?"

"To get a better feel for Caprize ... by going through her place."

* * *

At nine, Cash and I were seated in my Jeep, Rey and Linda in Linda's Toyota Camry XLE V6, three doors down from Caprize's dark house. The only sign that anything was out of the ordinary was the official seal.

A light rain had started to fall a few minutes ago, as it had off and on most of the day and evening. It was still hot and humid. The street was devoid of traffic and pedestrians; given it was Sunday night, people were likely readying for another work week and/or avoiding the mugginess.

"Your cousin's still eating Twizzlers and listening to music on her MP3 player," Cash announced wryly as he turned back to me, binoculars in hand.

"She's developed a thing for licorice and Il Volo." I took the binoculars and peered at the house. "Think we should go in?"

"You mean, *break* in," he mocked. "Maybe you should have taken your friend Gail's offer of accompanying us. Having a member of the police in tow is never a bad idea, especially when caught."

"We didn't want *her* to get caught if *we* got caught, but that's a big if, because we won't," I replied firmly. "You should have stayed home, too. The last thing you want is for your drug-dealer persona to be detained doing something 'suspicious'. Ald Ives would just love to get you behind bars."

"Didn't you just say we *won't* be caught?" he teased.

"Ha-ha … uh."

He squeezed my hand. "Too bad I'm heading back so soon. We haven't had much 'we' time."

"Not 'up close and personal time' anyway." I offered a quick smile and scanned his face in the dimness. "I still can't believe how different … un-aggressive you are this trip." I leaned close and peered into his eyes. "Who *are* you really? What have you done with the arrogant and abrasive Cash Layton Jones?"

"People change."

"*That* much?"

He smiled, but again there was no cheer. "Listen, there are some fairly tense and serious things going on in my Richie J life and lifestyle right now—"

"More than the usual drug-dealing, weapon-wielding routine of an undercover agent slash drug lord?" I asked with a sardonic smile.

"Things are coming to a climax," he responded flatly, then shrugged and sighed. "Look, this isn't the best time to tell you this, but it may be the only time …"

I tensed, sensing something in his manner and tone that promised to be unpleasant. "So, go for it."

"Given who I am and what I do in Florida, and what's going down, I've kind of been seeing a kingpin's daughter for a few months now."

"Kind of?"

"… We've kind of become engaged."

"Kind of?" I repeated disdainfully. "Someone twisted your arm? Or is this a shotgun wedding?"

"I can't share the details, because—"

"Yeah, yeah, they're classified and, therefore, confidential. Something like that," I said sarcastically.

An urgent tap-tap-tap on the window caused us to jump. Rey's face was pressed against the glass; it meant business.

"Time to rock and roll." I hopped out of the Jeep and managed not to slam the door—but barely. I should have known. It had been too good to be true. When had Cash entered and re-entered my life and *not* done something to irritate or drive me crazy? Always expect the unexpected—and disagreeable (to put it lightly)—from the man with the penchant for expensive Aloha shirts. I *really* needed to walk away once and for all time.

"Oh-oh. A fight?" Rey asked quietly, scanning our expressions under the dim street lighting.

"Where's Linda?"

"She thought it best to keep guard."

"What good is that going to do if we're in the house?" I questioned with a frown.

"She'll be in those shrubs." My cousin indicated the hedges bordering the house to our immediate left. "She'll do one of her bird calls."

"You're the one with the bird calls," I reminded her. "And how will we hear them if we're inside?"

"She's learned to buzz like a Golden-Winged Warbler. And we'll make sure a couple of windows are open as we check out the place when we're in there."

I raised a skeptical eyebrow and looked at Cash, who'd just climbed out of the Jeep. "Ready?" I asked coolly.

He nodded once and Rey tsked twice before motioning us forward.

* * *

Inside the two-story townhouse, we slipped on latex gloves before ensuring blinds and shades were properly drawn and lighting was minimal. To guarantee that we heard Linda's potential warning "buzz" we also opened windows a fraction. With muttered promises to work quickly, Rey took the basement, I the rest of the house, and Cash the studio/*ohana*.

Rummaging through drawers and closets provided little of interest. In truth, I had no idea what to look for, but I was pretty sure that if something important were to be found, I'd recognize it. In the cupboards and desks on the first floor were floral and agency photos, receipts, brochures, notes and recipes, and kitchen and office stuff. For a second, I considered dumping them all the photos into my knapsack, but then decided against it. They'd probably be of little value and if Ald ever found out, he'd not be happy; I could hear the heated lecture now.

The second floor didn't provide much of note either. It was only after pawing around underneath her bed and bedroom nightstand that I discovered something of note—a key to a house. The one off Makaniolu Place maybe? I tucked it into my jeans.

The last place to investigate was the walk-in closet. Bright light on, I took a swift look-see at countless clothes. Nice. Expensive. A lot of it vintage.

Four-dozen shoe boxes were stacked in one far corner. To open or not to open? With a sigh, I quickly went through them. The second box from the bottom revealed an interesting find: six photos of Caprize in various poses on beach sand, one of her dressed in a 20s flapper with accessories of the period, and two wedding photos of Caprize and someone who could have been Slim, given the build and close-set eyes. Both were rather grainy —for effect?—but the twosome made for a happy-looking couple. So, was this what Slim looked like without make-up or costumes? Or was he sporting expertly applied theatrical make-up? Hard to tell. Curious. Why didn't Alaina-Lei Mei have more photos of her son? Or had she lied and said she had only the one? I took a wedding shot and put the rest back in the box.

There was a "bonanza" find in the very last shoe box: wrapped in a red-and-blue polka-dot scarf was an overstitch wheel roulette, and a costly one at that. The type of tool that GRP might have used on his victims. Holding it cautiously, I peered closely but saw no blood. It looked new, so it might never have been used or, if so, maybe only once or twice, then methodically cleaned. Into my knapsack the box went.

A glance at my Fossil watch told me I'd been searching for more than thirty-five minutes. Time to catch up with Rey, collect Linda, and meet Cash back at the Jeep.

* * *

"Anything?" Linda whispered, moving alongside, as Rey and I slipped from the house and hurried toward the cars.

"A photo, a key, and a roulette," I replied and turned to Rey. "You?"

She stopped us before the Jeep, not far from Cash, who was leaning by the gas tank, arms crossed. "Howdy-Doody's driver's license ... in a silver frame, no less."

Linda whistled softly. "We should drop off your finds at the station."

"You call Ald and tell him Rey and I will head over, or meet him somewhere if he's not there." I jerked a thumb at Cash. "Why don't you take lover boy back to the house? We'll meet you there as soon as we can."

Linda, Rey and I looked at him, which prompted him to straighten and eye us expectantly, and perhaps a little worriedly.

"Keys," Rey requested firmly, holding out her hand. "My cous and I have a stop to make. You're with Linda."

"I—"

"Hand 'em over or else." She stepped up to him and leaned in close.

He looked like he might argue, then thought better of it; when Cousin Reynalda had that tone and expression, you listened. *Or else.*

CHAPTER THIRTY-FIVE

"Perfect timing," my cousin murmured as we entered a small coffee shop near the intersections of Kalakaua and Ala Moana. At 10:30 it was still busy. Guess no one had worries about ingesting caffeine so late in the evening.

Ald Ives was seated at a corner table, dressed in designer jeans and a black long-sleeve hooded T-shirt, sipping a beverage while reading what appeared to be—given the horses, hats, and badges—a western. He glanced up, his expression neutral, and waited for us to sit.

"So, you did some B&E," he said with a salty smile, placing the book beside a huge half-empty mug. "I'm no longer surprised. And, oddly enough, not angry or even annoyed."

"… We checked out Caprize's place," I responded. "And found some items of note."

He motioned the waitperson, who was strolling by with an empty tray. "Two hot chocolates drizzled with caramel, heavy on the whipped."

Rey thanked him and pulled out Howdy-Doody's license. "Nice, huh? Vera Wang frame, no less."

He remained silent as he scrutinized the legal document.

"In my knapsack," I motioned, "is a photo and a roulette. No, there's no blood on it, at least that I can see."

"We think Slim Mei's GRP," Rey announced, leaning forward and staring intently.

"And you have proof, besides what you've presented this evening?" he smiled drily. "While interesting, these things don't serve as proof of anything illegal—unless we find DNA from a victim, which I seriously doubt. Nor can I take your word that this Slim guy is the killer."

"For heaven's sake, Detective Need-to-Have-Proof-Slapped-in-the-Head," Rey snorted. "It's a murdered guy's license! In a frame!"

"That you had no warrant to go and 'take' ... and she isn't around to explain. If memory serves correctly, she was talking to him that night. Maybe he dropped it and she found it."

"And kept it *and* framed it?" she demanded. "You don't keep something like this for no reason."

With a frown, he eyed the license lying on the table. "It's unfortunate we don't have a clue where Mr. GRP is."

"He's close," I affirmed. "Probably watching us at this very moment."

Like a Kit-Cat wall clock, our eyes moved from left to right, right to left.

The hot chocolates arrived and we sipped in silence for several minutes, surreptitiously scanning the shop and the sidewalk and street. Finally, Rey and I offered Ald all that we'd learned or considered over the last couple of days.

"Intriguing notion," he said, "that Jimmy C might have seen two faces and, hence, the reference to 'two-faced'."

"More than intriguing," Rey spat. "Quite probably *fact*."

He tilted his head one way and then the other.

"Maybe you should compare this photo with the one Linda and I received from Slim's mother and my sketch of the stalker?" I suggested, thinking we'd do the same. Linda had taken a couple of photos of the wedding photo I'd taken, as well as Howdy-Doody's license, so we had them handy.

He nodded. "Even if there are similarities—"

"You won't jump on it," Rey scowled. "Couldn't you call Slim Mei a 'person of interest' and pursue that angle?"

He didn't respond, merely stared.

Rey rolled her eyes and turned to me. "You wanna head back?"

"I think I'll stay at a hotel tonight." A just-in-case overnight bag always rested in the rear of the Jeep, so I'd be fine for two days, if necessary.

"We can become guest-free. I only need to say a word or three."

"It's quite likely he's already left, given he's got things to, uh, see to," I said quietly. "I'll think I'll just stay at a hotel, if you don't mind."

She eyed me keenly, then nodded. "I can take the Jeep if the detective here drives you. Is it hard to drive stick-shift?"

My eyebrows nearly flew from my forehead. "You don't know how to drive."

"Wrong-o. I've been taking lessons secretly." She smiled proudly. "I'll be ready to take my test soon."

"Well, you can't drive without a license and unless your lessons have included stick-shift vehicles, I don't think you'll be taking the Jeep," I replied with a wry smile.

"Head over to my townhouse, Fonne, and I'll drive your cousin home," Ald announced, standing. "There's a key to the place at the base of the third terra-cotta planter."

"Is that wise, having it readily available like that?"

"No, but it's smart." He winked and looked at Rey. "Ready, Ms. Fonne-*Weird*?"

"Sure, *Hives*."

He simpered and motioned her to lead the way.

* * *

The townhouse was within walking distance of a pool and recreation center, whirlpool and tennis courts, and beach lagoons. The complex in a word: beautiful.

After locating the key in the third terra-cotta planter from the townhouse door and not from the entrance (the man had eight in total), I stepped into a lovely home with a vaulted ceiling and lots of space. I ensured the opaque roller shades were down on all the windows before I allowed curiosity to take control. Slipping off my flats, I took a quick tour.

The three-bedroom, three-bath place—with a full bath on the first level—had neutral wood flooring and ceiling fans everywhere. The kitchen contained new stainless appliances and just to the side was a large laundry. Very nice indeed. Two bedrooms and an office-den were also on the ground floor. There was a private upstairs lanai off the huge master bedroom—tastefully, masculinely decorated—with a large private bath. The man had good taste.

Hearing a car pull up, I ambled back down and opened the front door.

"That cousin of yours can be quite the chatterbox," he said, slipping past. "Or is that blabbermouth?"

I closed the door behind him and chuckled, imagining the spirited drive home.

"I'll show you to your room so you can change and whatnot. If you like, we can share a nice Californian merlot."

"I'm in." I grabbed the overnight bag and followed him to the first bedroom, a small L-shaped room painted and decorated in shades of shell and sand.

"There are a couple of fleecy robes in the closet, as well as a few pairs of slippers in different sizes. You'll find new toothbrushes and wash-up stuff under the sink."

"You're well prepared."

"Like a Boy Scout." He closed the door behind him.

I took a quick shower, slipped on an oversize, super long Under Armour T-shirt and one of the fleecy robes. As I sat on the cushioned bench before the bed, I wondered if I wasn't acting childish, trying to avoid Cash. Maybe. Probably. But the fact was, I didn't feel like facing him right now. That he was engaged to some kingpin's daughter was ... too much, I supposed. Yes, he was an agent and that required him to do certain things that wouldn't prove agreeable to everyday people—and occasional lovers—who led everyday lives.

A knock preceded Ald's entry. Dressed in white chino shorts and a black V-neck T-shirt, he padded in on bare feet, two crystal goblets hanging from one hand and an uncorked bottle of wine in the other. Filling the glasses, he placed the bottle on one of two gray scallop-decorated nightstands and slipped onto the bench beside me.

I accepted the glass he handed me and smiled. "Thanks for the hospitality."

"I couldn't have you sleeping with a drug lord now, or have your cousin piss him off, could I?" he asked with a tart smile, toasting me. "She could get that pretty face altered."

"Cousin Reynalda can handle herself."

"True, that she can," he smirked.

I sipped. "Nice."

He sipped as well. "Very nice, indeed." He scanned my face and smiled. "You know, I used to have a thing for you."

"Used to?" I asked drolly.

"I got over you ... pretty much." Ald laughed.

I laughed too.

"I guess you only ever had eyes for that loser drug dealer."

"Successful *alleged* loser drug dealer."

He sipped again. "Can I ask? What's with you two?"

I shrugged. "I guess I'm one of those girls who's attracted —*was* attracted—to bad boys."

"He's now a thing of the past? You're not into him anymore? You both seemed so tight."

Another shrug. "He can be a colossal pain in the neck."

The detective smirked. "So, you're here to avoid said pain in the neck?"

I took several small sips, then smiled ruefully. "Something like that."

"Very mature," he joked.

"Very safe," I grinned.

He laughed and we drank in thoughtful silence for a few moments.

"Another glass?"

"Please."

"You know, having you over for the night had always been on the agenda, though not because you're avoiding a jackass," he said, refilling glasses. He gently clanged his against mine as he sat back down. "Welcome to *Chez Ald*."

I looked around the tastefully decorated room. "Nice room and nice digs. You have excellent taste."

"I had help." He eyed me keenly. "That very first day I first laid eyes on you and that abrasive cousin of yours ..."

He didn't finish the sentence but leaned over and kissed me lightly on the lips.

"Was that everything you imagined it to be?" I asked with a dry smile.

"Let's aim for a *real* kiss. Then I'll answer your question."

* * *

"Oh ... wow."

"That good, huh?" Ald mocked.

"No, I mean ... wow, that we're here like this."

"Is that bad?" Ald's hand slipped around my neck and drew me close.

"Not," I whispered, "bad at all."

He pressed his glass to my lips. I mimicked his move and we drained the goblets.

I scanned his attractive face, recalling our history, and murmured, "This is ..."

"Weird?"

"Unexplainable." I laughed lightly.

"Then let's try to *explain* it."

When his lips captured mine; I, like a romance heroine, had no desire to liberate them.

CHAPTER THIRTY-SIX

I headed home at noon after having coffee with Gail and stopping by the office to see that all was still standing, I headed home. Linda was volunteering at a homeless shelter and Rey had advised she was working from home and that Cash had left early that morning (so there was no reason to avoid the place anymore).

"Hey-ho," Rey said cheerfully as I strolled into the kitchen and placed my cell phone and overnight bag on the counter. She was slicing a multi-grain baguette for a brie-and-cuke sandwich. "Care for one?"

"Sure."

"The kids are with Eddy, by the way." She looked up and those grass-green eyes scanned mine, then narrowed. "You slept with Hives!"

How my cousin always knew when I'd been with a guy was beyond me. Maybe she had some extrasensory thing going. Or maybe I just wore guilt like others wore clothes. Not that I truly had anything to feel that guilty about. Ald and I had shared the bed and a lot of kisses and canoodling, but that's where it had stopped. Seeing no need to respond, I went to the fridge to get a couple of cans of club soda and a plastic container with pre-cut slices of lime.

"Like, *really*? I want details."

I was about to respond when I saw Cash standing not far to her left. My mouth fell open; his pulled into a taut line.

"Uh, he dropped by not long ago because he forgot something in your nightstand, so I sent him up. I, uh, yeah well." Rey chewed her bottom lip and resumed slicing, her gaze focused on the task but her ears unquestionably perked.

Cash scrutinized my face for several seconds, then offered a curt nod. "Forgot I'd tucked my wallet in there. Take care, ladies." The tone was brusque, the expression sullen. With that, he strolled past and left via the front door, which closed with a deafening slam.

"Well, that was tense."

"That would be an understatement," I sighed.

"So, how was he?" my cousin asked flatly. "You beginning a new *relationship*? Should Linda and me get used to having the detective sleep over?"

"I'm not sharing my evening escapade with you but, no, I am not beginning a new *relationship*. There'll be no sleeping over." I drew a quick breath and offered a transient smile. "It was just—"

"One of those things?" she asked blandly, slipping four thick slices of bread into the toaster oven.

I grabbed the overnight bag. "I'm going to change. Be down in five."

I stopped. Bongos, sounding strangely like those from an old B-movie beach flick, announced a call on Rey's cell phone. I arched an eyebrow in amusement and she shrugged.

"Hey, you," she said with a smile in her voice. "No worries. That's fine. Keeping checking, if you can… Yeah, catch up soon." She looked at me. "Shane found the marriage license your some-times-uh-former boyfriend did—you know, Maye's. Couldn't find any photos or any more info on this Maye guy. And nothing was found on Slim Mei's or anyone named Pree, either. Not yet anyway."

I sighed and went up to my bedroom, where I slipped into an airy, floral sundress. Just as I was about to head back down, I noticed a flash of red. On the nightstand, in a tall slim vase, were two long-stemmed red roses. Beneath them, a card bearing a small gold heart.

It read: *One day I'll be back on Oahu, working in another capacity. Please accept what I do as something that (hopefully) contributes to helping make a small part of this world a better, safer place. I'll be back soon and I'll make it up to you. Promise. Luv ya.*

Luv ya. An expression he used when he'd spoken to his ex, me, and likely dozens of others. A flippant, unemotional statement. Like "gotta pick up milk" or "I better fill up the tank". Luv ya. A phrase with no passion or promise. I exhaled noisily and brought the vase downstairs.

"Guess you won't be getting any more of those from your 'sometimes boyfriend'." She motioned the table, where the sandwiches and two ice-filled tumblers with soda rested.

"I guess not." I placed the roses and my cell phone on the blue-veined counter, grabbed a jar of spicy pickled veggies from the fridge, and took a seat. "Men."

"Men." She flipped her hair, revealing two pink flamingo earrings with rhinestone feathers.

We ate in silence for several minutes.

"The Saint's back."

"I hear."

"You going to keep Simon Templar waiting?" my cousin smirked.

"I'd like to," I admitted.

She got up and answered. "… Uh-huh. Sure, okay … yeah, gotcha. Hold on." With a solemn expression, she returned to her seat, folded her hands on the table, and watched the kitchen entrance.

Puzzled, I looked there as well.

In walked a man of medium stature, sporting an oddly familiar face, sort of a cross between Shaggy (reddish hair, wide ski-slope type nose, and quasi goatee) from *Scooby-Doo* and Mr. Peabody (oversized black-framed round glasses and bow tie) from *Mr. Peabody & Sherman*. His face bore obvious "pancake make-up", thick and visible. He was dressed in black jeans, an ash-gray sweatshirt from which peeked a white shirt with the aforementioned bow tie, and black Nikes. In a latex-gloved hand was a short-range tranquilizer pistol.

"Where's lovely Linda?" he asked with a husky, croaky voice, perhaps disguising it, given the actor he was.

I managed to push aside disbelief that GRP was standing before us. "You mean you, the ever-watchful, don't know?"

He offered a trim smile, the pistol poised as he hoisted himself onto the counter. "I'm not omnipotent. But knowing you as well as I've come to, I'd say she's volunteering at a shelter, visiting Jimmy C, or attending a blog-related function."

"You've certainly got balls," Rey stated, eyeing him up and down.

GRP smiled again.

"What brings you to our little grass shack?" I asked casually.

"I thought I'd ratchet up the game a bit."

"I didn't take you for a gun man."

Close-set eyes a unique shade of cadet blue (contacts?) glanced at the revolver and a slight frown tugged at wide lips. "I'm not, and it's not a real gun, but a tranquilizer pistol. It seemed necessary for this visit, just in case you decide to do something silly, like knock me over or pursue a citizen's arrest, that kind of thing."

"Now that you're here," Rey said blandly, "why don't you tell us why you killed Caprize?"

There was silence for several seconds, then he laughed. Heartily. "Mom gave me your message."

She looked like she'd been smacked with a wet towel. "You *don't* deny you're Slim?"

"I could, and probably should, but what's the point? That would merely delay the inevitable." He crossed strong legs and motioned the fridge. "Do you think I could have a soda? Please pour it over ice and put it over there." He motioned a spot three feet away.

"Your mother is going to be so very disappointed," I said, getting a cola from the fridge and pouring it into an ice-filled, plastic tumbler.

"I'm a good son."

I plonked the tumbler on the counter. "You're a serial killer."

"You say poh-tay-toe, I say pow-tah-toh."

"You're a *murderer*." I retook my seat.

"And speaking of, let's get back to why you killed Caprize, your pawn, if we read your 'silver' message right," Rey prodded. "She was your wife, right ... S.G. M-a-y-e?"

He simpered. "Yeah, okay. She was."

"Why kill her?"

He stared at Rey for several seconds, as if deciding how much, if anything, he wanted to reveal. Finally, he shrugged. "She screwed up by letting Jimmy C see her face."

"He was drugged. He couldn't remember what actually happened," she pointed out.

"It was a screw-up, nevertheless. Just like the time she'd messed up killing that freckle-faced red-haired guy in the alley."

"Howdy-Doody?"

"Good one. That fits him perfectly." GRP gave a thumb's up. "She fumbled with the actual killing and couldn't do much with the roulette. She had the desire, but not the skill."

"She was trying her best, I'm sure," Rey stated coolly. "Like helping you with the foursome by the canal. She did help with that, didn't she?"

He arched a shoulder.

"She probably loved you to death, uh, yeah."

"She did. I loved her, too. We were thinking of having a baby. I'm rather sorry that's no longer possible. But, to be honest, I was beginning to feel weighed down, and getting more and more annoyed."

"How'd you win her over?" my cousin inquired, regarding him intently.

"I was playing chess in Plummer Park and Caprize happened to be taking a break from a conference. She saw the guy I was playing with leave, so she sat down and asked if I'd be interested in a game of action chess. She played amazingly well. We got to talking and found we had a lot in common: theater, Oahu, theater, chills and thrills, and chess, of course. The two of us probably fell in love that very afternoon."

"I'm guessing you didn't share your 'thrill' of killing right away?" I asked with a flat smile.

He returned the wry smile. "Not *right* away."

"And your killing people didn't upset her?"

"When I finally shared that, she got excited, intrigued ... she wanted to watch *and* partake."

"A marriage made in hell," Rey murmured.

I concurred quietly. "You know we have to go to the police."

"You've already shared your thoughts with them." He looked from me to Rey and back again. "And sharing this little visit won't help much. You won't find me once I leave here. All you'll do is confirm who the Rose-Pin Killer is," he chortled. "Not overly original, and certainly not written in stone, but it has a certain appeal."

He was probably right. "I feel for your mother," I said with a shake of the head. "When she finds out—"

"She doesn't follow the news, JJ, so maybe she'll be spared." He sighed. "For a while anyway."

"Wishful thinking?"

"*Very* wishful thinking," he replied ruefully. "She's done so much for me, stuck by me ..."

"Like the time you were apprehended for mutilating that cat? Was the old guy—Meyers 'Juniper' Beenie, if I recall correctly—your first murder?"

"The guy fell—drunk as a skunk, as that silly expression goes."

Rey eyed him skeptically. "You *really* didn't kill him?"

"No, Rey, dearheart. I did not. He got smashed on gin and tumbled to his death, as reported in the media." He held up a gloved hand. "T'is true. And, contrary to popular belief, as a so-called 'serial killer', I did not—do not—mutilate or kill animals. I respect them and would *never* hurt one. I guess that makes me ... a limited edition."

I chuckled darkly while Rey released a raspberry.

"It's true. I find them quite wonderful. As for Beenie-Boy, he came a across as a nice, quiet kind of man, but he had a mean, dark streak. Not many saw it, but I did. Or rather I *sensed* it. He did kill animals, hundreds I'm sure, but no humans to my or anyone else's knowledge."

"Seeing as we're being so open today, why do you engrave floral designs on your victims?" my cousin asked. "And immerse them in water?"

"Flowers, particularly roses, are an homage to my mother. She loved them. Before my twit of a father divorced her, he destroyed her prized flower gardens. Why? Because that young, big-breasted boob of a wife-to-be—Myrtle, of all stupid names—was allergic to flowers, so much so, she hated them."

"It wasn't as if your mother was going to continue living there and have access to the gardens," I emphasized.

"The ass set them aflame while she was pruning them one afternoon," he hissed. "They were such beautiful blooms. He could have waited until she'd moved out. It broke her heart. She'd won awards, you know?"

Rey and I couldn't help but express pity, not because we cared about GRP, but because we cared about Alaina-Lei Mei.

"So, you came calling today just to ratchet up the game?" Rey sneered, staring intently.

"That and to finally meet face-to-face. And to chat. I must confess, I do believe I will sorely miss having Caprize around for that. Oh well." He exhaled slowly, then chuckled. "I also came to advise that someone will perish—I do like that old-world word, don't you? Perish ... give up the ghost ... succumb."

"Anyone we know?" I asked drily.

"Yes."

"One of us?"

"We'll have to wait and see, won't we?" He winked and jumped from the counter with the pistol aimed. "I don't want to do this, truly I don't, but I can't risk having you follow me. I promise, it won't hurt much, and you'll have nice little naps."

Rey swore softly and before I could, it was light's out.

* * *

"Ballsy is right," Hammill muttered, holding up a ballistic syringe in a latex-gloved hand and eyeing it critically. "I doubt we'll find fingerprints, but we can hope."

"Do we need them?" Rey asked caustically. "We know who he is."

A uniformed officer knocked on the kitchen window and motioned the woman beside Hammill, who was checking something on a tablet. By the perpetually wheezing fridge, Ald was talking on his cell, taking surreptitious glances my way. We'd greeted each other when he'd arrived and had been amiable but, without question, we were experiencing the same degree of awkwardness.

"How ya girls feelin'?" Sallo asked crisply as he entered from the mudroom, the fedora hanging awkwardly from the back of his head. A short-sleeved beige cotton shirt was tucked into taupe pants two inches too short. "Better for taking those unexpected naps?"

My cousin rubbed her neck and scowled. "We've felt more lively."

Seated at the kitchen table, the two of us were drinking green tea, as were Hammill and Ald.

He smirked and strolled over to Hammill. "We got one good footprint—size 11—not far from the pool, by the fence, but that's it."

"Same size Jimmy C found near the stream that time," I said to Rey.

Sallo looked from me to her and back again with a scowl. "Hablador and Parleur are questioning the neighbors."

Hammill frowned. "They won't have seen much, if anything. Bet on it."

"An APB's out, so—"

"So?" Rey smiled sourly. "You don't actually believe you'll catch this guy?"

Before Sallo could respond, Linda raced into the kitchen, followed by Adwin, Sach, and Cash. "Those cop cars and legal sorts are not a good thing! What happened?"

"What the frig is this—a belated welcoming committee?" Hammill mocked.

Linda eyed him heatedly. "We all arrived at the same time and have a right to be here." She turned to my cousin and me. "Spill it! What happened?"

Rey gave a rapid rundown.

"Shit," came the very un-Linda response.

She and Sach hastened to our sides and gave us both hugs while Cash and Adwin glanced warily at each other and moved to the chairs by the counter.

"What now?" she asked Ald as he eyed Cash with obvious suspicion and aversion.

With a curse, he moved over to the teapot and refilled his mug. "We nab this S.O.B."

Rey met his fixed gaze. "Won't be easy, if even doable."

His lips pulled into a tight line and he looked at Hammill. "You better get the stuff we collected to Chapman."

Hammill nodded and left.

"Who do you think is next on the guy's hit list?" Sallo asked, eyeing the assortment of Honolulu Cookie Company shortbread cookies. He took a Kona Coffee and eyed it searchingly.

"It's eatable and delicious," Rey stated flatly.

He smirked, unwrapped it, and took a bite. "So? What's next?"

My cousin and I gazed at each other, then at Linda and Sach.

"Your guess—"

"Is as good as ours," Rey finished for me.

Ald leaned into the counter and started tapping his fingers. "I'll see you have 24-hour police protection."

"You think that's necessary?" Adwin asked anxiously.

"Of course it's not," Rey snorted.

"If he wants to get us, all the protection in the world won't stop him," Linda affirmed.

Sach agreed and I offered "ditto" with a flat smile.

Sallo snatched two more cookies. "You think he's aiming for you? Or someone associated with you?"

The three of us looked at one another. Rey crooked her head to one side and then the other, Linda shrugged, and I held out my hands, palms up.

"You know, I'm going to guess it's not Rey, Linda or me, but definitely someone we know." I met Cash's intense gaze and glanced at Adwin. Worry was written all over his attractive face while Sach's Groucho-Marx eyebrows grew even more tightly knit.

"Could be you or one of your colleagues," Linda suggested to Ald.

"It'll be some living target who won't see it coming." Sallo glowered. "F'g jackass."

Linda exhaled loudly, and Rey and I nodded.

"F'g jackass," we repeated in unison.

CHAPTER THIRTY-SEVEN

At seven, the night was breezy and warm, not quite humid, but close. The verbal exchange between Cash and I had been limited after the police left, with the six of us had discussing an impromptu dinner and then scattering to do what was needed.

Cash and Sach sipped light beers as they grilled steaks and shrimp. Linda and Adwin made hummus and potato salad from scratch while Rey and I organized appetizers (cheese and crackers, and clam dip) and prepared pitchers of non-alcoholic sangria.

As I mixed the dip, I mulled over the talk Cash and I had had ...

* * *

... "I've postponed my return flight for a short while. I didn't think we should leave it this way."

"Whatever," I murmured as I pulled celery and peppers from the fridge. "Thanks for the roses."

"Did you sleep with him?"

"If I did?"

"I guess that's your right."

"Of course it is ... just as it's your right to get yourself engaged to a kingpin's daughter," I responded sourly.

"It's part of the job."

I placed the vegetables on the counter. "Why are you back?"

"As I texted—twice—I didn't want to part on bad terms."

"We've done so before," I pointed out, getting a large wooden cutting board. "Why should this time be any different?"

"Hey, Rey and I are—uh, yeah." Adwin's mouth pulled into a tight line when he sighted Cash.

I met his gaze, smiled wearily, and prompted him to finish. "You and Rey are doing something?"

"Uh, right. We're going to pick up mayo, onions and olive oil at the grocery store. You seem to be out. We'll be back soon. Need anything?"

"Perrier and a couple of baguettes."

He nodded, glowered at Cash, and left.

Cash chuckled but not with cheer. "I'm feeling unloved. A guy could get a complex."

"You annoy or aggravate people at the best of times."

"Yet you have no objections to having this annoying, aggravating dude hanging around this evening?"

I met his probing gaze. "Even annoying, aggravating dudes have to eat." I offered a flat smile to his rueful one and grabbed a Swiss paring knife. "Besides, Sach invited you—spiritedly, I might add—so we could hardly *un*-invite you, could we? You better go help him. He's probably wondering where you've disappeared to."

* * *

"A pretty nice spread, if I do say so myself," our neighbor grinned, eyeing the laden side table and laundry-room bench that we'd brought out, and then looking upward. "And a pretty nice night to enjoy it all."

"Start helping yourself, boys," Rey said gaily, grabbing paper plates and passing them around.

Plates loaded and bums seated, we dug in. Despite the events of the day, appetites had not been in the least diminished.

"You think this guy's really going after one of us?" Sach stuffed a chunk of medium-rare steak into his eager mouth.

"Definitely, but 'us' comprises a sizable group," I answered.

"If he left a pawn to signify Caprize, then the king has to mean he's going after someone male," Rey put forth.

"That's a likely possibility." Linda took a sip of non-alcohol sangria and puckered her lips. "But there are several males GRP might consider as belonging to our 'us' group."

"The three of us here, members of the police, and your pal, Jimmy C," Adwin offered. "And maybe past clients are part of the equation."

"Where do you suppose he's hiding himself? How could he be *that* undetectable? Like, is the guy *invisible*, a figment of our imagination?" Sach joked with a feeble smile and furrowed brow.

Cash smiled darkly. "Unfortunately, he's very real. Remember, he does apply theatrical make-up and very well, so yes, he can be *that* undetectable." Eyeing a shrimp, he sampled it, apparently liked it, and speared three more.

"If you guys want to spend the night, feel free, we've got enough room," Rey offered.

"That's fine for one night, but we can't move in indefinitely," Adwin said with a tired smile. "Besides, as you said, if he wants to get one of us, he will—even here, with all of us under the same roof. He's smart, calculating, and bleeping lucky."

"Luck does run out eventually," Cash said casually.

We all nodded solemnly and resumed eating.

* * *

"Déjà vu," I murmured, slipping off my T-shirt and shorts, and getting into bed. I rolled onto one side and, propping my head on one hand to watch Cash undress. I still marveled at the intricate workmanship of the tattoo covering half his back: an intricate dragon coiled around a broadsword (black and gray work – fineline).

I couldn't explain how he came to be up here. I hadn't agreed to it, and he hadn't asked; we'd simply strolled up the stairs at 9:30 after Sach and Adwin left. Rey and Linda had wished us both goodnight without a blink or sideward glance. We were all exhausted—some of us beyond the "good judgment" stage.

He dropped alongside and mirrored my pose. "Think we can pick up where we've left off too many times of late?" He fingered my lower lip.

I stifled a yawn. "We can try."

Jade-green eyes scanned mine.

"I know what you're thinking and I'm not going to answer the question if you ask it again," I said aloofly. If he wanted to believe I'd slept with Ald, so be it. That was between the detective and me.

His smile was haughty and fleeting, and he held my chin between a thumb and index finger. "That's between you and the detective."

"You a mind reader?"

He laughed. "Among other things."

"Such as arrogant prick?" I winked.

"Such as awesome lover." He leaned over and turned off the Crate & Barrel lamp. "Care to have me demonstrate?"

"Only if you live up to that self-celebrated accolade."

We slipped under the basket-weave throw to determine just how awesome he was.

* * *

I woke up in a dazed state a couple of times during the night and it seemed as if I were alone. I was too tired to call out or check if he'd stepped downstairs or down the hall.

Shades up, sunlight streamed in through the window. My gaze swept from the alarm clock—it was 7:35 a.m.—to the ceiling. I rolled over to find Cash gone. With a shrug, I tossed aside the lightweight cover, grabbed a short-sleeved floral shirt and black jeans, underwear and flipflops, and went to shower.

Twenty minutes later, when I strolled into the empty kitchen, I found him coming in from the mudroom, sporting jeans and an Aloha shirt with predominant shades of lemon yellow and lime green, and carrying a tray supporting four extra-large coffees and a box from a local bakery. Something flickered on his freshly shaved face... *Guilt?*

"Hey," he greeted with little cheer. "I went to get coffee."

"I see." I extracted two small bottles of orange juice from the fridge. "I guess Linda and Rey are sleeping in."

"I haven't seen them." He placed the tray and box on the table. "So?"

"You lived up to the self-celebrated accolade." I held out a bottle.

"That's not what I was asking," he smiled as he took it. "I was asking ... so, are we good?"

"We're good."

He took a long sip and leaned into the counter. "I wish I could stick around and help you nail this bastard."

"We've done okay before," I said wryly. "We'll do fine. He'll trip himself up."

"He hasn't yet."

I leaned into the counter alongside him. "He's admitted who he is ... and he seems perfectly comfortable sharing thoughts and information. The police are looking for him. He's in the media, hailed as the Rose-Pin Killer, at least for the moment. And Ald said he'll likely release the photo of him that we found at Caprize's. Someone will have seen him. He can't remain hidden or unnoticed forever. He *will* be caught."

"But how many more people will die before that happens?" he asked drily.

I sighed and blew hair from my eyes. "You know, given the dislike for his father, I'm surprised GRP hasn't gone after him."

"He has a brother he hasn't touched either, right?"

I nodded. "I don't believe they have—or ever had—a brotherly relationship. I doubt they've stayed in touch ... but I could be wrong."

"You know a private eye worth his or her weight in gold would never leave a stone unturned, right?" He offered a quick smile. "Maybe you should check with the guy. Get a feel. It's always possible there's something going on there, like—"

"Familial support?"

"Anything's possible."

An interesting notion. Might Luc E Mei be assisting his brother? Had we been remiss in not pursuing him more closely? Very much so. Cash was right. We couldn't leave any stones unturned. I'd give him a call shortly. And then, to be that private eye worth her weight in gold—and not a mediocre one (as I was feeling)—I decided to call his partners, Henny Spieler and Beck Bild, too.

Speaking of calls, I should check in with Adwin and Sach— Adwin because he'd seemed forlorn off and on last night and Sach because he'd seemed tense and worried.

"When are you leaving?"

"I'm not sure. I still have to book a flight," he said with a shrug. "Soon, though."

"Back to the life of a husband-to-be drug pusher," I said drily.

"I'm not going to marry her," he said flatly.

"You don't know that. Things have a strange way of transpiring." I removed a cup of coffee from the tray. "Daddy Kingpin may arrange a surprise wedding for you two."

"I'm not going to marry her," he repeated, taking one as well.

"Is she pretty?" I felt compelled to ask.

"She has the face of a whippet and the body of a basset-hound."

"In other words, she's drop-dead gorgeous with a bod to kill for."

"Right on." He laughed and I grinned.

Rey and Linda ambled in, stifling yawns as they waved limply. Both had their hair in pigtails with satin bows—a new [fashion] trend?—and sported sundresses with plumeria themes. As they settled at the table and Cash brought them their coffees, I pulled out toast bread, two types of jam, butter, and more orange juice.

"Nice to see you two made up," Rey commented casually as I placed four whole-wheat slices into the toaster oven.

"And then some." Linda winked. "The walls aren't as thick as we thought."

I blushed and gulped back a chocolate-caramel blend that made me wince. Nice for lattes or ice-cream, not so much for coffee.

"Is it worth heading to the office today?" Rey asked, peering into the open pastry box Cash held before her. She smiled and pulled out a cherry-mac danish.

Linda said, "I'd like to return to the house off Makaniolu Place. I'm sure there's nothing to be found, but I feel an over-whelming need to see it again."

"Let's do it," Rey said. "But before we do, we'd better call Professor Vatten and Nasa Wasser regarding those cistern water tests. We should have heard back by now."

"Let's call around nine. I'll take Vatten, you take Wasser," her best friend instructed. "I'll check in with Jimmy C, too."

"I believe Gail's off today. Why don't we take her with us?" I suggested.

Rey gave a thumb's up and then pointed to the toaster over. "Leave it another few seconds, and you'll have charcoal."

I raced over and yanked out four dark slices of toast, burning my fingers. Still edible. Just.

Cash and I took seats at the table, and the four of us sipped silently as we slipped into our own thoughts. A few minutes later, Cash stood. "I have things to tend to. Want to meet for drinks around one? Barefoot Bar?"

"Sounds like a plan," Rey answered merrily.

"Count me in," Linda said jovially.

Cash looked from one to the other, then to me.

I laughed. "I'll be there ... with my cohorts ... or without."

He shook his head. "See you later ... with or without."

"He's a cutie," Rey said as he slipped from the kitchen.

I smiled wryly. "And an ass."

"*That's* pretty cute, too."

Giggling like schoolgirls, we planned the daily schedule, and sucked back another round of flavored [but not flavorsome] caffeine.

CHAPTER THIRTY-EIGHT

We drove to the house in the Jeep and listened with grins and giggles as Gail merrily updated us on the recent trip to Japan and ensuing adventures. There was a new guy named Igor in her life, one she'd met at a local coffee shop. She wouldn't reveal much, preferring we first meet the professional zombie. Yup, that was his job and a lucrative one it was. As an FYI, zombies weren't just Halloween material anymore. They were popular at birthdays, bar and bat mitzvahs, communions, and staff parties (and a little less so at seniors' festivities).

Agreeing to have her and her new beau over for a barbecue next week—sans zombie costume and make-up and lumbering —we proceeded to enlighten her about all that had transpired, ending with the calls made earlier today.

Luc E Mei hadn't answered, so I left a message. Ditto for his partners, Spieler and Bild, who weren't available. The call re the cistern-water test results were more productive. Vatten and Wasser —as well as Ald—confirmed that there were traces of biological contaminants, such as legionella, coliform, and enterovirus, and chemical contaminants, such as arsenic, cadmium, and lead. Nitrates and atrazine were also in the cistern water. The scientific explanations had gone over our heads, but we'd gotten the gist. It appeared that a body (or bodies) had been in the cistern previously and that the water had been changed. It was quite probable that GRP had kept some victims in there. Not lately, though. Too bad our serial-killer pal hadn't explained about the significance of the immersion. But maybe there was no reason or logic. Maybe it had simply been convenient at the time(s).

Gail, seated beside me, removed black-framed Oakley sunglasses and rubbed her sun-kissed brow as we parked a block from the now owner-less abode. "So, for all we know, GRP is watching us right now."

"He certainly has eyes in many places." Linda gazed around with a pensive brow.

"Given all he's done and shared with you, it's almost as if he wants to be caught."

Linda shook her head. "He enjoys the 'game'. It's part of the fun, part of the competition—"

"Part of the fact he thinks he's an invincible winner," Rey interjected flatly, opening the car door and sticking out a long lanky leg. She was wearing jean shorts with a blinding white T, as were Linda and me (some telepathic thing the three of us seemed to share more often than not). Hooking a canvas Coach tote bag over one shoulder, she glanced around as she waited for Linda to step out, then closed the door. "I don't see anyone or anything suspicious, but then GRP could be disguised as a koa tree."

Gail and I grinned. After locking the Jeep, we made our way to the house, keeping a furtive gaze on the area, lest any nosy neighbors came over to see what we were up to.

"Doesn't look like a death house," Gail murmured, eyeing it as we strolled toward the crushed-stone driveway.

"What does a death house look like?" Linda asked with a grim smile.

"Ominous."

Rey turned slowly, scrutinizing the neighborhood. "Nothing

to see. Not even a cat. Looks like we're okay, but let's head in from the rear by coming around the trail."

Linda and I exchanged anxious glances. If we knew Rey—and we did—it was B&E time. But how else could we enter? Not that we truly expected to find anything, but it was possible the police had overlooked or missed something. We needed to—*had to*—risk it.

* * *

Once inside, we ensured the curtains were properly drawn. It was dim, but with the sunlight that peered through the edges, we could see enough. And, smart private eyes that we *could* be, we carried a couple of flashlights, just in case.

It was much like we'd glimpsed the first time and as Rey had described it after she'd been held captive: a planked hip roof reminiscent of Aunt Sue Lou's Maine cottage, a gleaming mirror running the height and length of one wall, tiny windows draped with speckled-gray linen fabric and two doors, a fake-oak, gate-leg table and an ash-gray armchair that looked like something out of a 50s comedy show. The scraped and scarred hardwood floor was clear of debris and dust.

"I wanna check what's behind the mirror." Rey stepped toward the door, took a deep breath, and pushed it open. "Holy crap!"

In the scramble, the three of us toppled like bowling pins struck by a clumsily pitched bowling ball; clambering to our feet, we came face-to-face with a man of medium stature standing beside a black-finish desk lamp that provided ample lighting. Bearing theatrical make-up and hairpiece, GRP resembled the Jim Carrey character from *Dumb and Dumber*, silly haircut, goofy teeth, and all.

A black-finish desk lamp provided ample light. A dart-gun rested in one hand and a tiny gift-like carton in the other. At his feet, on a crumpled sheet and rumpled blanket, sat a large make-up case and nondescript gym bag.

We froze. He smirked.

"What? You *knew* we'd be here?" Rey asked blandly, crossing her arms.

"You're *very* good," Linda said, visibly impressed.

"Not really." He chuckled. "I needed to pop back here. Merely a coincidence. But, this time, welcome to *my* little grass shack." He eyed Gail. "I believe you're HPD's Gail Murdock, yes?"

She nodded, revealing no emotion.

"Run out of places to hide?" my cousin asked, leaning into the doorframe.

"As I said, I needed to pop by, which I did around three this morning, in case you were curious. Thankfully the 'crime scene' is no longer locked down, but not so thankfully, as I was about to leave, Parker decided to take his Standard Schnauzer, Snuggy-Bugs, for a walk. As luck would have it, Snuggy-Bugs decided he wanted to meander around the property. Guess he sensed someone was on it." He offered a dour smile.

"You could have run off after Snuggy-uh-Bugs and his master left," Rey said, trying to keep a straight face.

"Woulda if I coulda. But Snuggy-Bugs wanted to 'bless' the grass a few times and his owner seemed to be fine with playing amateur sleuth. I came in here in case he saw something he shouldn't have through a window." He shrugged. "Thanks to media stories about my victims and known haunts, the ever-inquisitive and ghoulish came by the house early this morning and took photos."

Suddenly, he pouted like a tot. "I'm not liking the fact they're going with the Ha-Ha Killer now and not so much the Rose-Pin Killer, the original name. I really do like GrimReaperPeeper, even GRP, as you prefer."

Linda crossed her arms and regarded him intently. "Don't serial killers taunt the press?"

He sighed noisily and rolled his eyes.

Rey gestured. "So, Mr. Ha-Ha-Ha—"

"That's Mr. *Ha-Ha* Killer," he informed her with mock sternness and a twinkle in eyes that were hazel this time.

She offered a salaam. "So, you decided to look like Carrey's Christmas in the event someone saw you leave?"

"I wanted a disguise, just in case, so I went for a 'dumb' one. Like it?"

"It's pretty good. But flying that banner that time with HA-HA-HA-HA, now *that* was genius." Rey gave a thumb's up. "And darkly funny to boot."

GRP offered an exaggerated wink, then gazed from one face to the next. "Feel free to look around and tell your police friends I was here. But, before you do, please drop your purses behind you, away from the door. You know I'll use this. I may not hit all of you, but I will definitely get one of you. Who wants the honors?" The dart-gun rose higher, aimed at Rey's neck. "But if that doesn't deter you, I could blow you—us—up." He held up the teeny beige carton. "If I press this, it will set off a bomb."

"You'd blow up yourself?" Linda asked drily, obviously not buying it.

"It's better than being put behind bars."

"Or locked in a rubber room," Rey simpered.

He scanned her face, then chuckled. "Or that. The purses, please."

We dropped them.

He slipped to one side. "Step in here, please, so I can lock you inside. I'm sure you'll figure a way out. May I have the keys to the car you drove here with?"

"In the bag," I gestured my purse on the floor. "You don't have your own wheels?"

"Not nearby. Get the keys slowly, please, and then return to that spot. Maybe I'll take your car. Maybe I won't. But you won't be getting too far too quickly, either way."

"Question?" Rey.

He motioned us inside with the weapon and against the far wall. "Sure."

"Same one from the visit: why did you put your victims in cisterns like the one outside?"

He snickered. "You think there's some symbolic reason? Water immersion as in renewal of life and all that?"

She nodded.

"Solely convenience. In most cases, hiding the bodies in a nearby cistern or well was the best option at the time. But I haven't done so recently, as you well know."

Rey nodded crisply.

"Sorry, dearheart." GRP shrugged and sighed. "I'm not as complex as you—or the police and their medical specialists— might like to believe."

"But you *are* intense," Gail commented.

"In some ways, yes, I suppose." Another shrug. "Any more questions before I leave?"

"It was your dead ex with you behind the mirror that night I was here, wasn't it?" Rey asked.

He nodded. "She could be ten-thumbed sometimes. She dropped a bottle of soda that night. I am *so* much better off without that woman … though … I truly do miss her." He appeared bemused for a blink. "Strange."

"Are you still planning to off someone we know?"

"Yes, Rey sweetheart, I am." He motioned the gym bag and make-up case . "Linda, dear, please push those outside the door, then step back beside JJ."

She looked like she might refuse, but he extended the dart-gun. With a scowl, she did as instructed.

He stepped before the door. "You can shout and scream if you like, but I doubt anyone will hear you—unless they're very close to the house. And breaking down the door may be difficult; it's fairly sturdy and thick, as you can see. I advise you to put your heads together and figure out a better means of escape, one where you don't injure your pretty selves."

Our mechanical nods came simultaneously.

"See you soon."

"I hope so," Rey hissed.

Laughing, GRP winked at her, slammed shut the door, and locked it.

"Think it was a real bomb?" Linda asked, stepping before the two-way mirror. "And, if so, where is it hidden?"

"He'd never allow himself to be caught, and bombs aren't his style," I replied. "He wouldn't risk it ... but we couldn't either."

"Ya'd think the guy would *want* to go out with a bang," Rey scowled.

"Not before his time."

She scowled again.

Gail jerked a thumb at the door. "Let's not do any second-guessing and start figuring a way out of here, before the nutbar changes his mind and we do go out with a bang."

Rey pulled out her cell. "We're fine, ladies."

Linda stared into the next room. "For the love of ... the guy just blew a kiss... Okay, he's gone from view now. Why do you suppose the jackass 'needed' to come back here?"

"It couldn't be to check for—and collect—evidence," Gail answered, running fingers over the doorknob and lock. "The police scoured this place."

"But there was *something* he wanted, something he'd hidden *here*," Rey suggested. "Something that wasn't found, or he assumed couldn't be found."

We stared at one another for several seconds.

"Documents?" Linda.

"His passport or license?" Gail.

"Or other people's licenses?" Me.

We stared at one another for several seconds, then said in unison, "Trophies."

CHAPTER THIRTY-NINE

"Smart thinking, tucking your cell phone in your back pocket," Ald told Rey, giving her shoulder a slight squeeze, much to Linda's and my surprise. "That saved you all a lot of time and a major headache trying to get out."

Yes, smart thinking. Why hadn't GRP thought to check pockets instead of assuming we kept phones in purses? Rey had called Ald almost immediately and within minutes, police had arrived and broken down the front door, and then the one to this odd narrow room. On a call nearby, Ald himself arrived within fifteen minutes.

The place was being given the once- and twice-over. They'd not allowed us to do much except explain what had transpired. And, amazingly, Ald once again hadn't lectured about breaking-and-entering but, given the dour expression, we suspected that might come later.

Seated on the rear deck, we watched the team do their thing: secure the crime scene, take notes and photos, collect trace evidence, perform evidence management and crime scene security, among other imperative tasks.

"They won't find much of anything," Rey commented.

"I hope they find my Jeep ... in one piece."

"It's probably in the ocean," Ald said, slipping before us. "And he's no doubt changed his facial looks again."

Gail said, "I'd bet he has a few disguises on the ready."

I scanned the sky that had started to collect a sundry of low-level Nimbus clouds; rain wasn't far off. "Let's go home and pick up Linda's car and check in with GRP's brother."

Gail looked at Ald. "Care to give us a lift?"

He called to an officer walking past. "Officer Otto will drive you all back."

* * *

The plan to meet Luc E Mei was postponed until tomorrow morning. An assistant named Botho called to advise he was on Maui and scheduled us at the Mei house for nine.

Due to the teeming rain, Cash and I opted for cappuccinos and dessert at a small European café on Manoa Road. I'd updated him about the preceding few hours and he'd told me he had arranged to return to Florida the following morning after a night of dinner, drinks and a lush suite at a hotel.

"You're certainly a wealth of surprises on this trip." I forked the last of a scrumptious Sachertorte past appreciative lips.

He smiled thinly. "A *wealth*?"

"I still can't get over how you're ... not like you used to be. It's ... weird."

"People change." There was a note of abruptness, or maybe impatience, in the response. He took a sip of cappuccino and scanned the small crowded room.

"Do they?"

"They can."

I decided to ignore the tone and offered an easy smile. "I still say the real Cash Layton Jones has been kidnapped and replaced by a doppelganger."

With a fleeting smile, he motioned the server for the bill.

"Let's take you back and collect your gear for a fun evening. I booked the Lotus."

"Lovely place, but I'm sure your hotel room would be just fine." I winked. "But don't you still have people to see and things to do?"

"I've rearranged them," was the dull response. "Besides, you never know who may be watching."

"So? Didn't you tell once tell me a few people knew you had a relationship with a private eye here on Oahu? And, if someone *were* watching, wouldn't they have seen you at the house on more than one occasion?"

"I'd prefer a suite for this evening." Another fleeting smile.

I knew Cash well enough to know when he was skirting the truth. Did I want to call him on it? Of course, I did. "Where *are* you staying? I don't believe you mentioned it."

He met my penetrating stare with his own. "Rayna's."

"Your ex's."

He nodded.

"She must be enthralled having you out and about with your *sometimes girlfriend*."

His lips drew taut.

I rose and nodded to the server when he returned to the table. "Your treat, Mr. Layton. I'll meet you by the car."

* * *

"Another fight?" Rey asked blandly as I strolled onto the lanai.

She and Linda were lying on a large blanket on the grass in tiny black bikinis, well-oiled, and sun-kissed. The pigtails sported different colored bows—strawberry-red for Linda and blueberry-blue for Rey. While Linda sported diamond studs, BFF Rey wore long sparkling bacon strips (my cousin did exhibit an odd sense of humor when minded).

The rain had ceased ten minutes before Cash pulled up before the house and I hopped out—with a grenade-exploding bang. The tires must have left marks on the street, because his Audi R8 peeled off with a deafening screech.

"That doesn't look like the right type of sunscreen," I said dully as I grabbed a can of diet cola from an ice- and can-filled bucket and sank to my knees before them.

"It's three and we've only been out here for a half hour or so," Rey advised, rising up on her elbows. "What did you two fight about this time?"

I shrugged. "He's been staying at Rayna's."

"No!"

I nodded.

"The blighter," Linda said with a wry smile.

"What the frig is that?" my cousin asked.

"Someone who's looked at with contempt or annoyance. Or pity."

"The blighter," my cousin declared with a nod, then eyed Linda keenly. "We better share our news."

She nodded once and motioned her to proceed.

"Ald called not long ago—"

"Not Hives, but the first name, and the correct one at that?" I joshed.

"Ha, ha—uh. He called to say there was a Lloyd Christmas sighting at Ala Moana Center by a Carrey fan. In Macy's, to be exact. And one at a juice bar in the food court an hour later by the same fan. He managed to get a sort-of shot—there were some heads in the way. He sent it to the boys and girls in blue."

"I'd have thought he'd ditch the look, knowing we'd have told the police."

"Part of the game," my cousin said flippantly, sitting up. "All part of the f'g game."

"And thrill." I glanced from one face to the next. "You both okay?"

"We're just eager—antsy, if you like—to catch the dude," Rey replied. "We can't let him win."

Linda rolled onto her stomach and propped her chin on her fisted hands. "He won't. But we have to outsmart him—"

Rey glowered. "Checkmate him, you mean?"

"Exactly." Linda scanned my face. "There's more."

"I'm waiting with bated breath," I said with a pained smile.

"There was a black rose on the side table here. It wasn't there when we popped out on the lanai at two to make sure the rain wasn't drenching anything it shouldn't be. But it was there at half past two, when we stepped out."

"A reminder that one of us is next?" I asked astringently.

"There was no note or card, but that'd be my guess," Rey replied.

"Let's call Sach and Adwin and Jimmy C and have them stay the night. We can have a wine and steak party," Linda suggested.

I agreed. "That would help lessen the stress—"

"And keep us safe as a group, even if only for this evening," Rey added. "And while we're sitting around getting tipsy, we can come up with a plan to trap our crazy, game-loving friend."

"Let's keep the Tasers and gun handy," Linda proposed.

I winced. A weapon in our hands was like a shotgun in the clumsy fingers of Elmer Fudd before the cartoon folks decided he should no longer have one.

"It's good that the pets are still with Eddy—oh-oh." Rey paled.

"GRP likes animals, remember?" Linda said soothingly. "I don't think he'd harm their sitter. He kills people for a reason, offbeat as it can be. Eddy is no threat to him."

"I believe you're right. Eddy's no threat to GRP," I reiterated, getting to my feet.

"But we should be extra vigilant now," Linda advised.

Rey scowled. "For *how* long?"

CHAPTER FORTY

At eight, the wine and steak party had turned into a pajama party, because the rain had returned with a vengeance, pounding walls and windows. And before the wine was opened, we'd decided it might be fun to put on pjs and lounge on fleecy blankets in the living room, before the sofa and armchairs.

Sach wore a blindingly colorful jungle-print robe over pink cotton pajamas while Adwin sported a long-sleeve neon-green T-shirt over pansy-purple fleece pants. We couldn't help but joke that the two must have shopped together. Jimmy C's bedtime ensemble was subdued with simple cotton-poplin drawstring pants and a white T. The three of us? Shorty pajama sets. Rey: red pouty lips. Linda: dancing frisky felines. Me: black-and-white prison stripes.

The last half hour had been spent discussing GRP and all that we knew to date, with theories as to where he might be.

"I say he *has* to be staying with someone," Rey stated over a full glass of merlot.

"I can't see him trusting anyone." Linda.

"Or anyone trusting *him*." Adwin.

She tapped her nose and pointed. He raised his glass in response.

"He's probably got an apartment somewhere. He's ballsy enough to hide in plain sight. Even with the photos and sketches in the media, he can disguise himself well enough to not be 'seen'." Jimmy C leaned back and sipped.

"And yet, surely *someone* has?" I put forth.

"Why haven't they come forth then?" Sach asked, puzzled.

"Fear of retaliation or being in the spotlight," Adwin answered. "Some people simply refuse to get involved."

"That's *so* wrong." Sach's eyes widened like checker pieces. "Is that the theme from *Vegas*?"

"You're good. You know your retro TV." I reached over for my cell phone and in a sing-song voice said, "Tanna Investigations."

"Huh? Tanna who?" asked Cash, clearly confused.

"What do *you* want?"

"I just thought I'd let you know I'm leaving tomorrow, first thing," he advised in a businesslike tone.

"I believe you already mentioned something to that effect. Have a safe flight." I severed the connection.

Rey looked from me to Adwin and back again, opened her mouth to speak, then hastily gulped back wine.

Vegas announced a call again. I sighed and answered the unknown number. "I said have a nice flight, so bugg—"

"Dear, lovely lady, hello."

"You should move in, given we're in constant contact. In fact, we're having a pj party. Care to join us?"

"That's a thought, but unfortunately, I must decline. I'm in the middle of something," GRP said gaily.

"How unfortunate indeed."

"JJ, are you missing anyone? Maybe misplaced him or her?"

I tensed as I glanced from one face to the next; they tensed in return.

"No? Well, no matter. I'm sure you'll hear from Detective Ives soon enough."

I found my voice. "What have you done?"

"Exactly what I said I would—no, nix that. I haven't killed yet. I'm going to give you twenty-four hours to find us. If you succeed, your friend remains a living, breathing entity. If not … well, that's on you."

Before I could respond, he was gone. I drew a quick breath and told the others what GRP had said.

Rey hopped to her feet. "This party just ended. I'll put on a pot of coffee. We have to be sober and smart and figure out where he has whoever he has. Linda, call Ald!"

Before she could, the agency phone rang. Rey had it in a nanosecond. "Yeah!?"

Six uh-huhs and three nods later—accompanied by visible paling—she hung up. "Gail's missing. She was with Igor at the movies like she told us she'd be, but after they ordered drinks at a nearby bar, she went to the ladies' room and didn't return. Igor got a hold of Ald ten minutes later—he knew about GRP and had a 'gut feeling' something was terribly wrong. Ald called her cell. No answer. So he sent Hammill to the bar. A waitperson said she saw someone who resembled Gail hurrying through the fire exit when she rounded the corner."

"Opening the exit didn't set off an alarm?" Linda asked, stunned.

"Apparently not," she shrugged. "Let's get dressed, peeps. We have a damsel in *serious* distress to rescue!"

* * *

I sat back down at the kitchen table after refilling mugs with a second round of Kona coffee. Ald hadn't returned my calls but Hammill had, only to sternly state that everyone was putting in 150+% to find Gail Murdock and they'd not cease until the mission was accomplished.

"I refuse to sit here another second and *not* do anything," Rey declared angrily, pushing aside her pineapple-shaped mug and slapping the table. Thunder chose to boom at that second.

"Nice touch," Linda said drolly. "But maybe you should add a little more drama by flinging your arm toward the rear door and commanding we charge like the cavalry into the stormy night."

"As they used to say: *bite me*."

Adwin chuckled and Sach gave an OK ring gesture. Jimmy C smiled into his coffee.

Linda simpered and turned back to us. "You know how GRP likes to walk on the edge?"

"And then some." Sach snorted like a dog who'd inhaled a snoot-load of ocean foam.

"He stayed at the Makaniolu Place house—"

"Only because Snuggy-Bugs and owner decided to 'water' the grass and crime-scene enthusiasts were eager to snoop around and take photos," I pointed out. "He couldn't chance leaving and being seen."

"Still, he took a risk staying," Linda declared.

"Okay, he took a risk," I shrugged.

"Why wouldn't he be inclined to return to another familiar place?"

We stared at Linda as we pondered a very valid question.

"You mean Caprize's Kahala house?" Sach finally asked.

"Why not? It's a quiet street. The house is well concealed with trellis fencing and panels and shrubbery. The lighting at night is pretty dim. And the traffic is fairly non-existent after seven."

"It would make for a perfect hiding place," Adwin stated, regarding Linda with a furrowed brow.

"And don't forget the *ohana* ... and the cellar, which is unusual here on Oahu. Why couldn't there be more to the place, like a hidden room, one the police wouldn't have been looking for? The tortures and killings had to have taken place *somewhere*, so why not there?"

"Yeah, why not there?" Adwin nodded solemnly.

"*Now* I'm going to be dramatic." Rey smiled darkly. "Gear up! Grab the Tasers and gun. We're heading over." She pointed to the rear. "We'll meet at the back door in five minutes. We'll take two cars and have develop a plan of attack once we're there."

* * *

It was a little after ten when we parked several houses down from GRP's ex's. The teeming rain had lessened to a drizzle. For how long, remained to be seen.

Linda, Sach and Jimmy C would sneak up to the *ohana* and investigate the interior, Tasers and flashlights in hand. Rey, Adwin and I would steal around the main house and see what, if anything, might be going on inside, flashlight, Taser, and gun in [my] hand. I sure hoped I didn't have to use it; with my luck/aim, I'd likely shoot a neighbor or pet, like Mrs. Kotter's Dalmatian, Angheim.

We'd all donned dark sweatshirts and beanie hats—fortunately, Rey had a solid selection. Phones were on vibrate. Standing by the lanai, amid a fragrant *alahe'e* hedge, we surveyed the two-story shadowed house. Save for the drizzle and occasional sound of a distant horn or plane, there were no signs of life. The place was as dark and quiet as it had been the last time we'd been here.

"You really think he might be here?" Adwin asked quietly, a note of apprehension in the question.

"It wouldn't surprise me," I whispered. "But I don't know how he could *not* be detected."

"If he's in the cellar or a hidden room, who'd ever notice? There'd be no lights to give him away and the house is far away from the street, so who'd notice much—"

"Save for those twisted folks who like dropping in on murdered people's homes," Adwin interjected flatly.

"We ready?" Rey asked somberly.

"As ready as we'll ever be," Adwin and I answered simultaneously and gave each other a quick high-five.

"Cute." She punched my shoulder and nodded to the side door. "Like Chuck Berry once sang, 'let's boogie'".

"May we should fasten poochie harnesses on one another," Adwin joked.

"Funny *not*, Cousin Jilly's ex-boyfriend."

I swallowed a chuckle and slapped them both in the back. "Let's find Gail."

Cautiously, slowly, methodically, we circled the house. All the blackout fabric roller shades were drawn and there were no cellar windows to be found. All was still. Again.

"Enter via the side or front door?" Adwin whispered tensely.

Rey pulled out her infamous B&E kit. "Side should do it."

"But if GRP's in there, he'll hear us," I pointed out.

"He'll hear us no matter where—or how—we enter," Rey stressed. "We just have to be prepared."

"For *any* contingency," Adwin added solemnly. "Okay, Fonne-Werde, can you work your breaking-and-entering magic in this wet gloom?"

She stared. "I'm not just good, Addy, I'm great." She motioned the side door and stepped forward, and sailed onto her butt, as did a curse—into the night. The B&E kit flew onto the grass.

"Nothing like making an entrance," my ex-beau said drolly. "If GRP didn't know we were here, he does now."

We helped my cousin to her sneakered feet and handed her the tools of a burglar's trade.

Adwin and I kept watch—not that we'd see much—while Rey quickly, expertly (scarily), opened the door. "Thank God there's no alarm."

"You have to wonder why," Adwin murmured, perturbed.

"Let's move," she urged.

We closed the door softly behind us, then waited for our eyes to adjust to the darkness.

"Turn on a light?" Adwin asked, his lips tickling my ear.

"We'll use our flashlight." I removed a mini one from my jean pocket. With a deep inhalation, I turned it on and pointed it around the dining room. A narrow sage-green cellar door was barely visible alongside a sizable, handsome two-glass door cabinet.

We looked at one another, nodded, and I pulled out the Luger LCP 380 that Cash had once given me; it, like the Beretta M9A3 I'd purchased many moons ago, had been lying in a drawer. I *really* hoped I didn't have to use it.

Rey held out her Taser and we stepped before the door. Gently, she opened it and, happily, it didn't creak like some haunted-house entrance.

"Stay behind, just in case," I instructed Adwin under my breath.

"I'm not letting you two—"

"You may need to get help in a hurry. *Please*."

He shook his head but pressed up against the wall and stayed motionless; I felt the scowl more than saw it.

I pointed to the light with the Luger and Rey and I descended the steep narrow stairway. The special grow lights that had once brought life to lush plants had not been on since Caprize's passing. The result: limp, dead plants.

"To hell with it." Rey strolled over to a light switch by a tall metal shelving unit and flipped it on. An ocher sheen bathed the room painted vivid shades of blue and purple.

We gazed around and then looked at each other and shrugged. She gestured the small metal pantry door with the Taser. We entered and turned on the LED lighting strip that lined two walls. The pantry, or cold room, looked undisturbed, just like the main cellar room. Jars and bottles sat on two shelving units, while boxes and plastic crates were propped against a wall.

"Guess we lucked out." Rey looked discouraged and helpless —much like I felt.

I turned back to the rear wall. A circular 20" mirror with a lattice-like, copper-finish frame was suspended in the middle, surrounded by a half dozen bronze-framed floral prints. Pretty enough. Something you'd have in a cottage or cabin, but not something for a cellar pantry.

I aimed the gun and Rey's grass-green eyes widened. I shot and—for the first time in my short shooting career—*almost* hit the intended target. The left side of the border splintered.

And, slowly, the wall slid open to reveal a small rectangular room.

Five feet before us, bound to a ladderback chair, with a floral gag around her mouth and a black rose pinned to her strawberry-red blouse, sat Gail. Her eyes, hazel this time, were open but appeared unfocused. Still, she seemed aware enough to know that Rey and I were standing in front of her and that GRP's hearty laughter was flowing through a tiny speaker at the base of the chair.

A frenetic drumroll commenced and tiny red rose petals, the size of confetti, streamed down.

"You won the big deal of the day, ladies."

CHAPTER FORTY-ONE

Rey cursed and Adwin came crashing down the stairs into the room—and into us. Down we went like the bottles in a fairground milk pyramid. His cremini-brown eyes were as round as pizza pies as we struggled back up on two legs. "What the—you found her!"

I nodded grimly and sneezed as I inhaled a teeny petal.

"Addy, why don't you help untie Gail? JJ and I have a nutbar to find."

"Goo-ood luck, lovely Reynalda," GRP said liltingly. "Toodle-loo. Until we meet again."

Snap, crunch. The speaker went dead.

Rey and I looked at each other, then at Adwin, who had started to remove the gag from our dazed friend's mouth. My cousin strolled over to a 60" LED magnifying task floor lamp with 360-degree rotating lens, which stood alongside a stainless-steel workbench, and turned it on. Along two walls, near the back, where metal cabinets with multiple drawers.

"Charming," she murmured and motioned the workbench. "Could be an autopsy—or torture—table, couldn't it?"

"Could be," I concurred. "That lamp would certainly assist with the, uh, job."

I moved to the wall where the mirror had hung and noticed the two-way looking glass enabled a limited view of the cellar beyond. Had GRP been hiding in here those times we and Sach had visited?

Rey stepped to the cabinet nearest her and began searching through drawers, swearing now and again as she reached in to finger something. Out came a black rose. "No question, Cousin Jilly. Besides the rose, there are some pretty damn sharp tools in here. This is the place where our sick friend did his work."

Adwin, who didn't much care for swearing or cursing, released a few colorful expressions that made even Rey's [non-delicate/non-innocent] ears color.

Rey chuckled darkly, tossed the rose aside, and moved to the other cabinet.

"I am so p'o'd that he got the better of me. I knew better than to follow him into the alley, but I couldn't chance losing him when I saw him moving toward the fire exit," Gail said groggily, rubbing her wrists. "How'd you find me?"

I quickly explained what had transpired the last couple of hours as Adwin and I helped her to her feet. He draped an arm around her shoulders, and she leaned into him.

"Let's get—"

"Hey, there's a small, super narrow staircase here, behind the cabinet!"

The three of us turned to find Rey nowhere in sight.

"You two head up and out," I instructed. "I'll follow Cousin Reynalda and meet you by the Jeep. Keep a vigilant eye."

"No need to tell me," Gail muttered, hooking an arm around Adwin.

With a solemn nod, I slipped around the cabinet and sighted the staircase. It was incredibly narrow, maybe a foot wide. And steep. And dark. I beamed the flashlight on the high steps and began my ascent.

A minute later, I found Rey. She was before a wooden door maybe five feet in height and trying to open it.

"It probably has some sort of grab latch—you know, the kind you simply push open."

"Let's have at it."

Several seconds later, the door opened—to reveal our three colleagues standing but a few feet away, two Tasers, a flashlight, and a camera raised. The flash went off.

"Talk about perfect timing," Jimmy C stated elatedly.

"Man, you blinded me. Damn. So? What? You *planned* to take pics of the place?" Rey asked wryly, squinting. "Hoping for the ultimate big scoop?"

"The ultimate, you bet," he grinned, lowering the camera.

"We found Gail," I announced. "Adwin escorted her to the car."

"GRP had the room, probably the entire house, bugged. Guess he reckoned we'd figure it out," Rey said. "Shit, we should have grabbed that speaker. Oh well. The police'll get it."

Linda tucked the Taser in her jean pocket. "Do you think GRP's in here somewhere?"

I shook my head. "He's close, but not within reach."

"We didn't find much, except a well hidden beneath some dense shrubbery to the far rear of the *ohana*," Sach said. "And then, just when we were going to leave, we discovered this passageway."

"Purely by accident," Jimmy C said with a self-conscious smile. "I tripped into it and it opened."

"This place has suddenly become *very* creepy," Sach grimaced.

"Did you lock up the *ohana*?" I asked.

Linda nodded. "Behind us, as soon as we entered."

"Then let's head back this way. Given Ald's incommunicado, we'll call Hammill on the way home."

"Shouldn't we call him now?" Jimmy C asked. "He and his team members would probably prefer we stuck around. And I'd certainly like to. Maybe I could get some cool details for my story."

"This place could be boobytrapped and, if it is, we may find more than confetti raining down on us," I advised. "Let's not take chances."

"I'm in total agreement." Sach pointed forward. "Let's get out of here, and fast!"

* * *

Three blocks away, Rey put in a call. Hammill answered ten rings later, just as she was about to give up. He hooted when he heard the news, congratulated us, and then told (ordered) us to return to Caprize's house. Our response in a word; no. He or one of his colleagues could come to our place, and arrive without wailing sirens or flashing cruiser. We'd be waiting with fresh coffee and cookies (which we'd picked up at Foodland on the way back).

Rey and Sach escorted Gail to the hospital—much to her annoyance and vocal opposition—to ensure all was okay. She'd insisted she was feeling fine, but she didn't look fine, considering she was leaning into the car door with lackluster eyes, so we weren't taking chances.

Back at the house, I put on coffee and got mugs, sugar, and milk organized while Linda took care of cookies. Adwin, opting for herbal tea, prepared a pot for himself and Jimmy C. Then we all ambled into the living room and dropped onto the sofa and armchairs to await our "guests".

Jimmy C crossed his legs as he sat before the coffee table with his laptop and leaned back. "I wonder if he talked to her. I wanted to ask, but ..."

"She wasn't too with it to answer questions," Linda pointed out, hooking a leg over an armrest. "No matter what she claimed."

A loud knock-knock-knock resounded throughout the house.

"Hit the door with any more force and they may as well knock it down," Linda muttered, hastening to let the police in.

A few seconds later, a grim-visaged Hammill followed Linda, who was trailed by a young burly officer in uniform. The detective jerked a thumb behind. "This is Officer Lecter."

My eyebrow shot up. "His first name Hannibal?"

He regarded me as if I were the cannibalistic serial killer himself. "Where's Gail?"

"At the hospital, being looked at," Adwin told him.

He turned to Lecter. "You wanna patrol outside? Keep an eye out for *any* little thing that seems out of the norm. We're dealing with a very crafty creep." When Lecter had left, he sat in the free armchair. "Sallo's at the house. Ives is on his way there. So's half the force. They're combing the area."

"You're wasting your time. You won't find that dude. He's too smart," Jimmy C stated flatly, then began typing.

Hammill's baleful glare went unnoticed. He looked toward the kitchen. "Did I hear something about fresh coffee? Because I sure smell some."

"Coming up," Adwin said, hopping to his bare feet.

"I want each one of you to tell me what transpired—in *full* detail. And you, Carcanetta, if you're writing a story, I want to see it before you do anything with it. We don't want any info out there that shouldn't be. So, let's start with you, Linda." He removed a laptop from his messenger bag. "Then I'll head over to the hospital and, if Gail's up to it, I'll get her side."

An hour later and two rounds of coffee later, rapid rapping on the front door sounded. I got up, wondering if more police had arrived.

It was Gail, Sach, and Rey. All held large take-out coffees.

"That was quick. Aren't you supposed to be in a hospital bed, recuperating?" I asked, motioning them in and closing the door.

"The ER was—oddly enough—almost empty," Gail replied. "I got in quickly, let them draw blood and do a couple of tests, and then left ... while the nurse went to the nurse's station to get something."

"Gail all but yanked us out the entrance," Rey said with a

dark smile, sinking onto the sofa alongside Jimmy C and taking a long sip of coffee. "Too bad. I was hoping to see that doctor again. And what a name: Aloysius Samuel Farnsworth III. But he was as down-to-earth as his name was hoity-toity."

Slowly, Gail lowered herself onto the rug by the sofa. "Yeah, he was real nice doc," she said with a wistful sigh.

"*Hunky* doc," Sach murmured with a wistful sigh.

"*Real* hunky doc," Rey declared with a wistful sigh.

Linda grinned and I swallowed my laughter. Adwin shook his head and stared at the ceiling while Hammill and Jimmy C looked at each other and shrugged.

"He recommended Gail drop by around nine," Rey said. "Maybe I'll go with."

Gail gave her a high five.

Hammill's cell phone rang. "Yeah. Sure." Two minutes of a one-sided conversation ensued. "Okay, I'll tell them."

"Ald wants us at the office *tout de suite*, right?" Linda.

He shook his head. "Tomorrow at eleven. It's going to be an all-nighter at the house."

"Anything happen? Anything or anybody found?" Rey queried, leaning forward.

He shook his head again. "We'll check if those rose petals and that speaker were purchased anywhere local. Are you up to sharing the details now, Gail? Or would you prefer to wait until the morning?"

"Do you mind waiting?" she asked wearily. "I'll be there at eleven with my friends here."

He smiled fleetingly and rose. "I'll collect Lecter and see you at the station tomorrow. Lock up tight folks. You know, I could have someone stay here—"

"We'll be fine," Linda advised, waving him off.

"We should probably call it a night," Rey said, watching the detective leave.

Jimmy C leaned forward, eyeing Gail closely. "Mind if I ask

… did GRP talk to you?" Jimmy C asked, leaning forward, eyeing Gail closely.

"He did a bit. He told me to relax. Mentioned the weather, I think. I wasn't that out of it at first, when I was on the floor in the back of his car, but before he got ready to carry me inside the house, he shot something into me." She snorted softly. "He was playing Red Velvet. Never thought of him as someone that might like pop music. Odd, huh?"

"You mean, you never thought of him as a real human being?" Linda asked with a wry smile.

"Who's Red Velvet?" Rey asked, puzzled.

"A South Korean girl group," I answered.

Gail gave a thumb's up. "A good one, too. Anyway, that guy's strong, too. As he was tying me to the chair, I recall him telling me how much fun he was having playing this game with you, and welcomed me as a new player." She took quick sips of coffee and stared ahead with a pensive brow. "He was kind of nice, actually, almost charming, even a little … regretful maybe. He said he hoped he wouldn't have to kill me, but per the rules of the game, if you didn't find me, he'd have no choice."

"Did you see his face?"

"He had no qualms about me seeing it." The pensive brow again. "He bore a striking resemblance to Stuntman Mike, forehead scar and all."

"Who?" Adwin and I asked in unison.

"The main character—a serial killer, as it were—from Tarantino's *Death Proof*," Rey answered with a smug smile.

"A very good movie, in fact, save for some longwinded dialogue," Jimmy C added. "What an interesting choice. He must have spent a few hours getting that make-up just right." He turned to Gail. "Do you mind if I get some facts and feature you in my story? I'll call it, hmm … *Escaping the Crazed Cruel Clutches of a Scheming Serial Killer*."

"Sure, but you better work on that title," she winked, standing and stretching.

"Too much?"

"Way too."

CHAPTER FORTY-TWO

"Dan Tanna wants ya," Rey said with a cheeky smile and, leaning into the mudroom doorframe, took a sip of Perrier from a tall tumbler. She'd changed into a short lacy nightie, displaying lanky legs, ones gumshoes—private eyes of yesteryear—might have called "great gams".

I grabbed my cell from the kitchen counter, glancing at the clock and absently noting it was four minutes after midnight. Linda had already gone to bed, as had Adwin and Jimmy C. Sach was seated at the kitchen table, eating a Granny Smith apple as he reviewed tomorrow's must-do list.

"Whatzup?" I asked.

"Missing anyone?"

"You? *Again?*" I pressed "Speaker" and placed the phone on the table.

Sach looked up with those squirrel-tail bushy eyebrows raised high.

"Keeping the game interesting, and you all on your pretty toes," GRP said gaily.

"Keeping us something, that's for sure," I responded. "We're all accounted for."

"Are you?"

"GRP, Slim, I'm tired and I'm hanging up."

"Oh, of course you're tired." He clicked his tongue. "Okay, this one's a favor. How's that boyfriend of yours?"

My blood chilled and my stomach flipflopped. I gazed anxiously at my cousin.

She stood ramrod straight, her jaw taut. Sach sat back and started chewing his bottom lip.

"That loser you had that tiff with earlier this afternoon, outside that little café, has to be your boyfriend, what with the way you walked off in a huff and he got into that snazzy BMW looking like a smug-ass jerk."

"That's because he is," I said dully. "You were watching?"

"I watched Linda first for a while, then Rey, and then you."

"Nothing better to do?"

He chuckled.

"You called to bid us goodnight?"

"I called to tell you I have Mr. Smug-Ass. Would you like to experience the ultimate thrill?"

My heart skipped a couple of beats. "What's that?"

"Running a roulette along someone's body, someone who's done you wrong, someone who's a plain pain."

I could feel my face tense. I was about to provide an angry comeback, which Rey must have sensed or anticipated, because she began flapping her arms like a tornado-whipped windmill. "Be careful," she mouthed. "Play the game."

I drew a quick breath. "Done me wrong?"

"He was cheating on you, using you. He had a wife *and* kids. He went home after he left you."

"Wife? Kids?" I looked at Rey, wide-eyed.

"Rayna. Madison Taylor and Nathan Matthew."

"How did you find—"

"After I followed him, I sat around in the car and did some research. You can find names, addresses, anything, if there's a will and a way. It's pretty easy. So, JJ, do you want the supreme thrill? You can etch your name in his body so he'll *never* forget you ... at least while he's alive." High-pitched, rapid-fire laughter erupted, reminiscent of a relentlessly ringing bicycle bell.

I shot up and tumbled from the bed. Ouch. Glancing around the dimness, the laughter still resounding, I realized the bicycle-styled alarm clock I'd purchased recently was bidding me to rise and shine. I'd set it for 7:15.

Thank the Lord. It had been a dream—a *very* bad one.

* * *

"It's dee-vine," Rey murmured with an over-the-top smile that only the former B-movie actress could manage as she took another demure sip of a lovely dry and smoky coffee. "Thanks much, Ovarie."

Luc E Mei's father's "manservant", a small slender sexage-narian, nodded with equal demureness. "That would be Over-guard, ma'am." A brown-spotted, heavily-veined hand placed the Meissen porcelain coffee pot on a handcrafted square coffee tray and nodded again, asking us to please help ourselves to the croissants, blueberry muffins, and coconut turnovers resting on a lovely English platter etched with gold. Our cups matched it and the rest of the china.

Rey, Linda and I were seated at a round table at the edge of one of two wrap-around lanais, near a heated, tiled pool at the rear of Richard Rijk Mei's magnificent oceanside home. It was so lavish, it could have graced the cover of *Architectural Digest* or *Better Homes & Gardens*). At 9:30, the sun was bright, the breeze light, and nary a cloud in sight. Catamarans, sailboats, and a couple of handsome anchored yachts—an Open Flybridge and Marex 375—were in view. Another happy day in Paradise.

We'd been engaging in small talk, a little about the agency and a lot about Mei's successful video game business. Proud of his credentials and accomplishments, he seemed innocuous enough, and a little arrogant perhaps but not obnoxiously so.

We'd not had the privilege of meeting the owner of the house, Mei's father; he had flown out the day before to attend a convention in Boston and visit colleagues while there for a week. The wife, Myrtle, had left with a girlfriend to spend a few days in France.

Eventually, we turned to the topic at hand: his brother, Slim Gevaar Mei. Also known as GRP.

Mei smiled tartly as he took a sip, pinkie raised, sporting a multi-diamond pinkie ring. He watched a couple of Cattle Egrets where the grass met a small swath of sand that served as their private beach. Dressed in a Versace print silk shirt and Brunello Cucinelli jeans, the handsome (not born-with) features, gave him the look of a GQ model. He spoke with a hint of a "highbrow" British accent; given he'd rarely left the Islands, save for the odd Mainland business trip, you had to wonder how he'd acquired it.

"What makes you think I'd know anything about Slim and his affairs?"

"Surely you've kept in touch?" Linda asked nonchalantly, taking a croissant the size of a 747 with obvious glee. A big blob of boysenberry preserves landed alongside the fragrant crescent-shaped roll.

When he didn't respond, I felt compelled to ask the question again. "You haven't remained in touch then?"

"Just greetings on birthdays and certain holidays." Mei broke a tiny piece from his muffin, popped it into his mouth, and looked across the water. The man's family had a beautiful view as well as home. "Why the interest, if I may ask?"

"He's integral to a case we're involved in," Linda responded reticently.

He popped another piece into his mouth and chewed slowly as he regarded her intently. Ocean-blue eyes, like the expression, revealed no emotion.

"You've *not* seen him?" Rey prodded, pouring more cream into her coffee.

His gaze on her sparkling rhinestone crustacean crabby-crab earrings, he finally offered a thousand-watt smile (those gleaming-white choppers had to have cost a few grand),. "He's into theater. I'm not. We have little in common," he replied, evading the question.

"We understand there was friction between you two," I offered.

"Does that have anything to do with your case? Or is the case information confidential?" Another thousand-watt smile. "And, not that I mind having breakfast with three pretty women, but is it common practice for *everyone* in an agency to come calling?" He motioned Overguard and pointed to his empty cup.

The man, who'd been standing the shade of an awning, had to amble several yards; it would have been easier, and quicker, for Mei to refill his own cup. Ah, the life of the privileged.

"Let's cut to the chase," Rey declared. "Are you protecting him? Hiding him?"

"Why would I do that?" he asked blandly.

"Because he's the guy who's been gracing the headlines—you know, the one leaving black roses on dead, tortured bodies."

Mei's full [enhanced] lips drew into a tight line. "His name's not been mentioned in the papers or media. Do you have proof he's behind those killings?"

"We heard it from his very lips. Up close and personal."

He chuckled briefly, drolly. "Slim was always a joker—and a twisted one, at that."

"Where can we find him?" Rey persisted.

"I wouldn't know." He rose and bowed regally. "Overguard will see you have more of our personally blended brew. I have an appointment at ten." He offered a quick salute. "It's been ... interesting ... if not entertaining. You know, I wouldn't take Slim too seriously. He can be quite the prankster, among other things. *Adieu*, ladies."

With that, he strolled along the flagstone walkway to the four-door garage.

Overguard topped up our cups. "Please allow me to pack up these lovely pastries for you to enjoy at home."

Linda smiled and told him that would be most appreciated and we watched the man return to the house with the platter.

"What do you think? Could it be that GRP—Slim—really is joking around? Pranking us?" Linda asked drily.

"No," Rey and I replied simultaneously, and my cousin scanned the dwelling. "Is he in there, ya think?"

"Yes," Linda and I answered in unison.

"Dare we?" she asked with a twinkle.

Linda slapped her hand playfully.

Rey slapped back. "Let's see what sort of security system Mei's daddy has before we go find the bastard."

"We don't know anything about circumventing security systems, Cousin Reynalda," I reminded her.

"We can learn," she replied determinedly.

Linda and I regarded the luxurious two-story dwelling. My cousin was right. We could learn. But how quickly?

* * *

"Here's hoping we fully absorbed Petey May's twenty-minute tutorial re beating security systems," Rey murmured, eyes glued to the Bushnell binoculars as she surveyed the vast Mei property from our vantage point two [mega] houses over.

We were behind dense shrubs, alongside a granite flagstone curved wall of a vacant for-sale property that apparently no one was interested in purchasing; it had been on the market for five months (Linda got curious as we were keeping surveillance). You would never see us from the street or the Mei place unless you were *really* looking—with a telescope or binoculars.

Petey May, by the by, was a Big Island P.I. we'd befriended during our first official case, where we'd had to discover the "secret" of a millionaire's pretty young wife, but soon discovered her murdered instead. Reminiscent of a 50s

TV hardcore private eye, Petey frequently provided professional advice. I smiled as I envisioned his deaf, fairly toothless sidekick, Barney Fife, a cross between Irish Setter and English Springer Spaniel. Hopefully, we'd get to sit down and share a couple of pizzas again soon (if was a favorite of the pooch, too).

It was four in the afternoon and Luc E Mei had arrived back at his father's house ten minutes ago. Given the shiny-clean Boxster remained on the gray-paver driveway, it appeared he wasn't staying long.

"We won't be entering the place tonight, so we can review it again tomorrow. Good idea taping it, Linda." I scanned the neighborhood. Save for a landscaper and a middle-aged lady walking a pot-bellied pig, no one was about.

Rey passed the binoculars to Linda. "I thought I saw shades move in the *ohana*, but it might have been the air-conditioner blowing them or the sun playing tricks on my eyes—the reflection's pretty strong."

"It would be the logical place to conceal GRP, or Slim, as the case may be. Overguard probably doesn't go there often," Linda offered, staring at it through the powerful optical device.

"It's possible Overguard is aware," I said. "I mean, if Luc's brother were staying there, why would the man think anything was out of the norm? He'd view Slim as a sibling, not a serial killer."

"He might have seen the media's pics," Rey said airily.

"Why would Overguard believe that the killer might be Slim, if he even saw them? One's a sketch and one's a cropped, grainy photo. He resembles a lot of guys: nondescript."

Linda lowered the binoculars. "And Luc, if he does know the truth, wouldn't share it with the butler."

"Hey! Mei's leaving," Rey announced. "Wait—he's walking toward the *ohana*."

"Interesting," Linda and I said in unison and glanced at each other with quick smiles.

"I think we should sneak in there tonight," my cousin declared.

I shook my head. "We don't know how long Mei's going to stick around. Besides, tomorrow night he'll be back on Maui, so we're guaranteed no interruptions."

"Except when GRP, uh, Slim finds us snooping around," Linda stated blandly.

Rey's strong jawline set. "We'll be prepared."

"What if he's not in the *ohana*?"

Rey eyed her best friend. "Then we check the big house. We'll just have to find a distraction for Overguard and that housekeeper."

She offered a limp shrug. "I know the answer, but I'll ask anyway. Shouldn't we tell Ald?"

"We have no proof GRP, ugh, Slim's staying here," I answered. "Maybe you're right. It wouldn't hurt to call—"

"No," Rey interrupted firmly. "He'll only tell us to stay put, maybe even post some boy or girl in blue at our door to make sure we do. Slim's *our* collar, as they say in cop shows. The dude pulled us into this perverted game, so we're staying in it until it officially ends ... by us taking him in."

Linda looked edgy. "We better invest in extra sturdy disposable restraints."

"Aluminum chain-link ones might be better," I said sarcastically.

"What the hell. We'll get a sundry."

* * *

Adwin and Sach joined us at seven for dinner on the lanai. The guys were grilling chicken breasts and ahi, and us gals were making salads: Caesar and niçoise. Dessert was a decadent blueberry-lavender gelato and nothing stronger than soda was on the drinks menu.

"You're *not* going it alone," Adwin declared for the second time, waving a long-handled spatula for effect. "Sach and I are coming and that's that ... or I'll call Ald Ives."

"Tattletale." Rey stuck out her tongue as she arranged cutlery on the side table.

"You may be professionals now, but you don't have that many cases under your belts," Sach stated firmly, brushing the chicken with an apricot-chili glaze. "We're coming and that's that. We'll hang back, but we'll be there, ready to pounce if anything goes wrong."

"We'll have cell phones and Tasers handy," Adwin added.

Rey sighed loudly. "Fine. You two can follow us in Linda's car. We've got a small, dark rental lined up for tomorrow that our guy won't recognize."

"Unless he follows you to the rental agency," Sach said drily, checking the ahi.

Linda grabbed a can of club soda from an ice-filled bucket. "That's a good point. GRP—Slim—has a habit of doing that."

Rey dropped onto the chaise longue. "We'll have to be extra watchful tomorrow."

"You'd think he'd be more cautious now and stay put. In fact, if I were him, I'd have flown to a place far, far away," Linda stated with a black look.

"He doesn't have to be overly careful, given his talent with disguises," I pointed out. "He can blend into any crowd."

She nodded and poured soda into a tall plastic tumbler. "What if he's not at Daddy's place?"

Rey and I looked at each other with pensive brows.

Sach gestured the diet cola Adwin held in one hand; ginger ale was in the other. "You'll be starting from scratch then. Looking for a teeny needle in a mammoth haystack."

"Then we'll have to devise a plan to draw him out," I responded. "Maybe with the help of Jimmy C and his social media connections."

"Let's just get through tomorrow night first, then worry about new plans of attack," Rey said solemnly.

"I get that he might not be there, and you don't want to alert the police on a 'gut feeling'," Sach advised somberly, "but what if he *is* there? And you didn't communicate that to the cops? And what if he kills again before tomorrow night? That's on you, you know."

Rey shook her head. "Our detective friends won't check out the house on a whim. There's no proof, nothing to warrant a search ... nothing to warrant a warrant."

"How can you be so sure they won't? Maybe if you three shared—"

"Fine! Let's just do it. Go ahead JJ, *call*. Then you guys can shut up already and we can eat dinner without continuing to argue."

I complied, and was proven right. Ald said they couldn't check out the premises based on "greenhorn P.I. gut instincts". Dr. Richard Rijk Mei was not a man without [considerable] influence; we'd better have concrete evidence if we intended to go up against him. But the detective did promise to have an unmarked car cruise pass regularly. The plainclothes officer would keep an eye open for GRP sightings "up and above the dozen we're getting every hour on the hour".

And that was that, until nine the next morning when we arrived at the agency office after picking up the rental car.

CHAPTER FORTY-THREE

Three woodsy-scented North Shore Candle Company candles burned on the counter of the "sort-of" kitchen to offer the agency a pleasing non-stale-office scent. Lips drawn tight, Linda stared across the room while my cousin responded to texts and I reviewed the agency website, revising a bit here and there.

At 9:25, Beck Bild returned our call. He had an odd voice, rather like Bugs Bunny. When I put him on speaker, it took Rey everything she had not to laugh or comment, and I did everything I could to not laugh upon seeing her facial expressions and gesticulations. Linda merely shook her head and took control of the conversation.

"I don't know much about Slim. Never met him. Luc once told me they had an odd relationship. Sometimes they got along famously. Other times they didn't. And in the early years, never."

"Do they hang out together a lot now?"

"They get together on birthdays, sometimes."

"Has this been going on for years or is this just recent?" Linda asked casually.

"Recent. Last four years. Maybe five."

"What do you know about him?"

"Next to nil, other than the guy's into theater and does make-up and acting now and again. Oh, he's into chess and games. The guy's super bright. I believe Slim actually gave Luc the idea to start this company."

Henry Spieler called not long after his partner and his answers to my questions were pretty much the same as his colleague's. But he did add one interesting fact: Luc hated his father. Luc, however, never exhibited animosity, never made it known. How had Spieler found out? He'd overheard Luc on the phone one afternoon, telling the person on the other end how he loved the old man's money, but loathed the old fart's face, attitude, and "jackassness".

"Daddy Dearest had *real* control over Luc, but one day, Luc put his foot down and hard ... said he'd had enough and was moving out. That went over like a ton of bricks." He chuckled darkly. "Luc did get his own place of course, eventually, but he's at the old man's house more than he is at his own. Poor guy. It's hard for some people to snip those f'g apron strings or, in this case, purse strings." Another dark chuckle.

"One last question?"

"Sure, but then I have to run. Meetings abound today."

"What sort of business do you have on Maui? Luc seems to fly over quite frequently."

"We don't have business per se, but a game designer we hired lives there. He's working on one that involves the components of chess, but not on a board."

"Slim's concept?" I asked nonchalantly.

"Yeah." He laughed. "Luc and the designer, Theram—Joy-Boy's his gamer name—hit it off so well from the get-go, that Luc flies over as often as he can."

I thanked him for his time and disconnected.

"So Slim's cozier with his brother than he likes to admit," Linda stated with a pensive brow.

"And Luc hates the old guy as much as Slim," Rey nodded,

slipping her cell phone into the pocket of her collarless open-front jacket.

I walked over to the pedestal table and sat on the edge, arms crossed. "Are we good for tonight?"

"We're good," Rey confirmed. "We got our tools, weapons, restraints. Adwin and Sach'll play watchdogs."

I looked from my cousin to her best friend. "This isn't going to be a walk in the park."

"I think we know that," Rey said saltily.

Linda nodded. "And what do we want to do about Jimmy C and his connections?"

I scanned her grim expression. "I thought we decided to wait, depending on what happens tonight?"

"Let's make the game more interesting." Linda offered a wicked smile. "Why not have Jimmy C post that the serial killer that has this island on edge is about to be caught?"

"Slim wouldn't believe it," I responded drily. "He'd think, rightly so, that we put Jimmy C up to it."

"Then let's add something to it to piss him off." Rey's eyes sparkled mischievously. "Let's have him say something like the police know who it is and are—"

"You want to piss off *Ald*?" Linda interjected, stunned.

"Suggesting the police know who it is before they're ready to, Rey, is *way* dangerous," I stated, standing and ambling to the window. I peered onto a drizzly, car-heavy street.

A homeless man with a cart filled with bags and boxes was sauntering along the sidewalk. A plastic bag covered his battered soiled sun hat. Another man remained dry by sitting on the ground, his back against a vacant storefront. Two young teens with no-name baseball caps and heavy knapsacks on their lanky backs sauntered along, listening to music, and sipping sodas.

"Crap, isn't the luau tonight?" I asked, suddenly recalling Mink's reminder email.

"Dang, it is," Linda confirmed with a frown.

"Too bad, so sad, but we have something more important." Rey's tone leaned toward caustic.

Before Linda could respond, I hastily said, "Back to posting about him being caught soon—we don't have to mention the police. Just say clues and evidence—and witnesses—have been forthcoming. Let's make him nervous." With a what-do-you-think expression, I looked from Linda to Rey and back again.

Linda shrugged. "It *won't* make him nervous and it *won't* do anything except maybe get us another call, but what the heck? Let's stir the pot a bit."

* * *

At two, we were back home, getting things ready for the "visit" to Dr. Mei's estate. We'd be wearing black leggings, black long-sleeved Ts, black canvas runners, and black beanies. For now, we were in shorts and tanks, sipping Perriers as we sat in the living room, reviewing plans and double-checking that everything was packed. Adwin and Sach would be by around six. The rental car was parked several blocks over, just in case Slim swung by to see what we were up to. Everything, so far, was going as scheduled!

Jimmy C had posted on social media and his blog about the upcoming capture; he'd also be on the evening news, reiterating his encounter with the Rose-Pin Killer, aka the Ha-Ha Killer.

Murder She Wrote announced a call and Rey grabbed my cell before I could. She stuck out her tongue, pressed "Speaker", and chirped, "Howzit?"

"My favorite private eye," Slim chirped in response. "How goes it, Rey dearheart?"

"Fine, now that you called," she crooned, cranking up the volume.

"You knew I would. That's why you had Jimmy C put out that feeler."

"Then we won. Again."

He chuckled, but not with humor. "You really believe you'll be capturing me soon?"

"If we don't, someone will," she said merrily. "But I'm gonna bet it's us."

"You know, I'm gonna give you that," he said with equal cheer. "Do you have an idea where to find me?"

"What if we did?"

He laughed. "You know, we could call this a stalemate."

"And what? Go our separate ways? Forget all that's happened?"

"Why not?"

"You play to win, Slim. So do we," she affirmed crisply.

"*Slim*? Okay, farewell to GRP, we knew thee well." He laughed again. "I'll be awaiting your citizen's arrest."

Before Rey could respond, he was gone.

"Do you think he has a sense we know where he is?" Rey asked, placing the phone on the coffee table.

"We were at his father's house. He knows we dropped by, either because he saw us—because he *is* there—or Luc told him." Linda got up to get three more cans of soda and passed them to us. "But whether he really is staying there or not, at some point he's got to be thinking that we'll head there."

Rey's sipped thoughtfully for several seconds. "If he *is* staying there, do you think he'll wait for us to 'figure it out' and show up … that he'll sit tight, like a hunter waiting to take aim at game birds?"

"If he's not staying there, I have a feeling he may head over to 'greet' us," she replied with a firm nod. "I think he wants this game to end as much as we—and everyone else—do."

* * *

After a quick dinner of tuna-salad sandwiches, Sach and Adwin, and the three of us packed the cars, reviewed plans, and then sat back a wee while in an effort to relax. We'd enter the Meis' *ohana* at eleven or thereabouts and if one of us didn't "check in" with the boys within thirty minutes, Ald would receive a call.

Both cars were parked three blocks over, at the for-sale house from where the three of us had recently surveilled the Mei mansion. On the way over, the guys had picked up Jimmy C, who'd called just after completing the interview.

The blogger-writer had come across cool and collected, and knowledgeable. He'd relayed the facts of his kidnapping and drugging, and the few details he could relate (like the serial killer's taunting calls to "private-investigator colleagues"). He didn't mention the police, as agreed, but did state that there was "substantive evidence" and some "forthcoming witnesses", and he was certain "apprehension was imminent".

Had Slim seen the interview? If so, what had he thought? Was he worried that he was about to be caught? How would he react? Would he run? Or retaliate?

Bidding the boys well, Rey, Linda and I slowly made our way over.

"All quiet on the western front," Rey joked quietly as we surveyed the estate. Save for a dozen elegant brass path lights, the place was fairly dark.

"World wars are hardly worth making light of," Linda murmured, referencing the WWI premise of the book of the same title as she adjusted the small knapsack on her back.

"Don't get those knickers in another knot, Lindy-Loo," she replied drily.

"Play nice, kids," I advised, gesturing ahead. "It's show time!"

* * *

"It worked," Linda whispered triumphantly, closing the rear door softly.

We'd successfully circumvented the security system and snuck across to the *ohana*. Moonless and cloudy, the night was perfect for surreptitious detecting or, as Rey jestingly worded it, covert ops.

Overguard was still awake, so we assumed upon sighting a pale light in the second-floor corner window over the garage. Clarissa, the housekeeper-cook, had been with the family ten years. We figured her room was probably the one at the rear of the kitchen, with the added exterior exit/entrance; it was dark.

"Turn the *ohana* lights on?" Rey asked quietly. "Or just use flashlights?"

"No lights at all," I replied softly, waiting for my eyes to adjust to the dimness.

"Gun ready?" my cousin inquired.

"Uh-huh."

"Taser, Lindy-Loo?"

"Uh-huh."

"Do we separate?"

"Uh-uh," Linda and I answered in unison.

"You know, we could just call out for our unflappable friend."

Linda's mouth dropped as Rey called out. "GRP? Slim?"

"Good grief." Linda groaned. "Here, let's just turn on the f'g lights and engage in a sing-along."

I grabbed Linda's arm before she could flip the switch. "We don't want to alert anyone in the main house."

"But the drapes are closed—"

"Ssh," I hissed, silencing Rey's loud voice. "Let's stop yammering and start searching."

"Upstairs first?" asked Linda.

I nodded. "You two go up. I'll stand guard here, behind the stairwell, in case there is someone upstairs—namely GRP, uh, Slim—and he decides to scurry down here while you're up there."

"If he sees the two of us, he'll know you're down here," Rey pointed out.

"So, we'll have a face-to-face."

"Or a roulette to the heart. *Yours,*" she said flatly, turning on the mini flashlight and beaming it around. "Nice."

The furniture was high-end Ethan Allan traditional: comfortable and classic. Prime colors: tan, taupe, and chestnut. Lamps were elegant hand-painted ceramic. The artwork: various farmscapes and landscapes. Mosaic tiles covered the floor.

She shone the light on the winding stairwell lined with a soft, woven carpet runner bearing a Berber theme. "Ready, Lindy-Loo?"

"Sure, Rey-Poo. Let's do it."

I watched them head up and then slipped alongside the stairwell, gun firmly in hand.

My eyes had adjusted to the lack of lighting. We were close to catching/confronting Slim Gevaar Mei, of this I had little doubt, but how it would all end was as much a mystery as Mona Lisa's smile.

Who or what would my colleagues find? I couldn't hear any footfalls, which was good; they were being stealthy. Still, we'd made enough noise already to alert anyone inside the *ohana*.

I scratched a persistent itch at the base of my neck. My cell advised it was 11:25. How much time had elapsed since we'd stepped in? Ten minutes? Twenty? It was hard to tell ... and it was hard leaning into the wall, waiting and wondering.

My cell phone vibrated. The display revealed an unknown number. Text message: *Olly olly oxen free. But it's not yet the end of the game. Exciting, isn't it? Will they or won't they?*

Damn. Was our killer in here? Or watching from nearby? More importantly:

will they or won't they *what*?

CHAPTER FORTY-FOUR

My cohorts in crime soared pell-mell down the stairs as I was about to wend my cautious way up. I swear their feet didn't touch the ground, but we did ... when we toppled onto the patterned silk carpet like twister-propelled saplings.

"Oof."

"Ouch."

"Dang."

Disentangling ourselves, we struggled upright and nearly toppled again.

"He's up there!" Rey said breathlessly, gesturing dramatically.

"Slim?" I rubbed a sore elbow.

"Luc E Mei!"

"What!"

Rey retrieved the gun and mini flashlight from the floor. "He's wrapped in cellophane, like one of Aunt Gertrude's lunchtime, cottage-deck baloney and sauerkraut sandwiches! He's in a fancy-shmancy high-back executive chair, and there's blood oozing along the chest—"

"Courtesy of Slim's handy-dandy roulette," Linda interjected breathlessly.

"He killed his own brother?" I asked, stunned, taking the gun Rey held forth.

Linda nodded grimly. "We thought he might do that back when, remember? But with all that we'd learned, who'd have thought he'd *actually* do it?"

"Maybe Slim got worried that Luc would reveal that he was helping his brother," I suggested.

"That dude doesn't worry," Rey asked saltily. "No, he'd have done this just for the fun of it."

I showed them the text.

"Will they or won't they what? Find Luc?" Linda asked, bemused. "It wasn't that hard. He was in front of a window in a room that serves as an office and library."

"Yeah, but if we hadn't walked up to that window," Rey stated, "we'd not have seen him, because that fancy-shmancy chair was turned toward it."

"True," she conceded with a frown. "Imagine if we hadn't found him? Poor Overguard or Clarissa—or Daddy Dearest—would have."

I shook my head. "GRP-uh-Slim put him there for us to find. He knew we'd come here. And if we hadn't, he'd have delivered his dead brother to us some other way."

"So much for familial love," Linda said flatly.

"Did we believe it actually existed with these folks?" I asked sarcastically.

She and Rey snorted in stereo.

"I guess it's time to call Ald," I said.

"And alert the household," Linda added solemnly.

"I'll do it," my cousin volunteered. "You wanna go tell Adwin and Sach what happened? Leave the cars there, though. In twenty minutes, this area'll resemble an outdoor concert parking lot."

She nodded, took a deep breath, and left.

"What a mess," Rey stated, walking to the door.

"That would be an understatement," I said wryly and called Ald.

* * *

A little over an hour later the police and various teams had arrived to methodically process the crime scene. Linda, and I sat on reclining rattan chaises by the pool while Rey dangled her bare feet in the tepid water. Adwin and Sach reclined on floating padded pool loungers, faces directed at the cloudy sky, attempting to sleep. Overguard, bless his heart, had seen urns of coffee and tea were quickly available. We'd just finished our teas and were awaiting refills from a remarkably calm Clarissa; she'd just returned to the kitchen with her cart.

The *ohana*, house, and property blazed with light, as did the street—with hyperactive media sorts and prying spectators. Excitement and anticipation flourished. An arrest—everyone expected—was now imminent. Sure. In their dreams. Slim wouldn't be found any time soon, if ever. Idly, I wondered if Jimmy C was out there in the crowd; Adwin and Sach and Linda had lost him on the trek back to the house.

By the diving board several feet away, Sallo was vaping as he spoke into his cell several feet away. He was dressed in a short-sleeved beige shirt and black pants, and the signature fedora. Ald and Hammill were inside. We'd already provided statements and were hanging around at the request of Ald, just in case Slim called or texted, or they required more input/information. We didn't mind; this way we could get a firsthand account of what was transpiring.

"Jessica Fletcher's calling," Rey said drily, referring to the *Murder She Wrote* ringtone.

I answered the unknown number, expecting [hoping] it to be our serial killer. It was Cash.

"How's it going?"

"Does it matter?"

355

"Look, I couldn't sleep. I thought I'd call and we could have a civil conversation."

"Maybe. Another time." I disconnected. I had to give some thought to this bizarre relationship ... another time.

Rey got up, stretched, and motioned the property with dramatic flair—like ambitious Lady Macbeth gesturing doomed King Duncan. "Think he's out there somewhere?"

"Most likely," Linda replied. "And I'm going to bet he's on the water, which is probably where he was when we were here, chatting with his brother."

We turned to the ocean. Sure. He'd not been in the *ohana* but in one of the boats anchored close by. At this moment, I couldn't see any boats under the cloudy night sky, but that didn't mean there wasn't one anchored or docked out there. Note to self: check out boats in the a.m. No point in adding to Ald's workload if we were wrong.

"Of course. He was watching from one of the boats," Rey voiced softly, scanning the Pacific.

Sach stirred and Adwin sat up. "Whatzup?"

"We are ... still," Linda said wryly. "But we may have a new lead to follow."

"Not that it will help us much now," I said, discouraged.

"It may," she declared with an expression of hope on her shadowed face. "If we track down those boats, we may find Slim."

"Maybe."

"Ms. Optimistic you're not," Rey smirked. "Okay, so this case has been one major screw-up since the get-go. Doesn't mean it has to stay that way."

"It was never in our control," Linda pointed out.

"That's right," Sach agreed, standing, and embarking on triceps stretches. "GRP—Slim—has called all the shots pretty much. You're good P.I.s, but you're dealing with a crazy guy with super smarts."

"And doing a great job," Adwin declared. "Ald and his

people haven't been able to find much evidence, never mind him, so consider how much you've accomplished."

Sallo sauntered over, still vaping. I didn't want to think about how much nicotine he was ingesting.

"Anything new?" Rey asked.

"Nothing of note." He shrugged and then asked gruffly, "Anything from your pal?"

I shook my head. "No calls, no texts or emails."

He frowned. "Maybe you should head home. There's nothing more you can do here. And I have a feeling this guy's not going to contact you tonight—er, this morning."

I looked at Rey and Linda. They nodded in return.

"Will you keep us in the loop?" Rey asked him.

"Yeah, sure." The tone suggested he wouldn't go out of his way. He pointed to the next property. "If you walk that way, you should be able to avoid the media."

Adwin looked toward where they'd parked and sighed upon seeing the many headlights advancing slowly this way. "We can hope."

* * *

After watching Adwin follow Sach into his house, where he'd catch some sleep, we pulled onto our asphalt driveway. At 2:30 we were tired, yet pumped.

"Tea?" Rey asked as we slipped into the mudroom. "Might help us relax and sleep."

"Mint for me," I answered, removing my runners.

"Chamomile." Linda tossed hers on top of Rey's, which had just graced the top of the bench.

"I'll put on the kettle and check agency voicemail."

"I'm surprised he's not contacted us," Linda murmured, rolling up her sleeves as we ambled into the kitchen.

"Part of the game, making an unexpected move." I slipped into a chair at the table as Linda reached into a cupboard and pulled out a gallon tub of Donna's Assorted Cookies. Placing them on the table, she hastened from the room and returned seconds later with her laptop. "I'm all for checking those boats we saw the other day."

Rey stopped by the stainless-steel cordless kettle and prepared mugs. "Jimmy C called from the Mei place; he decided to hang around with a couple of TV reporters he'd recently gotten to know. Unless he hears back from one of us soon—that message was over an hour ago—and tell him to pop over, he'll be here around eight a.m."

"Any other messages?" Linda asked, cramming an oatmeal-raisin disc in her mouth.

Rey was about to respond when a shrill "shit" rang forth. She stared at the window and Linda and I turned to see what had startled her.

Sach and Adwin, tense-faced, were looking in, their eyes as saucer-round as Rey's.

Linda hastened to the door and the two men raced in like Kentucky Derby thoroughbreds. Adwin held an open self-seal, side-load bubble mailer, Sach a florist card.

My cousin took the mailer that Adwin held forth and peeked inside. "You touch it?"

He shook his head. "Just the envelope."

"And the card," Sach added with a rueful smile, handing it to Linda. "It was on top."

"Where'd he leave them?" I stepped alongside Linda and peered over her shoulder.

"On the mat ... the *inside* mat."

"Cocky bastard, ain't he?" Rey asked sarcastically and then requested Linda read the card.

"This trio of entwined roses is lovely, so much more than the single one I left with Luc, rest his stupid, self-centered soul. I thought you might like a memento of our time together."

"What does that mean? He's going away?" Linda asked, puzzled.

"Or he's changing the rules," Rey said drily. "Not that we ever really knew them."

"We should call Ald," Sach suggested.

"He's busy at the Meis'. This can wait," I said and stifled a yawn. "Water's boiling, Rey."

She got two more mugs and poured water over teabags while we began munching cookies and Linda searched for the boats.

A crash from the rear, the *ohana* maybe, garnered our attention. Linda put a finger to her lips while Rey and I soared through the rear door like nightjars taking wing to snatch meals out of the air.

It had started to rain lightly and steadily, and the grass proved slippery as we skidded across.

Sighting a shadow before the *ohana*, we tackled it like football linebackers. I caught the leg and Rey the shoulders. Down we went, onto the sodden yard.

"Hey! Get off! Damn!"

"Jimmy C!" we shouted in unison.

"What the hell?" Rey demanded, rolling aside and scrambling to her feet.

I got to mine and we both helped our blogger-writer to his.

"I decided to head over just after I left the message." He retrieved his messenger bag. "I thought I'd stick around a little while and when it started raining, I went to stand in the *ohana* entrance. On a whim, I tried the door. It was unlocked. In I went and got comfy ... so much so, I dozed off."

Rey and I turned to each other and simultaneously asked, "Did you forget to lock the door again?"

"Do you think we can get out of the rain, ladies?"

Rey and I linked elbows with his and escorted him inside, grabbing three hand towels on the way to the kitchen.

"Look who we found," she grinned, wiping wetness from her face.

"You have a free-for-all or something?" Sach asked, scanning us from head to foot.

"We thought we were felling Slim," I replied ruefully.

"That would have been nice," he said. "Perp caught. Case solved."

Jimmy C walked to the sink and washed his face and hands while Rey got him a mug of tea.

He took the mug and sat beside Sach. "Is it really Luc E Mei?"

"It is," Linda replied.

One eyebrow arched. "Usual M.O. ? "

"Usual."

"The old man's going to raise Cain."

"Maybe that's what Slim hopes he'll do," I said and rubbed the towel across my face.

Jimmy C eyed me curiously.

"He has no love for his father. Maybe he's hoping this will all blow up in his face."

"That seems … farfetched."

I smiled ruefully. "I said 'maybe'."

"Think we'll hear from him?" he asked.

"Already have." Rey pointed at the mailer and card on the counter.

Jimmy C's forehead crinkled like crumpled paper. "What about leads? Any?"

"The boats," Linda answered, her expression hopeful. "Only the boats."

CHAPTER FORTY-FIVE

"Maybe we should move the office here," Linda joked, referring to the fact we were gathered on the lanai at noon, about to chow down on lamb burgers Adwin had just grilled.

Sach had picked up two salads—Thai and Greek—and a couple of pâtés. Rey and Linda had gotten fresh fruit and veggies from a farmer's market, and I'd bought pastries at a local bakery. Jimmy C had driven off on his Vespa to purchase soda and light beer. Given the lack of sleep, save for a maybe three hours between four and seven this morning, we'd managed to complete tasks without incident.

"Get-togethers and GRP-slash-Slim certainly have gone hand-in-hand," I said, pulling a bottle of Kona Light from the ice-filled bucket.

We were seated under the sizable cantilever shade structure, enjoying the warmth and watching the drizzle that hadn't let up since early morning. When the "case" was finally solved, I rather hoped we'd do this regularly.

Adwin placed two fat burgers on plates. "Ald and Hammill had better be here soon or these will get cold and sauce-soggy."

Rey gestured. "They've arrived, looking more tired than us."

The jeans-and-T-shirt-clad detectives hurried forward and crowded onto the lanai sofa beside Linda.

"Help yourself." She gestured the bucket.

The men looked at each other, shrugged, and grabbed two beers.

"You get any sleep?" Jimmy C asked before sucking back the duck pâté piled on Ryvita crispbread.

"Two hours. Maybe." Hammill frowned and drew on the bottle.

"These'll put some pep in that fatigue." Adwin passed them plates.

"Whatzup?" Rey asked, licking ketchup-coated fingers. "Daddy Mei heard the news?"

Hammill nodded once.

"He's on a jet—should be here now. He wouldn't accept that Slim killed Luc," Ald said with a shake of his head and piled Greek salad on his plate.

"It's hard for a father to accept that type of news," Adwin murmured, sitting on a large sparkly neon-tone outdoor cushion beside the chaise longue.

"And the proof is still lacking. Doesn't matter if three private eyes can confirm that Slim told them he was the serial killer terrorizing Oahu," Rey added.

"Luc did say Slim was a prankster," Linda reminded us. "Come push to shove, as long as that proof isn't there, Slim could claim he was joking around."

"The guy threatened and darted you two, "Ald pointed out. "That's assault and battery—not the same thing as tossing a rock through a window."

"Mr. Peabody-slash-Shaggy darted us," I stated. "We've never really seen him without a disguise, other than the odd—bad—photo."

"We have to tread carefully when asking for public assistance in tracking him down—like via Crime Stoppers. Mei could have a legit lawsuit if we inform the public who we believe GRP, or the Ha-Ha Killer, is—good Lord, this guy has more titles than royalty." He looked at Jimmy C, who appeared rapt.

He held up a flabby hand. "No worries, Detective Ives. I'll only post what you've already revealed, with no mention of Slim, GRP, whatever. But it'd be most welcome if you gave me a tidbit no one else has." He presented a cute puppy-dog smile.

Which made Ald laugh. He looked from his face to mine, to Rey's, then to Linda's. "How about a trade? You have anything to share that you haven't yet?"

Rey threw up an arm and waved it like an excited, starry-eyed concert-goer, looking to attract the lead singer's attention (she did that well).

The attractive detective smirked. "Fonne-Werde?"

"We think Slim was on a boat anchored near the estate the day we were there—and maybe even several days before and after. The name of the Marex 375 was *Money & Mayhem* and it belonged to Richard Rijk Mei. It wasn't there today, from what we viewed on TV—courtesy of cameras from planes and helicopters flying over the property. Slim may be on it as we chat."

"More likely he's ditched it or is somewhere in international waters now," Hammill muttered. "But we can hope." He pulled out his cell, got up, and ambled inside.

"He also left a memento with a card," I advised.

Still standing, Adwin offered to get the items he'd tucked into a plastic bag before we retired.

"So?" Jimmy C smiled with hope. "Trade?"

Ald smiled wryly. "You can tell your followers—and inquisitive sorts—we have a fingerprint. Found on the plastic wrapped around the body. We're certain it belongs to the killer. Like sharks circling their prey, *we* are planning to circle in soon."

"Do you really have one?" Sach asked dubiously, leaning forward.

Ald merely grinned and focused on his burger.

"He won't take the bait," Linda stated flatly.

"Maybe yes; maybe no."

Hammill returned. "Sallo's following up on the boat. Mei's screaming about having Luc's body released. His wife's returning from Paris on an afternoon flight. And the media's chomping at the bit." He eyed Jimmy C intently for several seconds.

"That's really not much, and others will wonder how I got the tip re the fingerprint. They'll suggest I made it up." Jimmy C bit his bottom lip. "Can I add that we—you—have a lead on a boat? More details to follow once it's been located?"

Ald stared at him and I was certain he'd say no. To my surprise, he grinned. "Go for it, kid."

* * *

A little after six, the three of us were parked in Linda's Camry, not far from a couple of media vans, watching police sorts process *Money & Mayhem*. The Marex 375 was currently docked in Pearl Harbor, near a popular waterfront restaurant, but it had been found moored not far from Ford Island Bridge, also known as Admiral Clarey Bridge. A boater, who'd read Jimmy C's post and boat description, had noticed it and called the police.

Rey twirled a Twizzler, her pensive gaze on the bustling activity ahead. It was well lit, thanks to countless portable scene lights. "Think they found something?"

"That melon-round guy with the tablet has a confident look about him, as does the carrot-thin one looking over his shoulder," Linda answered, jumping when the phone rang.

Rey shifted forward so that she was once again halfway between the driver's and passenger's seats.

"Hi. That's rare, you calling me." She put Ald on speaker.

"I tried the agency number and got voicemail. Tried JJ's and Rey's. More voicemail. Took one last chance and I lucked in," he said dully. "As detecting detectives, you might want to keep your phones close at hand."

I checked my bag and found I'd forgotten my cell. Rey pulled hers from the bag at her feet and realized she'd put it on mute. "You got news?" she asked.

"Other than the boat being located, which I have a feeling you're at right now, no. I thought I'd see if you had any, like Mr. Nutbar calling."

"Nothing to report," Linda stated. "But your people are immersed in their jobs. How come you're not here?"

"Sallo and Onneton are on their way. I'm about to head over to Rue's lab to see what they found on your rose-triad 'memento', then stop off at the morgue to hear Smithers' preliminary findings. Here's hoping there's something useful or incriminating on the boat."

"It's quite possible Slim didn't have time to scour the boat like he did the house," she said. "He had to have been in a hurry."

"The guy has Lady Luck on his side, so I wouldn't bet on it." He disconnected and we went back to watching the police in action.

"He's got to feel the noose tightening," Linda murmured.

"Not likely," Rey snorted and pointed with the Twizzler. "Our favorite dick's arrived."

Sallo was climbing out of the passenger's side of a metal-gray Dodge Charger; Onneton had to be the fortyish, gaunt-faced woman who was getting out of the driver's side. Neither looked particularly happy to be in the other's company.

"They must have something," Linda said, holding out a palm.

Rey slapped three licorice rods on it. "Let's drop by the station later. Maybe Ald will have learned something by then."

Jimmy C pulled up on his shiny-cleans scooter as Linda and Rey stepped from the car. "Howzit?" he grinned as he pulled out his camera and scanned the area. "Anything?"

"We asked the very same not long ago," Rey replied, leaning into the car.

Quickly, he took a few photos, then looked at Linda's trio of

Twizzlers. Gleefully, he accepted the one she held forth. "In case you hadn't checked, I posted. No nibbles from our friend."

"None here either," I said, watching Sallo chat with an officer. He must have been in a hurry to get here; he wasn't sporting the signature hat. "I wish I were a *pinao*."

Jimmy C laughed. "I wouldn't mind being a dragonfly myself right now."

Sallo finished talking and scanned the vicinity and noticed us. The scowl said enough. He stomped off to join a quartet of men at the bow of the boat.

"Love you too," Rey muttered.

"You think Mei might be sheltering his crazy kid somewhere?" he asked, taking a bite of the licorice.

"If he believes he's innocent, maybe." Linda.

"No way. He and 'the crazy kid' never had any kind of relationship." Rey.

"That we *know* of." Me.

We pulled out more Twizzlers from Rey's mega-size bag and chewed thoughtfully as we stared at the attentive efficiency transpiring ahead.

We weren't expecting to see or learn anything new standing here, but there was nothing else to do or pursue for the interim.

* * *

Linda placed the tablet on the sofa beside her. She, Rey, Ald and I were seated in a small dim lounge on the second floor of the station, drinking Starbucks coffees we'd picked up before heading over. The room, painted gun-metal gray, wasn't particularly cozy, but it served its function: a refuge from the grit and grimness of the station itself.

Jimmy C had decided to remain at the crime scene to see what he could learn while the three of us had grabbed a quick Thai dinner—mango rolls, hot and spicy chicken, and jasmine rice—at a well-liked family-run restaurant.

The early-day drizzle had returned on the way over and promised to remain indefinitely. It had also grown sweater-required cool. The weather folks on the news had advised of such. Good thing we'd listened and, in addition to sweaters, had brought lightweight rain-jackets.

"So, he whacked his brother on the back of the head with a heavy, blunt object—like one of the golf trophies in the built-in cabinetry." Rey crossed her legs as she leaned back in the mesh-back swivel chair and scanned the wall lined with posters related to police notices and events. "Not his usual approach or style."

"Luc must have caught him by surprise." Ald rubbed his red-rimmed eyes.

"Or pissed him off."

"Or that," he agreed wearily.

"But otherwise the M.O. was pretty much the same." Linda.

"Pretty much."

"How long was he dead?" I asked.

"Maybe an hour and a half before you called it in."

"So, we just missed Slim," Linda said with an expression of awe.

"He was still alive when he was wrapped in plastic," Ald said. "But not by much."

Linda shuddered. "The poor guy must have been aware of his, uh, dilemma for some time."

He eyed Linda for several seconds, then shrugged. "Unpleasantly, unsettlingly ... possible." He glanced at his Movado watch, a handsome new one if I wasn't mistaken. "Walker should be calling about the boat."

"How amazing that hair and fibers were actually found," Linda said.

"I can't believe Slim'd be that careless," Rey murmured.

"Could have been there from before." Ald pulled out his ringing cell phone from his lightweight rain-jacket. "Yeah?"

Rey, Linda and I sipped tepid coffee as he went to a corner and turned his back to us.

"So?" my cousin demanded when the detective sat back down.

"Skipper Gill, the guy who'd noticed the boat and called us, suggested we talk to his 'dockmate', Heinie Higgins; he'd been around all day and might have seen something. Gill was right. Higgins recalls seeing a guy walk away from *Money & Mayhem* around ten. He'd noticed him because of the loud shirt with skulls and bones—'eye-squinching tangerine and melon'—and purple latex gloves. The baseball cap was jet-black like the runners."

"Good eyes." Rey.

"*Bored* eyes." Ald. "Higgins was waiting for his brother-in-law, Chaz, who was already an hour late for their fishing expedition."

"Face?"

Ald chuckled drily. "He didn't get a long or close look, but with the mustache and black, 60s-sytled hair, and oddball smile … he was reminded of Gomez Addams."

CHAPTER FORTY-SIX

An hour later, we were seated on big cushions alongside my bed, dressed in silly-themed pjs (we had a few) and drinking hot butterscotch cocoas. Beat, we'd opted to go to bed after huge mugs of heated liquid sugar.

"I miss Pigaletto," Linda sighed.

Rey sighed as well. "Yeah. I love having Bonzo's wispy whiskers tickling my face."

A third sigh. From me. "And snuggling with Boo-Boo Button."

"At least we know they're in good hands," Linda said.

"Loving hands," I added. "Eddy's so fond of them."

"He spoils them rotten." Rey finished her cocoa and placed the coconut mug on the nightstand. "Why hasn't Slim-slash-GRP-slash-Rose-Pin-slash-Ha-Ha-Killer contacted us?"

I extended my palms in a who-knows gesture.

"This is the weirdest case we've ever worked on," she murmured.

"Technically, it's not a case. And, if it were, it's only our fourth," Linda pointed out, placing an empty mug that matched Rey's alongside hers, and stretching her arms. "And weird doesn't begin to describe it."

"Maybe we need a day off, to get away from it all. I hear there are some great sales at the Center."

Linda eyed Rey with a critical eye. "You are such a sales whore."

The response: an incredibly loud raspberry and thrusting forth of the tongue (Kiss' Gene Simmons would have been proud). Rey hopped to her feet. "Think Mei'll talk to us if we call tomorrow?"

Linda's latte-colored eyes narrowed. "What would he tell us that he hasn't told the police?"

"The old man might be more willing to talk to three pretty faces—ones who know his son, and are sympathetic to him."

"Sympathetic to murdering offspring?" I snorted.

Rey sniffed. "We should follow any and all potential leads."

Linda and I eyed each other and shrugged.

"We can try," I said, then yawned.

"It sucks that there's nothing substantial that points to Slim Mei as the Ha-Ha Killer." Rey chortled. "Ald Ives is right. He does have more titles than royalty."

"No fingerprints, no witnesses, no DNA." Linda's expression was a cross between grim and angry. "He *was* here. He did dart you two. He sent texts. He hired a banner-flying plane to mock us. He—"

"Whoa Nelly!" Rey's hands flew up. "You got no argument from me, Lindy-Loo."

"We need to catch him in the act, preferably before he actually kills or hurts anyone again, or find *convicting* evidence in his possession or on his person." I stifled another yawn, sensing sleep wasn't far off.

"That goes without saying," Linda responded, rising. "I doubt we'll luck in with either."

"If he did keep trophies, I'd sure like to know what he's done with those."

Rey smirked. "The ones we thought he might have kept at the Makaniolu Place house?"

I nodded.

"Where do you suppose he'd keep them?" Rey asked.

"Either in a faraway cubby hole, his current lodging place, or a bank safety deposit box," Linda replied.

"I'd opt for the bank," I said. "He's quite particular—fastidious—and wouldn't want to have them on hand, just in case. He'd be quite cautious about where they'd be kept."

"You think a safety deposit box would be under his real name?" Rey asked dubiously.

"Not likely," Linda answered, scanning my face, then Rey's.

Who scanned hers, then mine.

In unison, we voiced the obvious. "Alaina-Lei Mei."

* * *

The next morning, we were at the agency at nine, ready to tackle our safety-deposit box theory with the help of Gail, who we'd texted before going to sleep. We asked her to try Slim's mother's name and, on a whim, added Caprize Marquessa de Sade. It was unlikely he'd use his wife's name—too obvious—but never say never, right?

"So, once again, no prints or DNA were found on the 'memento' or card." Linda was seated at the pedestal table, working on the agency Thinkpad.

"Did we think otherwise?" Rey asked wryly, placing a tray of fresh coffees on the kitchen counter. She removed her doe-toned twill jacket and flung it on one of the blended leather chairs. "Here's hoping Gail comes through."

She passed cups and we went about typical agency business for the next ninety minutes—Rey networking on the phone, Linda playing accountant, and me responding to email queries about the agency and our services.

One call came through from a journalist who wondered if we were the unnamed agency featured in Jimmy C's posts, the one whose team had received text taunts from the Ha-Ha Killer.

Most likely, J.K. Stiles had called all the agencies on all the Islands, hoping one would admit they were the party in question. We, however, wouldn't. I wished him well and was about to check in with Gail when Linda shot to her sandaled feet.

"I've had enough numbers for today. We're okay financially on a business level for now, but we'll need clients *soon*."

"Paying clients," I emphasized.

Rey, standing by the window, staring at the street below, finished her call. "You know, I swear I just saw Mr. Brooks—with glasses and bow tie—standing across the street and looking up here."

"Who?"

"Kevin Costner from the movie *Mr. Brooks*—about a dude with a dark, super dangerous side."

Linda and I looked at each other.

She appeared skeptical, then frowned. "You think ... ?"

"Maybe." I stepped to the window alongside Rey and peered below. The only people to be seen were two frowzy-haired women chatting by a hydrant across the street and an older Asian gent standing before a parking sign, regarding something on his Smartphone. "Maybe we're getting a wee bit paranoid and over-imaginative."

"We are *not*. And why the frig hasn't he called?" Rey grumbled.

Moving to the sleek steel-finish coat rack (yes, another new addition, thanks to Cousin Reynalda), I pulled off my denim jacket and draped it over my shoulders. The day was cloudy again and cool. "I'm all for taking Gail to the park for lunch. Let's pick up something in the food court at the Center. Maybe she'll have news for us by the time we arrive."

"Sounds like a plan," Linda said. "Let's not expect Slim to call and focus on finding bona-fide evidence ... like those trophies we've talked about."

Rey gave a quick thumb's up. "But if we can find *him* in the process, bonus!"

* * *

"You actually located one?" I asked Gail excitedly as she, Linda, Rey and I started heading to the parked Jeep a few blocks away from the police station.

The intention to lunch in the park had been changed as Gail had taken off the afternoon to help us with our investigation. Her outfit today consisted of lovely colorful elephant-print capris and a bright pink short-sleeve split-neck tunic top. Her lips were candy-cane red and her eyes a pretty shade of sage green.

"Ald's working on a warrant as we speak," she said. "He's eager to nab this jackass *toute de suite*. Besides scaring everyone on Oahu, he's putting a major damper on tourism."

"Think he'll get the warrant?" Linda asked.

"He'll get it," she said confidently.

"Which bank?" Rey asked.

"First Oahu."

"I'd love to be there," she said wistfully.

Linda nodded. "Wouldn't we all?"

"I hope Slim doesn't catch wind." I gestured the car a few yards ahead.

"Even if he does, he won't have enough time to clean it out. In fact, I'm sure Hammill's there now, waiting for Ald, and watching for anyone that might attempt to get into that safety-deposit box," Gail said with a dry smile.

"Slim'll know Hammill," Rey said, slipping into the rear when I opened the door.

Linda concurred and waited for Gail to get in beside Rey before she took the front passenger's seat.

"Maybe it won't matter to him anymore," my cousin said.

"That they find evidence?" I asked as I waited for an opening in traffic.

"Exactly."

"The guy may not even be on Oahu anymore," Gail pointed

out. "Usually he contacts you. He hasn't made any effort of late —hey, didn't you tell me you called his father?"

"We left a couple of messages, but he hasn't gotten back," Rey explained with a sigh. "Where're we headed?"

"The bank. At least the one I know, which is on Kalakaua. Is that the one, Gail?" I asked.

"Yeah." She smiled wryly. "Do you want to hang around there until Ald shows?"

"That could be a long while," Linda replied. "That doesn't sound productive."

I agreed, then shrugged. "Anyone have any better, *more* productive, ideas?"

"Yeah. Let's drop by the Mei house."

I eyed Rey in the rearview mirror. And grinned.

* * *

Reporters were hanging around, keeping a hopeful eye on the Mei property, no doubt yearning for the killer to make an appearance or longing to swarm Dr. Richard Rijk Mei when, if, he left the premises.

The three of us slowed down as we passed the tall iron swing gate. There was no one outside and shades on all windows had been pulled tight; no surprise there. Maybe the cosmetic surgeon and his wife had snuck to the water's edge and boated off somewhere. I'd have done that. But, from all we'd heard, he was an ornery sort, so he'd likely stick around and take on anyone who challenged him.

A media van was parked in the driveway of the for-sale house where we'd previously parked, so we kept driving and stopped two streets over, before a coffee shop. Rey offered to get four large caffeine infusions—with treats. While she did so, Linda called Mei. She got voicemail and left another message.

"Well? How do we want to pursue this?" she asked dully.

"We can't exactly march over and press the gate buzzer, hoping that someone will let us in," Gail replied with a sigh.

"We're kind of stuck at the moment," I murmured, watching people enter and leave the shop. It seemed to be popular. A good sign that the coffee had to be superior.

Linda's phone announced a call and she hastily answered it. She offered a couple of affirmative responses, one "really?", and an "okay, thank you". "Mei will meet us at our agency at four."

Gail and I peered at Linda, surprised. She smiled. "He doesn't have much to share about Slim but is interested in hearing what *we* can share."

Rey passed a cardboard tray and paper bag to Linda through the open Jeep window and noted our gleeful expressions. "Who called?"

"Dr. Mei," Gail replied. "We have an audience with the gentleman at four."

"Woo-hoo!" She punched the air.

"We may as well head over after these," Linda said, pulling a guava-filled cupcake from the bag and grinning.

Rey got in and we sat back and silently sipped and munched.

* * *

At 4:15, a light rain began to moisten everything below and a brisk breeze continued to blow. What a gray, mournful day.

Mei hadn't yet made an appearance. Nor had he called. So, we sat around, Linda and Gail playing gin rummy, Rey reading an on-line script, and me applying apple-red polish to my nails. Hey, it passed the time.

"Maybe I should text him?" Linda asked, peering up from her hand.

"We left two messages," Rey pointed out. "He's probably stuck in traffic."

"Or met up with Slim," Linda suggested with a frown.

"Or is avoiding being hounded," I offered. "He may have taken an alternate—longer—route to get here."

"Too bad they lucked out with the safety deposit box," Gail said. "Gin."

"Dang." With a tight smile, Linda tossed her cards onto Gail's.

"Too bad no one noticed Slim arriving at the bank," I said.

"Ald's checking security footage," Gail said. "But, given that our guy's managed to avoid security cameras and being taped to date, let's not hold our breath."

"They may have caught him on camera, but as someone else, considering his penchant for disguises," Linda said, standing and stretching. "They'll have to be diligent."

"They will be," the HPD Administrative Assistant assured her.

"I have a bad feeling." I rose and grabbed my cell from the sideboard and called Ald. He didn't answer and, instead of leaving a message, I tried Hammill. No luck there, either. Sallo? Ugh.

I called and he grunted, "Yeah?".

"It's JJ Fonne. Has anyone seen or heard from Dr. Mei?"

"I haven't, but then I haven't tried to make contact. What's up?"

"He, uh, well, was supposed to meet us at four."

"Really? Well, it's only a little after. Not everyone's as punctual as you girls," he said brusquely.

"If you talk to your colleagues, would you check with them as to whether they've heard from, or seen, him?"

"Yeah, sure. See ya." Translation: in your dreams.

"Can you get a number for the house?" I asked Gail. "Maybe Overguard has heard something."

She went to the corner and, while she made a couple of calls, I got four bottles of water from the fridge. Rey and Linda joined me at the table as we waited.

"A woman answered—the housekeeper—and said no one is

taking calls at the moment. She was quite stern and firm," Gail explained, slipping alongside Rey. "Another washout."

"This goes beyond frustrating," Rey fumed, taking the water I passed her.

Gail laughed upon hearing the expletives fly from her cherry lips. Linda merely smirked and I rolled my eyes. But she was right. $@>$@#!!!*~

* * *

Eight o'clock saw the four of us at Adwin's 600-square-foot Ena Road apartment, seated on two rattan sofas in a comfy L-shaped living room decorated in shades of butter yellow and olive green. We were drinking spearmint tea and chilling—literally. It had grown quite cool outside. Jeans and heavy, fleecy jackets were worn by all. Jimmy C had joined us and had just finished telling us about articles he'd keyed and would be posting later this evening. He'd offered some "theories" without revealing too much that he'd receive legal admonition or a lawsuit in response.

But Hammill, who'd called thirty minutes earlier, reported that Slim Mei had evolved from a "person of interest" to "suspect", and he wouldn't reveal what had transpired to change that. Meanwhile, Dr. Mei was still MIA. The detective said he'd see what he could learn but didn't promise to get back with any findings.

"You know, we found property in a spouse's names before. Maybe there's another property in Mei's name," Linda put forth.

"I'd bet dollars to donuts Ald's people checked." Gail sipped and leaned back with a sigh. "If they'd found something, they'd have gone to check it out."

I gave it some thought. "What about Alana-Lei's maiden name, Stark?"

She drew a shallow breath, her brow furrowed. "Okay, let's give it a shot.

Adwin added, "And try Luc E Mei, or variations thereof. You never know."

"They would have checked." Gail eyed him pensively for several seconds. "Let me call Rodney. If anyone can dig up something that's been buried, he can."

Off she went to make another call.

And, while she was on the phone, we received an update from Ald re MIA Mei. It appeared, as he was attempting to escape the persistent [hounding] press, he had a panic attack. Leaping from his Benz, off he raced ... onto a filled Floating Hippo bus-boat. In the endeavor to flee fast, he drove it off a pier, right into an Oahu Neptune's Retreat sub, which had just started a tour of the briny deep.

Broken arm, cuts, and frayed nerves aside, he'd be all right. It couldn't be said the same of the tourists. The word "lawsuit" was already on many of their lips.

CHAPTER FORTY-SEVEN

"Shades of William Pierponce Howell," Linda murmured, a strawberry Twizzler suspended from the side of her mouth.

In fact, we were all gnawing the tasty licorice rods as we watched a dark house with a partial wraparound deck and a carless carport. She was referring to that first official case where we'd had to discover that "secret" I'd mentioned previously of a pretty, young wife married to millionaire septuagenarian, William Howell. The poor thing was murdered not long after we took on the case, as were a few other unfortunate souls. Long story short, we discovered the conniver had put three properties in his wife's name (a variation of, to be precise). Upon checking out the one in the Ko'olauloa district, we'd found more than we'd bargained for. But, once all was said and done, we had tied up the case quite nicely.

We had left Sach and Gail back home a couple of hours ago to travel to Kailua to view the house we were now surveilling. It was set far from the road, at the end of a private lane, maybe a dozen blocks from Steaming Mimi's, with a rear view of the Koolau Range and Olomana Mountain.

It was eleven, cloudy and very cool. The moon: waxing gibbous. In addition to thick hoodies, we'd put on our fleeciest socks. Nocturnal animals, heard nearby and in the distance, added to the surreal, film-like scene. We were parked between two monkeypod trees on the opposite side of the quiet one-lane road, about a hundred yards away. Two pairs of Clear Vision™ Binoculars helped us surveil.

Jimmy C, wedged between Linda and Adwin in the rear, finished reciting our actions and [limited] observations. "If nothing else, I have some great fodder for a ghost or horror story."

"Too bad we can't start a campfire. We got the marshmallows and dogs," Rey chirped from the passenger seat beside me.

We'd stopped at a Foodland on the way here and bought a lot of unhealthy but tasty groceries for a laidback barbecue tomorrow afternoon at—where else?—our increasingly popular lanai. (We weren't anticipating any major detecting assignments or tasks, unfortunately.)

"Shouldn't we check out the place?" Adwin asked, placing his binoculars on his lap. "There haven't been any signs of life, but maybe we should make sure."

We turned back to "the place", a two- or three-bedroom clean and tidy house situated on a huge, fenced lot surrounded by trees and shrubs. It looked harmless enough, but who knew what lurked beyond the freshly painted walls?

"If he's in there, he may be watching—"

"The guy's gotta sleep sometime and, if he's not sleeping, he can't have eyes at all the windows," Rey cut off Linda.

"He may have security cameras focused on key locations, like the road and rear and sides," Jimmy C advised, leaning forward and scanning the property. Adwin passed him the binoculars and he scanned again.

"Only if he believed we—or the police—would be smart enough to check properties under his mother's name and find him," I pointed out.

"He's way too sharp," Rey said flatly.

"And exceptionally cautious," Jimmy C added.

"So we've agreed upon a few times." I pulled my hood over my head. "I vote for Rey and I taking a quick, roundabout look-see."

"I'm so with you," she announced, slipping her hood over her head as well. "I got a Taser tucked in here. You?"

"Same."

"Be careful and quick," Adwin instructed, concern in his voice.

My cousin patted his arm. "You three keep your eyes and ears open."

Linda drew a deep breath. "If you're not back in five minutes—"

"Ten."

"If you're not back in *ten*, we're coming after you."

"And calling the police," Adwin added firmly.

* * *

"Kinda like a sheriff and his deputy sidekick lookin' for the big bad outlaw," Rey quipped quietly as we cautiously walked to the house via dense shrubbery on the *komohana* side.

It wasn't easy to see far, so we took vigilant baby steps, not that it helped. Twigs and branches and dry leaves snapped and crackled under our sneakered feet.

"There any feral pigs and goats around here?" asked my cousin from the corner of her mouth.

"Probably."

"Great." She slapped a spindly sapling.

"What'd that poor little tree ever do to you?" I asked with feigned gravity.

"It dared to get in my way."

Ten seconds later, I grabbed her arm and we stopped fifty feet from the side of the house. Six steps up were two small windows and a narrow door.

"Whadya think?"

I scanned the building and then the metal bench and matching table beneath a breadfruit tree ten yards, give or take, to the rear. Six flourishing rose bushes stood nearby, encircled by gray landscape rocks.

"How do you want to do this?

"Tasers out. Let's stick together, Cousin Reynalda. You take up the rear." I glanced from *mauka* to *makai* and pointed. "We'll head that way and follow those shrubs. They circle the house and make for decent cover. See if you detect any light or movement as we walk around."

"If I do?"

I turned to her. "We do what you do best—B&E."

"That might alert him."

"Only if he's awake."

"What if there's no light or movement?"

"We do what you do best—B&E."

* * *

What seemed like an hour later but could only have been five minutes, we'd circumnavigated the perimeter and were back at the side door, with Rey expertly picking the single-cylinder chrome deadbolt lock.

We didn't even have time to swing open the door—a gun was pressed to Rey's neck and what felt like a sharp needle was jammed into my back.

"Stay calm, ladies. Nice to see you again," our serial killer's voice greeted us serenely. "Before you breathe or twitch, I will blow off your pretty head, darling Rey. The gun has a silencer as an FYI, in case you're tempted to tell me your Jeep-mates will hear it and come running like the cavalry.

"If you want to chance that I won't—considering it's not my usual M.O.—go for it. I'd be very sad, but that's life. And death. *Yours*, dearheart."

"Crap." Rey.

"Damn." Me.

This was *not* good. Before anxiety or dread could take control, I told myself to wise up. Would Bogie have fallen apart like an over-boiled dumpling? Would Holmes have cried into Watson's smoking jacket as Moriarty threatened deviltry? Would Nancy Drew have run from a specter flitting along a fog-shrouded showboat? No!

"So, what now?" I asked with more ease than I felt.

"I'll ask you both to walk to the rose bushes and beyond. There's an SUV fifty yards further. We'll have you drive, JJ. From what I know of your driving—or lack of—Rey, we don't want to end up in a stream or wrapped around a tree."

"Thanks. But I'm not that bad."

"Sure you are," slipped from my lips.

"Yeah? And you're—"

"Please, *not* now," he cut off Rey. "Please drop your Tasers and cells."

We glanced sideward at each other and did as requested.

"Don't move an inch, JJ."

The pointy thing left my back and a hand began feeling my back, sides, and—"Hey, watch that!"

"Nothing 'physical', JJ. Just making sure you aren't carrying anything else that might prove harmful to yours truly." Next, he did the same to Rey, then the pointy thing returned.

We'd not yet faced Slim and I was curious to see who he resembled. I had to ask. "Who are you made to look like tonight?"

"Sleep-interrupted *Slim Mei*. That's who."

"Ah, your true self. How clever," Rey said sarcastically.

He laughed lightly and pressed the weapon—whatever it was—through the hoodie. "Don't make me hurt you—good God, what a bad TV line. Over to the roses, ladies."

We saw to the Ha-Ha Killer's bidding. Given the gun was firmly pressed to Rey's neck and the pointy thing to my back, we walked slowly but steadily. I was sure Rey was thinking the same thing: how long before our Jeep-mates came looking and/or make the call?

We approached a recent-model gray Infiniti, one that looked brand new and freshly washed. Stolen? Or bought?

"JJ, the key is under the driver's seat. Rey, you and I will sit in the back. You can drive straight and along a path you'll soon see. Hang a left at the lava-rock wall and head *makai*."

I drew a deep breath, located the key, and started the engine as I waited for the two to settle in the back.

As we drove onto the path, I asked the requisite question as I peered into the rearview mirror. It was too dim to see much of either face, but I could glimpse the shiny gun bussing my cousin's cheek. "What happens next?"

"We review—maybe rewrite—the rules of the game."

"We're still playing it?" Rey asked acerbically.

"We didn't officially stop."

"Why'd you kill your brother?"

"Besides the facts he was vain and self-absorbed, and selfish?"

"If you killed every selfish vain dude, Oahu'd be minus a few hundred, if not thousand, males," Rey stated snidely.

"That's a rather pleasing image."

The Infiniti's clock read 11:58 when we finally pulled past the Lanikai Monument, a pillar dating back to 1924 that marked the entrance to the residential area of Lanikai. In fact, we were near Lanikai Beach. We'd driven about fifteen minutes. The car's headlights illuminated a trash bin, various trees, lots of sand, and a relatively calm ocean. Sounds were minimal; just a few nocturnal animals and birds, and waves slapping/lapping rocks.

"You going to make us take a swim, Slim?" Rey asked, the gun still pressed to her cheek.

"We're waiting for someone to pick us up."

"You have a partner?" I asked, surprised.

"Let's say 'helper for hire'."

"He bringing a car or boat?" Rey asked.

"A very nice boat that will take us far away from here."

"Another skill—you're a boater."

Slim chuckled and leaned back, but kept the gun pointed at her face. "Not much of one, to be honest. But Jack will get us where I want to be."

"Care to share the location?" I asked, my eyes on the rearview mirror and my hands on the steering wheel, as he'd requested earlier. Without question, the Jeep-mates had now checked and found us missing and called Ald.

They'd comb the area, maybe even track us here—a long shot, but never say never—but would a rescue transpire in time?

"We'll moor at a not overly popular marina on Big Island for two or three days, just in case they decide to canvas nearby waters. We can stock up on supplies there and head to Vanuatu."

"You need a crew?" Rey joked blandly.

Slim chuckled again. "I could use a cook and company—"

"We suck at cooking. You should have kidnapped Cousin Jilly's former boyfriend."

"Adwin?" He tilted his head to one side and then the other. "Too late now."

"Never say never," Rey said merrily.

He looked at her for several seconds. "Tempting, but you know? I'm not that fussy when it comes to food. But your company will be welcome. Jack's a little limited in the gray-matter department, but he's an excellent sailor and order taker ... and, actually, come to think of it, he's a decent chess player, too. I guess I'd better take back what I said about the gray matter."

"He's all that, for the right price," I added smugly.

"Quite true."

"We get seasick," I warned.

"Speak for yourself," Rey muttered.

"I am really going to enjoy this trip," he said happily.

"And just before we reach the final destination, you'll dump us in the briny deep, right?" I asked dully.

"If we become partners in crime, I wouldn't have to," he advised.

"You'd trust us to become—and remain—your partners?"

"No … but I might be willing to give it a try. Let's see how the next couple of days go."

I sighed, Rey snorted, and Slim laughed.

* * *

Ten minutes later, Jack arrived in a 10′ double-deck hulled dinghy. He was a boxy fellow who seemed to stand 5′10″ or 5′11″ and was dressed in a double-breasted peacoat and sporting a black narrow-crown mariner's cap. Given the shadows, it was hard to make out the face, but it would be ruddy and bristled (I'd have bet dollars to donuts at that moment).

He didn't say much—grunted twice when Slim told him the four of us would head to the boat together—but waited patiently with a S&W revolver, a .357 Magnum, poised.

Rey and I sat stone-faced on the molded seat by the bow while Jack sat at the aft and rowed. Slim, was seated cross-legged before us, surveying the dark, calm ocean. It wasn't as breezy as earlier but still cool and cloudy. I fought the sense of dread as we neared a handsome Catalina sailboat. From what I could see, it had cost a pretty penny, if Slim had actually purchased it. I suspected he had; he'd not want to risk having anyone, specifically the harbor police, searching for him.

"What time is it?" Rey asked.

"Does it matter?" Slim asked, watching her closely.

"Yeah. For some reason, it does."

With a shrug, he looked at his Fitbit watch. "A couple of minutes after midnight."

"Time doesn't fly when you're not having fun," she stated apathetically.

We reached the Catalina, named *CheckMate,* and Jack helped Rey board at the freeboard with the transom ladder. I followed, then Slim, and Jack focused on a tow line. Several seconds later, my cousin and I were seated at the settee in the port-side ultra-leather dinette.

"Shades of you and Linda with James-Henri on the boat that time."

"A lot of shades," I said with a dry smile. "But you're right."

"What are you talking about?" Slim asked, curious.

We turned to Slim and Rey answered. "Our last case had Linda and Cousin Jilly on a boat with an art-gallery owner who wasn't all he appeared to be. It got really dicey on the boat that night, but my two colleagues got the better of him."

"You did quite well with that case."

I looked over at Jack, who was on a small chair in the corner, drinking club soda from the can. He'd removed the cap and I was right—he was ruddy-faced, with a full head of black, wavy hair. Quite handsome in a dark, sinister way.

"You want I lock them in the aft cabin?" he asked gruffly.

Slim scanned my face, then Rey's. "You'd better tie them up, too."

"Like we're gonna jump overboard and swim," Rey scoffed.

"That's right. You're guppy-level swimmers."

"More like goldfish," I sniffed.

He grinned. "Jack will escort you below. I do hope you won't cause trouble."

"Would we do that?" I asked with a frown.

"You would."

CHAPTER FORTY-EIGHT

Twenty minutes later, we were underway—with Rey and I reclining on the teak-heavy double berth that sported a pretty paisley comforter. Four folded fleecy blankets sat on the corner with three cases of bottled water beneath. Warm lighting came from one of two halogen lamps. There was a seat, hanging locker, cabinet, and ample space for storage.

"Rather nice," she said, eyeing the sizeable cabin. "And comfortable."

I concurred. "Slim's a thoughtful man."

"Among other things. At least he agreed at the last minute not to have Jack tie us up," she said briskly and moved toward the rectangular cabin window and peered out. "Nothin'. Just lots of dark and wet. Think they'll be looking for us?"

"Of course they will," I assured her. "They already are, no question!"

"It won't take us long to get to Big Island." She exhaled softly. "Think they'll *find* us?"

"Of course they will," I stated with a nod, endeavoring to stay positive.

My cousin sat on the edge of the berth and regarded me for

several seconds. "We can try to get out of here and swim to safety or we can get some rest."

"Rest sounds the better—less dangerous—option."

"Well then, dream of how we're going to overpower those two dudes and escape."

"We'll need help, but this may give us a fighting chance." I pulled a 6.9" razor-sharp knife from its neoprene ankle-wrap sheath.

Rey eyed it skeptically. "You'd have to be quick *and* deadly, because if you're not, we're done for."

I stared at the weapon and nodded. "Let's aim for *debilitatingly* deadly. I'm not certain I can—or want—to kill."

"You have before. You got Colt right through the heart before he could blow you and your sometimes boyfriend away."

"Yeah, but not intentionally. I was aiming for the shoulder." Yessiree, I was so not a good shot. I returned the knife to its sheath, rolled onto my side, and pulled over one of the blankets. "Nighty-night, Cousin Reynalda."

"Nighty-night, Cousin Jilly."

* * *

The next morning, a strident rap-rap-rap preceded the opening of the door.

Jack, wearing a navy-blue cotton turtleneck and jeans, and sporting the cap again, peered in. The turtleneck was tight and showed how muscular he truly was. Not someone you'd want to engage in fisticuffs with, gauging from those biceps. "Coffee's on. You know how to make omelets?"

Rey gazed at him blearily. "You know how to fu—"

"We can do scrambled," I quickly interjected, certain that verbal sparring with this goon would not be in our best interest.

He scanned me from head to toe, then grunted, pulled out a small pad and pen from his back pocket and tossed them over.

"I'm going to buy supplies later. Better list what you'll need for the trip—clothes, food, women's things."

Rey opened her mouth, caught my warning glance, and waved limply. "Yeah, sure. Give us five."

He grunted again and closed the door.

"You notice he has a slight mid-west accent?"

"Maybe he once hailed from Nebraska or Kansas, or somewhere around there," I offered, sitting up and stretching.

"I wonder what his story is."

"You mean, how he hooked up with a serial killer?" I asked wryly. "You better list what we'll need, just in case."

Rey studied her sock-encased feet. "Think if I put a Glock 17 on it, he'll pick one up?"

I chuckled. "Only if it's made of chocolate."

Her smile was thin. "Thought as much."

"May as well wash up before we play short-order cooks."

"You gonna take your knife?"

I shook my head. "I won't be able to use it with both of them there. Let's keep it here for now."

Rey ran her tongue over her teeth. "I'd better put toothbrushes and toothpaste at the top of the list."

"Followed by mouthwash, soap, cream, tampons, nail items, combs and brushes—"

A hand flew up as she laughed. "You really think Jack can manage all the stuff we'll need?"

"He'd better or there'll be two testy 'crewmen' to contend with."

* * *

Noon saw Slim and Rey returning to the boat with a multitude of bags and boxes piled into a foldable utility wagon. We were situated at the very last dock of a small marina near Kailua-Kona. On one side you had a view of the ocean—calm today with full sun and no clouds or breeze—and on the other you could see other boats, a road, kiosks and buildings, two parking areas, and several Matson containers.

Earlier, Slim had taken one look at the three-page list, groaned and cursed, and changed plans; he and Rey would do the buying (Jack hadn't appeared overly confident about having to purchase our "supplies"). He slipped on a simple but decent disguise: a full lace cap of auburn, wavy hair and Dali mustache, and heavy-framed glasses. Rey had to be on her best behavior, wearing dark sunglasses and keeping the hood of her hoodie's hood over her head—or Jack would pragmatically and efficiently slice my throat.

When the two of them entered the galley, he said, "You two had better be worth the two grand I put out on clothes and things."

"*Two*?" I looked at Rey in awe.

She smiled innocently and extended both palms in a you-got-me gesture. "We got cool electric toothbrushes that match our pajamas."

I swallowed my laughter.

"And three cookbooks to help you in the culinary-skills department," Slim said sarcastically.

"And some awesome kitchen gadgets," Rey added enthusiastically.

Great. My cousin appeared to think we were embarking on a multiple-day, ocean-faring picnic.

"Let's have the porterhouse steaks with mushrooms and spuds around two." He turned to Jack, sitting at the smaller table, studying a large nautical map. "You should be back by then with our seafaring supplies, right?"

Jack retrieved the Browning Semi-Auto he'd slipped to the side and tucked it into the back of his jeans. Grabbing a faded denim jacket and small duffel bag by his feet, he stood and finally offered a "yeah". We watched him depart.

"Not a man of many words, is he?" Rey asked acerbically.

"Better that way," Slim responded as he pulled a Taser from

his two-button linen blazer. "You may as well go down for a couple of hours and rest or freshen up, or unpack, or whatever. Ladies, please grab a few bags and boxes, whatever you can carry."

He motioned with the electroshock weapon and, after we collected as many as we could manage, he followed us down and locked the door behind.

"Did you get a chance to leave messages or anything?" I asked as I started to unpack toiletries.

"He kept a real close eye and made sure I didn't lower my hood or take off the ashtray-sized sunglasses." She ran slender fingers through that shoulder-length, wheat-colored, sunshine-yellow streaked hair and shook her head like a dog who'd run through a sprinkler. "I did smile at everyone and blew kisses and flirted as much as I could in hopes someone would recall the 'flirty lady'. And I also manages to position some lipsticks into the word 'SOS'. Don't know if anyone'll notice, though. But here's hoping."

"Here's hoping." I squeezed her shoulder and moved the window shades so I could peer out. "I feel like a clam in a boiling pot."

She chuckled, moved alongside, and peered out as well.

"Lipsticks, huh?"

"I told Slim no woman likes to be without it. The watermelon-pink one in there's yours. So's the chocolate-brown mascara."

I had to laugh. "And he 'bought' that we needed all this stuff?"

"Caprize liked her girly-girl stuff, apparently, so yeah, he 'bought' it." She twittered and began pawing through a large bag holding T-shirts and shorts. "I think you'll like this Hilo T and these shorts."

I eyed them and nodded; seashell pink and sea blue were my favorite colors.

"I also got supplements and melatonin."

"You're joshing?"

She shook her head. "I told him I've been having trouble sleeping. If we put some melatonin in their drinks, maybe they'll nod off."

"We'd need a shitload to accomplish that—and they'd taste it long before they could ingest enough to get drowsy."

She sniffed. "Well, it won't go to waste ... but I may still give it a try."

"Whatever floats your boat."

"Ha-ha ... uh."

I scanned the ocean. In view: two catamarans and a fishing boat. "Did you think to get pens or markers?"

"Yes, ma'am. Coloring pencils and markers and adult coloring books—celebrations for me and mandalas for you—to pass time." She winked. "Just in case."

"You're good."

"Of course I am." She rummaged through bags and frowned. "Pooh. The pencils and markers are in one of the bags we left in the galley."

"It's okay. We'll use the lipstick—"

"No way! It's Yves Saint Laurent—"

"But we can write 'SOS' on the side, below the window."

She grimaced. "You think the guys won't *see* it?"

"Only if they're approaching from the water—"

"Jack took the dinghy, remember? He'll come in from the side."

"That's right, he did." I frowned. "I wonder why he did that."

"He probably doesn't want to be in immediate view, which he would be if he walked the streets. Who'd see him close up when he's on the water?" Rey suggested.

"You could be right. He may be on a wanted list or something, or would prefer to be not to be seen and, thus, remembered. Whatever. Right now, I'm fine with just freshening up."

"Given our situation, we're pretty calm, don't you think? It's like a day at the agency or something."

"Just biding our time, Cousin Reynalda," I smiled wearily. "Just biding our time."

* * *

While Jack ate his meal in his cabin, Slim joined us at the cockpit table. He sat beside Rey, who was settled beside me at the table that could easily seat six. We ate hungrily; the steaks weren't bad, either were the fried mushrooms or garlic-cheese bread. Diet sodas accompanied the late lunch. Dessert would be fresh papaya and lime.

"You really plan to head to Vanuatu?" I asked casually, stretching my legs and eyeing my bare feet and the chain around one ankle that shackled me to my cousin. With a sigh, I closed my eyes and turned my face to the sun.

"It's supposed to be beautiful." He popped a button mushroom in his mouth. "Lovely beaches to walk, beautiful reefs to swim along. Several picturesque islands. Explore-worthy caves and active volcanoes."

"Sounds like Hawaii," Rey said drily.

"But is Hawaii French, dearheart?" He grinned. "Do either of you speak it?"

"*Un peu,*" I said with a shrug.

"*Oui, oui,*" Rey said flatly.

Slim laughed.

"So, what game are we playing now?" my cousin asked.

He scanned her face but remained silent.

"You going to kill Jack when all is said and done?" I asked.

He merely smiled and returned to the last piece of steak.

"So, do you get urges?" I felt compelled to ask.

Another smile. "Certain individuals and situations *motivate* me, as I've explained. Urges? No, dear JJ. Soft inner voices don't bid me to kill. Faces don't appear in my dreams and chant or cackle or instruct me to do 'nefarious deeds'."

"Do you take trophies?" Rey asked. "We're pretty sure you do, given the bank scene."

Slim regarded her closely.

"You kept them at the Makaniolu house, didn't you?" Rey smirked. "That's why you popped in there that time—to collect them."

"What were they?" I asked with an innocuous smile.

"Maybe I'll let you look at them after we've set sail," he said simply, winked, and fell silent.

My cousin and I glanced at one another, shrugged, and stared across the ocean, where a dozen sailboats were in immediate view. We'd decided against the SOS at the side of the boat for the interim; others wouldn't get close enough to see it and people wouldn't be walking by, given there were no docks on our side.

Sticking with the knife seemed the better option, we'd decided, but the men couldn't both be around. Yes, it was a long shot—striking and felling one of them in order to escape. But what options were there? I was known to be a good "beaner" (ask Cash), but I suspected both Slim and Jack were too aware, mindful, to have some sort of implement clunk them unconscious.

If we couldn't strike tonight, we had to tomorrow, before we left the marina.

CHAPTER FORTY-NINE

Slim allowed us to sit in the cockpit for an hour, with the warning, "It's not likely anyone will hear, considering our location, but if you're inclined to shout or scream, I'll be here fast, with one of your Tasers and a cleaver, and we'll be on our way—you in considerable pain—before you can say Ha-Ha Killer three times."

Rey and I chose to catch a few zzzzzzzs and relax for the first forty minutes. The next twenty we yammered about this and that, like house-reno projects and having missed Mink's luau. She had to be pissed, big time.

I glanced around to see if there were any curious ears listening. "First things first, if he shackles us to the settee at dinner tonight, notice *where* he puts the key so we have fast and ready access."

"If Jack's with us, he probably won't bother." Rey braided her hair as she stared across the glistening water. "Maybe I could load melatonin in the gravy?"

"You're still thinking that'll work?" I grinned, envisioning their faces plopping onto laden plates. "Have you planned the menu?"

She chuckled. "I was thinking roasted chicken thighs, corn on the cob, and those little red potatoes."

"I'm game to try making chocolate mousse."

"Go for it, Chef Jilly."

"I guess the plan to head out after breakfast tomorrow is still on?"

"That's what he said," Rey confirmed, fastening the second braid. "If we don't strike tonight, tomorrow morning is our last —and only—chance."

We eyed each other grimly.

"Time is not our friend," she said ruefully.

"No, but resourcefulness is," I assured her, conveying hope I didn't much feel.

* * *

Dinner, oddly enough, was a pleasant affair, as far as dining with a serial killer and his henchman went. Maybe it was the rioja or maybe the melatonin-infused gravy had mellowed the boys (Rey and I had gone gravy-less); both were fairly relaxed. Slim was personable and Jack even conversed a little. We learned Jack had lived on a farmstead in Nebraska for the first sixteen years of his life. His father was a bitter drunk at night, but a decent worker during the day. The mother, a spiritual woman, left when Jack was eight. He didn't seem angry about it; it simply was.

Unfortunately, dinner didn't allow for any knife-thrusting opportunity. Instead, we watched the two men engage in a game of chess on a handsome walnut set that had obviously cost a pretty penny.

After escorting us to our cabin shortly after 9:30, Jack bid us good night and advised we'd be setting sail at seven. With a quick salute, he locked the door behind.

"At eight a.m. we'd better be on terra firma, without our escorts," I murmured, removing my jeans.

"You know, Slim's not a bad guy, murderer-torturer aside."

"He has a certain likeability," I concurred wearily, slipping beneath a blanket, then getting up again when I realized I'd forgotten to perform my usual pre-bedtime tasks.

"Jack seemed almost human tonight. He even complimented you on your mousse—which he ate with obvious gusto, I might add," Rey said with a tired smile.

I nodded and moved to the adjacent head. "Too bad the melatonin didn't do much.

"You were right. We'd have to have dumped three bottles in the gravy for it to have been effective," she joked, removing a bottle from the waterproof storage bag on the cabinet and eyeing the label. "Well, at least they'll sleep well." She popped two into her mouth. "Maybe I will, too."

"Too bad the cavalry isn't coming to our rescue."

I turned and eyed her keenly. "Did we *really* think it would?"

"We *hoped*."

"This one's on you and me, Cousin Reynalda."

"I always thought I'd do better *riding* to the rescue than *swimming*." She simpered. "Who do you want to be? The general or the captain?"

"The *admiral*."

* * *

"Ready?" Rey asked as she watched herself apply an avocado-based cream in the gold-plated mirror she'd perched on the cabinet.

I'd always thought her pretty in an old-world cinema way (rather like Marlene Dietrich or Carole Lombard), but I wasn't aware just how much so ... and told her so.

She closed one eye and peered at me with the other as she studied me. "We're not gonna die or get hurt, so no need to get schmaltzy or anything like that. I ask again: ready?"

I offered a thumb's up and checked the ankle sheath and knife hidden beneath my jeans. "Ready to rock and roll." Slipping on a lightweight cotton sweater, I grabbed hers from the corner of the bed and tossed it over. The early morning breeze bordered on nippy.

Rey put on hers and motioned the door. Slim had unlocked it twenty minutes ago to advise coffee was brewing; he'd also requested we grace the breakfast table with pancakes.

"Where's Jack?" I asked casually as we strolled into the brightly lit galley. "Are we making pancakes for three or four?"

"Make them for five. I'm hungry," he winked. "Jack'll be back at 6:30."

I glanced at the gold-finish clock across the galley. "It's only five after *five*?"

He chuckled and zipped up his wind-repellent racer jacket. "The early bird catches the worm."

"I'm not a fan of wriggly jigglies," Rey muttered, stepping before the coffee machine and filling a 14-ounce copper mug. "I'd rather catch me more shut-eye."

He chuckled again and she filled a second mug for me. "Does Jack know what you do, who you are?"

"He watches the news. And I'm all over it now. So are you actually."

I took a seat beside him. "You're so calm about it. No worries?" I asked nonchalantly and nodded at Rey as she passed me a mug and sat opposite our "host".

He looked at me, then at her. "We'll be en route in a couple of hours. No one's found us yet and I'm fairly certain no one will."

"Ya gotta admire confidence like that," Rey said blandly and sipped.

I eyed him closely. "You take out people *you* believe have wronged. Do you see yourself as some sort of god or something?"

He burst into laughter, then wiped his eyes. "That's good. No, JJ. I'm more a … a punisher maybe. Or an avenger, maybe. Far from divinity." He eyed his empty mug. "Actually, what I am is a cleaner-upper."

Rey and I glanced at each other with like-really? expressions and she asked, "Care to share your plans for when we arrive in Va-uh ...?"

"Vanuatu."

"Yeah, there."

He started to talk about the provinces and marinas and places of interest. We smiled and nodded appropriately, and I kept a close eye on his face and form—taking notice of how he spoke, sat, gesticulated, blinked. I thought about when I might remove the knife without him spotting that and where to strike. I'd have to be within close reach and my cousin would have to distract Slim at just the right second.

"Rey hon, let's start on breakfast. Why don't you get bananas and peel and mash them while I put together the batter?" As I rose I motioned the island; she caught my keen look.

"Where is Jack, anyway?" she asked, stepping toward the built-in refrigerator-freezer.

"We took inventory late last night and decided we'd better pick up a few more items, including extra lifejackets and a raft. Jack thought a rifle might come in handy."

"You gonna shoot fish?" my cousin asked wryly, accepting a heavy ceramic bowl from me and moving to the counter.

"You never know who you might meet on the ocean."

"He can buy one here? At this time of the morning?" I asked, truly surprised, as I pulled out bowls and mixing implements.

"They have all-night outlets here, too," he grinned. "And connections."

"You must be paying him well," I said, bending down to get a pot and quickly removing the knife and slipping it alongside a large cutting board. Yes, there were other knives around, but this one was lightweight, easy to grasp and handle, to swing and debilitate.

Annoyingly if not frighteningly, Jack chose that moment to enter, a two-gun floating case perched on one shoulder. He placed it beside the fridge. "Lifejackets are on deck. So's the rest of the stuff." He nodded at Rey, then at me, and moved over to the coffee pot. He frowned, shrugged, and took the empty pot to the sink.

Damn. He was back way too early. Rey shot a look at me the same second I did her. *What now?*

* * *

"Guess we're ready to head out as planned?" Rey asked as she mashed bananas.

"Guess so," Jack replied as he stood by the coffee machine and watched it do its thing. He'd removed the peacoat and sported the same turtleneck and jeans as yesterday. No question, he was handsome, save for the hard lines pulling his full lips into a perpetual frown and intensifying the crinkles around eyes that viewed the world with a significant degree of distrust.

Scanning the galley, I wondered where Slim might have hidden his weapons. I'd have preferred a Taser to the knife, but beggars couldn't be choosers, right? I glanced at Jack. Yup, he sported some serious muscles. The guy could probably handle three opponents simultaneously, with little effort. The only chance Rey and I stood against him was if he were incapacitated.

"Mac nuts would go well with the bananas, doncha think, Cousin Jilly? Grab some for me, will ya?"

I glanced over and caught the almost imperceptible nod. And clued in. The rifle. The nuts were within reach. But was the ammo?

Jack raised the mug. "Think I'll take this and check everything one last time before we sail."

"I hear we're in for rain," Slim said.

He nodded. "I picked up a newspaper. It's on deck. You're front-page news, by the way."

Slim shrugged, disinterested. "I've been front-page news for a while now."

"But now they know who you are." Jack's chuckle sounded

like a locust's chirp. "Cute headline. 'The Ha-Ha Killer Won't Have the Last Laugh'."

"Not bad," Rey commented, edging toward the rifle.

"I'd be curious to see why they're saying that and who wrote that," I said innocuously as I whisked the batter. Would Slim take the bait and head up to grab the paper?

He frowned and looked from me to Rey. "Jimmy C wouldn't have, would he?"

Rey extended both hands in a you-got-me gesture.

His frown deepened and he rose. "Where is it?"

"Beside the lifejackets," Jack replied, moving to the doorway, mug in hand.

CHAPTER FIFTY

Rey focused on the mac nuts and I returned to the batter, feigning nonchalance as Slim and Jack stepped from the galley.

As soon as they were gone from view, we sprang into action. I removed the rifle from its casing and found it hadn't yet been loaded. "Damn." I crammed it back in and returned it to its resting place.

Rey's expression changed from hopeful and determined to thoughtful and worried as I grabbed the knife from behind the cutting board and tucked it into the front of my jeans—and sliced myself. I slipped the kitchen washcloth over it as the f-word flew from my mouth like a stock car shooting forward from the start line. I slipped it behind the batter bowl just as Slim re-entered, newspaper in hand, Jack on his heels.

His expression suggested suspicion as he eyed us and then the galley.

"Expecting us to set it on fire?" Rey asked sardonically, popping a fat mac nut in her mouth.

"Expecting you to do something, that's why I returned so quickly." He shrugged and smiled fleetingly. "Obviously I was wrong. Maybe I can trust you after all."

"Pishaw."

He chuckled and watched Jack perch himself on the corner of the settee. He tossed over the paper, grabbed a fresh coffee, and sat across from him.

Rey and I exchanged glances, nodded once, and the rest happened in slow-mo, much like Lee Majors from *The Six-Million Dollar Man* taking after a villain. My cousin seized the bowl of mashed bananas and flung it at Slim's head. It clunked him smack-dab on the nose. His head snapped back and smacked the wall and with a grunt and a curse, he stood and did an odd two-step. While that transpired, I launched the batter-filled bowl at Jack, who'd charged forward. Intuitively, I gripped the knife and sprinted forward to jam it into his shoulder. Instead, I caught him in the base of the neck.

Jack groaned, gurgled, grabbed for the weapon, and dropped when I shoved him from behind. That jammed the knife in more deeply when he tumbled face-forward and hit the fridge with a resounding (bone-crunching) thud.

There was no time to worry or gag. I kicked Slim where it would hurt the most and Rey did the same. I felt for Slim when I heard the shrieks, but I felt for us more.

Rey clutched my hand and off we raced, down the fixed walkway and past the slipway, undoubtedly resembling a stumbling, bumbling silent-movie comedic duo.

* * *

Timing was everything. When we rounded a tour operator's brightly-decorated kiosk, we stopped short, as if we'd hit a plexi-glass wall. Ald and Hammill stood standing, guns in hand, looking as if they were readying for action. Thirty feet behind, before a small building belonging to a sailing club, stood Linda and Jimmy C. Two officers—a tall young woman and portly middle-aged man—were approaching from a cruiser parked at the edge of a fairly empty parking lot.

Linda raced forward, as did Jimmy C, and threw her

arms around us. Pulling us close, she laughed with glee. Then, Ald did the same, much to our surprise, but as quickly as he'd wrapped his strapping arms around us, he retreated.

He opened his mouth, but Rey beat him to the punch. "Slim and Jack are in the galley of the last boat—the *CheckMate*—and they're both out for the count!"

Hammill ordered the two officers, now beside Jimmy C, to follow him and—weapons drawn—they raced forward.

Ald looked as if he planned to pursue them, but then dropped his arm and eyed us up and down. "You okay?"

"We're fine," I assured him. "We were never mistreated. In fact, Slim made things relatively pleasant."

Jimmy C stepped alongside the detective, concern crinkling his high, perpetually glowing forehead and darkening cola-brown eyes. "You had us so worried. We thought, well, uh—"

"That we were two more names on the Ha-Ha Killer's victims' list?" I asked wryly, giving him a quick hug.

He offered a woeful smile.

"You look like you spent a lot of time worrying," Rey grinned, slapping his arm.

He glanced down at his cotton pants, and wrinkled shirt and jacket, and offered another smile, this one embarrassed. "I—we —didn't get much sleep."

"Is Adwin all right?" I asked worriedly.

Jimmy C nodded. "He's with Gail and Eddy and the pets at the house, drinking coffee by the potful. In fact, I think they're pacing the walls and roof."

A car screeched to a stop and we turned to see another cruiser and an unmarked police vehicle arrive. Two more officers and a detective disembarked, and hurried forward.

"Ald Ives, it's been a while." A giant, pockmarked man of thirty-five, sporting a lightweight tan suit sans tie, extended a large, fleshy hand.

Ald shook it. "Big Island looks like it agrees with you, Hart."

He requested the two officers hasten to the boat to assist the others.

Hart slapped Ald's back and advised he was heading to the boat as well.

"How'd you find us?" Rey asked, leaning into the wall of a small closed marina shop.

"The 'SOS' and furious flirting at the super store helped," Ald smirked, scratching a rash at the side of his neck as he scanned the marina. "But the clerk, Aaron, a keen amateur sleuth, thought there was something strange about an 'odd couple' spending a lot of money on 'everything and anything'."

Rey eyes widened. "He's sharp if he saw through Slim's disguise."

"Good ol' Slim didn't do that great a job concealing the shape of his face or lips this time. And the hair—whoa!"

"He *was* in a hurry," she said. "So this keen amateur sleuth called the cops?"

Ald nodded. "Unfortunately, Aaron is known to be overly enthusiastic and has often gone to the cops to report sightings of kidnap victims or most-wanted folks, so Captain Kailu didn't take him overly seriously when he dropped by to say he'd sighted the Ha-Ha Killer."

"What made the captain change his mind?" I asked, sitting on a small timeworn bench that had seen many sunsets and bums.

"First, my call—after we got wind that a boat called *Checkmate* might be in and around this island."

I searched his face.

"Second, your drug-dealing boyfriend's," he lowered. "He called me personally and wouldn't let me get one word in. I had to hang up, which only got me another call, and then another. Finally, my captain marched in. He was *very* vocal about us getting our asses in gear and saving your lives." He said angrily, "We were on it, for heaven's sake."

"You mean, JJ's sometimes boyfriend called your captain?" Rey asked, puzzled.

"It appears that may have been the case, but I'm not sure," he scowled.

Cash had demanded action by going over Ald's head? I glanced at Rey and she shrugged.

She sat down to my right and Linda dropped on the left and hooked an arm around my shoulders. "I texted him when I found him in your cell phone contacts. I thought he should know."

"Apparently, he cared enough to take time away from those profit-yielding drug-dealing duties," Ald stated with a dark smile.

I peered across the parking lot to six small round tables before a snack bar that was lit by a solitary and sad-looking neon sign and looked as if it hadn't been open to the public in months. In the waning morning dimness I envisioned Cash seated on a Harley-Davidson SuperLow, under a date palm a few yards over, tight designer jeans and T, and Converse runners. Sporting that arrogant smile, he gave a quick salute.

Good Lord. You're dreaming of a romance ending, where Mr. Smug-Ass Hero, aka Cash among other names, pulls you into his arms, passionately kisses you, and you ride into the sunrise? Like really? I shook my head and refocused on Ald.

"Anyway, Aaron took it upon himself to do some serious sleuthing and check less frequented marinas. He sighted Jack very early this morning. We'll catch you both up on it all later. Right now, we have a f'g nutbar to bring in." He took a step, then stopped when he saw Hammill sprinting toward us.

"Oh-oh. Maybe not," Jimmy C stated, grim-faced.

"The one guy's dead, but our main guy's jumped ship, pardon the pun."

Rey, Linda and I gazed at one another, stunned. *How?*

* * *

Rey and I hadn't particularly cared to return to the boat and happily hopped into a cruiser with Linda and a stern-faced officer who drove us to the local police station. We'd left an eager, photo- and story-hungry Jimmy C with Ald and Hammill at the crime scene. After giving our statements, the three of us sauntered across the street to a small coffee shop and caught up. Munching peanut-butter cookies and sipping freshly brewed Kona coffee, Linda relayed what had transpired from the moment Slim had "escorted" us to the Infiniti.

"When you two didn't return after ten minutes, we got out and circled the house. Fortunately, Adwin sighted a glow from one of the cell phones and found the other one not far off. He contacted Ald immediately while I called Sach to let him and Gail know what was going on. He wanted to drive over right then and there, but I told him it was better that he—they—stay put, in case someone called the house or dropped by. Then, well, I texted Cash. I don't know why, but it seemed the right thing to do," she said with a rueful smile.

"Did the dude respond in a timely manner?" my cousin asked drily.

"He returned my text with a call about fifteen minutes later. He asked for details and I gave them as we knew them at the time, which wasn't much," Linda replied with a limp shrug. "Anyway, Ald called almost immediately after that and said he was on his way with Sallo and Hammill to meet us, as well as some uniforms. They were there within thirty minutes, give or take. And it wasn't much after that they issued an APB."

A neighbor, Mr. Mason, had noticed the new Infiniti behind the house when he was taking Goliath, his Great Dane, for a walk—as it hadn't been parked there previously, he'd mentioned it to the questioning officer. That got the police scouring security cameras in the area as well as traffic cams. The Infiniti was sighted near Keolu Drive as well as by Kailua Beach. Hammill was the first to voice the notion that Slim had likely made an escape on the ocean. More questioning ensued.

"They learned of a boat—*Wunderbar*—that had been moored in the vicinity for a couple of days. A honeymooning couple wanted to enjoy some 'solitary' quiet as too many visitors were coming to the marina to bid them good wishes and all that. Anyway, they noticed Slim's boat because of a guy who had started rowing away from it."

"They noticed Jack in the dimness?" Rey asked, surprised.

"As he was getting into the dinghy, he'd knocked over something that made a racket. He must have checked to see what he'd done because, for a few seconds, there was a bright beam of light pointed at *Checkmate*. If that hadn't happened, the Enrights might never have noticed anything."

"Talk about luck," I said with a grateful smile.

Linda nodded and grabbed another cookie. "One thing led to another, and thanks to amateur-sleuth Aaron, they found you."

Rey leaned back and released a lengthy exhalation. "I wonder when they'll find Slim. There must be a trail of blood to follow."

"He'd have jumped overboard if he were smart, which he is, so there won't be any trail." I stared across the coffee shop that was filled to capacity. "I'm guessing he's on his way to Vanuatu."

"You think he'll still head there?" Linda asked, astonished.

"I do."

"He'll lose himself on one of the islands," Rey said with a nod. "I wonder if we'll hear from him again."

Before I could respond, Ald and Hamill entered.

"No luck finding him, right?" Rey asked flatly.

Hammill scowled and Ald lowered, then strolled to the counter to order coffees.

A group by the window left and we took over their table.

"So?" Rey prodded as Hammill watched Ald pay.

"As you said, no luck finding him," he replied gruffly.

"Crap."

He looked at Linda and the corners of his mouth twitched.

"No one saw anything either?"

He shook his head. "Too bad Aaron hadn't stuck around. There's someone who makes for a great witness." He chuckled briefly. "Maybe we should recruit him."

Ald stepped up to the table with a tray supporting large mugs of coffee and muffins.

"We've got divers out—"

"He's not dead and they won't find him," Rey said blandly, taking a mug when he placed the tray on the table and murmuring thanks.

Ald sat and inhaled at length. "Too bad Jack can't talk."

"Any leads on where he resided or anything?" Linda asked, helping herself to a coconut muffin.

"Not yet."

"I guess we can fly back," Rey said, sipping.

"We're on the noon flight to Oahu," Hammill said. "The media's going to want your stories."

Rey perked up. "Ya think?"

Ald smiled wryly. "I suggest you keep mum for a while."

She didn't seem to hear him as she peered around eagerly. "How come there aren't any reporters around?"

"They don't know you've been rescued," Hammill responded, gazing onto the car-heavy street. "We're keeping this under wraps for as long as possible. The public doesn't need to know a serial killer's escaped ... and may run amok again."

"He won't do anything," I said with a shake of the head. "He's going to get away as far, as fast, as possible."

"Maybe," he said to the window.

"Gail and that neighbor of yours, Sach, are still at your house. Eddy and the 'kids' are there too, eagerly awaiting your return," Ald said with a fleeting smile. "No one wants to do anything until you're back safe and sound."

Rey smiled, then frowned. "Hell! Our stuff's still on the boat."

"'Our stuff' that Slim bought?" I asked wryly.

"It was nice stuff," she pouted, then chuckled. "As long as we get our cell phones back, I'm fine."

I agreed and looked out. The day was gray and breezy, and almost as cool as it had been pre-sunrise. People were walking with destinations and tasks in mind—like us. Given our flights were at noon, we'd be heading for the airport shortly.

Once back at home, life should return to normal. No more Slim/GRP calls and texts. No more victims, at least not courtesy of the Ha-Ha Killer. What about us? Would we soon have a case? Would Rey sell her/our story? Would my "sometimes boyfriend" see how things had fared? I suppressed the simper, leaned back, and nibbled a taro muffin.

CHAPTER FIFTY-ONE

Eight o'clock found the house filled with a few friends and police personnel. Through blaze, Adwin had found a good caterer—*No 1 'Ono*—and food was delicious and plentiful. So was wine and beer.

The news focused on the Ha-Ha Killer's escape, his cohort Jack's death, and "the abducted female private investigators' astounding escape". The events were the talk of the town, Islands, and Mainland. Rey wasn't keen on the "abducted" spin as she felt that might bode badly for the agency, but Linda and Gail emphasized the fact we'd escaped by taking out the two men. That brightened her mood a bit, and when Jimmy C said he'd write about how we'd *adeptly* and *courageously* accomplished that, she glowed like lava flowing from spewing Kilauea Volcano.

In fact, media folks were parked outside in the cool drizzle, waiting fervently for photos and interviews. They could wait until "pigs fly", as Rey huffed. She'd had a change of mind re interviews when we'd arrived and she'd slipped on the grass, and a reporter got an unflattering shot of her backside as she'd scrambled to her knees. The only one to receive an interview had been granted a couple of hours earlier—to Jimmy C (with a *flattering* photo).

Ald, Hammill and Sallo were tired, much like the rest of us, but a short respite this evening was welcome. Tomorrow, it would be back to tracking Slim—with a vengeance.

Rey and I got bottles of wine to bring to the living room, and while she saw to filling glasses, I moved over to the corner where Gail and Linda were chatting with Eddy. He'd come downstairs to fill two plates (he had a hearty appetite) before returning upstairs to sit with the kids. He preferred the company of pets to police sorts, which he found intimidating.

Gail grabbed a heart-shaped cracker with *fois gras* and apricot chutney from the platter resting on the coffee table and eyed it critically. "Am I going to like this?" she asked Linda, who was sipping from a fancy flute that had come with a bottle of champagne we'd found in the kitchen.

"The price says yes."

Gail tee-heed and took a dainty bite, chewed for several thoughtful seconds, then offered a maybe-yes-maybe-no gesture.

I slapped her shoulder playfully and took one myself. I'd not eaten since the muffin on Big Island this morning. I wasn't overly hungry but drinking wine on a relatively empty stomach was not a great idea.

Jimmy C sauntered over and asked if Linda and Gail would like to read his copy and comment on it before he submitted it. They agreed and followed him into Linda's room.

Rey sauntered over with two glasses of red and my cell phone. "*Matt Houston* was announcing a call."

I grabbed it gratefully. "I am *so* happy Ald let us have these back."

"He probably copied our contacts, including you-know-who," she said with a wry smile.

I checked my calls. The last one had a local area code. Curious, I hit the "Call" icon. Ten rings. No response. No voice-mail. I gave up.

"No luck?"

"Nope. It was someone local, though."

We eyed each other.

"Ya think … ?"

I shrugged.

"Shit." She took a long sip.

"Crap." I did the same.

We eyed each other again and then chuckled. Clinking glasses, we moved into the kitchen and found Adwin refilling half-empty platters.

"Welcome, lovely ladies." Sach raised his glass of wine. His nose was red—from too much sun or *vino* was hard to say.

"Speaking of lovely." Rey indicated his outfit: a buffalo-plaid shirt, flamingo-pink jacquard pull-on shorts, and periwinkle nubuck-leather loafers. She winked and pulled out a bottle of water from the fridge, and emptied it in four gulps.

"To use an old saying, when ya got it, flaunt it," he winked.

Matt Houston announced another call and I removed the cell phone from my jean pocket. Same number. "Yes?"

"It's me."

Cash? "What are you doing on Oahu?"

"I'm not. Just using an Oahu number. I had to get rid of the other one."

"What's up?"

"Checking in. Are you all right?"

"Rey and I are fine. Unfortunately, as you heard, Slim—the Ha-Ha Killer—got away."

"They'll catch him."

"… Maybe."

"What are you doing?"

"Having a bit of a get-together with Adwin, Sach, Ald, Sallo, Hammill, Gail, Eddy.

"… I was worried."

"… Were you?"

"Yeah, babe, I was."

Babe? Ugh. "I have to go."

"Luv ya."

Sure. I hung up without responding.

* * *

A strong hand clamped itself over my mouth. "I'm right next to you, JJ." Slim's whispered words warmed my neck.

Good Lord. He was here—*beside me.* I tried to break free in the dark of my room and clutched at the fingers; they were padded, soft. They were ... my pillow!

I sat up, breathing heavily, and turned on the nightstand lamp. The bicycle clock said it was 5:35. Well, at least I'd slept a solid six hours.

Raking a hand through my hair, I looked around for Button, then recalled she and her playmates were in the guestroom with Eddy. The sweet kid would probably be up around six to feed and walk them—yes, even Bonzo. He'd taken to having the Checkered Giant rabbit accompany the dog and pig enclosed in a little stroller, from which the bunny could watch the passing view. Too cute.

After a quick soapy shower, I slipped into jeans, a T-shirt promoting North Carolina, and a thick wool sweater. New fuzzy kitty-cat slippers warmed my feet. Would it ever get Hawaii-hot again?

In the kitchen, I turned on the light. It appeared to be another gray, cloudy day was ahead of us. Might as well set an impromptu breakfast table for everyone. I put on coffee and placed six eggs into a water-filled pot.

"Hey," I greeted Eddy, dressed in ash-gray sweats (baggy pants and top) and thermal socks, and old Converse sneakers in one hand while the other pushed the stroller.

He smiled and gestured his entourage. "We're off. Need anything from the store?"

I shook my head and gave his shoulder a quick squeeze.

With a nod, he entered the mudroom, slipped on the sneakers, and left with his charges. One large mug of coffee and ten minutes later, Linda strolled in with the company laptop. She was sporting baggy sweats similar to Eddy's, except hers were mustard yellow. Her hair was arranged in pigtails with two white satin bows. The bags under my eyes had to resemble those under hers.

"Is it ever going to warm up?" she groused, putting the laptop on the counter and pouring coffee into a glass mug advertising a car-rental agency, and topping it off with milk. "Guess I'd better make another pot. Rey'll be down in a few."

"Didn't sleep well?"

"Bad, weird dreams."

"Me, too."

"I guess we'll have them for a while." She leaned into the counter and sipped.

"Most likely."

She flipped open the laptop and started scanning news.

"Anything of interest?" I asked a couple of minutes later.

"Just speculation re Slim's whereabouts but nothing concrete. No Ha-Ha Killer sightings." She offered a salty smile.

"He's probably on the ocean—"

"In international waters," Rey interrupted, padding in, wearing a watermelon-pink tracksuit and two pairs of plum-purple, heavy-duty socks. "Out of sight, but not out of mind."

I grinned and Linda chuckled and returned to the laptop.

Rey filled her favorite mug and sat across from me. "We should get networking now. We need a case."

"Goes without saying," I chirped.

She stuck out her tongue.

"Ladies?"

"Uh-huh?" Rey asked blandly, eyeing the chipped nail polish on her fingers with annoyance.

"We have an email."

My cousin and I peered over.

"Dear lovely ladies of the Triple Threat Investigation Agency, the game is not over, just in limbo. We'll take up where we left off—one day, one year, one decade from now. Who knows? By the way, thanks for the disfigured nose. I was furious at first, but now I believe it kind of gives me character. And what's a little pain between pals? For now, dearhearts, *adieu*. Formerly the GripReaperPeeper, the Rose-Pin Killer, and also known as the Ha-Ha Killer (like really?)—and now your forever bosom buddy, Slim."

"Shit."

"Crap."

"Dang."

Dear reader,

We hope you enjoyed reading *Ha-Ha-Ha*. Please take a moment to leave a review, even if it's a short one. Your opinion is important to us.

Discover more books by Tyler Colins at https://www.nextchapter.pub/authors/tyler-colins

Want to know when one of our books is free or discounted? Join the newsletter at http://eepurl.com/bqqB3H

Best regards,
Tyler Colins and the Next Chapter Team

ABOUT THE AUTHOR

I possess numerous years of experience in freelance writing, editing and proofreading, as well as training in business communications and technical writing. My current focus: fiction. I (still) plan to reside in Hawaii permanently and embrace America, a country I've been enamored with since childhood. Besides writing, my passions include the aforementioned land of Aloha, animals in all shapes and sizes, fitness and athletics, the Good Lord and spirituality.

CONNECT WITH ME:

Twitter: https://twitter.com/UsBound3
Friend me on Facebook: https://www.facebook.com/tyler.colins.9
Visit / Subscribe to my blog: https://thewritersgrabbag.com/
Amazon: https://www.amazon.com/Tyler-Colins/e/B01KHOZAL2%3Fref=dbs_a_mng_rwt_scns_share

DISCOVER OTHER TITLES BY TYLER COLINS:

The Connecticut Corpse Caper
Can You Hula Like Hilo Hattie?
Coco's Nuts
Forever Poi

To discover what mis-adventures prompted the trio to become professional detectives, please check out *The Connecticut Corpse Caper*.

As proud owners of the Triple Threat Investigation Agency, the not-so-newbie detectives continue to hone skills as they take on challenging cases with curious (if not crazy) characters. The following prologue from *Disco's Dead and so is Mo-Mo* (tentative title) serves as a sample chapter in the continuing sleuthing escapades of JJ, Rey and Linda.

SNEAK PEEK TO DISCO'S DEAD AND SO IS MO-MO
SEPTEMBER 1978

This is the zany tale of Sammy Mohammed "Mo-Mo" Martine, a dime-store mobster as attractive as he was aggressive. How factual it is, is anyone's guess, but all gossip and hearsay, even that related to murder and mayhem, begin with some kernel of truth. And here, as I heard it, are a kernel or three …

… It was a warm, breezy night in the north end of Montréal (that's in Québec Canada, folks) off *rue* Jean-Talon. Little Italy, or *Petite Italie* if you're French, was a modest little community that consisted of family-owned restaurants and cafés, a sundry of small shops, numerous churches, a "community center", the requisite bocci court, and the splendid decades-old Jean-Talon market.

The odd person not still feasting on fresh *pesce* or homemade *zuppa* or sugary *torta*, listening to the news or sports, or watching the new prime-time soap, *Dallas*, was ambling along cracked, leaf-strewn sidewalks, enjoying the simplicity of being. Perhaps he or she was remembering the events of the day, considering the new government led by Giulio Andreotti that had been installed in Italy with the support of the Communist Party, or contemplating the Camp David peace agreement between Israel and Egypt, or mulling over the plight of disco.

Parked on side streets lined with small but immaculate lawns and a few Madonnas (not of the singing variety), were typical cars of the period—a Ford Bronco, two Buick Skylarks, a Pacer, two Matadors, a GMC moving truck and, strangely enough, four Gremlins. Corvettes and Cadillacs were few and far between in the neighborhood, but certainly not unheard of, particularly if you enjoyed an affiliation with the Martine family.

Strolling along one of those side streets were three men—one would be reluctant to call them gentlemen, for reasons that would become clear much later—who had just finished a three-hour stick-to-your-ribs meal at Reg's Parmigiano, owned by gourmand-glutton Regulus Febrezia, a rotund and rapacious young proprietor. The dinner had consisted of *crostini de fegato, quaglie,* tortellini and tagliatelli, and osso buco, a favorite of Sammy Martine's, and three bottles of Regulus' homemade red wine, an intriguing little red number that might not have made the top ten list in *Wine Spectator,* but received rave reviews from the locals because of the way it pricked the palate with a salty-sweet astringency, not to mention the way it complemented any dish.

As always, Regulus' dishes were superb: fresh, rich, and plentiful. And the waitress, an equally intriguing little red number named Sonja, had been in usual fine form. The twenty-two-year-old redhead might not have pricked your palate, but she could have knocked you on your butt—with a bawdy verse or practical joke. And those 40C jugs—they were easy on the eyes as far as Sammy and company were concerned.

Thirty-one-year-old Sammy Mohammed Martine, called Mo-Mo by friends and foes alike was sauntering happily if not dreamily along, wedged between two burly fellows: Louie "The Lip" Walfisch and Isaiah "Dragonfly" Browne. The nicknames had been aptly granted. Louie had no upper lip, but a fat, ugly bratwurst-shaped and braunschweiger-sized bottom lip while Isaiah, whose father had a penchant for Hebrew prophet names, made an odd, buzzing sound when he spoke. It wasn't a lisp but a drone or persistent hum and, like a dragonfly, he tended to hover—right on the tips of people's toes.

The fellows were joking about guy things (probably those jugs) as they headed toward a colleague's house two streets over. It was unlikely they noticed what an astonishingly bright and starry night it was, how the burgeoning breeze was swirling subtle scents of vin du pays, smoked meats, and garlic around them, that someone had Tony Bennett cranked, perhaps to blast Paul Anka who was belting out what a lonely boy he was three doors down, or that a big fat black cat had crossed their path.

Louie took it first, ironically, in the lip. A .30-caliber, to be precise, whizzed across the narrow street and removed the bratwurst-shaped and braunschweiger-sized lip, sheared it off as easily and as quickly as if a gardener with an ephedrine buzz had gleefully taken electric clippers to an errant hedge. There'd be no opportunity to change the young man's name to Louie "No Lip" Walfisch.

The shot or scream—witnesses couldn't agree which—prompted Sammy to hit the dirt. Or maybe it was Isaiah's quick-thinking clout to the back. In any event, as Sammy fell, Louie kissed the sidewalk, not an easy feat for someone no longer sporting lips, and while flesh bussed concrete, the left side of Isaiah's leather-tough neck turned into striated red goo. He fumbled for his piece as Louie staggered to his feet.

The lipless one received a bullet in the shoulder, which prompted him to perform an odd step-close-step-close pattern, somewhat like a samba, making him appear as if he were in heat, denial, or having a grand old time. Another bullet caught him in the vicinity of the liver.

As the dance was taking place, Isaiah plowed into a natty rose bush, shouted "vengeance will be mine!" or "vermicelli with mushrooms!"—two witnesses claimed it was the former, three the latter—and remained still, slumped like a scarecrow that had had its stuffing removed.

A glossy-green, four-door Lincoln Continental sedan

careened to a stop before the immobilized trio and a tall man in black jumped out. Depending on who you wanted to believe, he resembled: Ernest Borgnine in a velveteen suit; Vincent Price in jet cape and tux; Porky Peters in his customary plumber coveralls; or Meatballs Avila, Johnny "Baloney" Vespuzzi's left-hand man (technically, he couldn't be a right-hand man because he'd lost it during a laneway free-for-all the preceding summer).

Sammy, stunned, stupefied and/or scared shitless, was thrown into the rear of the gas-guzzling submarine as if he were little more than a crushed cardboard pizza box, and was never heard from or seen again ... until today.

His remains had been found—bizarrely enough, in a tin drum not far from Bellows Field Beach Park. This had media dredging up history and theories. And had the three of us wondering which was the more pressing mystery.

How/when had Mo-Mo gotten from the eastern region of Canada to Oahu, given the kidnapping so many years ago? His disappearance had made the news for months. Many had claimed fellow dime-store mobster Johnny "Baloney" Tino Vespuzzi had wanted to take over Mo-Mo's turf and "enterprises".

Who had killed him by pumping two .44 magnum cartridges into his cranium? One had been found, still wedged in his skull and the other at the bottom of the drum. Was it Baloney, er, Vespuzzi? If so, how had they managed to transport the dead body here?

It was a head-scratcher ... and one we'd just been hired to solve.

Ha-Ha-Ha-Ha
ISBN: 978-4-86750-476-5

Published by
Next Chapter
1-60-20 Minami-Otsuka
170-0005 Toshima-Ku, Tokyo
+818035793528

5th June 2021